"RIVETING AUTOBIOGRAPHY FROM ONE OF SOAP OPERA'S QUEEN BEES!"

—*Kirkus Reviews*

"WARRICK'S LIFE MAKES SOAPS PALE BY COMPARISON..."

—*Publishers Weekly*

The husbands—the one who beat her...the one who proved gay...the one who drank...the one who tried to push their little boy into the fire...

The lovers—the college boyfriend the doctor ordered her to go to bed with...the boy genius who went off like a skyrocket in the Hollywood heaven...the superstar who wanted to make love to every woman in movieland (and almost did)...

The dangers—the studio heads who demanded that every actress share their couches...Orson Welles and the smashing success of CITIZEN KANE...the plunge into the TV "pits" that led to the peak of fame as PHOEBE TYLER on ALL MY CHILDREN!

The CONFESSIONS *of* PHEOBE TYLER

RUTH WARRICK

with Don Preston

BERKLEY BOOKS, NEW YORK

This Berkley book contains the complete
text of the original hardcover edition.
It has been completely reset in a type face
designed for easy reading, and was printed
from new film.

THE CONFESSIONS OF
PHOEBE TYLER

A Berkley Book / published by arrangement with
Prentice-Hall, Inc.

PRINTING HISTORY
Prentice-Hall edition published 1980
Berkley edition / February 1982

ISBN: 0-425-05202-8

A BERKLEY BOOK® TM 757,375
Berkley Books are published by Berkley Publishing Corporation,
200 Madison Avenue, New York, New York 10016.
PRINTED IN THE UNITED STATES OF AMERICA

This book is dedicated to
all my children,
Karen, Jon, and Tim,
and to my grandchildren,
Erik and Eliza.

Our mutual love and learning
have been my basic training for
ALL MY CHILDREN,
whom I also love.

CONTENTS

INTRODUCTION

by Jørn Winther,
Producer of ALL MY CHILDREN

How do you go about writing an introduction to any autobiography? The answer is obvious. You simply say those things about the author that the author could not possibly say about him- or herself. In *The Confessions of Phoebe Tyler* Ruth Warrick has provided us with all manner of fascinating information about her life and the life of her imperious alter ego, Phoebe Tyler. But by the same token she has also left some things out—perhaps because she didn't know about them or was too modest to write them or just plain didn't want them said. But I suffer from no such inhibitions, so here goes.

Before I decided to accept the position of producer on *All My Children*, I watched a few shows and saw Phoebe Tyler for the first time. I said to myself, "My goodness, this woman overacts something fierce. If I take this job she is going to be one of the first ones I replace." But after I had joined the show and watched her on a daily basis, I realized that there *are* people like Phoebe Tyler around and that Ruth Warrick was not only able to portray this kind of character, but to make her absolutely realistic and believable. Only then did it dawn on me what a truly fantastic actress she is.

I think one of the reasons Ruth is so convincing as Phoebe is that she really loves her. One aspect of this love is expressed in Ruth's passion for authentic detail. I am not speaking merely of costumes, make-up, or hairstyling. Absolutely nothing is too good for Phoebe. If Ruth had her way we would have real

Persian carpets on the floors, genuine antiques in the Tyler library, and all Phoebe's jewelry would come straight from Cartier. (And *All My Children* would probably be bankrupt.) As it is, Ruth makes certain that all the props and imitations Phoebe does use are as close to the real things as possible. If this sounds like fanaticism, it's not. It's professionalism of the best sort. Ruth is determined that nothing about Phoebe—neither the way she is portrayed nor any of her surroundings—will ever strike a false note.

Speaking of professionalism, some viewers at home may have noticed that Ruth is almost always the best lit of our performers. There's a reason for that. Even though our directors and lighting technicians carefully position every cast member in each shot, Ruth can sense how, by slightly tilting her head or leaning a little this way or that, she can make even the best lighting better. This is the kind of craftsmanship that comes only from experience and I've rarely seen it developed to the degree of perfection Ruth has achieved. The word on the set is: "Don't worry about Ruth; she'll always *find* her light."

In case anything I've said about Ruth so far leads you to suspect she could be something of a pain in the neck on the set, let me assure you that the reverse is true. Not only do we all profit from her professionalism, we know her to be one of the most cooperative and dedicated people in the cast, a real upper to have on the show. We've never had a problem we couldn't discuss and work out. Also, she's especially good with new members of the cast, helping them to learn the ropes, gain confidence, and become integrated into the *All My Children* community. And she is extremely generous with her time: Of all the performers on the show she does the most promotion for *All My Children*, traveling to every part of the United States giving interviews, speaking, and making appearances in "Soaps Alive" shows. Above all, she's downright fun to be with. She has a great sense of humor, a quality that shines through in her characterization of Phoebe. It's more than a matter of Ruth subtly poking fun at some of Phoebe's pretensions. Even at her most severe, you sense that Phoebe herself has never lost her potential for laughter, something that makes Phoebe rather endearing even when she's doing her best not to be. As a charming lady, recently arrived from the West Indian island of Grenada, once said of Phoebe, "She wick-ed, but she wonderful."

Although Ruth's humor is entirely natural and spontaneous, from my point of view it serves an indispensable practical function on the set. As Napoleon said of Italy, "If it didn't exist, it would have to have been invented." Our work schedule is arduous and unremitting, and tensions, no matter how well controlled, can build to dangerous levels. But somehow, just when the going seems roughest, Ruth always manages to come up with some piece of inspired nonsense that makes us all laugh and puts everything right again. For example, after some particularly long and frustrating wait while a technical problem is being solved and it appears we may be there all night, she may burst into a raucous version of "Tomorrow." Often she will appear in zany costumes of her own devising (once it was as Mercury running about bearing Christmas gifts, with little silver wings attached to her head and heels). And on one memorable occasion she actually did a lady-like streak across the set, leaving hilarious pandemonium in her wake. We all have many reasons for treasuring Ruth, and not least among them is the fact that she is so successful at brightening our days.

In view of what I've been saying about Ruth, it should come as no surprise to you that she is easily the most social member of our cast. I don't think she ever misses a Broadway play or any of the bigger charity events, and she constantly entertains, either in her Park Avenue apartment or in her house on Cape Cod. From personal experience, I can vouch for the warmth and elegance of her dinner parties, and I can also testify to the fact that she usually does her own cooking.

If all this makes Ruth sound too much like some sort of flawless paragon, let me quickly state that she definitely has her faults. One of the most maddening to me—and I daresay to other members of the cast and staff—is her apparently inexhaustible capacity for getting to work late. Yet it is impossible for any of us to be truly angry about this because her excuses are always so fascinating. Once it was a baroque and only partly comprehensible tale about how the elevator in her apartment was being redecorated. Another time it had to do with a tiger that had escaped from the New York Zoo and was terrorizing her neighborhood.

But there is one thing about Ruth I doubt anyone will ever

find fault with: her taste in clothes. She has to be one of the best-dressed women in the world, and if she were ever to give up acting she could probably make a fortune by opening a Fifth Avenue boutique and selling her own creations and selections. Phoebe Tyler may have many short-comings, but you can bet that being badly dressed will never be one of them. Ruth can be counted on to see to that.

To one of the central conundrums posed by this book—where the personality of Ruth leaves off and that of Phoebe begins—I have no answers half so good as the ones contained in the book itself. Obviously Ruth and Phoebe are separate and unique, yet they have much in common. All I can say with confidence is that they are both great ladies and that I love them.

FOREWORD

by Carol Burnett

I wasn't always a fan of *All My Children*. As a matter of fact, I was only slightly aware it even existed—what with my own television schedule and the brief half-hour lunch periods I had while doing *The Carol Burnett Show*.

I became intrigued by the hold it had over my three daughters. I started watching in bits and pieces. Before long I found myself asking the production department to try to arrange my lunch periods so they would coincide with the time *All My Children* was shown.

From then on, I was hooked. Watching the show became like eating Chinese food. Less than an hour after one episode, I began craving another.

What's more, *All My Children* brought me recognition in my own children's eyes. They took it for granted that I had my own show and was on television every week. Then, I did a brief guest appearance on *All My Children*.

That did it. I became a star.

*"In the midst of winter I
finally learned that there is
in me an eternal summer."*
ALBERT CAMUS

PROLOGUE

Plains, Georgia, 1976

IT'S A LONG WAY from the imaginary affluence of Pine Valley to the very real simplicity of rural Georgia, but it was a trip that Phoebe and I made gladly in the late summer of Jimmy Carter's first presidential campaign. I had come, at Miss Lillian Carter's invitation, to see this miracle up close.

To be completely truthful about it, I suppose I had invited the invitation. With a few free days on my hands, I had made an impetuous phone call to Carter-Mondale headquarters in Plains and asked to speak to Miss Lillian, to ask if I could interview her for my book. I had read that she was a fan. The anonymous voice in Plains had said Miss Lillian wasn't there, and was about to hand up.

"This is Phoebe Tyler calling," I had cut in quickly.

"Phoebe *Tyler*!" I could hear her telling someone nearby, "Hey, it's Phoebe Tyler!" followed by the diminishing echo of the name, repeated from one person to the next. Then the operator was back: "Why, Miz Tyler, you want Miz Lillian's private number," she said, and gave it to me.

I dialed it, and Miss Lillian answered.

"This is Phoebe Tyler," I said.

Before I could utter a word of explanation, Miss Lillian was off and running. "Why, I don't *believe* it," she said. "I was just now watchin' you on the TV. You were bein' so *mean* to Linc and poor Kitty. How come you ah such a *bee*-utch?"

After that, what could Phoebe do but go down to Plains and defend herself?

Not that I was a total stranger to Georgia. I had been there in 1946 for the premiere of Walt Disney's first live-action film,

Song of the South, and had returned to make personal appearances when the film was re-released twenty-six years later. The
thirty years between 1946 and 1976 had brought great changes
to the cities of Georgia—and indeed to all the South—from
the dazzling new architecture of Atlanta to the inevitable highway blight of shopping malls and fast-food chains. But these
changes still seemed barely to have touched the farmland or
the tiny back-country towns.

The main streeet of Plains comes as a mild shock no matter
how many pictures you may have seen. And for me, driving
my rental car in from the airport at Albany, it was a kind of
déjà vu as well. That single block of stores, all connected by
a continuous front, was almost exactly like a movie set. I half
expected that if I walked through a door, I'd find myself back
outside in the blazing sunshine.

But of course the stores were quite real, and the town's busy
life was going on behind those doors—as it was in the restored
train station where the Carter campaign was then headquar-
tered, and around the beer cooler in Billy Carter's gas station
over across the village green. (Billy no longer hangs out there,
but in that hot summer it was a busy gathering place, a veritable
bastion of good ole boys that Phoebe just had to invade.) I
found out just how real it all was when Miss Lillian insisted
on conducting a tour of the street.

As we went from store to store, being introduced to this
shopkeeper and that, we began to collect a sizable retinue. The
slacks and wide-brimmed Panama hat I'd worn were certainly
no part of Phoebe's wardrobe, but most people seemed curious
and pleased to meet a familiar television face.

I signed autographs and shook hands in one store, then
repeated the entire performance in the next one, and the next.
From Uncle Hugh Carter's Worm Farm and Antique Emporium
to the dry-goods store we went, and then to the grocery store
and on to what had once been Earl Carter's seed store, now
a souvenir shop. It was a two-hour journey down that one short
block, and the procession kept growing as we progressed.

Then, in one store, I noticed a teenage girl eyeing me with
what looked like suspicion. I saw her again a few minutes later,
looking me up and down from pants to hat and shaking her
head.

"Is something wrong, dear?" I finally asked her.

"Well, are you *sure* you're Phoebe Tyler?" the girl asked. "I mean, you don't look or talk much like her."

The smile on my face froze. I drew myself stiffly erect, and with chin elevated and eyes widened, I said haughtily, "My *dear* child, I can assure you I most certainly *am* Phoebe Tyler." The voice had deepened and grown sharp edges; the consonants were clipped with imperious precision. "I simply *had* to get away from Pine Valley for a bit, until Charles comes to his senses and ceases his disgraceful *dalliance* with that dreadful Mona Kane person."

The girl's eyes widened. Then she turned and dashed out the door. I could hear her, out on the street, shouting to her friends: "Hey, y'all, Phoebe *Tyler* is in heah!"

And so she was. For the next few minutes Phoebe held court, answering quite serious questions about Pine Valley and the problems of its people, the Martins and Tylers and Tuckers and all the others so familiar to the approximately ten million who watch *All My Children* daily. For those minutes Phoebe Tyler was entirely real—to the eagerly questioning fans and, in a curious way, also to me.

In a sense, that other reality of Phoebe and Pine Valley is what this book is all about.

ONE

Where Is Pine Valley?

PHOEBE STANDS BEFORE a great multitude, eyes downcast demurely. "Did you *see* what has been happening to me?" she asks them.

There is laughter and applause.

"Well, weren't you *shocked*?" Phoebe asks them.

"Yes!" They shout in unison, with clapping and nodding.

"Are you mad at me?"

"Noooo!" Heads shake throughout the crowd.

"Surely you don't think I should do it again?" Phoebe asks them.

Shouts of "Yeah! Yeah!" and cheers, as if Phoebe had scored a touchdown.

One woman near the front is shaking her head and frowning, so Phoebe asks her what is wrong.

"You're not gonna let that professor get all your money, are you?" She is very earnest, her question obviously genuine. "Can't you see he's a bad man?"

"Oh, I think you're being much too harsh on poor Langley, my dear," Phoebe answers. "He is really a quite charming gentleman." (He is, in fact, a con man, as everyone but Phoebe knows.)

The lady is shaking her head sadly. Phoebe Tyler is just too arrogantly stubborn to listen to anyone. At last, in desperation, she blurts, "If you let him take your money, I'll never *speak* to you again!"

I'd like to reassure her, but I cannot. And I am interested in the crowd reaction here in this bustling shopping mall, surrounded by thousands of fans of *All My Children*. Because something has happened to Phoebe in recent episodes that is

4

seemingly out of character for this soul of imperious rectitude, and I am wondering how the fans are taking it. Their cheers have answered most of my questions.

"I don't see why you dislike Langley so," Phoebe tells the upset woman. "Don't you think he's *terribly* attractive?"

The lady shakes her head vehemently, but many others in the audience cheer again.

"You know, it really is amazing," Phoebe tells them. "Ruth has been in the movies and theater for . . . well, a number of years." That evasion gets some smiles: Phoebe is touchy about the subject of her age. "And in all that time, even back in those Hollywood movies, she hardly ever even appeared in a bathing suit, and she was *never* . . . ah . . . *intimate*, shall we say, with a man." More smiles and knowing looks. "And now, all in one week, I have been revealed in a bathing suit, and I have been unzipped on camera. Isn't it amazing?"

More cheers and applause. Evidently my concern about how the fans would take Phoebe's fall from virtue was unwarranted. In fact, one middle-aged lady stops me after the show to say, "You may have been embarrassed to be unzipped on camera, but you certainly put some zip in *my* life that hasn't been there for a long time." Her eyes are moist and her cheeks are rosy as she presses my hand. "Thank you," she says.

These shopping mall appearances are part of a phenomenally successful program called Soaps Alive!, the brainchild of a New Jersey housewife and part-time PR expert named Harriet Epstein, who felt the stars of the daytime serials would draw crowds at least as large as those brought in by sports or arts-and-crafts shows. The huge crowds that have mobbed us at malls and theme parks from New England to Florida to California have proven how right she was. Countless thousands have turned out to see and meet their favorites from the soaps, filling the malls and hanging from the upper levels to shout questions.

As they are doing now, here in Massachusetts. I can see a lady in the front whispering in her small daughter's ear and nudging her. The child holds up her hand hesitantly.

"Yes, dear?" I lean forward and smile encouragement, though I can almost hear the question coming. "You wanted to say something?"

"How old are you?" the child asks. The crowds laughs.

Phoebe smiles. "Well, how old are *you*, sweetheart?"

The child holds up fingers and says, "Five."

"What a *nice* age to be," Phoebe says. "Are you in school?"

"Kindygarden."

"How wonderful. Well, you do well in school now, will you?"

The child nods, and the crowd laughs as they realize Phoebe has once again dodged the question. She has had a lot of practice.

"What do you think of Erica?" someone asks.

A tricky question. Erica Kane Martin Brent Cudahy is a spoiled, egocentric, manipulative resident of Pine Valley, but Susan Lucci, the beautiful young actress who plays her, is none of those things.

"Well, Ruth likes Susan Lucci a lot," Phoebe tells the crowd. "But I'm not sure how *I* feel about *Erica*." This brings smiles. I'm sure most fans would continue to believe Susan *must* be as devious as Erica, no matter what Phoebe told them.

Another hand goes up. "Where *is* Pine Valley, anyway?" This question is from a man, one of many in this audience. (And one of many millions who watch daytime serials regularly.)

"Well, I guess it's wherever you think it is," Phoebe answers. "Benjamin, here, always drives me, so I never pay attention to road signs."

The man laughs, and we move on. But the question is a good one: Just where *is* Pine Valley?

The question is also a tricky one, because in some ways the hometown of *All My Children* is *meant* to be wherever you think it is: small town, middle-American enclave, cross section, all the idealized roots some of us actually have and the rest of us wish we had as we move about in this mobile, rootless modern world. The town revolves around a hospital, several restaurants, a country club, a boutique, and a few homes whose rooms millions have grown to know almost as well as their own. Occasionally—and more often since the show went to a full hour daily—there are outdoor scenes, but they are shot in a variety of places and give no identifiable sense of locale. Pine Valley is Our Town, U.S.A.

A careful viewer might be able to place the geographical

location a bit more specifically. It is the suburb of "Center City," which somewhat resembles Philadelphia. And it is about ninety miles from New York City—close enough for illicit or clandestine adventures, but distant enough to avoid Fun City's distinctive flavor. In fact, Pine Valley occupies roughly the same map position as Bryn Mawr, the affluent Philadelphia Main Line community which is the home of a famous institution of learning.

Which is not surprising, since Bryn Mawr is also the home of a certain soft-spoken woman who has become something of an institution in her own right. She is Agnes Nixon, creator of *One Life to Live* and *All My Children*, and she is the acknowledged queen of daytime television serials, more commonly known as soap operas or simply soaps. Though Mrs. Nixon no longer owns either show (having sold them to ABC), she retains considerable creative control over her "children," and her influence is felt constantly and directly throughout the ABC daytime lineup. She seldom visits the set, but little that occurs there escapes her attention, whether she is watching from a New York City hotel or from the comfortable clutter of the television room in her historic Bryn Mawr home. She created the show, she continues to provide the principal story lines and themes, and she maintains a lively, though non-interfering, interest in all aspects of production.

Pine Valley might be said to have been born on the island of St. Croix in 1965. It was here, during a working vacation, that Agnes Nixon completed the final editing of what was to become the basic "bible" of *All My Children*. She had written the show for Proctor & Gamble, which optioned it to CBS conditional on another show going off the air. When CBS could not readjust its schedule, the *All My Children* project had to be put aside while Mrs. Nixon continued to work on her other, immensely popular, creation, *One Life to Live*. So impressed was ABC with *One Life* that in 1969 they asked Mrs. Nixon to provide them with a second show. She promptly gave them the *All My Children* "bible" and not long thereafter, in January 1970, Phoebe, along with most of the other people who now inhabit Pine Valley, suddenly became "real."

Have we located Pine Valley now? Is it Agnes Nixon's fictional town, near a city much like Philadelphia, ninety miles from glamorous and wicked New York? Well, yes and no. In one sense, Pine Valley can also be said to exist in a sprawling, concrete-floored, warehouselike studio on New York's West Side, a few blocks from Lincoln Center. It comes to life on the nine or ten sets assembled there on any given day, and in the dressing rooms and the makeup and hairdressing and wardrobe rooms that line the ground-floor corridors, and in the rehearsal hall and the tape-editing room and the offices and seldom-used lounges on the second floor. It exists, too, in the control room, a place featuring banks of monitor screens, vast computerized control consoles, a dozen or so people, and an atmosphere of serenity similar to that of, say, the bridge of the *Titanic*.

This building, with its hospital-white corridors and its constant bustle, is the ABC *All My Children* studio, and it is where Phoebe Tyler's day begins. At seven-thirty A.M.! That is when the actors who will appear on that day's show begin to straggle into the rehearsal hall, in blue jeans and sweaters, scripts in hand. We assemble, by twos and threes, for the day's first confrontation with our friendly nemesis and guiding spirit, the director.

Actually, the show has three regular directors, each paired with an associate director. Each duo works a five-day stint in rotation. On this typical day we face the most vocal, demanding, and generally flamboyant of the three, Henry Kaplan. He sits behind a steel table, a large man in jeans and red polo shirt, his associate director at his side and a heavily marked script before him. To an outsider, Henry's mordant sarcasm, often bordering on downright insult, might convey the impression that he holds the actors and the show in contempt. Nothing could be more wrong. He has been with the show eight years, and he loves his work.* He also respects the performers, who achieve remarkably polished results under stressful conditions that would send most stage or screen actors running for their lives. The biting tongue is just his style, always deliberately overplayed to the point of self-parody, often amusing and never intentionally hurtful. It is his way of playing ringmaster in this three-ring circus. We all understand.

*Editor's note: Since this was written, Mr. Kaplan has left the staff of *All My Children*.

Now, still subdued in these early hours, Henry nods at the yawning actors with their Styrofoam cups of coffee, stares across at the wall of floor-to-ceiling mirrors facing him, and picks up the green mimeographed sheets that list the day's cast and the sequence of scenes. He looks around to see who is there and ready.

The day begins.

I sit at a table, sipping orange juice and making cryptic notes and boxes on my script, which I have seen for the first time a few days before, along with two others in which I will appear later this same week. (These hieroglyphics are my own memorization system and a mystery to everyone else.) Hugh Franklin, who plays Phoebe's estranged husband, Dr. Charles Tyler, is trying not to look distinguished in his flapping Hawaiian sport shirt. He is succeeding, though his rumpled look has a temporary air about it, as if the familiar man-of-distinction image will click into place momentarily.

Julia Barr, who plays Phoebe's niece, Brooke English, manages to resemble a fashion model at a picnic despite the hour; and Tricia Pursley, who is Ellen Tucker Shepherd's daughter, Devon, on the show, strolls about looking like a high-school girl in her sweatshirt and sloppy socks. Others come and go.

Henry Kaplan opens his script, glances again at the green sheet listing the day's scenes, and says, "OK, let's do Phoebe and Mrs. Whatsername first."

Phoebe has two scenes today with Mrs. Valentine, the Tylers' long-time cook and housekeeper, and we run through them now, while Henry indicates what our movements will be on the set. He positions the clutter of chairs and tables to represent kitchen counters in one scene, library furniture in another, and directs Phoebe to walk to the counter on this line, turn around on that word, sit down at this point (slowly, of course, so the camera can follow the movement), and so on. We run through the scenes, noting these movements on our scripts along with the pauses (or "pa-houze," to our cast), counts, and other directions indicated by Henry. Pauses are inserted for emphasis or dramatic effect or to allow clear spots for cameras to "cut" from one actor to another. Counts are inserted to allow time for the camera to show another character's reaction to what has just been said; the dialogue will resume after the reaction just as if there had been no break—often a tricky matter when a scene heats up.

Since the pauses and counts have been worked out by the director in advance and do not appear on the scripts, we must note and learn them now, often by counting silently as we rehearse. (Occasionally, especially if an actor has fluffed a pause and has been loudly corrected, you will see his head bobbing as he counts. Sometimes, if Henry has been a bit too emphatic, the count will become quite audible in the next run-through.)

These counts now become essential elements of the script. They are noted during this first run-through, along with movements on the set, indicated by numbers of steps ("takes three steps downstage"), or by positioning of props ("moves to kitchen counter"). These notations, along with directions about body position ("leans in") or gesture ("turns, points at Charles") or other "business" ("answers phone"), must all be carefully worked out now, as we run through each scene among these shifting chairs and tables. (In a later scene with my daughter, Anne, three chairs become a bed, then shift slightly to represent a sofa in another scene.)

"Leans" are especially important, since they have a direct effect on the positioning of a camera: If one character leans-in toward another during dialogue, this signals the camera to follow in for a closer shot of the second character's reaction, or for a tighter shot of both characters together. If someone leans-in too abruptly, he or she may well slide right out of the shot, leaving the viewer with only scenery. Timing is crucial here, as in most other aspects of our performance.

Actual props are almost never used in this first rehearsal, but I can recall one memorable exception. For a time Phoebe was confined to an electric wheelchair, a situation that involved some very tricky coordination of movement with camera and sound equipment, not to mention the problems of maintaining concentration on dialogue while working the controls that could send the chair whizzing all over the place. We had the chair brought upstairs for those rehearsals and lugged back down for work on the sets, which involved coordinating the efforts of several unions and produced constant screams of anguish when the chair was not on hand at the required spot.

But the wheelchair was fun, once I got the knack of it, and it added an element of adventure to each show as I zoomed about the set with tipsy disregard for all traffic rules. Fans loved it, especially in one scene where I chased Benny onto the sofa with the chair, then spun it around and swept out of the room while angrily tossing my vodka over my shoulder, without looking back, to drench the poor man. The entire control room cheered.

But back to today. We finish a scene and Henry indicates a final run-through for time. We do it once again, uninterrupted, paying special heed to those beats while the associate director holds a stopwatch and writes down the precise duration in seconds. When all the day's scenes have been run through and timed, when the commercials and fade-outs have been allowed for, and when any pretaped segments (such as an outdoor scene or perhaps a flashback) have been added in, the director will have an accurate total, in minutes and seconds, for that day's show. Cuts can then be planned if the show has run too long, or additional pauses may be added to certain scenes to bring a show up to length. These changes, worked out over the next two or three hours, may be given to an actor just as the dress rehearsal begins. It is not unusual, in fact, to find several lines lopped suddenly from a scene you have rehearsed all day just as final taping is about to start.

Gwyn Gilliss, who has recently been cast to play Phoebe's daughter, Anne, is a fugitive from a mental institution at this point in the story, and our scenes are played with great intensity but also with bewildering changes of mood on Anne's part. In her disoriented state of mind, she must switch instantly from the "real" present, in which she is aware of her situation, to another time in which she is a young girl at home on vacation from school. The counts are crucial here, as are her expression and posture and my reactions to them. The viewer must be able to follow those quick jumps from fantasy to reality. We rehearse them several times, with Henry hovering and making changes in his notations. During the third try at one bit it suddenly hits me that the script has both of us referring to Mrs. Valentine, the cook, as Sarah.

"Why am I calling her Sarah?" I ask Henry.

"Maybe because it's her name?"

I pay no attention to Henry's sarcasm. "I mean, I have never, ever, called her anything but Mrs. Valentine in the last ten *years*."

Henry shrugs. "Do I write this stuff?" But he tells the associate director to check it with the writers, to see if the name is a slip or if it portends some change in the long relationship between the two characters. We continue with the scene. (The word comes down later: Call her Mrs. Valentine. More changes on my script.)

Phoebe and Charles have a long scene in the recently re-modeled library of the Tyler mansion, and we run through it several times to chart our courses among pieces of furniture that are no longer where they always were. Henry consults his diagrams to assure me that a certain move will not send me sprawling over the coffee table. Charles reads a line containing the word *HARassment*, and Henry stops to suggest that it be pronounced *harASSment*. Charles draws himself up and insists that the accented first syllable is correct. Henry mimes terrified submission. (Either pronunciation is acceptable, I learn later, but no one argues with Hugh Franklin on such matters. He is a man of some erudition, and his wife, Madeleine l'Engle, is a noted author.)

And so it goes, through all twenty-three scenes that will make up the Prologue and six "Acts" of this day's show, which will be seen by television viewers one week after the day it is taped. Actors wander in and out as their scenes are called, muttering to themselves and scribbling in the wide margins of their scripts. At one point Henry stops a scene and glares at two mutterers. There is a general decrease in the buzz. "Keep it up, keep it up," Henry warns. "Don't you see that the big people are *working* now?" Despite his protests, we all know that if something of general interest were being discussed, such as a new Broadway opening, Henry would stop the rehearsal to join in the chit-chat.

In fact, there is a great family feeling among the people who do *All My Children*, as if we were actually citizens of a small town like Pine Valley. We hear one another's troubles and offer comfort or advice, we bring news, and sometimes we simply compare notes on our "other families" in the real world. I remember one such tale-swapping session about how our children had reacted to their first explanation of sex and the making of babies. Bill Mooney, who plays Paul Martin on the show, topped us all with the comment from one of his twin sons. After listening to the unlikely explanation with big eyes, the boy said, "Gee, it's good you and Mommy had twins, so you only had to do that once."

By around ten the scenes have been run through and timed, and the cast is drifting toward the sets, preparing for the "blocking." I stop off on the way to check in on the editing room, where yesterday's tapes (there are always at least two, shot simultaneously for insurance) are being edited into the final master tape that will go on the air. While the associate director (the one who worked on that particular show) holds a stopwatch, the tape editor runs each scene to time its duration. To the end of each scene he will also have to add a dissolve, that slow fade-out to black that tells viewers they will now be turning to another location and group of characters.

The editing room looks like something from science fiction, with its two large television screens, each showing one of the tapes as it is run through, sometimes at actual speed and sometimes slowly, by hand, a few frames at a time. The editing of the tapes is a precise matter and the concentration is intense, despite occasional interference from actors who may wander in and out in their free moments.

"You can't cut there, with my mouth hanging open like the village idiot," says Bill Mooney.

The associate director agrees, and the tape editor stops the tape, grasps the big knob on the center of the reel and turns it backwards, frame by frame. After a few frames Paul's mouth is closed. The change is noted and the scene run again, the dissolve now beginning at the earlier point.

Tape editing is an art unto itself. Unlike film, which can be literally cut and glued back together at the desired place, video tape cannot be physically spliced. The directors and editors must select and carefully assemble the shots they want and then transfer them—that is, re-record them—on a final, master tape. If for any reason part of a scene has to be re-shot, the director must choose some earlier point on the original tape where there is neither movement nor sound. This will be designated a "clear edit spot." The actors must assume the identical positions they held at that moment, stand immobile as statues for a few seconds while the camera runs (this will produce what is called a "freeze-frame," then come to life and re-do the remainder of the scene. When the master tape is being assembled, the re-shot segment will be electronically cued in at the freeze-frame, erasing and replacing the defective segment.

There is, of course, far more to the editing process than this—more than I know and perhaps more than most laymen would care to know—but I hope this is enough to give you some impression of the sheer technical wizardry and precise, exacting work that lies behind those images that seem to float so effortlessly across the home screen. This, too, is a part of the world Phoebe inhabits.

We'll be returning to this complicated and hectic day in the studio many times, but for now I'd like to go back to the question *Where* is *Pine Valley?* It isn't on the map, though it may have been inspired by a real place, and it certainly resembles hundreds of other real places. It is brought to life every day by real people in a real studio, yet those people don't actually live in Pine Valley, which isn't quite the same thing as the studio anyway. It was born in the prodigious imagination of one person, Agnes Nixon, yet it now has a vivid existence in the imaginations of millions—so vivid, in fact, that it sometimes seems to many of us nearly as real as the places where we actually live.

I could go on like this, but I'm sure the point is clear. If Pine Valley is something less than real, it's also, in an odd way, something more than what we usually mean by fictitious. And the same is true of its inhabitants; all of us who play parts on the show must have had an occasional eerie feeling that the characters we assume are somehow more than just actors' parts. So if I have trouble answering the question, Where is Pine Valley?, imagine how much difficulty I must have with, Who is Phoebe Tyler?

Phoebe and I are not the same person. I didn't create her, I have only a limited control over her destiny, and I sometimes don't entirely approve of her behavior. Yet in at least one sense her whole being exists in me. I know all of her feelings and thoughts. I know what she will say and how she will act in any situation. I understand her strengths and weaknesses as though they were my own.

How can this be? What exactly is the relationship between Phoebe Tyler of Pine Valley and a New York-based actress named Ruth Warrick? Is Phoebe an extension of Ruth's everyday personality; or is she perhaps a projection of some hidden elements in Ruth's nature, elements of which even Ruth is only dimly aware? Which of Ruth's varied real-life experiences contributed to the creation of Phoebe's character? And in what subtle ways may Phoebe now be influencing Ruth's interpretation of Phoebe?

Perhaps this book will help me answer those questions. I'm not at all certain I know the answers myself, but it seems clear to me that Phoebe has somehow arisen out of my own life. She could only be as she is because I am as I am. At least part of her history must be composed of fragments of my history. But which?

I've called this book *The Confessions of Phoebe Tyler*, which surely implies that it is, at least in part, my own autobiography. But not entirely. Phoebe also owes her existence to many other people, and I'd like you to get to know them too—who they are, what they do, and how much Phoebe depends on them. And finally, of course, there is Pine Valley itself, that realm of the imagination in which Phoebe's existence is most fully realized. We shall have to know something about that, too, if we are ever to understand Phoebe—or the actress who has played her for more than a decade.

TWO

The Road to Pine Valley: St. Joseph and Points East

I'M GLAD TO SHARE PHOEBE'S WORLD because acting has been a large part of my life, and certainly my living, for many years. An actress who isn't performing is like a pilot without an airplane: What else could one do with the special skills one has spent a lifetime acquiring? But I have been tenacious and lucky, and I have always worked at the thing I have wanted to do, whether it was in movies such as *Citizen Kane* or stage musicals such as *Irene*, or in daytime serials such as *As the World Turns* or *All My Children*. I've bounced like a tennis ball between Hollywood and New York, but have always found a home in the only world I know.

It has been said that half the people in Hollywood are from New York. It has also been said that everyone in New York came there from someplace else. Neither of these things is really true, of course; but if they were, I would surely qualify as typical, because I was born and raised in St. Joseph, Missouri, about midway between and a long way from either.

We moved many times in my early years as my father changed jobs, but the locus around which our lives turned was a very large farm called Quiet Glen, the home of my mother's family, about thirty miles northwest of St. Joe. Though now gone the way of most nineteenth-century mansions, Quiet Glen was a childhood haven for me and my sister and cousins, a huge cool house surrounded by fields of grains, grasses, and sorghum cane, the center of an extended family large enough to suit any soap opera.

How to tell of Quiet Glen? The memories are impressions, not stories, but they are no less vivid for their fragmentation:

My grandfather Scott's evening ritual, the trip to the cool, dank fruit cellar to select one perfect apple from the barrels of Golden Delicious, Stark, Winesap, McIntosh. Then, sitting before the fire, he would peel it in one precise, unbroken spiral, which a waiting child could toss over her shoulder to see what letter it formed, supposedly the initial of her true love's name. And then a crisp slice of apple, proffered on the tip of the penknife with the panache of a maître d' spooning out beluga caviar.

Drinking cold home-pressed cider from Mama Scott's Waterford crystal; cracking and picking black walnuts with tedious care (we were told that the nutmeats sold for twenty dollars a pound in Paris); the Victrola playing Caruso, Galli-Curci, Sir Harry Lauder, Sousa marches, or the Minstrel Man, Bert Williams, singing "Nobody" or "The Preacher and the Bear." And games to feed the mind: flinch to teach mathematics, hearts to sharpen the memory, checkers for strategy, caroms as an illustration of geometry. Always there was something to do, and people to do it with.

Summer brought Chatauqua week, days of lectures and debates and musicales and dramas in the big tent at the high school in Whitesville, ten miles away. Picnics on the grounds, smells of grape soda and trampled grass, sounds of feminine laughter, the swish of palmetto fans. And peeking through tent flaps to spy on actors while they applied makeup, an arcane but somehow titillating procedure I recall vividly, even though the memories are overlaid with the hundreds of makeup rooms Phoebe and I have served time in since. I remember my mother, whose maiden name was Annie Laurie Scott (her sister was named Bonnie, in tribute to a favorite song and the family's background), singing a duet with her brother Freeman in the program for local talent. (She had once been offered a professional contract to travel with the Chatauqua troop. She had declined, of course, since ladies could use their talents only as social graces, never for pay.)

The big kitchen, domain of the Irish hired girl, Lily, but inhabited by all the women and children when pies or bread were being baked, center of social interchange (yes, gossip) that sometimes grew spicy enough to get "little pitchers with big ears" banished, origin of life's greatest smells and tastes, classroom in the joys and sorrows of human life. Lily, an orphan who had joined the family at twelve, dreamed for years of California, and finally—at thirty-five—decided to go there. After ten months of silence she was suddenly back to resume her life exactly where she'd left it, quiet on the subject of her trip except for one exasperated comment: "All I'll say is, if there's any *meanness* in you, it's gonna come out in California."

Working the foot treadle of Mama Scott's sewing machine for her by hand while keeping under the machine, using my "sharp young eyes" to thread needles I later learned she could manage perfectly by herself, being a part of that woman's world and learning what daily life contained. (Later, in a brief fling at modeling in New York, my wardrobe was the envy of all, and one clothes designer insisted on sketching what I wore for possible use in his line. No one could believe that all my clothes had been made by my mother.) Quilting bees in the parlor, which I was allowed to join as I got older, sitting with fifteen or twenty women and stitching the intricate pieces together, ears tingling with the gossip I was now permitted to hear. And in between, rummaging through Mama Scott's scrap bag for colorful fabrics, or sitting in the porch swing, listening to the evening songs of mourning doves and tree frogs while I carefully sewed my quilt blocks together.

Bible stories at bedtime and lying awake after the lights had been turned out, wondering if God would ever speak to me as He had to little Samuel. And then, perhaps, before drifting off to sleep, trying to concoct the next chapter of the ongoing story I would be telling to an enthralled younger sister and older cousin the following day. (Though I had never heard the term, I was already deeply involved in a soap of my own.)

Summers and holidays were spent at Quiet Glen, and the family returned to live there often in my early years, to rest up between the travels required by my father's changing jobs. We lived in various towns before I was six, but there was no feeling of permanence until we moved into the house on Olive Street, in St. Joseph, where we finally settled at my mother's insistence so I could attend a proper school. One memory, though, is especially vivid.

I had been asked what special treat I wanted for my fourth birthday, since I didn't know enough children to have a party.

Ever a romantic, I had asked for a boat ride. We lived in Wichita at the time, so the river was probably the Arkansas, though all I really know is that it had very high banks. Lolling back, trailing my fingers in the water while my mother fussed that I might dirty my pristine white organdy dress, I asked my father if I could have a box of Cracker Jacks. He rowed the boat nearer the bank, called a boy from the refreshment stand and *flipped* a dime (which was a substantial sum in those days) through the air up to him. My mother was indignant at this cavalier attitude toward money, but I was impressed by it, and even more enchanted with the Cracker Jacks, which stuck to one's fingers, clothes, and teeth, but which also had surprising toys concealed in them. The memory is trivial, but in some ways it sums up my early recollections of my parents: my father, ever flamboyant and impulsive; my mother, more practical, concerned with proprieties and duties. And yet I never doubted their love for each other or their wish for my happiness, though just how that happiness might be reached was something on which they would never agree.

Yet they did agree on one thing: their desire for me to excel. Success may have meant different things to each of them, but in subtle ways the pressure to do things well came from both of them. And I responded to each, though I did not realize it till years later, pushing myself to get the highest grades while at the same time attending every party in sight and involving myself in all sorts of school activities. I edited the school paper, sang in the church choir, headed the literary society, starred in the senior play, played violin in both high-school and St. Joseph Little Symphony orchestras, led the Baptist youth program, taught Sunday school, and even spoke from the pulpit. It was a pace that was to continue and accelerate through high school, and for which I would pay dearly at the end of my senior year.

In those early years I took for granted that we lived in a house filled with singing, and that my father would always return from his travels laden with sheet music from the latest New York shows. In my practice on the piano and later the violin (not to mention my sister's reluctantly approved clarinet, when she could be hauled down from trees long enough to play it), Jerome Kern, Irving Berlin, or George Gershwin tunes were as likely to turn up as "Amaryllis" or "Glowworm."

Though my father loved the theater, especially musicals, my mother tended to dismiss most popular music as frivolous. A talented singer, she belonged to a choral group that provided ensemble singing whenever touring opera companies came to town. I vividly remember one thrilling occasion when my sister and I, dressed in robes and sandals, were permitted to join the ensemble when it sang with a touring company of the Oberammergau Passion Players. On the last night, the open-air performance was presented in the midst of one of those dramatic electrical storms which are a midwestern speciality. At the height of the crucifixion scene, as Christ pronounced the words "It is finished," there came a thunderclap so awesome that the entire audience ran screaming down Golgotha hill. Max Reinhardt couldn't have staged anything more spectacular.

My father, on the other hand, was responsible for introducing me to an entirely different kind of musical theater. I remember him taking me on a visit to such a theater when I was very young, probably five. I hung over the railing of the first-row balcony seats in the Tootle Opera House, gazing down at the beautiful girls of "Blossom Time" in their pink dresses. Everything seemed to be pink, for that matter, including the makeup and the crepe-paper apple blossoms that floated down onto everyone at the curtain.

Hardly able to breathe for happiness, I turned to my father and said, "Oh Daddy, I want to be down there where everything's pink!"

Any serious theatrical ambitions I might have had then were given a serious setback in the next few years, however, due to a simple phenomenon. I grew. And grew, and grew. By eleven or twelve I was close to five feet seven, in a time when the desirable thing to be was five feet two, preferably with eyes of blue. Clearly the theater held no place for such a monstrosity! It was not till years later, when I was about sixteen, that I began to feel there was hope. The awakening occurred at a Saturday matinee of *Grand Hotel*, in which the spectacular Garbo, taller than I and with even bigger feet, swept across the screen and into my heart. At the end I swept out of the theater, spine straight and head back, convinced there was hope for me yet.

Shortly after, I was slated to write a skit for the annual high-school student show. I wrote one involving Garbo and, for reasons impossible to recall, Joe E. Brown. As writer-director I was expected to cast it, and I found the perfect boy for the other part immediately. (He was a satchel-mouthed, freckle-faced trumpet player I'd had in mind all along.) But the Garbo role presented problems. I tried out several girls, but none seemed right for the part. Finally one of them said, "If you're so particular, why don't you play it yourself?"

How could I refuse a dare?

I promptly wrote in a song, though Garbo had never sung a note. (It's handy being writer-producer-director.) And I set about making the costume, a long, black, slinky number with a great swath of gray fox, borrowed from my mother's coat, around the off-the-shoulder neckline. I was ready.

If I had flopped that night, Phoebe Tyler might never have been. But I faced the jammed auditorium, half my mind watching the performance in astonishment while the other half fairly wallowed in the approval that poured across the footlights and surrounded me. I was a hit. Fortunately, the sketch itself has been lost to posterity, but I will never forget the feeling of that night: There were the long, lonely hours I'd spent writing the script in my chilly room, and there was the warmth and excitement up on that stage. I knew where I wanted to be from that moment on.

It might not be stretching things too much to say that Phoebe Tyler was born that night, in the cheers and applause from that captive audience. But perhaps Phoebe had always been there, I realized in later years. We share so many things, not the least of which is a fascination with family background. My childhood was a forest of family trees, some with branches reaching back to Europe's Middle Ages. My father's mother treasured a silk-embroidered genealogy featuring such names as Goza (originally di Gozzi, her own maiden name) and Dupuy (her mother's name), both of which were said to have been borne by knights who rode to the Crusades. Another Dupuy, a captain in the palace guard of Louis XIV, married the Countess Susanna Lavillon. In my childhood I often heard the tale of how they narrowly escaped, on horseback and with his wife disguised as his groom, from the Huguenot slaughter in the late seventeenth century.

They settled in Germany, then Holland, but their son emigrated to America and married a woman who, coincidentally, bore his mother's name: Suzanne Lavillon. A descendent, Aaron Goza, became a wealthy plantation owner in the Big Bend bayou country of Louisiana, and served in the Confederate army as a cavalry officer. Family legend has it that he made one too many clandestine visits to his wife, and during one of them the house was surrounded by Union troops. His wife put on one of his old uniforms and rode off in the opposite direction, drawing the troops away so her husband could escape. She was caught, but released unharmed. The captain and his fearless wife were my great-grandparents, and with such stories a documented part of my family history, it is little wonder that I thirsted for romantic adventure. (It is also no wonder that my father insisted on enlisting as a cavalry officer in World War I, to my mother's absolute dismay.) In fact, it has always been a sworn truth in the family that old Aaron Goza conducted jousting matches from horseback every Fourth of July on his Louisiana plantation, and I do not for a moment doubt it.

Books could be written about the Gozas and Dupuys and Warricks (who can trace their ancestors to not one but two Mayflower passengers), from medieval adventures to antebellum Louisiana plantations to prosperous grain warehouses in St. Joseph, still in existence during my father's youth. His father had been president of the Kansas City Grain Exchange, in fact, and had been a major dealer until his speculations in grain futures went sour during the war. My father returned from the army to find the business sold, his job gone, and the entire grain business in such turmoil that no comparable jobs were available.

Much could be written, too, about the hardheaded Scotts, the Scottish forebears of my mother's father's family, and the Irish Smiths, direct descendants of Daniel Boone. They settled in Missouri to raise thoroughbred horses and, of course, mules; my mother's father prospered sufficiently to move from log cabin to the mansion at Quiet Glen in one generation, becoming one of the area's leading livestock dealers. His stock shows brought enormous crowds from all over the country, and were major events in the area during my mother's childhood. The family histories filled my childhood, obscuring to some degree the harsh fact that neither family was now at its zenith, at least economically. No one was really poor, but the great fortunes had gone the way of their romantic pasts. Even Quiet Glen was to be lost, though that would come later, during my adolescent years.

With the grain business gone, my father turned to selling on commission, working for various companies over the next few years, while we moved from place to place. Then when I was six, and eager to begin school, my mother put her foot down and rented a house in St. Joseph so I could get a decent education. The house was large enough, but we couldn't afford to run the furnace, and so spent much of the time huddled around the one stove in the dining room, rushing off to frigid bedrooms to scoot under covers and wait for our teeth to stop chattering. (I still remember taking breaks from my piano practice to warm my stiffening fingers at the stove.) My mother worried incessantly about how it was all to be paid for, warning of possible starvation. Her fears seemed strange and ominous to me, especially since our basement shelves were crammed with home-canned food from the farm, but I realized later that my father's constant job changes must have made her feel insecure.

We remained in St. Joe until my last year of high school, and during most of those years my father prospered, moving up at one point to become sales manager of a chemical company. When that job was lost we moved to Kansas City, where he hoped the pastures would be greener. They were not. He moved from job to job, often seeking help from his younger brother Dupuy, a prominent Kansas City attorney. We survived, but he never again seemed satisfied or truly happy, and the subtle pressure on me seemed to grow, as if my success in life could somehow compensate for his disappointments.

I forged ahead through my senior year, still the classic over-achiever, trying to be perfect in every way. It was about this time that I made a startling discovery that added even further stress to a life already filled with it. This revelation occurred on a hayride, during which I was pressed close to my current boyfriend for hours, under watchful eyes that could not have known the wild urges that were practically consuming me. I returned home feeling feverish, convinced I was afflicted by some shameful obsession that would surely doom me to a life of sin.

I held these urges under iron control, but the effort may have been one of many causes that contributed to a near breakdown that enveloped me right after graduation. It was as if all my emotional and intellectual circuits had been overloaded and had suddenly blown out. Dramatically, in good Phoebe Tyler style, I had simply fainted and folded over the choir rail as we rose to sing the closing hymn at Wornall Road Baptist Church. When I came to, there was a persistent ringing in my ears, and for a long while after, everything seemed to be far away, as if I were looking through the wrong end of binoculars. I walked about in a daze for weeks, doing little more than eating and breathing, and seeming not to care much whether I continued even those activities. Rest and exercise were prescribed, and talks with a doctor about the pressures I'd lived with. He made me understand that the root of my trouble was that I had been vainly trying to make the real world conform to various ideals and attitudes (some of them contradictory) I had absorbed from my family. He suggested that my parents back off a little and avoid trying—however unconsciously—to enlist me to their particular points of view. And he encouraged me to try to do only those things that *I* wanted to do with my energies and talents.

What I chose, that autumn, was to plunge myself into the study of drama, literature, and music at the University of Kansas City. After my very first drama class, I remember riding up in the college's little gilt elevator to the cafeteria, ordering a cream-cheese-and-olive sandwich, and sitting down with my professor and some other students for an informal chat. At that moment something inside me relaxed and smiled, and I knew I was "home," finally doing exactly what I wanted to do and knowing that it was right. To this day, a cream-cheese-and-olive sandwich can turn me on.

Having set me free in this respect, the doctor proceeded to another, delivering a prescription that shocked me and would have horrified my mother. I still remember the dialogue:

Doctor: "Don't you have a boyfriend?"

Ruth: "Of course I do."

Doctor: "Does he really care about you?"

Ruth: "Yes."

Doctor: "Do you feel fond of him?"

Ruth: "Yes."

Doctor: "Hasn't he ever made advances?"

Ruth: "Well, yes. But I couldn't do that."

Doctor: "Well, I'm giving you a prescription and telling you that you had better have it filled or you are headed for *serious trouble*. You are overly mature physically for your age, and you're suffering from several assorted repressions. So I want you to go to this young man and tell him that I want him to go to bed with you."

I delivered this news to my boyfriend, who was understandably impressed and quite prepared to do his part in my mental-health program. He scouted an available house, arranged a New Year's Eve alone there, and conducted a most tender and thorough educational program for my enlightenment.

It was, for me, a powerful experience. Afterward I was certain I was eternally in love with the boy and irrevocably committed. Fortunately he was more realistic and cautious, which is probably the only thing that prevented me from marrying him on the spot. Later on, when he overcame his caution and proposed to me, I had regained my own sanity and remembered my ambitions. We continued to date, but in time my refusal to marry him placed a strain on the relationship. Eventually we broke up, and a short while later he married one of my best friends.

If the doctor had thought his prescription would end those powerful urges that had so alarmed me, he was wrong. I've never decided whether I should have felt cheated by the somewhat clinical aspect of my initiation into love-making or grateful for the tender care with which it was consummated, but I do know that it opened a whole new level of experience for me.

At the same time, my interest in the theater also began to flower at college, helped along by a most remarkable teacher named Blevins Davis, who was directing plays at the university then. A graduate of the famous Yale Drama School, he had taken a job as superintendent of schools in Independence, but found his true love in directing. I appeared in several college productions that first year, and in the second year he phoned with a suggestion that seemed totally preposterous.

"Ruth, you've got to get down here," he said. "The Chamber of Commerce is picking a Miss Jubilesta, and I think you're just right for it."

"You've got to be kidding," I said. I had seen the ads for the tryouts and had heard the constant radio commercials, but that sort of thing was light-years from my mind. "I wouldn't parade around in a bathing suit for anybody," I told Blevins.

"No, no, it's nothing like that," he said. "It's more like a promotion job, to publicize the big fall festival that will open the new music center. Whoever they pick has got to have brains as well as looks. That's why I thought the job might interest you."

Next day I found myself among hundreds of other girls waiting outside the boardroom of the Kansas City Chamber of Commerce. When my turn came I confronted the businessmen grouped around a gigantic table and listened while they explained: The festival was to have about twenty headliners performing, including Jack Benny, Edgar Bergen, Fibber McGee and Molly, and many others, including the big bands of Eddie Duchin and Wayne King. There was to be a production of *The Desert Song* in the new Philharmonic Hall, and an ice follies—the first major Shipstad and Johnson's show to have appeared anywhere outside Minnesota—in the new skating rink. Miss Jubilesta (a word coined from *jubilee* and *fiesta*) was to travel all over Kansas and Missouri for six weeks, appearing at Lions or Kiwanis meetings or anywhere a group could be gathered, and was to deliver a short speech describing the wonders of the Jubilesta so glowingly that families would come to Kansas City and stay for several days. I was to imagine that I was Miss Jubilesta, they concluded, and was to deliver that speech for them right now.

I ad-libbed a speech without any difficulty, and to my amazement I won the contest. I left the building and went home in a state of exhilaration bordering on fever. All night I tossed and turned, awake, knowing my picture would be on the front page of tomorrow's paper, seeing visions of myself in glamorous clothes from Rothschild's, a fancy store in town that had agreed to supply Miss Jubilesta's wardrobe. I knew, somehow, that the next six weeks would change my life, though I didn't yet know how.

By the end of the first week I was already too tired to care, having visited several small towns, talked with the newspaper editors and made my little speech at local clubs in each place, and helped set up a beauty contest that would send local candidates to the final pageant, where a Jubilesta Queen would be chosen. I traveled with a chaperone, since it was not considered proper for a young woman to travel alone, and often rode in a truck outfitted with recording equipment, with the assignment to interview some local celebrity for broadcast later. In those pretape days the recordings were cut on old acetate disks, which were vulnerable to heat. More than once we watched helplessly while a prize interview melted into a glob of wax.

I rode on an elephant in one carnival and judged jams and jellies in another, and in still another town I recall singing numbers from *The Desert Song* between reels of a Fred Astaire and Ginger Rogers movie. In Oklahoma City, the largest town on my tour, the mayor said he had left a hospital bed to greet me, and to prove it he insisted I feel the scars of surgery on his stomach.

But in some ways the most memorable of all was the day in Springfield, Missouri, where I ran into the first real resistance to my pitch. Long resentful of upstate outsiders, they seemed determined to give me no newspaper space at all. Frustrated, I asked around and found out the only action going on in town was a baseball game that night. I headed for the ball park and marched into the press box to introduce myself and plead my case.

They were sympathetic, but explained that this was a sporting event and they could only cover what happened on the field. "Now, if Miss Jubilesta should appear on the field and do something, I guess we could cover that," one of them said. That seemed reasonable, so I agreed to be taken down to the dugout and presented to the coach as a pinch hitter.

He didn't buy that, but he did agree to let me swing at a few pitches during the seventh-inning stretch. I waited, and when I was signaled to the plate I strode up in my bouffant organdy dress and big picture hat, smacked the first pitch over the pitcher's head, and tore off toward first base, losing first a heel, then a whole shoe, and finally my hat on the way. It was only then, hearing the laughter from the dugout and the silence from the stands, that I realized I'd been had. No announcement had been made, the fans thought some lunatic was running amok, and the press boys were splitting their sides instead of pounding out their stories. I managed to keep my injured dignity intact until I was back in the hotel room, then broke into tears of fury at the way I'd been tricked. It was my only time at bat in the minor leagues.

By the time my tour was over and I returned to Kansas City for the big show, I was already a local celebrity because of the recorded interviews, which had been sent back and played on KMBC, the CBS radio station. The original plan had been to have one of the stars host the show before ten thousand people, but picking among the celebrities turned out to be a thorny problem. Big Names have big egos, and no one wanted to see anyone else singled out as the evening's major attraction, so at last it was decided that I should be mistress of ceremonies. I was ecstatic.

The evening went without a hitch, including the coronation—patterned on the ceremonies used to crown British royalty—of the Jubilesta Queen. Virginia, the girl in question, had a face and figure that would have been the envy of most movie stars, but she turned out not to have the slightest ambition for a career in show business. When offered a choice of a trip to Hollywood, where a screen test could be arranged, or to New York for sightseeing, she astonished everyone by picking New York. "I can't act," she told them, "but I sure would like to see New York."

The chamber of commerce gentlemen now began to realize that their gorgeous queen was painfully shy. And this was worrisome, since part of the point of her trip was to publicize Kansas City and its new cultural center. If they sent her she might easily annoy or bore reporters with her reticence. Their solution was to send their proven nonstop talker, Miss Jubilesta, along with her to handle the interviews.

From the moment they informed me of this plan, I knew that *this* was how my life would be changed. No matter how much I loved my family, and no matter how busy and productive I made my life in Kansas City, I knew it could not be the place where my future lay. I'd done all the acting I could in community and college theater groups, and I had even sung on a local radio station, but I knew that there was no real possiblity of a theatrical career there. And now I was being offered a free trip to New York, with the beauty queen and a chaperone to cushion the shock of a strange place. Surely it had to be fate.

My mother was nearly prostrate when I told her about the trip, because I think she understood that I planned to stay there if I could find a way. My father knew that too, but he was happy for me and encouraged me to go. I'm sure he shared some of my mother's worries, which were many and lurid, but he also must have taken some vicarious pleasure in my chance to venture forth into the exciting city he had so loved to visit. Years later I learned that he had always secretly hoped I would one day star in musical comedies like those whose songs he had come home singing in his traveling days. My mother hoped only that I would come home, preferably unsullied, and settle down next door.

Virginia and I were given a big send-off, beginning with a chamber of commerce luncheon which was covered by all the papers. From there we were whisked to the airport, loaded down with bouquets of chrysanthemums, and were photographed endlessly all the way to the steps of the plane. Finally, when the hoopla was over and we were ready to leave, we were bumped from the plane to make room for paying passengers.

Fate's little jokes, however, often seem to have O. Henry endings, and this was no exception. Just before we boarded the second plane, we heard that the one from which we had been bumped had been forced to make an emergency landing in an Iowa cornfield, with several injuries among the passengers.

Our flight was blessedly uneventful, and by morning we were happily settled in our rooms at the Barbizon-Plaza, a place that seemed to me the absolute pinnacle of luxury. When morning brought a "continental breakfast"—a stale roll and tepid coffee pushed through a panel in the door, to be eaten in bed— I knew I had arrived in the land of my romantic dreams.

Virginia and I were hustled about dizzily during the week of our visit, being interviewed and photographed and even trooped before the microphones of a radio show called *Vox Pop*, where I managed to spell correctly a word I had surely

never had occasion to use in my life. It was "chukker," a term
from polo that I summoned from some unknown cranny of my
mind where forgotten sports pages were stored. It was a week
that moved at great speed, organized by PR people to squeeze
the most publicity from the wide-eyed midwestern girls in sophisticated Gotham.

One stunt was covered by the papers and the cameras of
Movietone News: my visit to Mayor Fiorello La Guardia on
the steps of City Hall. We arrived at the scene by car on a raw
October day, and I climbed out in my suit and hat to be met
by the PR man and one of the largest and most unfriendly
turkeys I have ever seen before or since. The PR man explained
that I was to carry the bird up the steps of City Hall and present
it to the mayor, while the newsreel cameras and reporters recorded the proceedings for the "eyes and ears of the world."

I have climbed the steps of New York's City Hall many
times since then, but they have never seemed so long. I had
especially wanted to look good for the Movietone cameras,
since that kind of exposure might help launch the career I
envisioned, but now it was all I could do to hang onto the
turkey, much less avoid being upstaged by it. Half-way up the
steps the wretched bird managed to work one huge wing loose
and began to flap it wildly in front of me. Since I was afraid
to risk loosening my grip on the bird's body to gather in the
wing, I could do nothing but trudge grimly on. At the top, after
an endless climb, a mayoral aide whisked the infuriated turkey
offstage while I shook the mayor's hand and mumbled inco-
herently. Years later the adventure was immortalized by a com-
poser friend in a song called "She's the Girl Who Took the
Turkey to La Guardia," but I cannot to this day face a turkey
calmly.

The week ended at last, and the entourage returned to Kansas
City without me. For Virginia the memories were enough. For
me, however, they were just the beginning—though of what
I was not yet sure.

I had come to New York with two hundred dollars, which
had seemed a fortune in Missouri but which was now beginning
to look less grand. Obviously I would have to watch the pen-
nies. As soon as I could I moved from the Barbizon-Plaza to
a seven-dollar-a-week rooming house, an ancient building of
forgotten elegance at Fifty-fifth and Seventh Avenue, right in

the center of the theater world.

The first night was uneventful, but in the middle of the second night I woke up itching, with little red spots all over my body. All my mother's horror stories about what happened to young girls in big cities ran through my mind, so I rushed to the bathroom to scrub myself from top to bottom. Then I went back to the room, turned on every light, packed my suitcase, and sat bolt upright in a straight-backed chair the rest of the night, praying I hadn't somehow caught some unmentionable social disease. At dawn I fled, relegating the two weeks' advance rent to the cost of experience, and reluctantly went to the Ambassador Hotel, where my uncle Dupuy stayed when he was in town on frequent business trips. He was there, and he quickly solved the problem. The daughter of a Kansas City friend of his was in town and living at the American Women's Association Club (now the Henry Hudson Hotel), a haven that allowed no males above the lobby floor and no bedbugs at all. He phoned to arrange it, and I moved in at once, a bit disappointed at having needed family help but at least relieved to be safe from further vermin assaults.

I quickly learned the formula for survival in the city, at least the one applying then to reasonably attractive single girls. You lived where the rent was cheapest, you got orange juice and coffee and toast in the morning for thirty-five cents at the drugstore counter, and you tried to have a dinner or lunch date every day, at which you gorged yourself. In between you made the rounds, which in those days involved theatrical auditions (which you dreamed of cracking) and the radio studios (which could pay the rent if you were lucky).

Although I was not particularly lucky at earning money, I did manage to get myself accepted in a very good workshop for young actors being conducted under the aegis of Paramount Pictures. We met in a building in Times Square to do scenes together, under an experienced drama coach. I can still recall staring out the window at the rising bubbles of the Wrigley sign and the smoke rings being blown by the huge face on a cigarette billboard. The workshop represented some progress in my career, I felt, even if my money was dwindling rapidly.

Just before Christmas, after I had decided not to go back to Kansas City for the holidays, the director of the workshop informed me that the whole operation was being transferred to California. I was welcome to rejoin it there, he said, but I declined. New York was where I wanted to be—even if I starved, which was beginning to seem likely. I had invitations that would feed me though the holidays, but by January my money would be entirely gone. And I felt strongly that I would not ask my parents for help.

When I told the workshop director of my troubles, I must have touched some chord of sympathy. He said he wanted to show me something, and suggested we take a walk.

We went down Seventh Avenue a little way, and he stopped in front of a big building. "Make a note of this address," he said, pointing at the door. "This is the center of the wholesale garment district, and right after the holidays it will be packed with out-of-town buyers who've come to order their spring lines. They'll need all the models they can get."

I told him I had never done any modeling, but he assured me it didn't matter, that any girl with a good face and figure could do it. I thanked him, certain he was wrong, and we parted company.

By the evening of January 1, after counting my few remaining dollars, I had decided to give the garment district a chance. So early next morning I arrived at the building and stepped into an elevator.

"What floor, miss?" the operator asked.

I had no idea, so I said, "The top, please." Might as well start there.

I got off the elevator into sheer bedlam. A fashion show was in progress and the place was jammed. The elevator door had barely closed when a harried-looking man rushed up, grabbed my arm, and said, "Where in hell have you been? You're late."

Before I could open my mouth he had hustled me into a dressing room and ordered me to get into the first outfit, then raced back out into the bustling showroom. I changed into the clothes he had shown me, asked someone where to go, and in seconds was walking up and down amongst the customers with the other models.

By the end of the day I was huddled in a chair, close to total exhaustion. Suddenly the harried man came in and confronted me. "You're not Norma," he said accusingly.

I admitted it.

"Well, you did a pretty good job anyway," he said. "We'll get your name down right on the records. Be here at seven tomorrow."

I went home and collapsed, trying to remember who in the world had ever told me modeling was glamorous. It was hard physical labor, as grueling as any work I've ever done, but I stuck it out for two weeks and hoarded my pay. When I got an opportunity to appear in a showcase production of the Theater Wing, endowed by Antoinette Perry, I jumped at it. The owner of the garment firm was appalled that I would leave a career in modeling for the rough world of the theater, but I thanked him for his concern and went on my way, filing away for possible emergencies his assurance of future employment.

Luckily, times never got that bad again, and I never resumed my brief career as a Seventh Avenue model. But I never regretted it, either, nor any other work experience I've ever had, including the stint years earlier selling lingerie in a Kansas City hosiery shop, though that job left me with a permanent compulsion to refold things. All those experiences are part of the way one learns what one can do, and for an actress they are part of the reservoir to be drawn from throughout one's career. Good or bad, happy or tragic, no experience is wasted if something is learned.

And I was learning at a furious pace, and trying every path that might eventually lead to those exalted regions where Helen Hayes and Katharine Cornell waited to be dethroned. In other words, I made the rounds, including the radio studios where one might—if persistent and lucky—get a chance to audition for a play or a soap opera. My director and friend from Kansas City, Blevins Davis, had joined NBC under his old Yale Drama School buddy John S. Royal. With Blevins' help I got small parts in several of the network's *Great Plays* productions, and those credits helped open cracks in other doors. Survival began to seem possible.

One day in the lounge outside the CBS casting offices I noticed a very handsome, tall man watching me as I read over the material I'd brought along for a possible auditon. When I left a while later, he followed me into the elevator. He asked if I would like a cup of coffee at Colby's, the unofficial hangout for many of the top radio actors of the day. I had recognized his voice immediately, and of course I was thrilled at the idea of being among the famous in Colby's, especially with one of the more successful of them as my escort. So, putting aside my mother's dire prediction, I said yes.

His name was Erik Rolf, and he was one of radio's better-known voices at the time. As announcer for newscaster Boake Carter, as actor on *Gang Busters* and innumerable other shows, and as one of the masters of the dialects then popular on radio, he was high on the ladder of success I was just beginning to climb. I was flattered that he was interested in me, and even more so when he offered to help with my audition material. We had dinner at a place called Marnel's, and from there we went to his room at the Shelton Hotel, at that time still one of the elegant places to live in New York.

I was somewhat apprehensive about going to a man's hotel room, having been crammed full of warnings by everyone before I left Kansas City. But I was also feeling quite sophisticated, filled with the sort of French cuisine one did not get in Missouri and flattered by the interest of this handsome and successful man. Besides, this was business.

He brought out a bottle of brandy and poured two glasses, and we started to work on the audition material. And we stayed with it for a respectable time, with me sipping on my brandy while he had a second glass and a third. After a while we put the script aside and began to compare our backgrounds, which turned out to be quite similar. We talked on and on, and he drank glass after glass of brandy, and in what seemed a short time the night was over and the entire bottle of brandy was gone. He had finished the whole thing without seeming the least bit drunk, and he had not made a single pass, which left me feeling both relieved and slightly disappointed. But this was New York and Erik was a worldly man, attentive but considerate, so I left that morning quite unalarmed and eager to see him again.

I was "home" at the American Women's Association very little over the next few weeks. Instead, I was on a constant whirl around the city, under the guidance of the most charming man I had met in New York. We dined at the Rainbow Room and lunched by Prometheus in Rockefeller Plaza; we rode horse-drawn carriages in Central Park and walked from one end of Manhattan to the other; we went to movies and the ballet and the Metropolitan Opera; and always Erik was the gallant and considerate man I'd met that first night in the CBS elevator. He was handsome, charming, at the peak of his career; and rather than hinting at a future of housewifery, he encouraged my ambitions. Of course I fell in love.

I confessed my feelings to another boyfriend that spring, over Manhattans in a midtown restaurant. Gail Smith and I had enjoyed some pleasant weekends at his older brother's home in Connecticut (our families were friends in Kansas City), but I was not really aware until that moment how deep his feelings ran.

"You mean you're thinking of marrying this man?" he asked.

I explained about the many interests Erik and I shared, especially our mutual ambitions in the theater, and ended by saying we probably would marry, though we had not actually made any firm plans about it.

"But do you *love* him?" Gail asked.

"Of course I do," I told him. Did I? I was certainly attracted to Erik and flattered by his interest, and even though our sexual experiences had been less than earthshaking I was convinced we were ideally matched. Besides, my own strong sexual impulses had alarmed me a bit, as anything not totally under control tended to do. The main thing I wanted was to be an actress; and that was the one thing of which I was totally certain. Erik shared my feelings on that.

Gail was looking miserable, as if he might burst into tears.

"At least promise you'll wait till I graduate," he pleaded. "I'll get a good job, and then I'll be able to offer you the kind of life you deserve."

I realized then how little he understood me. How could he offer me the kind of life I wanted? Only *I* could do that, by pursuing my own dreams. Erik surely understood that, since we shared those dreams. With him I could have both marriage and career; with Gail and most other men the role of wife and mother would have to come first. Part of me sympathized with Gail's obvious hurt, but another part stood apart and weighed the emotions, thankful that I had somehow been freed from the need to be responsible for another's feelings.

"All right!" he said. "You want to be a star? Go ahead, be a star. But I'll tell you this: No matter how far you go or how big you get, someday I'll be able to hire and fire you!"

The boast seemed extravagant at the time, but I smiled and placated him, glad that he had an ambition to match mine.

On April 15, 1938, in Holy Trinity Lutheran Church at Sixty-fifth and Central Park West, only three blocks from the present *All My Children* studio, I became Mrs. Erik Rolf.

As I look back on the courtship and try to reconstruct the thoughts and feelings that led me to that wedding, I find myself wondering if I would behave today as I behaved then. Oddly, it is easier to answer on behalf of Phoebe. For her, the answer plainly would be yes. For me, the matter is less clear.

We continued our careers in radio, appearing on such shows as *Myrt and Marge* and *Grand Central Station*. And in the following months two things occurred that were prophetic, at least in terms of my later career.

The first was a small part in one of the leading radio soap operas of the time, *Joyce Jordan, Girl Interne*. The role lasted six months, and I moved on to other things, assuming I had left the soaps behind me. (Years later, in 1954, Hi Brown revised the show for radio syndication and asked me to play the lead, by then *Dr.* Joyce Jordan herself. I took great pleasure in having the principal role in a show that had formerly offered me dialogue consisting mainly of "Yes, doctor.")

The second was an incident that seemed trivial at the time. It began with another call from my old friend Blevins Davis, now an executive with NBC.

"Ruth, get down to the RCA building," he said. "They need a pretty girl who can talk for a demonstration of closed-circuit television."

"Television?"

"You know, radio with pictures."

"Oh," I said. Of course I had heard of television, still in the experimental stage. It seemed remote from my life, but a job was a job, so I did it.

Years later I realized that my career has spanned the history of television, from that early demonstration to the present multi-billion-dollar empire of which *All My Children* is a part. That brief appearance before the television cameras was, in a sense, an aspect of Phoebe Tyler's beginnings, though more than thirty years were to pass before her time would come.

Oh yes, there was a third incident, though this one was so unimportant at the time that I hardly recall now exactly when or where it occurred. It was on one of the many radio shows I participated in, sometime later that year. One of the actors appearing with me was a large young man whose activities were beginning to draw attention in other arenas. Though only twenty-three, he had already caused much talk with his all-black production of *Macbeth* at Harlem's Apollo Theatre, and had created a nationwide furor with his now-famous *War of the Worlds* broadcast. Even though he was being hailed as one of Broadway's most innovative talents because of his Mercury Theatre productions, he continued to do radio parts to earn a living, as most theater actors did at the time.

Little remains in my memory of that first encounter except that he arrived late, but our second meeting was to change the whole course of my life.

His name, of course, was Orson Welles.

THREE

Pine Valley:
Later that Morning

YOU GO THROUGH A DOOR and down a short corridor. On one side is the control room; on the other, beyond a glass window, are the tape library and sound consoles of the show's music director, whose job it is to select, record, and insert appropriate background music in scenes the director feels require it. These tapes, thousands of them, are filed and numbered under such categories as Turmoil, Agitated, Extremely agitated, Happy, Frustrated, Haunted, and the like. Sometimes there are subcategories, such as Love's awakening, Love's flowering, and Love's consummation. It is horrifying to think what confusion would reign in a scene if those last three were switched around.

In many cases the music may express more than the actual dialogue conveys in a scene, as when two characters of opposite sex stare silently into each other's eyes. The music may swell to an emotional peak to indicate love, or it may sink sadly to indicate a parting, or any number of other possibilities not evident from the dialogue alone. And then there is the "sting," that sudden burst of ominous music so like a shiver down the spine, indicating something tragic or crucial impending. (The old radio soaps, where the organ held emotional sway, could sting listeners so violently they would gasp. Modern serials, with full orchestration, are less crude, but our effete sting is still very effective.)

The music is keyed into the script by the director, but the musical director makes the selections from his library, and his or her choices are usually accepted. Occasionally the director may disagree with the effect of the chosen music on the scene for dramatic reasons, and sometimes music is rejected because it clashes with a development in the future story line known to the director and writers but as yet unrevealed to the rest of us. Sometimes the objections are less concrete, and lead to dialogue best kept from the musical director's ears. ("Shouldn't the music be...uh... *nicer*, there?" the associate producer may ask from the back row of the control room. "What the hell does *that* mean?" Henry says. "Oh, I dunno. Sort of... uh... *longer*?" Henry throws his hands up. "Nicer and longer? Marvelous. *You* tell Jim that." No one does, and the music stays.)

But now, as you pass between the music director's lair and the control room, things are quiet. At the end of the short corridor you face another door, this one festooned with warnings: No unauthorized persons beyond this point, No admittance when red light is on, etc. On the other side of this door is Pine Valley—the "real" Pine Valley, as seen on television screens five hours each week throughout the year. It is the ABC studio devoted entirely to *All My Children*, and it is worth a long look. You are hereby authorized to open that door.

Your first impression is that the place is enormous, covering most of a city block. The cavernous room, which would accommodate a football field, was originally two studios. But in 1977, when our show went to an hour, ABC had to knock out the wall between Studio 18, where we taped, and Studio 19, which had housed Agnes Nixon's other creation, *One Life to Live*. We made a party of the demolition, with Phoebe wielding the sledgehammer for the big breakthrough. The larger space was quickly filled with the additional sets needed for the longer show, and with two additional cameras, a third sound boom, and hundreds of overhead lights. Although these lights are activated by a two-million-dollar computer console that can be played like a keyboard or run on a preset program, they still must be positioned and adjusted by hand.

Let's take a quick tour, before the madness begins.

Today there are ten sets, seven of which have been trucked in from a downtown warehouse and assembled overnight, to be ready for the day's shooting. At the right end of the studio as you enter, the first thing that hits your eye is the familiar foyer of the Tyler mansion, with its sweeping circular stairway and its marble-tiled floor. Through a connecting door at the left is the Tyler library, which remained unchanged for years until

Phoebe was persuaded by the smooth-talking Langley Wallingford to have it completely redecorated. These two sets, since they are the most often used and the most difficult to reconstruct, are permanent. A third rather elaborate set at the opposite end of the studio is semipermanent. It is the richly paneled study of the Cortlandt mansion, home of the immensely wealthy, coldly ruthless Palmer Cortlandt and his sheltered daughter, Nina. This large room, with its entrances through which corridors may be seen and its elegant masculine look, will undoubtedly be left in place for as long as the Cortlandts remain active in the story line.

Moving counterclockwise from the Tyler library we pass a staff lounge in the Pine Valley Hospital, a glittery disco under construction in the Goalpost restaurant, the third-floor servant's room in the Tyler mansion where fugitive Anne is being hidden from authorities. Beyond the Cortlandt study, described earlier, is a hospital room where Erica's husband is recovering from knee surgery, the kitchen of the Tucker house, a hospital waiting room, and the kitchen of the Tyler mansion. (The latter pleases me, since there have been snide suggestions over the years that Phoebe has never seen her own kitchen. Today she will—though she certainly will not *cook* anything there.)

These rooms are not like rooms in a normal house, of course. For one thing they have no ceilings, so the lights, mounted twenty feet overhead on frameworks of pipe, can play upon them from all angles. As I've said, all the adjustments for the angle or amount of light have to be made by hand, or more specifically, by technicians using a long pole with a hook on the end of it. Once, in my never-ending quest for knowledge, I asked one of the lighting men what that piece of equipment was called. "It's a pole with a hook on the end of it," he explained patiently.

Sets are generally three-sided, like doll-house rooms, except that the side walls are seldom set at right angles to the back. These wider angles, which are not noticeable on the home screen, allow the cameras much greater freedom to maneuver than would a conventional setup. Sometimes walls have to be extended in great haste, when a camera swings around during rehearsal of a scene and suddenly runs out of set and "shoots off" into bare studio. This will be followed by cries of "Carpenter! Carpenter!" and a great scurrying and hammering. In seconds the wall will have grown another ten or twelve feet. Some sets, such as the Tyler library and the Cortlandt study, are permanent; that is, not returned to storage each night, as are all other sets. Sometimes smaller sets can be fitted inside them, rather like a nest of Chinese boxes. Some sets are partial sets, sometimes even half sets with only the portions completed that will be seen on camera—a bed, a restaurant booth, a pay telephone hanging alone on a short section of wall.

It is a few minutes after ten. The technical director's voice is now heard over the speakers, which are in every makeup room, hairdressing room, and dressing room: "Camera and booms, please. Five minutes until blocking." This is the call to battle stations for the people who operate the cameras and sound equipment, and a general warning to everyone else.

A second voice, this time the stage manager: "Good morning. In the Prologue I will need Phoebe and Charles, Palmer and Nina, Paul, Ellen, and Devon. On the set in five minutes, please." (Once we enter the studio we become the characters we play, by custom and to avoid the embarrassment of forgetting the name of a new performer—or even an old one.)

The actors, still in jeans and shorts and some in curlers, begin to assemble on their various sets, awaiting the director. They walk around, following the notations on their scripts, mumbling or silently mouthing their lines in preparation, stepping over the snaking cables automatically. They are oblivious to the bustle around them, the movement of equipment and the scurry of the people who make it all go. We are ready now for the second run-through of today's script, this time on the sets before the cameras. Indeed, this "blocking" is really *for* the cameras and sound booms and lights.

If you were a bird, and if you could see through the roof of the studio past those banks of carbon-vapor lights, you would see that this huge room, with sets constructed around its four walls, has a large open area in its center. This area is filled with men and equipment: There are five cameras, two positioned now toward each end and one in the middle, but all of them mobile, gliding on silent rubber wheels. The operator must move the camera himself, pushing, pulling, kicking, framing, and focusing, all at once. There are the three sound booms, mounted like huge praying mantises on their higher platforms over larger wheels, with microphones extended on long, movable arms like retractable fishing poles that can swing into position above the actors' heads. There are three podium-like objects, each with a microphone and a small monitor set mounted on it, and each also moving on invisible wheels. From each of these mobile pieces of equipment long cables extend across the floor, thick black snakes containing dozens of wires connecting the machine to its power source and to the control room. The cables, some the size of garden hoses, are every-where, yet as each camera or sound boom moves from one set to another it must do so without crossing its own or any other cable. It is a diabolically complex ballet that requires careful advance planning and quick footwork on the part of the camera operators (no, not camera*men*—one of ours is unmistakably female) and their assistants.

This choreography has been diagrammed in advance by the director, who has just entered the studio trailing an entourage of assistants and technicians. Henry is still wearing the jeans and red polo shirt, but he is no longer subdued or sleepy. He is moving quickly, checking his master script and lists of scenes and camera positions, looking around to see if all is ready and everyone is here—all the more than one hundred people (in-cluding makeup, wardrobe, control room people, and others not immediately in view but at work nonetheless) who make this complicated undertaking work, at a cost of thousands of dollars per minute of actual air time. He marches to the podium nearest the Tyler library set and summons Phoebe and Charles, who are in the first scene.

"Let's *go*, people," Henry calls. "Run run *run*."

From this point on the action will be continuous and breath-less as each scene is run through on its actual set, with lights working and sound booms maneuvered into place, and with cameras moving to their positions, two and sometimes three to each scene, half-ton machines that must be rolled by hand and manually raised, lowered, or tilted to the desired height or angle. Each camera has a card clipped to it, and on these cards are directions for that camera during a given scene. If you translated the arcane abbreviations, one such card might read:

Shot 2: Medium shot, Phoebe at bar pouring drink. Carry her to Charles, include him in two shot.

Shot 3: Bust shot, Charles.

Shot 4: Close-up, Phoebe.

Shot 5: Close-up, Charles.

Shot 7: Medium long shot, Phoebe and Charles. Phoebe calls Brooke into room.

What happened to Shots 1 and 6? They are on the second camera's card, which might read:

Shot 1: Take Phoebe as she opens door to Charles. Follow them into library.

Shot 6: Close, Brooke in hall, overhearing conversation.

Shot 8: Medium long shot, Brooke. Follow her into room, include all three.

Each camera will have a card for each scene, with the shots for the entire show broken up among the five cameras but all numbered consecutively. The director's master list will include all these numbered shots, running perhaps between seven hundred and one thousand for an hour show with the additional notation of the camera number for each: Camera 1, Camera 2, and so on through the five. As we run through this first scene in the Tyler library the director will cue each camera with the number of the shot, then will add instructions as he sees that camera's shot on his own monitor, sometimes tightening a shot (coming in closer), sometimes asking for a change in height or angle. These added instructions will be noted on the camera's card for that scene and then, hopefully, will be committed to the operator's memory, since he or she will not be able to see the card during the actual shooting of a scene.

The blocking of this scene will be stopped a dozen times while a camera is repositioned, props are moved, lighting is altered, or other changes are made as the director actually sees the scene working for the first time on the set. At Charles' entrance the planned camera angle may pick up a bit of bare studio wall, so either the camera must be moved to a new position or the set will have to be changed. The camera's

movement may be impeded by the structure of the set. Options
are discussed and solutions are reached. Some props are moved
slightly and the camera is tilted a bit. We finish the scene, and
Henry races off to the set where Scene 2 will be rehearsed,
and where the actors are already waiting.

This is a new set, a great and glittery mass of moving Mylar
strips that will be part of Erica's new disco, now under construction unbeknownst to her hospitalized husband. (At the
opening a few weeks later, Phoebe is to disco madly with the
professor while Erica dances with the evening's guest of honor,
Dick Cavett. Bathing suits, passionate bedroom scenes, disco
dancing, even being suspected of murder—what else lies down
the road for Phoebe, I wonder?) There is a platform in the
center with empty boxes and debris scattered about, and there
are two tall ladders standing amidst the clutter. The scene will
open with Wally high on one of the ladders, screwing light
bulbs into an arrangement of sockets.

Mona Kane, Erica's long-suffering mother and Charles Tyler's long-suffering lover, enters at stage right and looks
around, obviously bewildered in this unfamiliar glitter. The
bewilderment is real, since Fra Heflin, who plays Mona, has
never seen this set before and is unsure of her directions. She
hesitates.

"You walk to center stage, dear." It is Henry's disembodied
voice, edged with impatience. Mona takes a hesitant step and
stops again. "W-A-L-K," Henry spells out helpfully.

Mona moves to center stage, blinking at the shimmering
Mylar. "My, but this place is coming along," she says, peering
up at Wally on his ladder.

"Stop! Mark her," Henry yells. The stage manager, a man
wearing bits of colored tape all over his shirt, runs out to stick
a strip of red tape on the floor at her toes. Henry cues the next
shot, and Wally begins to climb down the ladder, talking as
he comes. At the bottom he tries to pick his way through the
debris and over the platform, stumbling over a box.

"Hold it," Henry calls. There is discussion; a property man
moves the ladder closer to the platform and Henry rearranges
the clutter, risking the ire of the prop man's union, to clear a
path for Wally. They begin again, marking ladder locations
and each position of Wally and Mona through the scene. Sat-

isfied at last, Henry rushes to the next set, a new one representing the garret room of the Tyler mansion where Phoebe's fugitive daughter, Anne, is being hidden from hospital authorities. It contains a narrow cot and little else, but its walls have been artfully dirtied, the yellowing wallpaper showing lighter areas where pictures once hung, thus indicating that the room has been long unused. They are artists, our set designers.

Phoebe is there, and the scene—a monologue spoken over the sleeping Anne—goes smoothly, with two cameras taking their cues as they jockey for different angles and close-ups. There will be two other scenes on this particular set today, and they will cause more trouble. In one, while Anne and I walk about this room, embracing and moving from window to door to bed, Anne's head keeps disappearing behind mine at awkward moments, and cameras must be repositioned. More taped marks are added in this scene, this time in a second color. (In the third scene, in which Anne appears alone, still another color of tape will be used for the marks, until the floor will begin to look like the game plan of a demented football coach.) These marks, so essential to camera direction, must be followed precisely by the actors—but this must be done without looking down at them. If the camera catches an actor squinting at the floor during a tense, emotional scene, it can be embarrassing indeed. Especially if the offender hears the dread cry of "Cut!" followed by Henry's elephantine sarcasm. "Let's all take a break while Miss Dumb finds her mark, shall we? Have you got it, dear? May we move forward now?" There is nothing to do but grit one's teeth and vow never to look down again. Silently, however, or one will hear Henry's favorite words: "Shut *up!*" He is not above spelling that out, either.

The pace accelerates, and Henry's red shirt is in constant flight from set to set. He calls for missing actors; yells for a carpenter here or a prop change there; comes dangerously near hysteria when a kitchen faucet produces no water, is assured that the pump needs only to be plugged in, suggests sweetly that someone go plug the wonderful pump in; races on.

The "someone" who will plug the pump in will probably be from "electric," if the problem concerns wiring or the power source for the pump. However, the pump itself might well belong to "property," the people who are in charge of all the movable objects that make sets seem real: furniture, pots and pans, plants, dishes and trays, even the food to be eaten in a scene, which the property men prepare in their own little kitchen. The range of props is staggering, from party hors d'oeuvres to the large truck that picked up Donna as she hitchhiked away from Pine Valley. They can include everything from jukeboxes and psychedelic lights for Erica's disco to working stoves, refrigerators, sinks, and even in one case a huge kidney-dialysis machine borrowed from a hospital. (When Agnes Nixon learned that patients were deprived of its use while we had it, she was horrified and immediately ordered a replica of the machine constructed.) If ice cubes are needed for drinks or nail polish is to be applied by a housewife preparing for a night out, those items must be on the correct set for the correct act, and it is the responsibility of "property" to see that they are—or hear yells of outrage from the director.

Of course sometimes even the most professional propmen make mistakes. Once Nick Davis was having a quarrel with Erica, telling her he was *not* marrying her and, though she had her bags packed to go with him, he was *not* taking her along to Chicago. At this intense moment the phone rang. Nick turned to answer it—but there was no phone! He shrugged, picked up a potted plant, held it to his ear, and said, "Hello?" But the invisible phone continued to ring. In a few more seconds the propman walked into the scene, opened the closet door, took out the phone, handed it to Nick, and said, "It's for you."

The third major group composing the stage crew is "carpenters," the men who erect and knock down the sets and who must be on hand to repair or add to those sets throughout the day. All these people have been at work together since four or five in the morning, erecting sets and moving furniture and props into place, arranging standing back lights to simulate daylight outside windows on some sets or perhaps moonlight seen through others, even wiring pumps. They will be on call through the long day as needed, then will join forces once again when taping is done—often late in the evening—to knock down the sets and deliver them to the ramp for loading onto trucks and transport back to the warehouse. (The loading and unloading at the ramp is done by a wholly separate crew, members of the Teamsters Union, and woe unto anyone who trespasses on *their* domain.)

"What the hell are you doing, the backstroke?" We are back with Henry, now at the new garret-room set, where Anne is supposed to be waking and looking around this unfamiliar place. They run through the bit again, and this time her arms do not flail about. Satisfied, Henry is off again, calling for Cameras 4 and 5 to the Cortlandt study.

"Cue Miss Wisp," he calls when everyone is in place, and Nina Cortlandt picks up the phone, which has not rung (that sound will be "laid-in" from a separate studio during actual taping). She begins to talk to the young doctor she hopes to see that night, against her father's wishes. Behind her her father enters, overhears, reacts, and tiptoes backward out of the room—and into a wall, which trembles.

"Marvelous," Henry calls. "But might we try that again, do you think? Without that last wonderful touch?"

They run through it again, and again to reposition a camera that has picked up the shadow of the sound boom, and then again because Nina has missed a cue. This time, as her father backs into the hall to eavesdrop, carefully avoiding the wall, Henry discovers that Nina's voice has sunk to a near whisper.

"How can he hear you out there?" Henry asks her sweetly. "*God* can't even hear you."

One more try, this time while one of the pole-with-a-hook-on-it men bangs on the metal flaps of a light over Nina's head. Everyone ignores him, or tries to. We have all learned to live with the constant noise and commotion that goes on all around us as we rehearse, though it can sometimes be quite disconcerting to be doing an intimate love scene while a man is whacking away at a light directly above you and someone else is nailing a new foot onto your bed. Although Ruth would never complain about this, Phoebe occasionally does, in a fire and brimstone voice that brings instant silence from one end of the studio to the other.

Henry dashes away again, trailed by cameras which are trailed by cables which are trailed by men who jump about, pulling those cables this way and that lest a camera run over its own or another machine's umbilical cord. (Apart from possible damage to the equipment, a bump over a cable during actual taping would ruin a whole scene, so it is crucial that all moves from set to set be worked out now.)

"Cue Boring," Henry yells at the kitchen set. Devon has

missed her entrance. We've all been dubbed "boring" at some time.

"You sit now," he reminds Paul Martin. "S-I-T." Paul collapses into a chair, and the scene continues.

At the next set two chairs are mysteriously missing, and propmen are sent scurrying to find them while the scene is played, a dialogue between Palmer Cortlandt and Dr. Charles Tyler.

"Oh, Dr. Tyler, one, two, three, how good to see you," Cortlandt says on the third try.

"By God, I think he's got it," Henry cries, mimicking Rex Harrison. "Now if Camera Three can get it we'll be just fine. That's a bust shot, dear. B-U-S-T."

"But my card says—"

"Shut *UP*! You'll get a *hit*."

The camera is moved forward, lowered slightly, and Henry applauds. The operator amends her card. Henry is off to the next set, shouting for "Phoebe and Mrs. Whatsername."

At last he is satisfied that all cameras have their cues, all props are in place, and all actors are in reasonable control of their moves. While the lighting director and his men make last-minute corrections, Henry heads for the control room, where he will run through the whole thing again with the technical director, the associate director, the lighting director, the assistant to the producer, the script girl, and whoever else might have the temerity to enter that sacred domain, including an occasional actor. They will work through lunch, with food brought in, while the actors and crew go where they will.

Phoebe heads first to makeup, since she will not have time later, and then out to a restaurant around the corner for a hasty lunch with some friends who've come to town to visit. But first, as usual, she must run the gauntlet of fans at the building entrance. They are there every day, cameras and autograph books at the ready, and no matter how rushed the actors may be they always try to talk with them, pose for their snapshots, sign their books, and try to convince them that no one in the cast really knows what will happen to their favorite characters in the future. It is the truth, mostly, but I'm sure many do not believe us. A few don't even care about scripts or writers; they simply want to warn Phoebe not to believe what that phony

Sister act: Ruth (8) and Margaret (6). *Inset:* My very first picture (6 months). No wonder Phoebe loves hats.

Top:
Radio:
soap operas
and dramatic
shows. Here I am on **Grand
Central Station** (1938). *Bottom left:*
Miss Jubilesta. My start in show business—a six-week tour of
Kansas and Missouri. *Bottom, right:* Mr. and Mrs. Erik Rolf
attend the **Citizen Kane** opening.

Top: Orson's use of lighting and angled photography was extraordinary for its time. *Bottom:* The famous breakfast scene from **Citizen Kane** (Phoebe says the ironing of the tablecloth is a disgrace).

Hollywood tries to find my "look" in these studio stills posed in the manner of famous stars of the day.

As Maureen O'Hara

As Greer Garson

(RKO)

As Joan Bennett

(RKO)

(RKO)

As Irene Dunne

Daisy Kenyon.

Henry Fonda and Joan Crawford watch as Walter Winchell, Connie Marshall, and I meet Dana Andrews.

(20TH CENTURY FOX)

My "classic" Hollywood portrait from **Guest in the House.**

(COLUMBIA)

Top: **Guest in the House.** The negligee scene was part of a studio effort to give me a more sexy image. *Bottom:* With Pat O'Brien in **Perilous Holiday.** Pat was an Irish charmer whose wit and blarney never ceased.

(RKO)

(RKO)

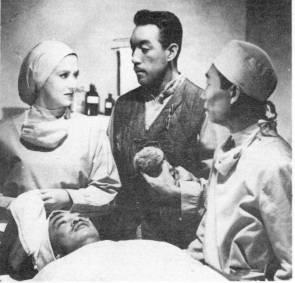

Top: **China Sky.** As I smiled at co-star Randolph Scott I was probably thinking of another member of the cast… *Bottom:* **China Sky.** Here he is, Anthony Quinn, almost unrecognizable in his Chinese warlord make-up.

(UNITED ARTISTS)

Top: With Douglas Fairbanks, Jr., in **The Corsican Brothers** (1941).
Between takes, I helped him study the navy officer's manual.
Bottom: With Carl Neubert, my second husband. We met at a
party and instantly became an "item".

Motherhood! Karen (16 months) examines new baby brother, Jon.

Top: McNamara's Band: Ruth, Tim, Bibber, Jon, Karen, and dog, Ricky. *Bottom:* At a **Peyton Place** cast party. Hannah Cord "marries" Martin Peyton (George Macready) in order to "legitimize" son, Steven.

Irene. Ruth, Monte Markham, Debbie Reynolds, George S. Irving, Patsy Kelly.

Bride and groom: Mr. and Mrs. Jarvis Cushing at their wedding reception.

Top: Mother and son, Dr. Jon Rolf, at a housewarming party for Debbie Reynolds. *Bottom:* Grandchildren Erik and Eliza visiting "WOOF," their name for me.

Campaigning for Carter. Ever since Watts, I've been socially involved.

professor has been telling her, or to plead with Erica to tell her
husband the truth for a change. We assure them we will try,
but "You know how Phoebe is, dear."

The fans are our most important asset, and we are all interested in how they will react to new twists in the plot, especially if those developments are a bit daring, or touch on
controversial subjects. But for the most part we cannot answer
their questions. Usually we simply do not know ourselves how
a given crisis will be resolved. We do learn what will happen
about two weeks in advance of air time, when scripts for the
next week's taping are delivered, but not many soap-opera
crises are resolved in a two-week time span, and besides, giving
even a little of the game away ahead of time only spoils the
viewer's fun. So we tell them to just wait and *see* how Phoebe
handles the professor, hinting that there are surprises in store.
And there always are, for the fans and for us.

One face in the crowd is familiar, and I quickly recognize
a very pretty young girl I have met before. An aspiring actress,
she had come backstage for advice and encouragement when
I was appearing on Broadway in *Irene* several years earlier.
I had advised her then to finish college first, and then come
back to give New York a try. To my surprise she took that
advice, a thing I did not do myself when I was her age and out
to conquer the world. She is back again now, full of hope and
news of bit parts on other shows, glowing with such expec-
tations that I find myself hoping she is tougher than she looks.
In our business failures are more common than triumphs, even
on a road that may ultimately lead to success. She'll need her
beauty, and all the talent I hope she has, and the guts to get
past those inevitable disappointments.

She joins us at lunch, which must be quick because it is
now nearing one o'clock and Phoebe must be back on the sets,
in costume, for the one-thirty dress rehearsal. As I gulp my
food I try, between bites, to offer the girl whatever words of
advice I can think of, to chat with my friends, and to watch
the clock while the minutes tick away. As I am apologizing
for my haste, a very handsome man stops by the table to say
hello. The young actress recognizes him as one of the longtime
leads in another daytime serial, and stares at his retreating back
with a look of awed admiration any director would love.

What she does not know, and what I cannot tell her, is news about this actor that has been buzzing through our tight little world: After many years on that show, his character is to die soon of a brain tumor. No one in this business is secure, because the very essence of drama—and of life—is change.

I gulp the last of my tea, say good-bye to my friends, and wish the young actress good luck. Then I sprint for the sets of Pine Valley, with a quick stop at wardrobe to pick up the day's costumes, and a fast check at makeup along the way. The preliminaries are over, and in about five minutes Phoebe's real day will begin. I pop into my dressing room to change.

In Phoebe's purple jersey Halston dressing gown, racing down a corridor toward the studio, I am still thinking about that pretty, hopeful young girl at lunch, and remembering how it was to be so young and certain that wildly wonderful things were sure to happen.

Well, why shouldn't they? Certainly my life has been full of wildness and wonder aplenty. There may be no great triumphs awaiting her, and if she is lucky perhaps there will be no terrible tragedies, but one thing is sure: Her life as an actress will not be boring.

FOUR

The Road to
Pine Valley:
Mrs. Citizen Kane

WHILE I WAS growing more enamored of Broadway by the day, my husband was becoming almost equally obsessed with Hollywood, enticed by visions of stardom and the good life of swaying palms and sparkling pools so well publicized by the media. To his chagrin I had turned down a couple of contract offers, contracts he knew as well as I could probably make me little more than another anonymous member of the huge stable of starlets crowding the studio lots. The studios were notorious for scooping up pretty, hopeful girls by the hundreds, placing them under binding contracts, and then picking from the catch at their whim, while the majority watched their careers stall and die. I wanted no part of that.

Erik, however, wanted almost anything that would provide entrée into that magic world of legendary, larger-than-life leading men, where he would stride the screen along with Gable and Grant. It was his dream, and I must admit it seemed quite possible to me. After all, he had the looks and the skills and a voice that had already made him one of the more successful radio performers. And if desire was a factor, he was certainly well endowed. He was one of the most fanatic movie buffs I had ever met, and I had come from a part of the country where the Saturday afternoon movie was almost a ritual. He lived for movies. For a while it seems that we practically lived *in* them, since his idea of a weekend was to pack his bride and his manager, Joe Stein, off to as many as three movies per day. I loved the first few triple features, but after a time I began to suffer some kind of sensory overload. Finally, one Saturday afternoon in the balcony of the new Radio City Music Hall,

I OD'ed on movies and went into a mild hysteria. It was agreed that I evidently needed more active participation and less spectating, and I was excused from some of the weekend movie marathons after that.

I had not wanted the starlet role, but I could see the wisdom of securing an agent to scout better parts for me, in Hollywood as well as the New York theater. After all, despite my burning ambition to tread the boards of Broadway, so far I hadn't progressed beyond small parts on a variety of radio shows. Clearly my career needed a boost.

The agent went to work, but he produced very little over the next few months. I became increasingly discouraged, and by spring I had decided to leave the whole scene for a while and pursue another ambition: to move to the country and start thinking about raising a family. So, with visions of bucolic motherhood replacing—for a while—my dreams of stardom, I set out with Erik to find a suitable setting.

The search stretched over several months, punctuated by appearances on various radio shows, commercial modeling (including a Miss Rheingold plum), and even one filmed commercial, possibly the first of its kind. (The product was another first: General Electric's pioneer garbage disposal unit, christened by some advertising genius the Electric Pig.) Then in May we located our dream home, a converted barn near Silvermine, Connecticut, outfitted with traditional stone walls, a stream that formed a lovely waterfall and millpond, even a group of resident swans paddling about, looking picturesque. Here I would grow heavy with child, baking fragrant bread and learning the language of swans while awaiting the miracle of birth. (I wasn't pregnant, but that seemed a detail.) It all appeared so much more satisfying than racing around from one radio studio to another in noisy New York. We took the train up, one sparkling spring day, to sign the two-year lease.

I was still dazzled by those swans when I got off the return train at Grand Central Station that afternoon, but I did remember to check in with my answering service, an act that becomes almost as automatic for actors as brushing one's teeth. And usually about as exciting.

That day, however, the faceless voice was almost shrill with excitement. "Where have you *been* all day?" she asked in the tone of a mother whose child has wandered. "We've been trying to contact you for *hours*. You had a one-thirty appointment in the Waldorf Towers. With *Orson Welles*!" The last was said in a tone of disbelief, as if my agent had somehow arranged for me to be interviewed by God Himself.

I looked up at the big terminal clock. Five-fifteen. Oh well, I thought, still drifting across that tranquil millpond with those languid swans—it doesn't matter.

"It will all work out," I reassured the operator at the answering service, and hung up to tell Erik I had an appointment to keep. I strolled the few blocks up Park Avenue to the Waldorf, announced myself, and was sent up to Welles' suite. He wasn't there. I sat down to wait.

In a few minutes Welles exploded through the door, looking as outsized and disheveled as ever, and twice as harassed. "Aren't you wonderful to wait for me," he said as he saw me sitting there. "I'm really so sorry, but its been a hectic day."

"Oh, that's all right," I said. "I did a thing or two in the meantime."

I knew, as did everyone in the theater, that Orson was casting for his new movie, after a year and a half spent on two projects that never got launched. His contract with RKO had been the talk of the trade when it was signed, and it had turned into a subject of ridicule as the months passed with no project before the cameras. Imagine signing one man to function as producer, writer, director, and star, with a blank check to make whatever movie he wished! Not since Chaplin had anyone been allowed to display such an array of talents, and this upstart Welles was not even twenty-five years old! But now, after a year and a half had gone by and the boy wonder had yet to shoot a foot of film, pressures at the studio were mounting. It was time for Welles to produce.

Actually, the months had not been wasted in idleness. During the first year he had completed a detailed, complex, highly original screenplay based on Joseph Conrad's *Heart of Darkness*, a treatment in which the main character was to be the camera, whose voice is heard but whose person is never seen. (That device was used a few years later in a Robert Montgomery movie called *Lady in the Lake*. And the Conrad story itself has most recently formed the basis for Francis Ford Coppola's

controversial *Apocalypse Now*.) But the outbreak of war overseas forced Welles to shelve that project, which was to have
been filmed in Africa. It also killed his second project, called
The Smiler with a Knife, when his leading lady was trapped
in Europe and unavailable for the part. His most recent project
was still a great mystery.

He explained a bit of the proposed movie to me that afternoon, sprawled in an overstuffed Waldorf chair and puffing
clouds of smoke from his pipe. The picture, he said, was all
ready to go, except for one part. "She is the main character's
first wife, Emily Norton Kane—the President's niece and a
lady of breeding."

I waited.

"I've tested and tested, and I've come to a conclusion." I
could see his sardonic grin through the swirls of smoke. "There
are no ladies in Hollywood."

I must have looked skeptical, because he went on: "I don't
mean someone who can *play* a lady; I mean someone who *is*
a lady. *That's* what I want."

He asked if there was any reason I couldn't fly out to the
West Coast for a test, and I assured him I could make it. He
said he would be in touch.

I left to phone my agent, since I knew no studio would test
any actress without an option for a firm contract. And then,
with the wheels thus set in motion, I went home to wait for
the next move.

I told Erik about the meeting, of course, but in a rather
offhand way in case nothing came of it. Privately I was convinced something *would* come of it, but I didn't want to get
his hopes up, or my own.

The next day the agent called to say Welles wanted to test
me right away. Could I catch a plane tomorrow? I said I believed I could make it, and then waited for Erik to come home
so I could tell him the good news.

He didn't come home. That wasn't unusual, since his radio
jobs often involved a late repeat for live broadcast to the West
Coast, and he often stopped for a drink with someone afterward.
So I waited. And waited.

At last I gave up and went to bed.

Next morning I discovered he had not come home at all.

I wasn't really alarmed or worried, though this was the first time he had ever stayed away the entire night without calling. I was a bit annoyed, though, what with big news and no one to tell it to.

The day went on and no Erik. At last, realizing that it would soon be time to catch the plane, I began to get ready. I was in the middle of packing when he came in.

"What are you doing?" he asked.

"Packing, obviously," I said icily.

"Why?"

"To go away," I answered.

"Oh. Well, I know I should have called, but I never dreamed you'd be *this* upset," he said, clearly worried.

By then I had had enough of revenge, so I told him the good news. He was delighted, agreed that of course I must do it, regretted that I would have to be away two whole weeks, but wished me terrific luck. And within hours I was on a plane thundering over Missouri on my way to what would turn out to be the major turning point in my life.

Within a few more hours I was pacing up and down the cavernous reaches of RKO Sound Stage 11, taffeta petticoats rustling and spirits rapidly falling. The place was huge, cold, dank, dark, with one small set forming a solitary point of warmth and light amidst the somber shadows. I felt tired and on edge, uncomfortable in the unfamiliar costume, unsure of what was to come. I wished Welles would stop bustling about with the crew and talk to me, but he went on plotting camera angles with Gregg Toland, and supervising sound equipment and lights as they were set up. I went on pacing, peering into the shadows and wrinkling my nose at a strange, fetid odor that seemed to permeate the place. It seemed to be getting worse by the moment.

Then I noticed the group of men, followed by a truck, moving toward the set. They were shadowy, sinister figures in long overcoats and pulled-down felt hats, an odd sight in semitropical southern California unless they were in wardrobe for a George Raft movie. They moved to the edge of that lighted area where Welles still fussed with equipment. The truck pulled up beside them.

Welles stopped his discussion with Toland and stared at the men.

One of them spoke. "We've come to offer congratulations on your first day of shooting," he said. "I must apologize for the condition of our floral offerings, but they were fresh when you were scheduled to begin." He signaled, and the truck up-ended its rear and dumped a huge, soggy mess onto the floor.

I moved closer and saw that the mound was a half ton or so of moldy, decaying flowers—collected from the refuse dump of Forest Lawn Cemetery, I learned later. The leader of the group smiled then, and Welles went forward to shake hands and to chuckle appreciatively at their little joke. I moved still closer to the set, but kept my distance from the odorous pile of dead flowers.

Welles introduced me, explained that we were about to do a test, and thanked them for stopping by. Then he stood there, his smile beginning to show signs of strain, waiting for them to leave and let him get to work.

Slowly it occurred to me that the men had no intention of leaving. They were the New York brass of RKO, I deduced from their clothes, and they were probably the ones who had drawn up that controversial contract with Orson in the first place. After all the delays and the ridicule they had endured, they were here to get a sample of what they had bought. Arms folded across chests, faces impassive, every line of their bodies saying "Show me," they stood their ground and waited for the genius to begin.

The situation was becoming clear to Welles, too, and his face began to glisten with sweat. He looked on the verge of panic. That seemed odd to me, since theater people are ac-customed to having all sorts of kibitzers around while they work. You ignore them and concentrate on doing what you know how to do.

Then suddenly I understood. This was Orson Welles' very first day in *front* of a movie camera! He was nervous enough anyway, but to take his first steps before this audience of stone-faced movie moguls? He was simply frozen on the spot!

Call it buck fever or shyness or stage fright or whatever, I recognized it and responded instinctively. Forgetting my ner-vousness, I went to Orson and began to talk about the scene we were to do. As I talked, I drew him to the other side of the set, away from the interlopers, and worked to build a feeling of intimacy between us, as if we were the only people who counted and those men didn't even exist. I chatted, laughed, asked questions, made suggestions, and all the while moved close to him and touched his arm. Little by little I felt the tension begin to drain away. Orson had said he chose me because I was a lady. I'd like to think that is what I was being then—a lady, putting a gentleman at ease.

The magic held, and we finished the test scene still oblivious to our visitors. In a while, to everyone's great relief, the men went away, and from that day forward the set was closed to all outsiders. It was our own tight little world, unlike any set I had ever seen before or have ever worked on since.

I stayed on for two weeks, doing other tests in various wigs and costumes, and watching Welles tighten his grasp on the technical intricacies of film work. But Welles postponed his decision about casting me, preoccupied with all the new toys at his command. At last, to spur Welles into a decision, my agent advised that I return to New York. So I caught a night flight, and went instantly to sleep.

Sometime later I woke up feeling queasy and headed for the lavatory. I never made it. The next thing I knew I was stretched out on my back in the aisle of the airplane with an oxygen mask being held over my lower face by a concerned fellow passenger. I had reacted to a change in cabin pressure by simply passing out cold, and he had been the first one to my aid. I looked up beyond him and saw other wide-eyed faces.

I moved the mask away and smiled at them. "Don't worry," I said. "I think I'm probably just pregnant."

And I was. I'd had the usual warning signs, of course, but it was as if renting that house in Connecticut had confirmed things. I had said, "This is the place to have a baby," and my body had responded. But now, of course, I would have to balance choices: I could sit and watch swans while my waistline grew, or I could grasp the unique opportunity to make my first movie—with the legendary wunderkind of the Mercury Theatre, at that.

I counted and calculated, and at last decided it would be possible. The opportunity was too good to miss for the little girl from St. Joe who had barely got her feet wet in the theater. So I would try to do both, and keep my fingers crossed that things stayed on schedule.

We began shooting in July, with a cast that was every bit as experienced in moviemaking as its director. In fact, not a single one of us had ever made a movie before, so we all entered this unfamiliar world with a sense of adventure compounded with confusion and spiced with the knowledge that we were long-shot outsiders. The equipment was strange, the techniques were totally different from those of the stage or even radio, and none of us really understood what was required of us. I had done that screen test back in May, and all I could remember of it was the consternation caused by those taffeta petticoats, whose rustling was picked up and amplified by the sensitive sound equipment until it sounded as if we were having a conversation in the middle of a forest fire. Now we all faced the cameras and sound booms with the suspicion of children approaching a dentist's chair.

Except Orson. He had been busy in the intervening weeks exploring the wonders of a movie sound stage: the giant cranes for zooming in and out of long shots, the huge jungle gym of girders for lighting, the sound system waiting like a mighty organ to be played. He was endlessly fascinated, his mind on fire with all the possibilities of this new medium. As he said that first day, "This is the biggest electric train any boy was ever given to play with."

He had also been busy trying to get a shooting script on paper, to reflect the clear sense of the story that existed in his mind. Realizing at last that he needed help, he hit upon the idea of hiring Herman Mankiewicz, a brilliant but undependable writer, but only on the stipulation that Mankiewicz be sequestered in a cabin on a dude ranch near Victorville until the work was done. The location, a small desert town about ninety miles from Los Angeles, would insure the privacy to work as well as the distance from friends and bars that might interfere with that work.

Mankiewicz's contribution to the script was certainly no secret, then or later. I was in the production office more than once as the daily courier arrived with sheets from the desert cabin, and I remember well how Orson would look them over, chuckling with pleasure or scribbling furious notes for rewrite. The final product was an amalgam of Mankiewicz and Welles, as the screen credits clearly indicated. They read, "Written by Herman J. Mankiewicz and Orson Welles," with Welles' name on the second line. Orson always acknowledged the contributions of others; even so, there was little doubt that the original ideas and driving force behind the script were his, and when he was given an Academy Award for that original screenplay Mankiewicz claimed no part of it.

By the time shooting began we were working from a script, and each scene was carefully planned in advance, to the most minute detail of camera angle and lighting. In a close partnership with cameraman Gregg Toland, Orson would scribble and question his way through each scene, exploring new possibilities and making new demands constantly. When he questioned why one part of a set was always out of focus while another was sharp and clear, Gregg set out to correct the problem. It meant creating a new wide-angle lens that had not been used before, and then putting ceilings on the sets because this new lens included a wider area than had previously been seen in a shot. This, in turn, brought problems with the lighting, since the new lens had to be stopped down so far, requiring more powerful lights which the new ceilings blocked out. The solution was to make the ceilings of a fine white gauze that looked solid to the camera's eye but still allowed light to pass through.

This sense of adventure, of testing the boundaries, was always there, and it led to innovations that seem obvious after the fact but were not until Welles used them. In one scene, for instance, Charles Foster Kane was to be consumed by a towering, gargantuan rage at Boss Jim Gettys, who has discovered Kane's love nest. Gettys now threatens to use it against him politically. Welles was not satisfied with any camera angles, and he and Gregg fussed with the scene for hours. Finally the solution hit him: Why not simply dig a hole and put the camera and its operator down into it so the scene could literally be shot from ground level? This meant ripping up part of the studio floor and then digging a gravelike pit, but everyone went at it with the enthusiasm of Tom Sawyer and Huck Finn digging for treasure. The resulting scene is startling, giving Welles an overpowering dominance, and it is considered innovative even today, when technical trickery is virtually unlimited.

We worked as a team in our private little world, disciplined but not driven, a group sharing an experience and giving to it levels of performance that often seemed beyond our capacities. Orson literally drew the best from us, somehow reaching into depths we had not known existed to bring forth miracles. Our celebrated series of breakfast scenes, a two-minute montage that spanned a marriage and defined its dissolution, was done without the great fuss and preparation most people have assumed it required. Orson was aged through use of makeup and rubber contrivances of his own design, but I depended mainly on changes in hairstyles and wardrobe to add years. Beyond that, we simply shot the scenes, and as Orson drew apart from me in growing coldness, I played the effects of this coldness on Emily, whose love was being extinguished at the same time that her values were being scorned and her very being excluded from his life. Orson projected the stimulus and my reaction came from deep inside me. It was one of those rare blends of artistry and magic no studio mogul could buy. With Orson, such things happened because he willed them to, and because he made us all believe without question that we could make them happen.

That brief montage has been widely studied by students of film, and has been shown on network television at least three times. The first was when Orson was given a special Academy Award in 1972; the second was in 1975, when the American Film Institute gave him its Lifetime Achievement Award. It was shown a third time in 1977, when the institute acclaimed *Citizen Kane* as one of the ten best American films of all time in a gala ceremony attended by President Carter and a sizable crowd of luminaries. (When I rose to take my bow I threw a kiss to the President, who gallantly threw one back.) The high point of the evening was the presentation speech by Milos Forman, who had declined to appear until informed that he was to speak of Orson Welles. He said, "As a boy I went to every film I could, but I was always puzzled by the credits. I understood why the actors' names were there, and even the men who supplied the music, but why the director? Then I saw *Citizen Kane* and I saw what the director could do. I decided that's what I wanted to be."

Orson mastered illusion, the essence of film. He created the feeling of a crowded opera house with a few strategically placed lights and four actors in a box. He added apparent age to the actors with his own makeup inspirations and artful lighting. (And, in his own case, aided by the uncorsetting of his normally ample figure. He had lost vast amounts of weight for those scenes in which Kane is young and slender, but even so he had to struggle into a corset every day and hold himself in with superhuman effort. The scenes in which Kane aged and put on heft were a great relief to Orson.) Novel use of lighting and camera angle were constant, and the overlapping and inter-mixing of sound and speech, hailed as innovative when used in recent years by such directors as Robert Altman, were Welles' answer to the artificiality of much standard film dia-logue.

Every shot in the entire movie was elaborately preplanned before a foot of film was run; every movement and every still position was diagrammed exactly. For the cast, Orson's preoc-cupation with the visual aspects made for a curious reversal of the customary emphases: We were encouraged to bring our own interpretations to the reading of the lines, but we were given no leeway at all in our positions or movements. As a result, every frame of the movie, when seen as a still, shows a sense of composition and a balance of light and shadow remarkable to this day.

To Orson every nuance of a scene, however trivial or com-plicated, was important, and worth whatever extra effort was required to achieve perfection. Such an atmosphere should have been crackling with tension, but it was not. Welles had too much respect for the people involved—especially the actors—to crack whips at them. Certainly he gave as much as he had in him and expected that from everyone else, yet we were a family, supporting and sustaining one another in a common enterprise. I have sometimes thought that we were all a little bit in love with Orson then, in our various ways. He wanted so much from us, and he tried to give so much himself, that we all lived in an atmosphere far beyond mere comradeship.

All of us, that is, except one. The solitary exception was Dorothy Comingore, who played the waif Kane befriended and later married, only to leave her broken and booze-sodden at the end. Orson treated her with a discourteous contempt that was often painful to watch, while making an obvious display of elaborate courtliness in his dealing with me. I found this embarrassing and asked him not to imagine that I was flattered by such overt favoritism.

He shook his head. "You just don't understand," he said. "I treat her that way because she has got to hate my guts when we get to the later scenes. When she yells and screams and finally walks out on me, I want her to feel every bit of it in her bones."

"Oh, come now," I said. "An actress doesn't have to' be bleeding to show pain."

"But that's just the point," he said. "She is *not* an actress. She *is* Susan Alexander, and she'll probably end up just like the woman she's playing." He shook his head. "No, I'm not mistreating her. I treat her exactly as she *expects* to be treated. She wouldn't respect anything else."

His view of her seemed terribly harsh to me, but Dorothy's later life seemed to bear out his prediction. Her next movie, opposite William Bendix, was unsuccessful, and her performance in it was a disaster. Parts were few after that, and several years later her marriage ended in an unusual divorce, with her husband retaining custody of the children. She began to drink heavily, sitting in Musso-Frank's and bending any available ear with her tale of injustice. After that I lost track of her for a while, but in New York during the midfifties I was shocked at a newspaper account of her arrest for soliciting from a car parked off Hollywood Boulevard. The accompanying picture, with the harsh flashbulbs revealing the marks of her life, looked eerily like the face of Susan Alexander Kane as seen in the final scenes of the film. Sadly, I remembered Orson's words, and I recalled them again a few years later when I heard of her tragic death.

There had already been one casualty, however, though none of us knew about it until months later, when the movie was done. That was the long-time friendship between Orson and his partner and business manager, John Houseman. If Orson was the crown prince of the Mercury Theatre, Houseman was its prime minister, the conservative elder statesman who respected the younger man's flash and brilliance but who nevertheless saw the need for a strong hand on the organizational and business side. Orson was, and is, a man of excesses, headstrong and somewhat arrogant in matters of money, a profligate spender with utter contempt for the balancing of books. It was Houseman who had always seen to it that the finances made sense and the company stayed on firm ground.

The RKO contract was for Orson, but Orson and John were a team and the Mercury Theatre was their company, so the whole operation was simply packed up and moved to Hollywood. (I was the only New York actress brought in for a role.) All went well at first, but when, after months of work, the first project went down the drain, there was restlessness among the company. After the second was abandoned, the impatience to be at work threatened to get out of hand. In an effort to quell the insurrection, Orson gave a dinner party for the whole company at Chasen's. He listened to their complaints, then rose to reassure them—in that rolling voice that could melt stone—that the new project was almost ready to begin and all would soon be well. He turned to John for support.

To his astonishment, Houseman agreed with the dissenters and argued that it was time to return to New York and the real world of the theater, where they belonged.

Orson reacted as though he had been betrayed. With eyes bulging and veins throbbing, at a loss for words for perhaps the first time in his life, Welles reached out blindly and grabbed the first object at hand, which happened to be a lighted chafing dish on a serving cart in front of him. He flung the thing at Houseman, narrowly missing him and spattering the wall.

Houseman's face, even then a mask of patrician iciness, was expressionless. He said nothing else, and the meal went on. So did the movie, with John remaining to see it through without revealing the slightest trace of tension. But as soon as it was finished, John moved back to New York, and he never worked with Orson again. I have always wondered, as have many others, what Orson's later career might have been like if he had not alienated the man who had so faithfully guarded his flank. As for Houseman, after years in the theater behind the scenes—as a producer at MGM and later as head of Juilliard's famed drama school—he made his acting debut in his seventies, winning an Academy Award nomination for his role in *The Paper Chase*.

Orson's excesses, which have grown legendary in his later years, were striking even then. When we began shooting *Citizen Kane*, Orson was suffering from the effects of caffeine poisoning as the result of consuming thirty or forty cups of coffee a day, so he decided to switch to tea, reasoning that the trouble of making each cup separately would cut down on the quantity he drank. It didn't. Someone was on call constantly to brew tea, and within two weeks Orson was the color of tannic acid. He would go for long periods without eating, then put away two or three large steaks with all the trimmings at one sitting. And his work habits were similar: He could film for thirty-six hours nonstop, then be hurt because Joe Cotten and I wouldn't go out at dawn to eat and drink with him.

For a man notorious for his disorganization, Orson ran a very tight ship during the filming of *Citizen Kane*. As a result, the movie was finished in just under ninety days, and on a budget that was amazingly low even in those preblockbuster times. We wrapped up the final takes in September, and I returned immediately to Connecticut to take up where I had left off with the swans. Because while Orson had been producing a movie, I had been engaged in a production of my own, which was already beginning to add noticeably to my waistline.

The aftermath was in some ways more remarkable than the making of the movie, as most students of film well know. What may not be known is my own inadvertent contribution to that chaotic chain of events. It occurred the following January in the 21 Club, where I had been summoned for my first full-fledged solo press interview.

The meeting had been arranged through the RKO publicity office, and I came down from Connecticut, bulging in my eighth month of pregnancy, to confront a reporter from *P.M.* *Citizen Kane* was scheduled to open on February 14 at Radio City Music Hall, and was to play there through the Easter season, the most coveted booking a movie could have at that time. I had seen little publicity, sequestered in Connecticut's snowy seclusion, but I had not given the matter much thought. Since no one from RKO had appeared at the interview to advise me, I plunged in exuberantly, quite unaware that this was the first interview anyone had given the press about Welles' mysterious new picture. During the four months since we had finished shooting I had had little contact with anyone connected with RKO or the movie.

"What's *Citizen Kane* all about?" the reporter asked.

It seemed a reasonable question, so I launched into an enthusiastic description, remembering Orson's eloquent words to us on the set. "It's about the kind of powerful, rugged individualists America tends to see as its heroes," I told the reporter. "We all know them, the despoilers and corrupters who live beyond the normal laws and rules of society. O'Neill and Dreiser wrote about them, the titans who forged economic empires and who have achieved a kind of mythic stature—men like Hearst and Insull and Fall."

I had noticed a certain transfixed look on the reporter's face as I talked, and his pencil had dropped from his hand unnoticed. Suddenly he said, "Excuse me a minute, I've gotta make a phone call," and he dashed from the table.

I took his words at face value and waited patiently for him to return. But as the minutes went by I began to grow uneasy. Then, after a long while, the maître d' appeared at my elbow with a bottle of wine and a menu.

"The gentleman sends his apologies, madam. He was called back to his office by some emergency, but he wishes you to order whatever you like and enjoy your lunch."

It seemed a shame that my first meeting with the press had ended so quickly, but I did have a lovely lunch. And afterward I caught a train for Connecticut, blissfully unaware of what I had done. In fact, I didn't learn the details till years later from Robert Wise, now a top director, who had been the film editor on *Kane*.

The cross-country wires must have been humming from the moment the reporter got back to his office, for in a matter of hours a suspicious Louella Parsons was on the phone to the RKO brass demanding an immediate screening. And what Lolly Parsons wanted, she got. Her power to make or break was awesome in those days, and she wielded it with a sanctimonious air of infallibility, even to passing judgment on the most private and personal aspects of performers' lives. (Each Christmas her station wagon would make the rounds of the stars' homes, returning after each trip laden with the most extravagant gifts their quaking hands could summon.)

Lolly watched the film aghast. Her boss, William Randolph Hearst, like Charles Foster Kane, was a quixotic despot who commanded a far-flung empire of yellow journalism unmatched before or since.

Like Kane, he lived openly with his mistress (Marion Davies) in an immense fairy-tale castle (San Simeon). But Hearst wielded such power that no newspapers ever ran photos of the two of them together or even mentioned their liaison. Though his life-style was anything but conventional, his privacy was sacrosanct, and woe to anyone who breached those walls.

When the movie ended Louella was almost purple. "I want you to go immediately and get the master negative," she croaked at the assembled brass. "And then I want it burned, right here in my presence."

George Schaefer, the New York banker who was then head of RKO, weighed months of work and the hundreds of thousands of dollars against the certain wrath of Hearst. He tried to point out that the script had passed the review of the Hays Office, which set production codes and which was notoriously conservative, but Parsons would hear none of it.

"I want that abomination burned *now, here*," she repeated, pointing to a large ashtray.

Firmly, but no doubt sadly, Schaefer declined. The studio was committed; the movie was to open in a matter of days.

Hearst's representatives summoned the heads of the major studios to a meeting and told them of the effrontery. Louis B. Mayer and Jack Warner listened, along with other studio brass, to the tale of the latest harebrained affair of the upstart Welles and of the eastern outsider, Schaefer, with mounting indignation. They also listened to Hearst's threat of a congressional hearing into the morality of motion pictures, precisely the sort of publicity the movie industry was trying hard to avoid. No one doubted that Hearst headlines could bring the wrath of Congress down on them all.

Under pressure from Warner and Mayer, the other studios joined in an offer to RKO: They would jointly pay for the production costs—around $800,000—and the film would be shelved permanently. The alternative, they warned Schaefer, would be unpleasant publicity for the whole industry *and* a total ban on all RKO advertising in the Hearst press, to say nothing of the strong possibility of litigation against RKO.

A tug-of-war began within the studio's board of directors, with half of them defending the film and the others advising a retreat before the ominous fury of Hearst. The $800,000 offer was refused, but the Music Hall opening was cancelled while the argument raged on in the RKO offices. A ban on advertising in the majority of the country's newspapers could cripple the studio, it was feared, especially when Hearst made it clear he would extend the boycott to any theater that showed the film. The long-term effects of this would be devastating, but even the immediate repercussions went beyond *Citizen Kane*, since it was part of a bloc of five movies being sold together to the theaters. (The largest chain, Fox-West Coast, solved that problem by buying the bloc, including *Kane*, and scheduling only the other four. Most other chains, it was feared, would pass up the whole bloc.)

In late January Orson announced his lawsuit against RKO, demanding that they either show the film or sell it to him so he could arrange for independent exhibition through unaffiliated art-theater houses. At an Author's Club luncheon in Los Angeles, just before he left for New York to press this suit, he quipped, "As soon as I get *Citizen Kane* off my mind I'm going to do a great film on the life of William Randolph Hearst."

Attorneys for RKO agreed that Hearst had no real grounds for court action, especially since the movie bore the Hays Office's Production Seal of Approval, indicating a careful review prior to shooting. However, the attorneys also advised that Welles' suit did have merit, that he might well win, and that he would certainly make the studio look bad in the process. Faced with this unwelcome advice, the studio at last decided to proceed with the opening.

But where? The Radio City Music Hall was now fully booked, as were the other major movie houses in New York. They were willing, the RKO brass assured Welles, but they had no place to premier the movie. Welles was implacable, so the studio was compelled literally to produce a theater, which they managed by refurbishing and reopening the old Broadway vaudeville temple, The Palace.

While all this activity went frantically forward, I was preoccupied with my own private premiere. In the freezing early

hours of March 13, in Harkness Pavilion, Karen Elizabeth Rolf
had made her grand entrance. She had taken a full ten months
do to it but, at that, she still beat the movie by more than a
month. As I held her, marveling in the way of all mothers at
this remarkable miniature person, I was certain she had more
beauty in her little finger than the greatest film ever made.

At last, on May 1, 1941, *Citizen Kane* opened simultaneously at The Palace and at the RKO Pantages in Hollywood.
I attended the Palace opening, still too ecstatic over the new
baby to be much concerned about the attention Orson lavished
on his new fiancée, Dolores del Rio. He stood tall that night,
but even so he was dwarfed by a replica of himself, a twenty-
eight-foot cutout looming in the spotlights and wreathed in
spouting jets of steam meant to symbolize the too-hot-to-handle
nature of the movie. Joseph Cotten was there, along with Ev-
erett Sloane, George Coulouris, Ray Collins, and others from
the cast. Agnes Moorehead appeared in an ermine wrap nearly
identical to the one I had borrowed for the occasion, which
amused at least one of us. The screening itself is a blur, now,
but I recall the audience reaction as enthusiastic, unlike the
confused silence that greeted the West Coast showing.

The next day was too filled with packing and moving for
much thought of the movie, and that afternoon I boarded the
famed Twentieth Century Limited, walking down the red-car-
peted platform with Erik at my side and baby Karen bundled
in my arms, on our way to California. There were crowds of
friends bearing champagne and caviar into our drawing room,
and the farewells went on and on, with the baby gurgling
happily in the midst of it all and totally upstaging her parents.
(Erik bore a noticeable resemblance to Orson, often commented
on by friends, and baby Karen resembled them both, a thing
that was to cause much embarrassing surmise in years to come.)
At last we were off, and we all fell into our berths exhausted.

Next morning we were up early and off to the dining car,
where a white-jacketed waiter seated us at a table on which a
copy of *The New York Times* lay open to the theater page. I
stared at it in disbelief. There, instead of the five or six inches
usually given to a movie review, was a solid half page, six
columns wide, devoted entirely to *Citizen Kane*. That Bosley

Crowther review, dated May 2, 1941, is worth recalling. It began:

> Within the withering spotlight as no other film has ever been before, Orson Welles' "Citizen Kane" had its world premiere at the Palace last evening. And now that the wraps are off, the mystery has been exposed, and Mr. Welles and the RKO directors have taken the much-debated leap, it can safely be stated that suppression of this film would have been a crime. . . . "Citizen Kane" is far and away the most surprising and cinematically exciting motion picture to be seen here in many a moon. As a matter of fact, it comes close to being the most sensational film ever made in Hollywood. . . .

Crowther continued with words of praise for the direction, the script, the score, and all the performers, and then concluded:

> You shouldn't miss this film. It is cynical, ironic, sometimes oppressive, and as realistic as a slap. But it has more vitality than fifteen other films we could name. And although it may not give a thoroughly clear answer, at least it brings to mind one deeply moral thought. "For what shall it profit a man if he gain the whole world and lose his soul?" See "Citizen Kane" for further details.

Other reviews heaped equal praise on Welles and the film, but there was utter silence in the Hearst press, and the boycott on advertising, or on any mention of anyone associated with the project, continued. The effect was precisely as feared: Silence in a majority of the nation's papers spelled financial failure at the box office. Ironically, this landmark movie, which has been shown constantly over the past forty years and acclaimed as among the most innovatively brilliant of all time, made little money during its first release. It was at the same time the beginning of a brilliant career for Welles and a portent of things to come.

Like all the cast, I remained a nonperson in the Hearst press for several years, though the ban resulted in almost comical

feats of omission. The first occurred at the release of my third
movie under the RKO contract, which involved a loan-out
arrangement with United Artists. It was a swashbuckler called
The Corsican Brothers, and in it I played the aristocratic Countess Isabelle, who is wooed by twin brothers—both played by
the dashing Douglas Fairbanks, Jr.—and whose kiss with one
arouses passion in the other, hundreds of miles away. It was
precisely the kind of film fare the Hearst papers touted, and
since it was not a product of the hated RKO, it was given full-
page layouts in the Hearst Sunday supplements across the nation. The top portion of the page featured the movie's most
elaborate set, a grand ballroom scene, and smack in the middle
of it—in bejewelled gown and foot-high pompadour, the center
of all eyes—stood the officially banished Mrs. Citizen Kane.

I can imagine what discussions must have gone on in the
Hearst editorial offices. They could hardly excise the sole leading lady from the still, yet they had orders. Their solution was
simplicity itself: They ran the picture, listed the cast beneath,
and omitted my name.

I somehow survived and even flourished during my exile
from the powerful Hearst press, but there was no doubt that
being pariahs made good parts elusive for most of the *Kane*
cast. Finally, after I'd served four years in limbo, my agent,
Kurt Frings, felt it was time to heal the breach. Through the
offices of publicist Henry Rogers, a luncheon was arranged
with Louella at Romanoff's. I was nervous, remembering that
a press luncheon had gotten me into this mess, but I entered
the restaurant wearing my most confident smile.

The smile faltered during the long lunch, and by the end
of it I was sure I had committed a second disaster. Lolly had
virtually ignored me throughout, chatting with table hoppers
and waving to friends while I tried with growing desperation
to say something that would get her attention. She made no
notes and seemed hardly to hear me, yet to my great surprise
the interview in the Sunday supplement was filled with quotes,
a couple of them even accurate. Under a large picture of me
with my two adorable little children, gathered at the piano, she
informed her millions of readers that my role in that nameless
movie had been a mistake, and quoted me as saying, "I was
too young at the time to know what I was doing." That was

not what I had said, but I was in no mood to quibble. I had been officially forgiven, and this was the signal that I could henceforth be mentioned in the hundreds of Hearst papers. The closing lines of Lolly's column, in fact, almost could have been written about the yet-unborn Phoebe Tyler: "Ruth is a very determined person. Whatever she sets out to do, you can be very sure she is going to do it."

As for Orson, *Citizen Kane* was followed, the next year, by *The Magnificent Ambersons*, which he directed and narrated, another classic that still causes heated discussion. Immediately after that came *Journey Into Fear*, based on the Eric Ambler mystery thriller set in the Middle East, in which I played Joseph Cotten's wife. It was the only other movie I made with Orson and another critical triumph, though not of the magnitude of *Kane* or *Ambersons*. Already the hints of Orson's later problems were evident: the heedless, spendthrift, live-for-the-moment ways that were to lose him the support of the very people he needed most. And then, not long after *Journey Into Fear*, Orson went to Brazil to film location scenes for a movie to be set partly during Carnival in Rio. One scene was to take place in the opera house, the pride of the city, and it was there that Welles committed an all-too-characteristic faux pas that was to cost him dearly. Frustrated by problems of lighting and restricted camera range, he ordered his crew to knock a hole in the wall of the building. The local officials viewed this as something close to an act of war, and Welles was hustled out of the country under armed guard. He returned to Hollywood in disgrace with studio management.

After that fiasco he found backers few and production money scarce. Frustrated, he fell back on his early love and opened a magic show in a tent on Santa Monica Boulevard, a move that attracted great publicity and drew huge crowds. He also used his formidable powers of persuasion to entice Marlene Dietrich into appearing as his stage assistant, and each evening those lovely legs stuck out of one end of a box with her head protruding from the other while Orson sawed her in half. She was a great draw, of course, but when she was compelled to leave his show a while later he pulled an even greater coup and persuaded the reigning sex goddess from Columbia, Rita

Hayworth, to replace her. Every day she was on the set of
Gilda, and every night she was in Orson's tent, under the saw.
The publicity flacks were ecstatic.

Orson and Rita complemented each other so neatly it was
as if the gods had planned their liaison. Orson—the gifted,
brilliant, silver-tongued wonder—was widely thought of as
unsexy in Hollywood; Rita—painfully shy and almost inarti-
culate—was the very essence of sexuality. A professional dancer from the age of twelve, she had been rigidly sheltered by
her father, who was also her dance partner. Her first marriage,
to an older, exploitative man, had done nothing to build her
self-confidence, so she must have been flattered to be linked
with Orson, first professionally and then romantically. And
Orson, it was quickly noted, must be sexier than anyone had
thought if this dazzling creature found him attractive. It was
symbiosis of a high order, and the resulting marriage was probably inevitable.

Even so, the day I heard of their surprise wedding I sat in
the middle of my bedroom floor, trying to decide whether to
laugh or cry. My feelings for Orson were still a confusion, a
large measure of admiration bordering on love, but mixed with
impatience at this profligate man-child who could never deal
with women as anything other than playthings. Poor Orson:
first Dolores del Rio, whose every serious utterance made him
laugh, and now Rita, so shy she could barely speak at all. A
strange combination, it seemed to me then—a man who commanded attention every moment and a woman who sat in corners at parties, smiling uncertainly and speaking to no one. A
friend who spent an evening with the couple described how
Orson held forth all evening, totally ignoring Rita as she sat
patiently by the fireplace radiating an almost painful beauty.
His only words to her all evening were a curt instruction to put
more wood on, which she did silently, returning to her passive
place by the fire. She did not compete with Orson, but she did
in some way enhance him, the way a beautiful painting might.
It was said that he once dragged her out of bed in the middle
of the night to prove to friends that she was really that beautiful,
even without makeup.

I began to understand, but understanding made it no less
sad. I felt sympathy for the poor, beautiful Rita, a sex goddess

to millions but little more than an objet d'art to her husband.
I saw little of Orson after *Journey Into Fear*, but I continued
to hear reports through friends. And I was not really surprised,
a few years later, when I began to hear rumors of their breakup.

I *was* somewhat surprised, however, when Orson phoned
one night and begged me to visit him. He was sending his car
at once, and I simply *must* come. He had no one to talk to, he
said, and he repeated the line he had used when we first met:
There were no ladies in Hollywood, no one with the depth and
compassion to understand him.

After that, of course, I went. I found him lolling in great
mounds of pillows, looking pale and sallow, as if playing a
scene from *Mayerling*. We talked a little, and he berated the
"money men" for their lack of faith and their crassness. "Any
man whose ability is simply to make money should get down
on his knees and beg a man with creative talent to make something of value with that money," he said angrily. "But they
don't seem to know that their money has absolutely no value
in itself." He was bitter about the turns his career and his life
had taken, but it was characteristic of him to philosophize rather
than to complain.

Still, he was terribly depressed, and after a time the talk
stopped because we no longer needed words. I, too, in my own
life, was beginning to have some need of comfort, and we
soothed and held each other through a long evening.

And yet, returning to my home later, I knew that somehow
I, too, had been used by Orson, that I was a handy balm for
a momentary hurt. It was not a role I felt good about, yet I
knew there couldn't be any other with a man such as Orson,
for whom women could be pursued and even admired but never
really accepted as equals. When he called the next evening to
renew the comforting, I refused. I have not talked with Orson
again since that night.

Yet messages have come: through Arnold Weissberger, the
distinguished attorney who has been Welles' longtime manager
and confidant; through José Quintero, the gifted director who
was told by Orson to "Find Ruth and do something with her";
through Milton Goldman, and many others.

The incident with Milton Goldman stands out clearly in my
memory. We were lunching with Dana Andrews and his wife

at Four Seasons just before Christmas a few years ago, and
Milton insisted I go with him to meet some people at another
table. Milton is so compulsive about introductions that he has
been known to introduce husbands to their own wives at parties,
but I humored him and went along.

As I got closer I saw that one of the people at the table was
Arnold Weissberger, whom I knew, and I recognized the older
woman with him as Orson's wife of more than twenty years,
the beautiful Italian Countess Paola Mori. The third person at
the table was a much younger woman, and when she stood to
be introduced I almost gasped. She was strikingly beautiful—
a tall girl with the wide-set eyes and squared jaw, the full,
sensuous mouth and distinctive hairline that I had known so
well. It could only be his daughter, Beatrice, now a grown and
lovely young woman. My eyes misted over, and the thought
suddenly shot through my mind: *This girl could have been your
daughter!*

Beatrice seemed even more startled and moved than I was.
"I've dreamed about meeting you all my life," she said. "At
least once a year since I was a little girl I've watched *Citizen
Kane*, and I grew up thinking you were the most beautiful and
elegant lady in the world."

Once again, as I embraced Beatrice, I hardly knew whether
to laugh or cry.

A few years ago, during a cruise on the Norwegian-Amer-
ican liner *Vistafjord*, I sat through two showings of *Citizen
Kane*. Walking the deck later, I thought about the movie, now
forty years in the past but somehow still fresh and sharply
pertinent today. In a curious way the life of Charles Foster
Kane was a prophesy of things to come for Orson, and an eerie
parallel to his own odd career. Like Kane, Orson was brought
up by a guardian after his mother was lost in his childhood;
like Kane, he took over a major undertaking at an early age,
with little experience, and made a great success of it. Orson's
unhappy experiences with women may have had their coun-
terparts in Kane's inability ever to empathize with women,
no matter how strongly he felt about them. And again like
Kane, Orson has become more and more the proud loner who
walls himself off from a harsh and unappreciative world. Both
isolated themselves, Kane behind the walls of his art-engorged

castle and Welles behind the portly disguise of a witty court jester, sharp of tongue and prodigious in appetites, familiar to the viewers of those Caesar's Palace celebrity roasts.

I remembered another press interview after the release of the movie. A reporter asked what I thought of Orson, and I said, "He's a genius, all right, but it will be a race against time; whether he'll grow up, or destroy himself, first." Somehow, it's still a dead heat.

But whatever the strengths or weaknesses of Orson Welles' character, the towering brilliance of his Hollywood years cannot truly be denied. His use of camera and lighting, the overlapping of sound and dialogue, the depth of focus, the use of visual symbols to underscore the message of a scene, the bold examination of the avaricious materialism of America's tycoons—all these things and many more mark the film as strikingly innovative. The music—for the first time an integral part of the movie, composed by Bernard Herrmann working with Welles as the scenes were shot—is in itself an important departure from the usual background syrup of the day. (And it may not be entirely coincidental that Welles appeared in Carol Reed's *The Third Man*, whose zither background music is among the most memorable of all time. Whether Welles contributed directly or not, his influence was most certainly felt.) The script, though written by Herman Mankiewicz in the physical sense of putting words to paper, was in every other way, from conception to execution, Orson's unique creation.* He once said there was no point in making a movie at all if you didn't have a poet behind the camera. The visual impact of *Citizen Kane* still stands as proof that Hollywood once had a poet of the first magnitude.

You can see this most clearly, I think, in the reaction of young viewers who see the film for the first time. To them, for whom so much of the early Hollywood product seems utterly silly now, *Citizen Kane* retains its capacity to startle and to move. Like all genuine art, it remains forever contemporary.

For me, walking the moonlit deck of the *Vistafjord*, it was

---

*The hotly argued question of just whose original idea it was can get even more complicated: Geraldine Fitzgerald, who was living with Orson at the time, claims that she suggested the basic idea to him. But whoever planted the seed, it was certainly Welles who cultivated it and harvested the fruit.

contemporary in a different way. I recalled vividly those electric days when we worked together, driven and stroked and cajoled and transformed by Orson. And I recalled what Paul Stewart, who played Kane's cynical butler, said to me at the Palace premiere: "From this night on, wherever we go or whatever we do in our lives, we will always be identified with *Citizen Kane*." For most of us his words have been remarkably true, but for me they have had a special significance. I realized many years later, when I was a long-established member of the *All My Children* cast, that in many ways the young, proud, aristocratic Emily Norton Kane represents an earlier incarnation of Phoebe Tyler. It is as if the imaginary girl who was Kane's wife had grown into the woman who influences so many lives in the imaginary world of Pine Valley. When you think of it, the two are remarkably similar. Both Emily and Phoebe placed their children first in their lives, and both were married to men more preoccupied with career than with home and family. And both, of course, are much concerned with their status in the community and the esteem of their peers. Since Emily's character owes much to the compelling hand of Orson Welles, so, indirectly, must Phoebe's.

Not long ago I saw a commercial on television; there, behind his formidable paunch and neat beard, was Orson. That voice, still with the mellow roll of distant thunder, was extolling the virtues of a California wine. As I watched him praising the product, my eyes drifted to the corner of my apartment where a genuine Rosebud sled leans against the wall, a present from my son. It was foolish, perhaps, but for a moment I wished I could reach out and take Orson's hand, and that we could go together for a daredevil ride down some mythical hillside. The portly man sipping wine on the television screen could not go, of course, but the old Orson would have.

FIVE

Afternoon in Pine Valley

WE ARE ALL ASSEMBLED and in place, the entire cast for this day's episode of *All My Children*. The cameras are placed, the actors are in costume and waiting on their first sets, the sound booms are positioned, and all is in readiness for the final run-through of this day's show. This will be our one and only full rehearsal on set before the actual taping of the show. (Back when the show was only a half hour long, we had time for a run-through *plus* a full dress rehearsal; but with a full hour to tape, the two had to be combined.) We are about to begin.

But where is the director? He is now ensconced in the control room, in the first-row center-seat spot from which he will observe, on the bank of television screens that cover the wall before him, the full march of scenes and ballet of machinery we have seen choreographed earlier. Tapping the control panel with a conductor's baton, Henry will call out the camera cues and relay instructions or comments to the technical director and lighting directors at his left. They in turn will relay those directions and cues to appropriate assistants through audio headsets, while orchestrating the complex play of lighting and the changes from camera to camera via panels of switches that make the cockpit of a jetliner seem simple by comparison.

I cannot pretend to understand fully the workings of those intricate consoles, and I suspect a full explanation would quickly leave most of us at sea anyway. A visitor's first impression of the control room is certainly bewildering, and even after years of familiarity I still find the place awesome. Oh, the function of the two large television screens in the middle of the monitor bank is simple enough: They show, in full color, what is to be recorded on each of the two tapes at a given moment. But what of the eighteen smaller screens arrayed around the two larger ones? Again, the complexity is confusing to all but the experts: One shows the teleprompter, so the control-room personnel can follow the exact line of script being spoken at the moment; others cover various sets not immediately in use, provide technical information on tint or lighting, and fill a variety of other functions. All are flickering with images or codes throughout the rehearsal and taping of a show, a dizzying spectacle to the uninitiated but essential to the various technicians observing them.

To Henry's right sits the associate director, script in hand, and to her right a production assistant clutches a stopwatch, her pencil poised, to check the precise timing of each scene as the run-through progresses. Behind them sit others of the production staff and occasionally a visitor, who quickly learns that no chitchat can be tolerated here. Producer Jørn Winther enters. He will observe every move of the rehearsal, give detailed notes to the director, then hurry off to a team "summit meeting" upstairs with Agnes; Jozie Emmerich, the vice president in charge of ABC's East Coast Daytime programming; and head writer Wisner Washam. A few cast members have already begun to speculate that this meeting could portend some major story line changes. Does this mean that the requirements of plotting will result in someone getting a plum story line for the next six months? Or maybe the reverse? Whatever the decision, no one will take it personally, for we know the story must always come first.

The actors are poised on their sets, the camera operators are crouched behind their lumbering devices, sound booms hover overhead, the control-room personnel are at the ready—and Henry taps his baton, the order for the circus to begin. Down on the Tyler library set the cue is given, the red light on Camera 1 goes on, and Phoebe speaks her opening lines to Charles. The Prologue is under way.

In the control room Henry leans forward, simultaneously following the dialogue on his script and watching the actual scene on the two monitor screens, a feat of double vision all directors find child's play. He raises his baton, his head nodding as the dialogue reaches the point at which Camera 2 will cut

in, then brings the stick down and says "Two!" The technical
director punches the control board, and the monitor shows the
scene as viewed through the second camera.

And so it goes, from one camera to the next, according to
the plan rehearsed in the morning blocking, until the end of
the scene. As the last lines are spoken and the camera tightens
in for a "freeze frame," Henry cues the second scene and the
monitor screens immediately pick up that set as seen through
Camera 3, one of the two already in position there. That is why
there are five cameras: so that there can always be at least two
in position to begin a scene just as the previous one ends. Even
as the lights go up on the second set, the cameras from the
first scene have already begun racing to reach the positions for
their next assignment. It is not unusual for performers to be
whispering sweet nothings in a delicate scene while a half-ton
camera goes barreling by, followed by assistants swishing cables about, on its way to a set halfway down the studio.

These "delicate scenes" often involve two people in bed,
seemingly unclothed, just before or after lovemaking. Such
intimacies cause the censors' antennae to quiver, lest anything
improper appear to be happening on camera. The actors' hands
must be in view outside the covers at all times, and naturally
no proscribed parts of the body should be visible. And yes, the
performers *are* wearing clothes, though sometimes skimpy
things not suitable for public appearances. One exception was
Francesca James, who plays Kelly Cole, the speed-freak twin
sister of Lincoln Tyler's dead wife, Kitty. One scene called for
Kelly to overdose on drugs while taking a bath, and for Eddie
Dorrance, her manager and supplier, to wrestle her out of the
tub and into her bed while she is unconscious. The scene was
done with the skimpiest possible clothing, since realism was
important to the effect, and the set was cleared of all but the
most essential personnel and closed until the taping was done.
(One amusing note about Francesca's return to the show as her
own twin, after an absence: One irate fan wrote to demand
why, if we had to have Kitty's twin sister, we couldn't at least
have found an actress who *looked* like Kitty.)

Incidentally, at Kelly's murder trial *all five* cameras were
used at once, four positioned about the courtroom set and one
hidden behind a sliding panel in back of the judge. The hidden

one was used for close-ups of the two attorneys as they approached the bench, with the panel opened while the camera
was on and then quickly slammed shut so that the wall behind
the bench would look solid when seen by another camera. This
"magic" allowed viewers to look right over the judge's shoulder, seemingly through a solid wall. It also made for a most
hectic day, since those cameras had to be whooshed all over
the studio for other scenes, causing much lashing of cables and
gnashing of teeth.

The Prologue scenes end, and there is a pause in the control
room while the time allocated to commercials and opening
credits ticks by. People trade bits of gossip, tell quick jokes,
munch apples during these two-minute pauses, then snap back
to full attention as if they too were controlled by switches. The
next scene begins. And the next, and the next, through the
various takes that make up the twenty-four scenes comprising
the Prologue and six Acts of this day's show.

There are other breaks to time segments that will be "rolled
in" from another part of the building, including, on this particular day, two scenes filmed previously on outdoor locations.
Outdoor scenes, which have added much to the sense of reality
on the show, have been used more frequently since we went
to the full hour length. Most locations are simple exteriors,
showing the houses in which Pine Valley residents live, or the
town's hospital or train station. Some of these scenes have
been filmed at various actual houses used by the show, and
one location, a fifty-two room mansion in New Canaan, Connecticut, was used to tape an entire two-week segment of the
story. Ever since the location shooting of Erica's Virgin Island
honeymoon, response to these outdoor scenes has encouraged
the show's producers to use them more frequently, despite the
added costs. (Exterior shots of the Tyler mansion are actually
done at Rose Hill, in Southport, Connecticut, a lovely house
built by a Captain Wakefield of the China clipper trade early
in the nineteenth century.)

An hour has passed—an hour of rushing from set to set,
dodging moving cameras and sound booms, running through
the entire show, scene by scene, without break. As the last
scene finishes and everyone sags against the nearest available
solid wall, the speakers begin to crackle in the studio and

throughout the building. In a moment a voice says, "Red chairs in five minutes, everybody. Five minutes to red chairs."

Red chairs. Our moment of truth. Our one and only all-out confrontation with our director, as *performers* rather than objects to be moved about on various sets while cameras and sound booms get all the attention. It is a great surprise, especially for visitors who are accustomed to a theatrical director's intense preoccupation with the way lines are read, to find that the *All My Children* cast seems virtually ignored throughout the day's various blockings and run-throughs, as if their reading of the lines were unimportant. Far from it. In fact, Henry has been making notes, on his script and in his mind, all through the day and particularly during the dress rehearsal we've just finished. He is literally bursting with comments, criticisms, complaints, instructions, and a few carefully chosen snide remarks, but he has not had a chance to brighten our lives with any of these things during the tightly structured doings of the day. Now is his chance.

The session is called red chairs for the very prosaic reason that it takes place in an improvised classroom composed of rows of collapsible canvas chairs which, in our studio, happen to be red. (Does the director on *Guiding Light* yell "yellow chairs"? I don't know.) The cast assembles on those chairs, scripts in hand, to face the music.

Our three regular directors have different personal styles, but each, in his or her own way, is a thoroughly accomplished professional. Jack Coffey is both a specialist in relaxed Irish charm and a marvelously incisive, inventive director whom Jørn calls "as close to perfect as you can get." The gifted Sherrell Hoffman brings a valuable feminine point of view to her direction and never fails to astound us with her phenomenal memory. Since it is Henry Kaplan whom we face today, we know we can expect a session composed of flamboyant gestures, theatrical modulations of voice, witty barbed comments ... and beneath it all, a formidable professional talent and genuine human concern. Today he seems relaxed as he looks us over, and his smile is beatific. It is as though he had no intention in the world other than to heap praise on one and all. Of course none of us believes this for a minute.

"Well, let us now begin," he says, stopping the chatter.

"And let us start with Phoebe. I refer to your soliloquy, love, in the garret scene." His smile is all sweetness. "Now weren't we Sally Soap in *that* one."

"In what way, Henry?" *Sally Soap* is his term for overacting, and I am secretly aware that I may have been a wee bit heavy-handed in that scene. But I will not admit it so easily. Actors do have their pride. Besides, I enjoy the byplay.

"Well, let us say that you are *not* doing Medea, and you have *not* just murdered your children. In fact, your daughter is sleeping right there before you, and if you carry on like that you will wake her *up*."

"You want it softer, more contained?"

With killing sweetness, "Is that possible, do you think?"

"It can be managed," I tell him, scribbling notes on my script.

"Good," he says. "And now we come to wonderful Mona Kane, in her scene at Tom's bedside."

Fra Heflin, sister of the late Van Heflin, frowns a bit. "Yes, Henry, I wanted to ask you—"

"*I* will ask," Henry says sharply. "What were you doing in that scene, attacking Erica or defending her?" (Erica, you may recall, is building a disco at the Goalpost, a fact her mother feels Erica's husband should know but hesitates to tell him.)

"Well, that's what I wanted to ask—"

"Don't ask, answer!" Henry snaps. "You've come there worried about what Erica is up to, and you're afraid to tell Tom. So how come you're defending her in such a nasty tone?"

"Well, I wanted to ask about the line—" Fra's soft voice seems near tears now.

"Shut *up*!" Henry shouts. "This isn't twenty questions. Let's just get it *right*."

"BIG BLOODY DEAL!" The voice, suddenly anything but soft and gentle, freezes every stagehand throughout the studio on the spot. It seems impossible that such an expression could have come from Fra, and at such volume, but it did.

Henry pretends to cringe in terror. "You wanted to say something, sweetheart?" he says almost pleadingly. By now everyone is laughing, and I hear a stagehand shout, "You mustn't say things like that in front of Phoebe!"

Fra, too, is laughing. "Well, what I was trying to ask is

whether that line about Erica's efficiency was meant to be sarcastic or straight. It's hard to tell from the script."

"I see," Henry says. "Well, why didn't you just *ask* me?"

The tension, now, has broken, and they discuss the reading of the line, which Henry assures her was *not* meant to be given ironic inflections. And now he moves on to ask Palmer Cortlandt why in hell he keeps rushing through his scene with Charles Tyler as if he's trying for a speed record.

"I forgot those counts again, huh?" Palmer asks.

"Again and again and *again*," Henry tells him.

Henry's tongue-lashing technique is usually taken in good part, and can be quite effective, but it can also sometimes backfire. We all still remember a day when Susan Lucci, who plays Erica, had great trouble with a line that was supposed to draw a laugh. It kept coming out flat, and she couldn't figure out why during the rehearsals. Henry explained that she was omitting the counts that would set up the funny line, but on the final run-through the line still fell flat. During red chairs Henry came down hard on her.

"Don't yell at me like that," she complained. "It's *hard* to remember those counts."

Henry's patience snapped. "Well, if you could remember how to *act*, we wouldn't have to put those counts in."

She flinched as if he had hit her. "I can't *act*?" she said. "Well then, get someone who *can*." And she ran sobbing from the studio, minutes before taping was to begin.

Realizing that he had inadvertently stepped over the fine line that separates good-humored taunting from genuine insult, Henry rushed after her. He apologized, cajoled, swore that he had not meant the words, explained that it was her inexperience with *comedy* he'd been referring to, and at last got her feathers smoothed back down enough so that she could return to the studio. We all felt it was a tribute to her skill, in fact, that she was able to compose herself and within minutes tape a difficult scene looking beautiful and serene.

By the way, lest anyone infer from this incident that Susan is a prima donna, she's anything but, as another incident will attest. It happened when some Con Edison workers came to repair damaged equipment in the building's basement and left a trapdoor open in the wardrobe room. None of us knew that trapdoor even existed, and we had all entered that room thousands of times over the years, so when Erica came rushing in for a costume change it never occurred to her to look down at the floor before her. The result was a horrifying twelve-foot plunge into the basement. Bruised but amazingly unbroken, she tottered back upstairs, got into costume, and was on the set within minutes ready to do her scene. And the remarkable thing is that no one found it remarkable. Such events are considered routine by performers, imbued with the belief that the show must go on no matter what.

So far, today's red-chairs session has passed in relative calm. Midway through, Sylvia Lawrence, head makeup artist and resident den mother, appears with a large plastic bag of fruit and begins passing it out, one of the few concessions to our comfort and well-being in this hectic day. The confusion of choosing amongst apples and pears interrupts Henry's discussion with Devon about how to time her exit, and he frowns.

"Well, it's Fanny Fruit," he says. "How wonderful for us all. Now do you think we could manage to munch our bananas *and* pay attention all at the same time?" Sylvia finishes and disappears toward the waiting stagehands, who will relieve her of anything left in the bag. We continue, and in a few minutes we finish the red chairs without further catastrophe. We head for Makeup for repairs or to Wardrobe for costume changes, still munching our apples and pears.

Before we leave this particular red-chairs session for good, I'd like to make a point about it that may not have been altogether apparent to you. It is that we cast members don't merely put up with Henry's flamboyant sarcasm: We both understand it and profit by it. Red chairs with Henry is like a master class in acting. With uncanny precision he goes straight to the heart of every scene, and by caricaturing his comments he makes it impossible for us to miss his points. Even his needling is purposeful. He wants to get our adrenaline flowing before we go on the air. In a sense, he uses sarcasm as a substitute for the stimulus a live audience would provide. For any actor, to sit in on a red-chairs session with Henry is a privilege. For any young actor, just starting out, it's an experience virtually beyond price.

One of the questions often asked by fans is, "Do you make

up the dialogue as you go along?" (Another version, somewhat more aggravating, is, "Do you have to memorize all that stuff or do you read it off cue cards?") I wish those fans could watch a red-chairs discussion some time, and a taping. Not only are we required to memorize all the dialogue, along with movements and counts and marks, but the positioning of cameras and the playing of emotional scenes would make reading cue cards a complete physical impossibility.

By now, in the few hours since we arrived with scripts none of us had rehearsed before, we have somehow progressed to a solid grasp of the scenes we are to do. Which is fortunate indeed, since it is now late afternoon and we are minutes away from the actual taping. With only one full-scale dress rehearsal and one intensive session of direction, we must now do it "for the money." This rapid progression from the fumbling beginnings in the rehearsal room to the finished performance, a sequence requiring weeks in the preparation of a stage play, is a wonderful and sometimes frightening thing to actors who come from other media into the world of daytime television. It requires the kind of control that can only come with experience, and often seems impossible to performers not accustomed to the pace. So if the people of Pine Valley occasionally stumble over a word or pause a second longer than seems called for, keep in mind the demands we must all meet to produce an hour-long show every day. (A movie, only slightly longer, may require many months, and each scene may be rehearsed for hours and then shot dozens of times until the last tiny blemish has been erased. Time, taken for granted in Hollywood, is one luxury we do not have in daytime television. Another is money. Although daytime television accounts for three quarters of network profit, our budgets are tiny when compared with prime-time shows.)

At four-thirty the speakers crackle once again: "Taping in five minutes. Five minutes till taping." We all head for the studio and our particular sets.

In the interim, we have been rushing to get our makeup touched up and our costumes changed, so we will be wearing the right clothing for the early scenes when taping begins. It is a close bit of timing, as are most of the activities of our day, with little room for such frivolities as trips to the bathroom. Once, when we were still in our old studio, I had made it through a particularly busy and stressful day of nonstop emoting in increasing need of relief, so when a five-minute break came I streaked for the ladies' room, which was up a flight of stairs and some distance down a corridor. No sooner had I arrived than the PA speaker began to crackle with peremptory commands: "Ruth Warrick to the set. Ruth Warrick to the set." Big Brother invading the last sanctuary! It continued without letup while I concluded the urgent matter at hand, rearranged my clothes, ran down the corridor and practically flung myself down the stairs.

It turned out that the stage manager had forgotten to deliver some trivial instruction about positioning, something that could certainly have waited. Furious, I stormed into the control room and shouted, "How *dare* you do that to me! I have a *right* to go to the john!" The assemblage, having no idea of what had happened, stared at me as if I had lost my mind.

Back in the control room now, the same personnel are in their same spots, with Henry again in the middle facing the bank of monitor screens and fussing with his baton. The atmosphere is less relaxed, since we are coming up on the real thing. The technical director is poised over his control board, face inches from the mike that will convey his commands to the people down in the studio, invisible from here except as seen on the various screens. He is in charge of all equipment— sound, lighting, cameras, music, sound effects, everything except stagehands and props—and he, in turn, takes his instructions from the director. The lighting director is at his side, hands poised over the console that will activate banks of lights above each set as needed.

The T.D., as he is called in the trade, has been at work in the control room during our red-chairs session, preparing for the actual taping and checking out the equipment. About forty-five minutes before taping was to begin, he issued a call over the speakers for the cameras to "go to charts." Each camera in the studio was then positioned in front of a targetlike chart composed of lines and concentric circles, so the complex process of focusing and aligning the image can take place. Since a video picture is composed of hundreds of lines varying in intensity and color, and since those lines may drift in electronic current to cause distortion, it is important to get them lined up precisely and to see that the three principal colors register on them with equal intensity. Shades of gray on the chart are used to balance the colors, and to recheck that balance before each scene.

"Are we ready?" Henry asks.

Nods, mumbles to right and left.

"Then cue Prologue, Scene One," he orders.

The associate director calls into her mike for tints, and the gray tones show briefly on one of the monitors. "Okay, roll the tapes," she says.

The T.D. flips switches, leans toward his own mike, and says, "Roll Able and Baker," to the operators of the tape machines elsewhere in the building.

"Let's have the slate," says the associate director, and immediately the stage manager appears on one of the center screens holding a chalkboard bearing the date, name of show, and number of scene. An electronic tone sounds, and he steps out of the screen.

We are on.

But not for long. The first scene, a dialogue between Phoebe and Charles, appears to have a jinx on it this day. Although we ran through it perfectly in rehearsal, as soon as tapes begin to roll the gremlins start their games. In moments I heard the T.D.'s voice order "Cut," and word is relayed that I have omitted a key line, without which the rest of the scene will not make sense.

While we wait on the set, concentrating on our lines, there is a hurried discussion in the control room about how far they must back up the tape to get a freeze frame, in which the camera has been held on one character in one spot for several counts. One is located, Henry instructs that we take it from a certain line, and the T.D. relays the instructions to the set. Charles and Phoebe resume the positions they had occupied (marked with those bits of tape, remember?) at that point in the scene, and the tapes are started again, with the camera holding on my face for a second. I then run through the scene from that point, this time making sure the missing line is there.

I am concentrating so hard on that problem that I hardly

notice what Charles is saying until I hear, "Oh, hell!" They hear it in the control room too, and instantly tapes stop and the conference begins again. It seems Charles has informed Phoebe that their daughter is "not in full possession of her mental facilities." The word should have been "faculties," a slip that might well have escaped notice by everyone except Hugh Franklin. Again the tapes are backed up, we resume positions at the indicated point, and begin again, this time getting the whole thing right.

Tape can never, of course, be edited as quickly or cheaply as film, and until a few years ago it was not always easy to gain access to the few existing tape-editing machines. Before the show went to the full hour, entire scenes would have to be reshot, and our studio time was too limited to permit such indulgences. We raced through from beginning to end, with commercials rolled in as we went, and with no breaks in the half-hour continuity. Now, with a somewhat larger budget, more time, and our own tape-editing machine, we have been given the luxury of a few retakes. But few is the key word. Time still weighs heavy, and retakes are costly.

Many things can break the smooth flow of taping, and some of these are beyond human control. Shadows from the sound boom may suddenly be noticed in a scene, and it will have to be reshot with the boom repositioned. Cameras may suddenly—for no known reason—malfunction, breaking the picture into fragments or introducing a wild color or even going totally blank. Why these things happen is the subject of much speculation, ranging from electrical storms or atmospheric quirks to fluctuations in the voltage of current supplied by Con Edison. Whatever the cause, their effect is the same—they result in expensive, frustrating delays while repairs are being made and armies of highly paid people are standing idle.

But tonight we are lucky, and all the equipment works, including the two exterior scenes that are rolled in from a third tape machine in some far reach of the building. These, too, are timed carefully in the control room, though their length is known. Both are scenes in front of the Pine Valley Hospital, and in one there is dialogue between two nurses, which must be recorded in the studio as the tape rolls in.

Agnes Nixon has been most innovative in the use of such

devices as flashback and dream or fantasy sequences, which are also shot separately (or—if flashbacks—picked up from an earlier taping that was carefully labeled to be saved for later use) and then rolled in. This is done by having the camera move in very close on a character's face, then superimposing the remembered or imagined scene as a double exposure. Slowly the frozen face fades and the imaginary scene continues, then as it nears its end the face reappears and we are back in the present, or reality. Flashbacks are used to underscore the importance of a scene, or to show what a character feels now about what happened *previously*, or at times simply to remind viewers of something they may have forgotten or missed in the passing weeks.

Fantasies or dream sequences, which are great fun for the performers, are often used to show what a character wishes would happen, and usually have little to do with reality. In one such scene Estelle, a former prostitute, imagines how it will be when Benny brings her home as his new wife and introduces her to Phoebe, his employer. In the daydream Estelle drips with diamonds and Phoebe burbles with joy, calling for champagne and insisting that they make the Tyler mansion their home forever. It closes with Benny, splendid in white cutaway, informing Phoebe that they are departing to make their fortune in Fairbanks, Alaska, an announcement that virtually dissolves Phoebe in anguish. Such scenes, which give the performers a welcome chance to step out of character and play games, are also favorites for the fans.

Another interesting device used in color taping involves a process called Chromo-Key, which is based on the separation of colors during the camera's transmission of what it "sees." A video camera has three buttons on its control panel, one for red, one for blue, one for green. Normally the colors are mixed, but it is possible to suppress one color and thereby blank out anything of that color in the scene. Suppose, for instance, two people are to be shown in the front seat of a moving car. The two actors are seated in front of a solid blue backdrop. When the blue color is suppressed during that scene, the effect, as seen on the monitor, would be to show the two people suspended in midair. At that point a film of moving background, as seen from the rear windows of a car, is rolled in "behind" the actors on the tape. Though none of this is visible on the actual set, the viewer at home sees a totally convincing picture of two people in a car.

Such scenes are often tricky, because the actor must remember at all times that he is supposed to be driving a car at highway speeds, though he is in fact sitting motionless on a set before a blue wall. I remember one such scene in which Erica's half-brother, Mark, had been talking to Ellen about their coming honeymoon. Henry had been scathing in the red-chairs session. "It's a love scene," he had roared at Mark. "You're not doing a travelogue on Niagara Falls, you're trying to sell her on a passionate honeymoon."

Mark heeded the advice, and during the actual scene he concentrated so intensely on Ellen that he ignored the "road" entirely to gaze romantically into her eyes. From the control-room speakers came Henry's wry voice: "Congratulations. You have just killed fourteen pedestrians."

We have no Chromo-Key scenes today, though, and we are nearing the end of the taping, with the T.D. calling for a check of the tape after each scene. Not until the tinny voice responds, "Okay, we have tape on Act Four," does the next scene begin. And not until that same voice, from the mysterious regions where the tape machines are housed, announces, "We have tapes—that's a wrap," can the evening end.

Since the last scene has been taped, there is only the "beauty spot" to be completed. This is the silent scene that runs at the end of each day's show behind the credits. Today's beauty spot was to have Ellen working in her boutique, but Henry discovers that she has changed costumes in order to tape two scenes for a future show. These scenes, rare exceptions to the do-it-all-today rule, include an actor who must be away for personal reasons, so they will be taped now and held for insertion when the script calls for them. Henry finally decides to go ahead with those scenes and then to hustle Ellen off to wardrobe for a change back into the correct costume for the beauty spot. Since none of those things involves Phoebe, I walk wearily back to my dressing room to change.

It is now well past seven P.M., almost twelve hours since I arrived at the rehearsal room to begin this day. And I am on call tomorrow at eight A.M. (union rules forbid calling an actor back to the set less than twelve hours after a day's work has ended unless additional compensation is paid). That leaves time for dinner with friends, a lesson in disco skating I've been promised, and a few hours of sleep before the morning begins once again.

The day in Pine Valley is done, but tomorrow is already beginning in the studio, where the crew is dismantling this day's sets, stacking the components on rolling platforms, and setting up the sets to be used tomorrow. This process can last until past midnight, and sometimes till two or three in the morning. Tomorrow's call for the same crew can be as early as five A.M., though any turnaround of less than four hours requires that ABC provide hotel rooms at company expense.

Life never stops in Pine Valley.

SIX

The Road to
Pine Valley:
Hollywood

IF PHOEBE TYLER was born in *Citizen Kane*, she spent her
adolescence on the back lots of RKO, United Artists, Columbia, Universal, and even the Walt Disney Studios. From the
beginning I had been firmly typecast as a leading *lady*, and the
publicity mills of the studios worked to build on the image. I
was married, a mother, a member of Welles' prestigious Mercury Theatre company, and I successfully portrayed a forth-
right, dignified, straight-arrow woman who could be a wife
(usually betrayed) but never a wanton. I might be glamorous
but never quite sexy. No seductive vamps for Mrs. Citizen
Kane was the word from on high, and the mills ground ac-
cordingly. The Phoebe Tyler-like characterization Welles had
elicited from me had suddenly become my persona as an actress.

The first job on my new RKO contract was a light comedy
with Edmond O'Brien called *Obliging Young Lady*, in which
I played the guardian of a young girl named Joan Carroll, who
was fresh from a Broadway triumph opposite Ethel Merman
in *Panama Hattie*, and regarded as a potential new Shirley
Temple. (Eve Arden had a single memorable scene, as a reporter locked in battle with a phone booth as she tries to call
in her story.) Little was done to promote the movie, which
nevertheless surprised everyone by outgrossing most RKO
films in 1941.

Obliging Young Lady was followed by *The Corsican Brothers*, a swashbuckling costume drama with Douglas Fairbanks,
Jr., filmed at United Artists on one of those loan-out deals that
were so common then. (Simply put, the studio that held your

contract could rent you out to another studio for any amount the market would bear, though none of this profit went to you. You got your normal salary, and the dubious privilege of being traded about like chattel.) *Corsican Brothers* is a legend of another kind in that it holds some sort of record for the number of times it has been shown on television. Doug Fairbanks often bemoans the lack of vision that caused him to sell out his share of the movie for next to nothing on the mistaken assumption that a black-and-white picture would be cast aside with the coming of color.

Between takes I helped him study the navy officer's manual, which meant that we spent considerable time together. Near the end of shooting he told me that working with me was the most fun he'd had since "punting on the Thames with Gertie Lawrence." I wasn't precisely sure what that meant, but I knew a compliment when I heard one.

Both films were released in 1941, on the heels of the *Citizen Kane* critical triumph, and at the same time I began work on another movie with Orson and Joseph Cotten, *Journey Into Fear*. Again I was the wife, with chin up in adversity, though this time it was Joe Cotten who played my husband. This role— a sort of Phoebe without claws—was to repeat itself with many variations over the next few years, in a kind of typecasting that seemed unbreakable. In movie after movie I was the reserved, poised, competent wife, loving but rarely passionate, and certainly never sultry. In fact, the role that followed was that of a wife and mother of no less than seven children in a war movie called *The Iron Major*, opposite Pat O'Brien. The story of Frank Cavanaugh, the famous football coach who became a hero in World War I, it was one of those inspirational movies, combining elements of *Knute Rockne* and *The Fighting Sullivans*, so typical of the wartime years in Hollywood.

Pat, of course, was an Irish charmer whose wit and blarney never ceased. He went on and on about how enchanted he was by my bright eyes and long legs. "Look at the whites of her eyes," he groaned one morning when his own bloodshot eyes bore bleary witness to a night of celebration. "They're so clear she must scrub them with a toothbrush."

When his birthday came around I searched long and hard for the one appropriate gift, which I presented, lavishly wrapped, at a party on the set. It was a well-turned leg from a store-window mannequin, wearing a black mesh stocking and a red satin garter. Pat gallantly said he loved it almost as much as the real thing.

At the studio preview for cast and crew, several members of the real Cavanaugh family who had acted as technical advisers were invited. During Major Cavanaugh's deathbed scene, with all his children gathered around him, each in a uniform of some branch of the services, someone in the front row began to sob uncontrollably, until we could almost hear tears splash on the floor. Everyone assumed it was a Cavanaugh, but when the lights came up, there sat Pat, bawling his heart out at his own deathbed scene.

Although Erik was working in radio during the exciting early months of my burgeoning Hollywood career, the movie parts he had hoped for eluded him. The character roles that were available, and for which he was perfectly equipped, were not at all what he had in mind. He worked less, played tennis more, and began to drink more heavily. The birth of our second child, Jon, seemed to give him no particular pleasure, though the later stages of my pregnancy did compel him to seek work to replace the income lost when the studio suspended me. He signed a contract at Columbia and did several character parts in war movies, playing Nazi officers with a faultless German accent and a most convincing aura of menace. He might well have continued a successful career and joined that company of distinguished character actors who were often paid more than lead players. But after Jon's birth allowed me to return to the studio and my regular paychecks, Erik returned to the tennis courts, the increasing liquor consumption, and the growing bitterness.

The Iron Major was released in 1943, as was my next movie, *Forever and a Day*, which featured such luminaries of the British film colony as Herbert Marshall, C. Aubrey Smith, Sir Cedric Hardwicke, Merle Oberon, Ida Lupino, and Brian Aherne. As an American girl who has come to claim her ancestral home in England, I was one of two Americans in the film. The other was Kent Smith, who had just completed a movie called *The Cat People*, said by some to have been the studio's economic salvation after the financial setbacks resulting from Hearst's advertising ban on *Kane*. Shortly after the release of *Forever and a Day*, several members of the cast were invited to the White House, where we presented a check representing the film's proceeds to FDR on behalf of British War Relief.

We were brought into the Oval Office one at a time, after being announced from the door. As I walked across that historic room, that famous voice boomed, "Ah, yes, I'd recognize you anywhere, my dear." I melted.

I often seemed to melt when confronted with childhood heroes or heartthrobs. During a scene in *Forever and a Day*, as I was emoting from the balcony of my stately English home while watching the bombing of London, Herbert Marshall strolled to the edge of the set. He had been a special crush of my childhood, and when I saw him, for the first time in my professional life, the lines went completely out of my head.

The director yelled "Cut!" and climbed down off the crane camera. He clambered up the two stories to my balcony and peered at me with a worried look. "What's the matter?" he said. "Are you ill?"

"No, I'm all right," I gasped, "but please ask Mr. Marshall to stand somewhere where I can't see him."

If this seems strange, I can only say that most theater people I've known were starstruck as children, which may be why most of us—even Phoebe—try to be patient and friendly with our own fans. My personal idols, in addition to Herbert Marshall, Greta Garbo, and just about any actress who stood tall enough to make my own height less catastrophic, had also included many figures in the world of music. I had devoured the records of the virile baritone Lawrence Tibbett, and when I saw him on the screen with Grace Moore it was easy to imagine myself in her shoes, held in those manly arms and bathed in that powerful voice singing "The Cuban Love Song."

During my freshman year in college I had heard that Tibbett was to give a concert in the auditorium of St. Joseph Central High School, my alma mater. I persuaded my current boyfriend to take me, convinced that Fate had decreed this meeting. And I sat through the evening electrified, my heart pounding.

However, wonderful as it was, sitting in the audience was simply not enough for me, so just before the last number con-

cluded I slipped out of the auditorium and through the corridors
I remembered so well to the stage door, which opened onto a
corridor leading to the parking lot. Moments later Tibbett came
striding through that door into the corridor. Waiting assistants
leaped to hold his coat and hat, which he slipped into without
breaking stride, and he headed for his limousine, waiting just
outside the door. Giving thanks for my own long legs, I kept
pace with him, trying to get his attention.

I succeeded. As we neared the door, he swept me up under
his arm and hustled me along, smiling down from his great
height and saying things I was far too ecstatic to hear. In
seconds I found myself in the backseat of the car and heard
Tibbett instructing the driver to take us to his hotel.

The fog lifted for an instant and I remembered my boyfriend
waiting in the auditorium. As the big car started to move I
opened the opposite door and slid out, then stood there trying
to regain my composure as the taillights disappeared into the
night.

I've never been quite sure just what fate my quick thinking
saved me from, but I must admit I've tried many times to
imagine it. I also must admit I've never been quite as friendly
with fans as Tibbett was that night, but I have certainly understood their feelings, as I'm sure Herbert Marshall did on the
set that day.

That same year saw the release of a Walter Reade movie
called *Petticoat Larceny* (reviews praised "the reserved Ruth
Warrick"), followed by another war movie for Columbia, *Secret
Command*, in which I once again played Pat O'Brien's wife.
In *Guest in the House*, a United Artists film produced by Hunt
Stromberg, some attempt was made to free me from the prison
of typecasting by way of a rather passionate bedroom scene in
which I got to wear a revealing negligee. I was still the wife,
but this time I was fighting to rescue my artist-husband (Ralph
Bellamy) from the clutches of either his curvaceous model
(Marie MacDonald) or his future sister-in-law (Anne Baxter),
a neurotically predatory woman who was the guest in our house.

A feature story in the Los Angeles Sunday *Times*, which
carried pictures of me and my children and praised me for
having so successfully combined career and motherhood, had
a large, ego-boosting headline: "Ruth Warrick Nears Great-

ness." However, most reviewers ignored the negligee scene and repeated the by-now-familiar praises for "that established character actress" and her performance as "the perfect wife," though one did add that I had "emerged as a full-fledged leading lady" in the film. In truth, whatever good the sexy scene might have done was offset by a fan-magazine article featuring full-page photos of Marie MacDonald and myself on facing pages. Under Marie's picture were the words, "The Body." Under mine it said, "The Brain."

The die, it seemed, had been cast: I might get leading-lady roles, but never the juicy ones offered to Rita Hayworth or Paulette Goddard or the other sexy beauties of the day. Still, there was some consolation in the thousands of letters that came from GI's, assuring me that if they could get a wife like me they would marry the instant the war ended. "The kind of girl you want to bring your paycheck home to," as someone put it.

Yet I could hardly complain. If I had wanted more, I was nevertheless aware of how much less I might have achieved. Whatever disappointments I might have had, I was, after all, a movie star, still the most glamorous and envied job in an actress's world in those days.

Among the decidedly pleasant fringe benefits of Hollywood were the publicity junkets, with VIP treatment that could truly spoil a girl. There were posh hotel suites, the best theater tickets, elegant wining and dining, and a whole studio wardrobe from which to borrow one's finery. (When Pat suddenly whisked me into an impromptu Irish jig in Boston and I split my gown, a new one was rushed to me.) I had dinners at "21," a special table at El Morocco, and a limousine at my disposal. I'd come a long way from St. Joseph.

A bit later I was part of the last of the big-time junkets, when oil man Glen McCarthy opened his Shamrock Hotel and invited an entire trainload of celebrities down for the ceremonies. It was like a whistle-stop campaign train, with fans turned out all along the route from Los Angeles to Houston. The bar was open twenty-four hours a day and the party was continuous.

Pat O'Brien was in heaven, singing and dancing up and down the aisles with a glass forever in his hand. Instead of sleeping, he would simply go for a refresher in the barber shop. (Yes, Virginia, there were barber shops on trains, as well as elegant dining cars, lounges, staterooms, bedrooms, and porters dedicated to your comfort.) Then, shaved and bathed and massaged, Pat would return to the fray.

By the second day Pat's wife, Eloise, was fed up. Not a drinker herself, she decided to teach Pat a lesson.

"Waiter, bring me a bottle of brandy," she ordered.

As the brandy bottle emptied, she filled with life, and by evening she had danced her way into everyone's heart—and every man's lap. Pat, who seemed to be sobering up fast, pleaded with her to slow down and take it easy, but she seemed delighted with the way the tables were beginning to turn.

A bit later that evening the train stopped at Lubbock, Texas, and a large delegation of gray-haired ladies boarded, bearing a huge shamrock-decorated cake for Pat. While Eloise sat at a table by the window and fumed, Pat pinched cheeks and spread the blarney generously. The cake was placed on the table, Pat sat down across from her and leaned over to inspect the cake, and, as the train pulled out, the beaming ladies blanched to see Eloise calmly reach out and push his head all the way into its gooey depths. The evening's object lesson was complete.

Not all junkets were quite so glamorous. I recall one proposed appearance, for a premiere in Marshalltown, Iowa, that brought no stampede of volunteers. However, since it happened to coincide with a wedding I wanted to attend in Kansas City, I agreed to go on the condition that I be put on an evening flight out of Des Moines. I was assured that I'd make the plane, so I went cheerfully through the day, ending with a cocktail reception at the Tall Corn Hotel.

And then it was time to go. The man who'd volunteered to drive me to Des Moines came with his car, accompanied by a friend, and off we went, with the men making the sort of nervous, flirtatious small talk I had come to expect. Local businessmen often got somewhat adolescent when they found themselves with a visiting actress. We often wondered what sort of fantasies they might be constructing, and whether those fantasies might not turn into "fact" when they got back among their cronies.

They suggested that we could have a great time in Des Moines if I missed my plane, and I chided them for their naughtiness, as expected, while sneaking peeks at my watch. We really didn't have much time to spare, so when they began to horse around with the car, stopping to clock the speed of their starts and the like, I began to worry. And then it suddenly dawned on me that they were really trying to make me miss the plane.

I was furious, and told them so rather vigorously, which produced an immediate acceleration and profuse apologies. We screeched up to the terminal on the dot of departure time, and I raced for the ticket counter while they struggled with my bags.

There was no one there! The terminal was absolutely empty, as only a small-town air terminal in wartime could be. I flew to the door of the boarding area and peered out toward the runway, where I could see the plane, lights blinking as it moved into position for its takeoff run. Yelling at the puffing escorts to follow me, I ran onto the field.

Once there, the scope of the problem hit me. How does one stop a moving airplane? The only thing I could think to do was to dash into the middle of the runway, which brought men rushing out from all directions, screaming that I was crazy and ordering me out of the way.

"The only place I'm going is on board that plane," I said grimly. "It's not taking off till I'm on it."

Amazingly, they wheeled out a boarding ladder, and with help from the Marshalltown businessmen, I and my bags boarded the plane for Kansas City. Phoebe would have been proud of me.

The junkets, however, were a minor part of my life, most of which was taken up with what the *Times* article had called my successful combination of career and motherhood. That same story had mentioned that my husband's career was also looking up, but this bit of information had far less basis in fact. In truth, Erik's career was at a standstill. As it became evident that his dreams of joining the ranks of leading men would not come true, he withdrew more and more into the spacious Spanish house we had rented above the Hollywood Bowl, and into drink. We seldom went out, and almost never attended any of

the social functions of the movie business, since Erik claimed
he found the Hollywood crowd shallow and stupid. The little
social life we had revolved around friends from other times,
particularly people he had known from his days at the University of Minnesota. Though many of them were now connected with the film industry, to them Erik was still the center
of attention, and when he was with them, he found it easier
to ignore—and even ridicule—my own growing celebrity.

I understood and even sympathized. I would have given
anything if his career could have matched or outshone mine.
He had been helpful and encouraging when I was the wide-
eyed innocent, and it was largely at his insistence that we had
come to Hollywood. Obviously it would be difficult for any
man to watch his wife's career grow while his own went nowhere. But his surliness and his refusal even to try to face the
reality of the roles he was physically suited to play created
tremendous tensions that gradually eroded our relationship and
took most of the joy out of living. His ill humor made it virtually
impossible for me to attend publicity interviews or any sort of
social function in his company, yet excluding him only served
to feed the bitterness.

But to be fair about it, perhaps I wouldn't have fitted all
that well into the Hollywood scene anyway, even without Erik's
caustic rudeness. There had been signs that I was something
of a maverick from the start. On the very first day, reporting
for work under my long-term contract, I had been informed by
the studio's head of talent that I would be sent to Dr. So-and-
so to have my teeth fixed.

"Why?" I asked him.

He seemed surprised at the question. "So you'll look good
in close-ups," he said. "It's standard procedure."

He said the last words in such an offhand way that I was
immediately irritated. I pulled my lips back in a maniacal grin,
exhibiting two rows of even, white teeth. "What's wrong with
these?"

He peered at them, then shrugged. He tilted his head for
a survey of my nose, which apparently he found adequately
straight. Finally he said, "Okay, but you'll have to get those
cheeks fixed. You look like a chipmunk."

I knew my cheeks were somewhat more round than was

considered ideal by that year's starlet standards, but round or not, they were mine, and I had no intention of letting anyone hack at them, certainly not on the authority of this pompous man.

"Claudette Colbert has apple cheeks, and she seems to be doing all right," I told him. "I think I'll keep mine."

He was annoyed, but I was adamant: no dentistry or plastic surgery. Later this same man was convicted of having taken kickbacks from some of the doctors to whom he had sent performers, but at the time such cosmetic surgery was considered a standard part of the star-building procedure.

It has been said that glamour left Hollywood with the demise of the star system, and that may be true to some extent. But it is also true that the system meant virtual slavery for the stars themselves. The studio simply took control of one's life, dictating appearance, dress, social behavior, standard and style of living, even acceptable love interests. It was a well-oiled machine, perfectly designed to produce, nurture, and promote precisely the image of glamour and mild titillation the public would buy, and to cast aside anyone who didn't fit the mold.

I was a problem for the machine. For one thing, I was already married and a mother; and even though I was of starlet age, I looked older. I had convincingly played an older woman in *Citizen Kane*, and I was to be cast in roles several years beyond my actual age in virtually every movie I made thereafter. Furthermore, I was an Orson Welles protégée, and Welles was hardly a model of Hollywood conformity. In other words, I was an outsider who had breached the Hollywood walls by other than the standard route. And to make matters worse, I exhibited signs of having a will of my own, a quality considered as inappropriate in an actress as, say, a taste for miscegenation.

This odd phenomenon was detected early, when a delegation of those same New York brass, wearing their same overcoats and pulled-down hats, visited me in my dressing room to discuss my salary. They were not supposed to discuss money with a performer at all, since all such matters were handled by agents, and they certainly should not have waked me from a much-needed nap to do it. I was not in the best of moods as I listened to their explanation of their problems, which involved great financial losses due to the war overseas. The bottom line was that they simply could not afford to give me the modest raise called for in my contract. They were sure I would be understanding and cooperative. Etcetera, etcetera.

I listened in growing annoyance, realizing that I was being gulled and patronized at the same time. Finally I interrupted their explanation of why they could not distribute films in their customary way because of that madman Hitler.

"Gentlemen," I said. "If I understand this, you say you are losing money because your *only* profits come from Europe. Well, if the money represented by my small raise will save the studio, by all means take it. But I would guess that any business set up so that its profits come entirely from a market that can disappear overnight is going to need more than my few hundred dollars to set it right."

They looked at me as if I had spit on the flag, and departed. I had done the unforgivable: I had questioned their judgment. Instead of remaining pretty, docile, and obedient, as befitted a girl being groomed by the system, I had dared to use my head.

In addition to being uppity and suspected of possessing a working brain, I had made it clear from the outset that I did not intend to play the casting-couch game that was virtually *de rigueur* in the world of Louis B. Mayer, Harry Cohn, Darryl Zanuck, David O. Selznick, and even the peculiar and elusive multi-millionaire producer who would later control RKO, Howard Hughes.

My first sight of Hughes was at Palm Springs, during a weekend Erik and I spent there with his Minnesota friends. We had been in Hollywood only a month or so, and I was still wide-eyed in this world of celebrities. I quickly spotted the tall, gaunt man as he entered the elegant dining room of the Racquet Club and was seated, surrounded by his lackeys, at a table near ours. Already a world-famous pilot and something of a legend in his business and personal life, he would have been hard to miss in any crowd. Here his dirty sneakers and open-necked white shirt were in striking contrast to the splendidly dressed company.

After the initial surprise, I forgot about him, until a short while later when a waiter edged up to me and slipped a note into my hand surreptitiously. Startled, I opened it up in full view and read it aloud to my husband and friends.

"'My limousine will call for you at your bungalow at midnight,'" I read in amazement. "It's signed 'Howard R. Hughes.'"

If the note amazed me, the reactions of our friends were nothing short of astonishing. They assured me that this was my big break, my ticket to stardom, the chance of a lifetime. Certainly I must go, they insisted. Even Erik seemed intrigued, which truly shocked me.

"You are all out of your minds," I told them emphatically, and ripped up the note.

I had been warned of the way the system worked, of course. But the more I heard about it the more determined I became not to play that game. Not that I considered myself saintly, or even that I was all that consecrated to undying virtue. But I knew myself well enough to know that cold-blooded "bedding for business," however glamorously disguised, would still be prostituting myself, a form of instant self-destruction. It wasn't a decision I had to make; it was quite simply not possible. Besides, there was the basic matter of pride: I was determined to prove, at least to myself, that an actress could make it in pictures on talent alone, without ever having to buy or sell favors.

I learned how difficult that would be even before we moved to the West Coast. David O. Selznick, impressed with my work in *Citizen Kane*, had my agent send me to his office. After a minimum of small talk he got quickly to the point, which was that I would have a far brighter future if I were to become his personal protégée. Self-preservation dictated that I avoid cries of outraged virtue, so I reminded him politely that I was already under contract to RKO. No problem, he assured me: He could always buy my contract (and me, his look implied). I thanked him for his interest but assured him I was quite happy under my present arrangement. It was my first and last meeting with Selznick.

A similar suggestion came from the infamous Harry Cohn, during an angry meeting he arranged through my agent not long after the release of *Citizen Kane*. He stormed up and down his vast office, smacking his riding crop against his polished boots, demanding to know how in hell that upstart Welles had managed to steal away one of his brightest stars. The "star" in question was one Linda Winters, a minor actress whose contract Columbia had allowed to lapse. Orson changed her name back to Dorothy Comingore. Cohn was outraged at this perfidy.

I listened to his idiotic tirade, assured him that I had had nothing to do with the theft of his property, and then was surprised when his ranting suddenly gave way to leers and crude suggestions about how I could further my career under his personal guidance. When I failed to show the proper enthusiasm by eluding his grasp as he chased me around a mercifully huge Louis XV desk, my promising career abruptly lost all promise and I was dismissed.

It was not that I held some special charm for these men. For Cohn and Selznick and the other monarchs of Hollywood such propositions were made as a matter of course, and it was rare when their advances were repelled. Rare, and dangerous for the actress who chose to be so fastidious. Although few actresses ever achieved real stardom without talent, everyone knew of talented women that had been cast aside for daring to antagonize someone in a position of power.

Darryl Zanuck was legendary for his treatment of young actresses, especially Marilyn Monroe, whose insecurities he exploited with a ruthless lechery that may well have contributed to her early death. He propositioned virtually every actress who crossed his path, including me, though I didn't cross his path until I had been in Hollywood for several years and had already achieved some success. His proposition to me was a bit perfunctory, since the word was out by now that I was uncooperative in such matters, and my polite refusal was shrugged off. Even so, he got his revenge a short while later, at a dinner party held in a restaurant featuring the kind of banquette seating that makes escape impossible. Zanuck arranged to be seated between his wife and me, and throughout the dinner he pawed me under the table without saying a word, knowing I dared not make a scene in his wife's presence.

I never worked at MGM, so I escaped the attention of that studio's equally legendary boss. But a minor incident sticks in my mind that may say something about my maverick attitude toward the system. It occurred at a cocktail party at the Beverly

Hills Hotel, where everyone was buzzing with talk of a dinner party many were invited to later that evening at the home of Louis B. Mayer. The guest of honor was to be no less than a famous Italian cardinal, who was visiting the city.

There was much discussion about the appropriate way to greet a pope. If you were Catholic it was proper to kneel and kiss his ring, but what if you were not Catholic? Should you kiss the ring anyway, or bow at a discreet distance, or would a simple American handshake be in order? And how, for that matter, should one address a cardinal?

The discussion went on and on until I began to get bored with the whole thing. At a lull I made a suggestion.

"If you non-Catholics feel that kissing the ring is too much, maybe you could just stand back and blow it a kiss," I said.

That got a round of chuckles.

"However, one thing still bothers me," I went on. "This party is at Louis B. Mayer's, right?"

Nods.

"Well, when you're at Louis B. Mayer's house, isn't there something else you have to kiss?"

There was a shocked silence, and in moments I found myself standing alone in the middle of the room. The lesson was clear: In Hollywood you could make jokes about almost anything, including God and the pope. But you could *not* make jokes about Louis B. Mayer.

Somehow, despite my failure to blend in, I did manage to survive and flourish. *Guest in the House* had been a solid role, and I was working hard, with a sense of achievement in my career that helped to offset the growing problems at home. I was loaned out to Columbia for an odd little movie called *Mr. Winkle Goes to War*, in which I played the Phoebe Tylerish wife of a mild-mannered putterer whose skill at repairing things becomes vital to the defense effort. Mr. Winkle was Edward G. Robinson, oddly cast as the meek and kindly fix-it-man whose ambition his wife cannot kindle. Needless to say, I was once again the competent and supportive wife, part of whose job was to avoid looming over the stocky Robinson in our few tender moments. (My height was often a problem, and more than once it cost me the chance to test for a role opposite a major star. The producer of an upcoming Alan Ladd film once took me aside and said, "Forget it. We have to dig trenches for his leading ladies to walk in as it is, but with you we'd have to put him on a ladder.")

Erik's drinking increased, compounded now by another problem. His doctor, in a misguided attempt to calm his nerves, had prescribed phenobarbitals, and Erik was popping these pills in ever-increasing quantities. I could see that he was becoming less coherent and less capable of simple self-control, but I didn't understand until years later what devastating things this combination of drugs and alcohol were doing to him.

Nor did I know until much later of the homosexual liaisons he had entered, even in the early months of our marriage. In those innocent days I thought of homosexuals as men who wore lipstick and carried chiffon handkerchiefs, which certainly did not fit Erik's size and booming voice. The closest I came to suspecting was at a birthday party, when Erik, who had always refused to dance, suddenly invited me to the dance floor. As a surprise, he had been taking ballroom dancing lessons, and now he led me proudly into a turn around the floor. The dancing was tentative but adequate, yet something was terribly wrong, and my whole body was getting the message. I cannot explain it, but it was a message that years of living together and bearing two children by him had somehow failed to convey. I pretended to be overcome by the thoughtfulness of his gesture, and fled to the ladies' room in tears. We never danced together again.

Perhaps it would have been better if, at this period, I had fully understood Erik's problems, but I did not. All I knew was that whatever love we might once have shared had long since been ground underfoot, and that all physical intimacy had long since ended between us.

More and more there was a split in my life, as if there were two Ruth Warricks: one was the movie star, hardworking, respected, supported by hordes of attentive studio personnel; the other was the wife, who came home to a confused household and a husband who treated her with seething contempt. Those were the only places I inhabited, it seemed, and they were on different planets.

Finally there was an episode that could not be dismissed lightly, even by Erik. One brilliant, windy Sunday afternoon, after a day of drinking, he suddenly decided to take a stroll around the neighborhood, past the homes of Claudette Colbert, Max Reinhardt, and author James Hilton—totally nude! Whether this was an act of defiant hostility or of self-destruction, it was certainly a bid for attention that worked—in the worst possible way. Because my father, who had chosen that afternoon to pay a visit to his daughter and grandchildren, encountered Erik on his ramble. From that moment on, my carefully guarded marital problems ceased being a secret. My parents were so upset that they urged me to divorce him, which must have been extremely difficult for those devout Baptists. But I wouldn't hear of it. Erik was my husband and the father of my children, and I would somehow simply have to make the best of things.

Erik, momentarily sobered, was persuaded to enter therapy. In fact, he entered therapies of all sorts, from vitamin and hormone treatments to psychoanalysis, but through them all the drinking and drug taking continued unabated, and his feelings of inadequacy continued to be masked by a surface manner of arrogant superiority. At one point, in a conference with his doctor, I admitted candidly that my love for Erik had been virtually snuffed out, and that although I would help him all I could, I found it all but impossible to maintain faith in a man who seemed determined to destroy himself and everyone around him. The doctor seemed shocked and a bit dismayed at my honesty, but by now I had come to some understanding of my own feelings, and of the siege mentality that was building in me.

After Mr. Winkle went to war, I returned to RKO for another film, called *China Sky*, based on a novel by Pearl S. Buck. Among the cast was a young actor named Anthony Quinn, playing his first major role, a Chinese warlord. I was elated because my part had been slated originally for Claudette Colbert, which meant it was a true star role. I played a doctor in love with a fellow doctor, Randolph Scott, who was unhappily married to Ellen Drew. (In one scene Ellen was to slap me, and after several unconvincing fakes I told her to try the real thing. She did, so realistically that I couldn't see for several minutes afterward.)

Several of my "love scenes" with Randolph were played in operating rooms, with only our eyes visible above the surgical masks. Critics later noted that I had expressive eyes. What they were expressing, however, was something the critics could not have known about. A remarkable thing had happened to me on the set, a kind of chemistry that was actually not unusual among leading men and women in movies and was, in fact, tacitly encouraged by the studios. Star dressing rooms were really private bungalows or apartments, making romantic interludes easy and temptations great. And the stirring of real passions could often enhance an on-screen performance, just as hostilities could make convincing love scenes almost impossible. Directors took whatever help they could get, and made no moral judgments.

For me such an affair was probably inevitable, given the problems in my marriage, but it was not my leading man who presented the temptation. It was young Tony Quinn—himself married to Katherine De Mille and the father of several children—who diagnosed my problem and prescribed an age-old treatment. We had become friends during the weeks of filming, and Tony had made no secret of his amorous exploits. "I want to impregnate every woman in the world," he once told me, though I didn't realize till later how literally he meant it. And so when he read poetry to me, held my hand, and told me I was too much of a woman to live without a man's arms around me, my whole being responded. His diagnosis was accurate, his prescription was wonderfully effective, and, I might add, his bedside manner was superb.

On our first tryst we left the studio in separate cars, but I was instructed to drive to a certain intersection and wait there for him. He arrived, got into my car, and uttered a line I shall never forget: "I trust you are not expecting some immortal words from me at this moment." Though my body was singing an aria, my mind reacted to the cold-shower message. I grew up quite a lot in that instant: With the right man at the right moment, perhaps one need not be in love forever to justify intimacy. Perhaps a man could be considerate and caring, before and after lovemaking, without being caught up in a cosmic relationship.

Our affair lasted through the shooting and was enriched by a sharing of confidences, tendernesses, and dreams to a degree I had never before approached. (Even on our honeymoon my chill Scandinavian husband had not allowed me to walk hand-in-hand with him.)

Tony brought records to the studio and taught me to dance the tango on the set; we explored the Mexican barrio of Los Angeles where he had grown up, desperately poor but determined to grab life by the throat and force it to yield satisfaction. We bought each other foolish but love-laden gifts. We shared fears, too: He was very insecure in his first major role and I tried to counsel him as best I could. By the same token, he well knew how insecure I felt as a woman, and he filled that well of loneliness to overflowing. We didn't just make love; we wove a fabric of trust and affection around our vulnerabilities. Perhaps it was only possible because we knew that it would soon end, that we could share for the moment without worrying about the future. And even though the parting, when it came, brought considerable pain, it also left me with a new knowledge of myself. For the first time in my life I was confident I was a woman who could be a full and pleasing partner to a real man. Before he ever left this continent, Zorba the Greek taught me to dance on the seashore of life.

Though there was no real marriage to be unfaithful to, I still felt sorrowful and somewhat guilty about my extra-curricular activity. And the guilt no doubt had a part in causing me to agree when Erik decided we must buy a house we couldn't really afford. He had learned that his parents had managed to save ten thousand dollars, and he persuaded them to lend it to him, arguing that owning his own home would give him a sense of stability that would make it easier for him to control his drinking. To my embarrassment they agreed, and the money was entered as a down payment on a house in Westwood, with the understanding that I would continue the payments and see that their investment was protected. I had great misgivings about this high-handed takeover of their life savings, and knew it was not in the least relevant to his problems. Erik had always maintained full control over all our finances. All my earnings went into the bank account he managed, and what he wanted he bought. I may have been the breadwinner, but Erik was always lord of the exchequer.

We moved in while I was working on *China Sky*. Erik was pleased for a time, but instead of controlling his drinking he stepped it up, so that by most evenings he was barely coherent. He was no longer working at all and he rarely left the house, except for an occasional game of golf. (Tennis was now beyond him.) There was no question now of his accompanying me on publicity junkets, which were only possible for me because we had a wonderful live-in housekeeper and a nursemaid to care for the children. Increasingly, those infrequent trips came to seem heaven-sent respites from the tense atmosphere at home.

China Sky was followed by a tough private-eye movie called *Perilous Holiday*, in which I played a chic, wisecracking reporter, once again opposite Pat O'Brien. It was a delight, since I adored playing comedy and was thrilled to be the first star gowned by the famous couturier Jean Louis. Moreover, though not a major movie, the role was a step out of the perfect-wife typecasting that had plagued me.

It was to plague me again that same year, 1945, which was to be one of the busiest and most traumatic of my life. I had just been cast, along with child-actor Bobby Driscoll, in a Walt Disney movie based on Joel Chandler Harris' Uncle Remus stories. *Song of the South* would be the first full-length feature movie combining animated characters and live actors, and was to be filmed at the Disney studios and on location in Phoenix, Arizona, whose red clay soil and weeping willows made a surprisingly convincing Georgia.

I was to be the child's mother, but no one had as yet been cast to play the father, who would appear only briefly at the beginning of the movie and again at the end. I was mildly curious about who would be chosen, but I was hardly prepared for what happened next. Walt Disney called me into his office and told me he had a wonderful surprise for me. They had decided, for reasons of publicity, to cast Erik as my husband. Didn't I think that was a marvelous idea?

I was too stunned to speak. Erik was a talented actor, and there was no doubt that he could play the part—if he could pull himself together and stay sober long enough. On the other hand, suppose he resented being cast in a lesser role and let his resentment show? It could be his chance for a new career, or it could easily be a fiasco that would hurt both of us personally and professionally. The wise thing would have been to discourage the idea, but I just could not do that to Erik. I knew that deep down he needed the challenge of a job. With great misgivings, I agreed it was a fine plan, even though the scenario was too close to home for comfort: The couple was separating, and the mother was taking her son, Johnny, to stay with her mother on the family plantation.

As it happened, Erik was delighted, and if he resented riding his wife's coattails he concealed his feelings well. He was sober and charming on the set, though his evenings were still a fast slide into alcoholic stupor. His genuine intelligence and talent sustained him until his scenes were done and it was time for the cast to move to location without him. Then he began to drink heavily again, and grew morose because he felt excluded. I left for the weeks in Phoenix feeling somehow more worried about Erik than I ever had before.

In Phoenix I was a girl again, delighting in freedom and alive to the overwhelming beauty of the desert. At home my problems seemed immense; under this big sky they seemed almost to shrink to nothing. I haven't the art to convey to you how strong this feeling was. It came on me suddenly and shook me so profoundly that I wept for the joy of its coming. To compare this sudden sense of shining, cleansing peace to divine revelation would be impertinent. I can only tell you that it happened and that my life has never been quite the same since.

I embraced God's beautiful world, vowing never to live again in the cave of exclusion and tyranny. I swam, played tennis, rode horseback among the purple mountains, went on chuckwagon barbecues, and worked, all with an almost drunken sense of joyful release. Many of the scenes were shot along the banks of an idyllic, willow-bordered stream which was actually a sewage canal, but even the stench could not dampen my spirits. I felt like skipping and singing "Zip-A-Dee-Doo-Dah" along with the cartoon critters.

Too soon it was over, and I returned home to find Erik even more remote than before. Trying to get him out of the house, I persuaded him to go with me to the opening of *Othello*, starring Paul Robeson and Uta Hagen. Erik became so hypnotically involved in Robeson's powerful performance, it was as if I had ceased to exist. Then, at the climactic moment when Othello, maddened by jealousy, strangles Desdemona in her bed, Erik's eyes went to mine. For once we left a play without discussion or criticism of the performances.

The next day he drank heavily, and that evening he built

a roaring fire in the library fireplace, though we still had not gotten around to buying a screen for it. The children came in to see it, and two-and-a-half-year-old Jon toddled up to the hearth for a good look.

"Stay away from there!" Erik ordered.

Jon backed away to my side, but in a few minutes curiosity got the better of him and he took a couple of tentative steps back toward the fire.

"I told you to stay away!" Erik yelled, and before I could move he gave the child a hard push—straight into the fire! I lunged forward and pulled the screaming boy out, quickly looked him over, and assured myself that he was frightened but not really hurt beyond some singeing of hair and eyebrows. I hugged the terrified child and turned to Erik as if I'd never seen him before.

"Why on earth did you do that?" I asked him.

"To teach him that fire burns," he said. "I told him to stay away and he disobeyed me, so I had to show him." He turned and left the room.

I put the children to bed and stopped to reassure my mother, who was staying with us while my father was out of town. She was terrified of Erik's moods. Then I went out for a walk, to calm my nerves.

When I got back I found Erik pacing up and down in the library, the inevitable drink in his hand and a look of absolute rage on his face. I was tempted to slip by, but that would only make things worse. So I went in to get it over with.

"How dare you humiliate me before my own children," he stormed at me. "How can they respect me when their own mother doesn't? Their mother, the great movie star." His tone was scathing, and he began a litany of my faults and short-comings.

I had heard it all before and was prepared to endure it again, but suddenly he launched into a speech from *Othello*, as if to prove his own talents were real. His voice, a deep and resonant instrument much like Orson's, thundered Shakespeare's lines, and his eyes widened and rolled as if he had gone mad.

"'O perjured woman! Thou dost stone my heart, and mak'st me call what I intend to do a murder,'" he bellowed, and suddenly I was flat on the daybed and he was crouched over me with his hands on my throat.

"'A murder, which I thought a sacrifice: I saw the hand-kerchief!'" His choking hands pressed harder, and I began to lose consciousness.

I knew instinctively that any attempt to struggle loose could cause him to strangle me. I called on all my discipline as an actress to lie still, thankful that he was so fascinated by the sound of his own voice. And then, as he spoke again, I began to draw my legs up slowly until my knees were almost to my chest. I was dizzy from the choking, but I managed to get my feet against him and to push as hard as I could.

He fell off the bed and sprawled on the floor. I screamed for help.

Erik was struggling to his feet, his face red with fury, when a most unexpected thing happened, and with bewildering speed. Our new maid came running from her room, grabbed Erik in some kind of judo hold, threw him on the floor with his arm pinned under him, and sat on him! (She was a large woman, over six feet tall, and I later learned she had once worked as a bouncer in a nightclub, but even so I doubt if she could have overpowered a man of Erik's size if it had not been for the combination of liquor and surprise.)

While she held him and I watched in a daze, with no notion of what to do next, I heard sirens. Almost instantly two officers were in the room, taking charge of Erik and leading him up-stairs. Moments later two more officers appeared and sat in the living room with me, waiting while their partners talked with Erik. They asked no questions, and I was too stunned by the rapidity of it all to volunteer information, so we just sat there.

Finally, for lack of anything better to do, I fell back on my early training and made cocoa and cinnamon toast for the three of us, evidently reacting to some childhood memories. The policemen sipped politely, like guests at the Mad Hatter's tea party, while Alice nibbled on her cinnamon toast as if it might somehow restore sanity to this surreal scene. We were still sipping and nibbling when the other two officers brought Erik downstairs, his arms handcuffed behind him. He seemed sober and very angry.

"You aren't going to let these people take me away, are you?" he demanded, glaring at me as if this whole silly business were my fault.

"She has nothing to say about it," one of the officers said

quickly. "On this kind of complaint it is the law that we have to take you in for psychiatric examination and a hearing."

Erik was still glaring at me, and I was on the verge of arguing with the police on his behalf. For such a long time I had conditioned myself to hide or explain away his behavior, but this time, for the first time, I felt real fear. "Try to think of it as a chance to rest," I told Erik, astonished at my own bravery. "Besides, you were complaining about the pain in your arm, and the doctors there can treat it." I promised I would call his psychiatrist first thing in the morning, and watched numbly as the two officers led him down the steps to the patrol car. One of the other officers came to me with a paper to sign, and I wrote my name on it obediently while the police took my husband away. Dawn was streaking the dark horizon as the second patrol car pulled out. The night was almost over.

The nightmare, however, went on. I sleepwalked through the next few days, trying to keep the house running normally for the children while I awaited the hearing and whatever was to follow.

The mystery of the instant patrol cars was also solved. I learned that my father, increasingly worried about Erik's erratic and threatening behavior, had alerted the police in our precinct to possible trouble. "If you ever get a call from this address, get there fast," he had told them. "It could be a matter of life and death." They had been keeping an eye on our house, and when my mother called that night they had raced over at top speed. (Mother, who was already fearful of Erik, had been afraid to leave her room when she heard my screams, but she had been sleeping with a telephone in bed with her, and the precinct number on a slip of paper clutched in her hand.)

At last the hearing was held. Two psychiatrists gave their findings, Erik's doctor read a statement, and all seemed agreed that Erik was not psychotic but that he needed treatment for alcoholism. The judge listened, then called Erik to the bench and began a stern but benign lecture.

"You should be ashamed of yourself, son," he said in a manner reminiscent of Judge Hardy chastising Andy for some prank. "You are a fine-looking man; you have a beautiful wife and two sweet children; you have a lovely home. Why don't you straighten yourself out?" He went on to explain that no sentence was indicated, but that he was ordering Erik to commit himself for drying out and treatment. "I'm sure your wife can afford it, just like she's managed to pay for all these other doctors of yours," he added, nodding to indicate that Erik was dismissed.

It was all over. I picked up my bag and prepared to leave, wondering dully how I could face the rage I knew would come when Erik got home. And then suddenly Erik's voice was booming out in all its basso profundo power.

"Just a moment, Your Honor," he declaimed. "There is more here than meets the eye, and I will not be railroaded in this conspiracy. *I* am not the one who should be standing here before the bar of justice, but the real culprits are present in this room." He extended his arm in a sweeping, theatrical gesture, ending with a finger pointed toward the table where I sat with my father and Erik's own psychiatrist and attorney. "They are right over there, Your Honor."

The judge stared at him with a look of total astonishment. He frowned, shook his head, gave a long sigh, and then lowered his head onto his arms, folded in front of him. Finally he looked up, and in a weary voice he said, "I'm sorry, son. I hereby sentence you to Camarillo State Hospital, where you will undergo examination and treatment for mental illness."

As I watched, totally stunned, Erik was led off. Incredibly, at the very moment when he could have walked away scot-free, his inner demon had forced him to that grand, melodramatic gesture of self-destruction, as if he had been so preoccupied with his own internal struggles that he had not even heard what was happening around him.

I could scarcely comprehend what had happened myself, but in a while I left the courtroom and headed for home, trying to figure out how to explain the situation to our children. Jon was only two and a half, and Erik had virtually ignored his existence anyway, so I wasn't really worried about how he would take his father's absence. But not-quite-four-year-old Karen was her father's boon companion, his "princess," and so would certainly be well aware that things were awry.

I decided to send her to visit her Missouri relatives, hoping a vacation on the farm, which she loved, would be a diversion

that would somehow make things easier. It didn't fool her for
a minute. The day she came home I found her standing in the
kitchen with a puzzled look.

"Where's Daddy?" she asked.

"He's gone away for a little while," I told her, trying to
keep my voice light. "Daddy's not well, and he's gone to a
place where they can make him better."

She frowned. "If Daddy's sick, why aren't you taking care
of him?" she asked.

I reached down to pick her up, feeling that if I could hold
her on my lap and hug her it would make it easier to explain.
She ducked under my arms and ran outside into the yard.

I stood there, unsure of what to do, while the pattern of
sunlight cutting across the kitchen counter and over the lino-
leum floor engraved itself forever in my memory. I wanted to
run after her, but I was afraid that would frighten her further.
At last I decided to leave her alone, to let time heal the hurt
for a while.

I was too optimistic. For many years Karen carried the
wound of that experience, and the feeling of betrayal. She froze
every time I touched her, suffering my kisses but never returning them. Not long after that she developed bronchitis, and
the doctor recommended that I hold her bare body against my
own for body heat, to relieve the spasms that sometimes seized
her. I did so gladly, and I noticed that as she slept (or pretended
to sleep) she would hug me very tight, as if she could only
then let the barriers down and accept my love. It was not until
her late teens that Karen really understood and forgave the
mother who had "sent her Daddy away." I could not bring
myself, then or later, to destroy whatever positive image the
children might have retained of their father, so I never at-
tempted to explain to them the depth of his troubles, telling
them instead of his many talents. Whether right or wrong, I
only know that the price I paid, in Karen's case, was far too
high for both of us.

I visited Erik, and within a few weeks, removed from drugs
and alcohol, I found him sane, sober, and impatient for his
release, which his father was already working hard to obtain.
However, he was also still bitter and angry. He gave no appearance of having come to grips with his problems or having

gained any understanding of himself. I simply could not make myself believe that things would be any better for us when he got out.

I realized I had a terrible decision to make when he was freed, and that the time would come very soon. I talked with several doctors who knew him, and was assured that there was little chance of inherited mental illness afflicting our children. Still, there were strong suggestions that constant exposure to Erik's neurotic behavior could create severe emotional problems for them. I loved Karen and Jon, and I was determined that they should have every possible chance for a happy, normal life. Erik was my husband and their father, yet his years of therapy seemed to have brought him no closer to self-understanding, and I was sure life would resume where it had left off the moment he returned. Reluctantly I filed for divorce, and informed Erik that our seven-year marriage was over. He took it better than I had expected, as if his intelligence forced an awareness of what his neuroses would not let him deal with.

I remembered how upset I'd become as a teenager when a palmist at the church bazaar had told me I'd have more than one marriage. I had gone home in tears. If she had told me I would be a murderess it could not have upset me more. Divorce had always seemed to mean failure as a woman, a heavy blow to anyone's self-esteem. Now my only salvation lay in being the best mother I could be.

I was working harder than ever, and in the next year made movies at 20th Century-Fox, Universal, United Artists, and even Republic, the citadel of six-guns and sagebrush. The Universal film was a rather strange departure called *Swell Guy*, in which Sonny Tufts was cast as a dashing war hero who turns out to be a failure and a bum. The film, based on a play by Gilbert Emery and produced by Mark Hellinger, was an attempt to upgrade the quality of Sonny Tufts' roles, but alas, the critics were unimpressed with his performance. They were much kinder to Ann Blyth, William Gargan, and Gargan's ever-perfect wife, Ruth Warrick, who this time almost slipped from virtue in her misplaced love for the returning hero.

Then it was Fox, for a really solid part in an all-star movie called *Daisy Kenyon*, along with Joan Crawford, Dana Andrews, and Henry Fonda, with Otto Preminger directing and with my own name given equal billing. It was an important step up for me, and working with such giants of the industry was to be a memorable experience. Henry Fonda, though now the veteran of dozens of starring roles, arrived each day wearing blue work shirts and carrying his lunch in the kind of tin box usually seen in factories. He was a joy to work with, and Dana Andrews became a friend whose affection I treasure still.

Joan Crawford, however, was another matter. Then in her forties, a veteran of motion pictures from the early days of sound, she seemed to live in a crackle of tension one could almost feel like a physical thing around her. She insisted that the air conditioning be kept going at such force that most of the cast went about shivering and blue from cold; I was told later that this was the only way she could prevent constant perspiration. At the time, watching her skip about in shorts and sleeveless blouses while the rest of us huddled in sweaters and fur coats, I thought her almost superhuman; it was not till later that I realized she was driven by such terrible insecurity about her career that it amounted to outright physical fear.

The recent revelations of her adopted daughter Christina may have shocked the public, but they could not have surprised anyone who ever worked with Joan. I can still see in my mind's eye a Christmas party, with Joan forcing her tiny children to open each gift, note down what it was, then go around and show each gift to every person there in a sternly directed performance that left no room for spontaneity or even pleasure. I remember a friend's description of an occasion when Joan invited her to lunch: When they went to sit down at the patio table my friend found that the two settings bore formal printed place cards. And most vivid of all, I remember the time when I heard Joan giving instructions to the small children and their nursemaid outside the door of my dressing room: They were to stay there until she had walked out onto the set, and then the nursemaid was to send the children running out to her, jumping up and down and yelling "We love you, Mommie dearest." They did as they were told, but the pathetically stiff performance fooled no one. Her fears and insecurities were huge, and they took their toll on everyone around her.

Doug Fairbanks always sent flowers to Joan on her birthday, even though they were long divorced and each had remarried.

"Poor Joan," he said to me once. "She tries so hard and is such a stern taskmaster with herself. But the one thing she could never achieve was to have our child, and it drove her crazy." (He might have added that the other thing she had never achieved was acceptance by her mother-in-law, Mary Pickford, a veritable Phoebe Tyler who never once invited Joan to Pickfair.)

After *Daisy Kenyon* my agent, Kurt Frings, got me a part in a serious Western at Republic for more money that I had ever been paid before. The movie, titled *Driftwood*, also starred Walter Brennan, Dean Jagger, Charlotte Greenwood, and a beautiful child actress named Natalie Wood. I, of course, played a virtuous schoolmarm, but the inflated paycheck took much of the curse off the role.

I sold the Westwood house and returned the money Erik had borrowed from his parents to finance the mortgage, moving myself and the children, along with the housekeeper, into a small bungalow in Santa Monica Canyon. It was modest but it had a beautiful view of the sea and some interesting neighbors, including Van Johnson, Laraine Day and Leo Durocher, and Leo Carrillo, the actor descended from one of the early California families, who raised splendid Spanish horses and peacocks whose screams could make your hair stand on end. Erik settled in at the tower suite of the Riviera Country Club (paid for by his parents), and came to take the children for outings and occasionally, when his parents were visiting, for entire weekends.

I felt these visits were important for the children, but I was worried at how upset and tense they seemed afterward. Finally one day Karen came home sobbing and asked me if they really had to go on seeing their father. I tried to find out what the problem was, but she would only say, "He scares me." (I did not learn till years later the sort of thing they were experiencing, but the final incident stands out still: On this visit to the club Erik had climbed out on the tile-roofed tower to take a picture. He slipped, caught himself near the edge of the high roof, and then teetered there deliberately, telling the children he might just as well go over, since no one loved him anymore. The more they screamed and cried, the more he taunted them, until they were near hysteria when he finally climbed back in. They did not tell me about the incident then, but for years afterward Karen would cry any time someone pointed a camera at her.)

On the eve of his forty-fifth birthday he went to sleep and did not wake up, leaving behind only a sad and painful feeling of defeat for me and no conscious memories for his children, though Jon's Rorschach test at fifteen brought forth his "father image" as "a big ape pushing me into a fire."

With all of Erik's manifold talents, he never mastered the simple business of living. He was a gifted actor, writer, sculptor, artist, singer, and photographer, but not one of his gifts was ever developed to its full potential. His mother had enlisted him early in her sarcastic ridicule of her husband, a distinguished Lutheran minister, and Erik had borne the scars of her neurotic contempt for men throughout his life. After Erik died, I had an odd dream about him. In the dream he told me that he now understood everything and felt no resentment. He seemed relaxed for the only time in my memory, and he assured me that all was well with him. I woke from the dream feeling strangely reassured, knowing it was only a dream but still convinced, deep in my heart, that it was true.

But this was years later. In 1946 we were both very much alive, and I was working harder than ever. Kurt Frings, my agent, had done much for my career and I was grateful. I even appreciated the screen test he had arranged for a Spencer Tracy-Katharine Hepburn movie at MGM, though the part went to Angela Lansbury, who was under contract to the studio and available. I shrugged and went on to the next thing, totally unaware that Kurt had gone to Frank Capra and ranted about the stupidity of the MGM management. Had I known I would have worried; that sort of thing could only cause trouble for an actress, and more trouble was something I surely did not need.

What I did need was a really juicy part. Again Kurt came through, arranging a screen test for the much-coveted role of the dying madcap heiress, Kate, who was Charles Boyer's first love and still-close friend in the planned film version of Erich Maria Remarque's novel *Arch of Triumph*. It was the third lead and a solid part that had been tested for by Joan Crawford, Sylvia Sidney, Barbara Stanwyck, and at least thirty others. The decision to give it to me was heralded with a blast of

newlines in the press, headlines that were to continue throughout the making of this controversial film. I was ecstatic over
the part, which I saw as a chance for me to break out of the
virtuous-wife mold.

I finished my work on the movie, totaling about forty-five
minutes of screen time, and then went off to publicize *Song
of the South*, which opened in Atlanta with a huge parade led
by an open car with the one and only "Ruth Warwick" waving
happily from it. (I did not notice the misspelling on the sign
until photos appeared in the papers next morning. It was not
the first time that *w* had crept into my name, and it would not
be the last.) The premiere, attended by five thousand people,
was a big success, and I went on to other cities with my head
in the clouds. In New Orleans, while we lunched, Walt Disney
began to talk of an amusement park he wanted to build, one
that would resemble a collection of movie sets. "It's magic,"
he said. "Everyone wants to come on the set, but there just
isn't room. I want to create that same feeling, where people
can come with their whole families and have a clean, decent,
but adventurous and magical time." It took him eight years to
arrange financing, but his dream finally became real in Dis-
neyland.

On the New York leg of the tour I came down to earth with
a jolt. I had known that Kurt and his wife were planning to
come East for Ingrid Bergman's Broadway opening in *Joan of
Lorraine*, and I had planned to go with them. But Kurt managed
to arrive a day ahead of Ketti and came to my hotel, planning
an evening together. I had already made a firm decision to put
an end to what was becoming an increasingly personal (and,
for me, awkward) involvement with Kurt. So instead of going
out on the town, we spent hours talking, with me explaining
how I felt and trying to reestablish our professional relationship
without rancor or hurt.

The next day, gritty-eyed and weary, I went through a grueling series of interviews in my hotel suite, ending with a lengthy
analysis of my handwriting. ("You are very trusting, really
gullible; but don't try to change the childlike quality in you.
That makes you a sensitive actress and is one of your greatest
charms.") A young man from the New York press office of
Henry Rogers, on hand to usher the press and magazine writers

in and out, kept wiping the ever-moist corners of his mouth with a folded handkerchief. All in all it was a tiring day, and when the handwriting analyst finally left I was decidedly behind schedule. I was heading for my bedroom to change for the Bergman opening when the doorbell rang again, so I told the press agent to please tell whoever it was that I was not available. He did, still wiping his mouth as he delivered the message that I was changing clothes and couldn't come to the door.

Unfortunately the visitor was Kurt, who had come early to escort me to the theater, and perhaps to renew his arguments. When I came out in my evening dress, ready to go, I found him pacing around the room in a rage.

"What's wrong?" I asked him.

He glared. "Christ, you'll do anything with anybody to get your picture in the paper, won't you?"

"What?"

"After all that fancy talk, you hop right into bed with a lousy press agent, just for free publicity."

Incredulous, I tried to explain how mistaken he was, but he wouldn't listen.

"You actresses are all alike," he said scornfully. "It's the casting couch all the way, isn't it?"

Outraged, furious beyond control, I leaped at him. He grabbed my wrists, but my fingernails still somehow found his face and I raked them down like claws, tearing away skin and leaving ugly red marks.

He stepped back and rubbed at his face in amazement. "Jesus, you're like a tiger," he said. "You must be crazy. I'll have you committed!"

I was as astonished as he was. I had a temper, but never could I have believed myself capable of such wild fury as that. It was as though some hidden part of my character had been suddenly revealed, as though the Phoebe in me had unsheathed her claws. To have lost a whole night's sleep trying to be kind to this man, and then to be hit with the crudest kind of insult, had just been too much. But now, looking at the red marks and anger in his face, I began to get frightened. He was a powerful man, physically and professionally, and there was no telling what he might do.

I tried to apologize, and helped him patch up the damage,

and we went on to the opening in silence. But before we got there he said one thing that really chilled my blood.

"You'll never work in movies again," he told me. "I'll see to that."

I knew he meant it. My instinct about mixing personal relationships and business had been all too accurate. Why hadn't I listened to myself? I also knew I would get another agent and go on with my career no matter what he said or did to hurt me.

When I got back to the coast, trouble was already brewing, though it was not of Kurt's making. Ads were appearing in the trade papers for *Arch of Triumph*, which was at last nearing release, and my name was featured along with Bergman's and Boyer's. It would be so featured in ads seen by the public, too, though by the time the film reached the theaters my presence in it was reduced to a few frames from which they could find no way to cut me. Kate, the dying heiress, was no longer in the movie at all.

What had happened? Well, for one thing the picture was considerably over the optimum length, and my character represented a forty-five-minute subplot that could be removed intact without altering the story line drastically. Beyond that, there had been problems with the casting from the outset. The picture opened with Ingrid about to jump off a bridge and Boyer talking her out of it. Then the script called for him to carry her up the stairs to her apartment, which was clearly an impossibility. In fact, robust Ingrid could more plausibly have tossed the slender Boyer over her shoulder and carried him up. Clearly, even these talented actors could not overcome the absurdities of their miscast roles. As for me, I was faced with the irony that one of my strongest performances was now on the cutting-room floor.

I was depressed, to say the least, since I had counted heavily on that movie to change my image. And now, with my old agent working against me and a new agent representing me, it began to seem that Kurt's prophesy would be fulfilled. There simply were no new roles being offered.

I did not disappear into instant obscurity, of course, though I worked very little in 1948 apart from a few radio appearances. In 1949 my new agent arranged for a part in a Fred Astaire musical titled *Let's Dance*, in which I played Fred's socialite fiancée, gowned quite glamorously by Edith Head. Betty Hutton was the waitress Fred danced with and ultimately married, but this happy ending didn't prevent Betty from becoming almost hysterical every time I appeared on the set in my elegant clothes while she frumped about in her waitress uniform.

After *Let's Dance* I had a solid part in a United Artists sequel to the successful *Letter to Three Wives*. The new one, imaginatively titled *Three Husbands*, was much less successful, as often happens with sequels. Both movies were released in 1950, and neither role thrust me to the top of the Hollywood star hierarchy. In fact, no new parts appeared, and it began to seem that my career had stalled, if not self-destructed.

Naturally I found myself wondering why that career, which had begun so brightly, seemed destined not to fulfill its early promise. There were reasons, no doubt, some of them obvious from the account you've just read. Perhaps another could be found in the early death, in 1943, of the RKO chief of production, Charles W. Koerner, who had shown great interest in my career after *Citizen Kane*. If he had lived, better parts might have been found for me despite my maverick reputation.

Still, I had lasted longer than the average female star. Men seemed to be permitted to age, but for women, seven years was about all the studios were willing to give before looking for a fresher face—the reason that most contracts were written for seven-year spans. Examples are legion, but one will do: Alexis Smith had starred in dozens of Warner Brothers movies opposite many of the top leading men, yet when her contract came up for renewal, at the ripe old age of twenty-six, Jack Warner dumped her. Fortunately she had a smart husband who encouraged her to do stock and road company musicals, where she polished her craft. She eventually wound up on the cover of *Time* as the star of *Follies*, many years after her Hollywood career had ended.

Most of the reasons for the collapse of my film career were obvious to me at the time, but one—perhaps the most important—only became apparent later. It was that the pictures in which I had played so many perfect wives were themselves dying out. Television had moved into that area of family entertainment with success, and Hollywood had turned its attention to blockbuster wide-screen extravaganzas or beach-party quickies. The maverick leading lady was no longer needed. Should I have seen this? And what should I have done about it?

What I did, alas, was to marry again, this time a tall, handsome Dane named Carl Neubert. (It is as if I were somehow specially tuned to men of Scandinavian descent.) We met at a party at the home of Marusia, the madcap Polish couturiere, and instantly became an item, as Hedda and Louella liked to put it. Carl was forty-two and had never married, which seemed incredible in view of his striking good looks and his courtly, elegant manner. I suppose I was responding much as Phoebe responded to Langley Wallingford, but in truth I think Carl was the more courtly of the two. Born in Copenhagen, he had come to this country with ambitions to act, and he had done some singing and had even appeared in a show with Mae West. But he had grown impatient with the long years required to build a career, and had gone instead into business, manufacturing custom furniture. He now ran a very successful interior-design firm.

Carl was the perfect suitor, with first-night tickets to everything and a flair for the good life. He loved to dance, having even mastered the intricacies of the classic Viennese waltz, and we made a striking couple at gatherings all over town, with our pictures constantly in the papers. He was attentive, generous to the children, and persistent. On the third marriage proposal I said yes.

He sold his rustic mountain lodge, I sold my house in Santa Monica Canyon, and together we bought a beautiful estate on Mulholland Drive at the top of Coldwater Canyon, with Beverly Hills at our feet and Catalina Island visible on a clear day. Our wedding in the huge living room was covered by AP, UP, and, wonder of wonders, both Louella and Hedda, arch rivals who rarely appeared at the same event. Everything seemed magically right—a safe harbor and a new life for me and the children.

Next morning, while I was sorting flashbulbs from the garbage as local law required, the phone rang. It was Carl, and he was frantic.

"Close the front gates, lock the doors, and don't answer the phone," he said.

"Why? What's wrong?"

"I can't tell you now," he said, and hung up.

After a long, lonely, puzzling day he came home, taut and silent. He began cleaning out a huge aquarium in the pool house, working furiously without looking up or speaking to me.

"Carl, what is the matter?" I asked at last, when it seemed he would never speak again.

"This marriage is a mistake," he said. And as I listened, stunned, he went on to say that he didn't want to be married, that he couldn't stand children, and that he wanted to call the whole thing off.

That was obviously impossible. I tried to tell myself he was suffering from the kind of jitters one might expect in a man who had made a drastic change in his life in his forties. I tried to reassure him, and finally asked what the phone call had been about that morning.

That was the second blow. It seemed that the lavish wedding, covered in all the papers, had aroused a veritable swarm of creditors, who all saw the opulent home and decided to demand payment—which he could not meet. It seemed that Carl, though a talented businessman with a substantial income, lived beyond his means and was heavily in debt.

Unfortunately, Carl was all too correct in saying he hadn't really wanted to get married. He was irritable and impatient with me and the children—really, I suppose, uncomfortable with us. And he was becoming increasingly gloomy about the state of our finances and "the terrible man at the bank." Though Carl bought me many beautiful clothes and furs, and even a Cadillac convertible to match his, and though we moved in an elegant social whirl, the moment the whirl paused and we were alone, another person took the place of the gay *bon vivant*. Carl had left Denmark because of his father's constant criticism, yet he seemed unable to see that he was following his father's role model exactly as he had described it to me.

Very soon I began to agree with Carl's view that we had both made a mistake in deciding to marry. I found it impossible to please him, and, in the circumstances, perhaps it was impossible for him to be pleased. At last, after two years of trying, I gave up. My departure, following some dreary maneuvers over property and divorce terms that ended with everything in

Carl's name, was in many ways typical of my life. I simply packed my clothes, a few paintings I loved, and my two children into my sky-blue Cadillac, and I headed East, leaving everything else behind me.

The trip was an adventure in itself. We camped out at the Grand Canyon and spent weeks at a dude ranch, while everyone tried to figure out what a movie star was doing wandering about like a hobo with a happy look on her face. What I was doing was finding myself again, savoring the freedom to be *me*, shedding a past that no longer seemed relevant or worth clinging to.

The dude ranch in Colorado was a delightful place, run by a remarkable couple from Illinois. They had a great joie de vivre which they transmitted to their guests. I wasn't really surprised when Jon and Karen asked to stay on with them the rest of the summer. Besides, I knew that settling into a New York apartment while their mother was out looking for work would be hard on them. I agreed that they could stay, and when the time came I drove on to New York alone, grateful at least that I had an apartment waiting for me there.

It was a three-bedroom place in Stuyvesant Town, a sublet arranged through Tommy Dorsey, a good friend from the movie years. I knew little about Stuyvesant Town, but I had been told that the apartment had a piano in it. No place could be bad that had a piano. And it would be *mine*.

In fact, it was the pits. A cramped, gloomy place in a huge, impersonal housing development, it could not have been farther removed from the pools and patios of Mulholland Drive. Somewhat grimly I unpacked and began to make the rounds.

One little episode stands out from the interminable summer while I was reestablishing my professional contacts and trying to adjust to Stuyvesant Town: One day Michael Myerberg, the producer, phoned to ask a favor.

"I'm doing a new play, and there's a young man I'd like to see in it. He's a Yale graduate and very good-looking, but he needs some help with the part before he's ready to audition. Would you consider coaching him?"

I agreed, and the next day I answered the bell to find a pair of the world's bluest eyes staring at me.

I worked with the young man and listened to his life story,

of his Ohio boyhood and his desire to be an actor, which his
father thought foolish. He talked about his wife, over in New
Jersey, and his young children, whom he loved, but mostly he
talked about the theater and how much he wished to be part
of it. He was effusive in his gratitude for the trouble I was
taking. His diffidence and freshness were totally charming.

The day came when we walked down Broadway to the
audition and discovered yet another secret we shared: an addiction to popcorn. We ate our way through enormous bags of
it on the way to the theater.

It didn't help him with the audition. The part, that of a
homosexual serviceman trying to renew a wartime love affair
with his married commanding officer, was simply not suited
to his appearance or talents. He didn't get the job and was
understandably disappointed, but a few months later he did get
a job in the William Inge play *Picnic*, as a handsome young
midwestern stud. Hollywood took one look at that charisma
and it was bye-bye Broadway, hello world.

Even now, whenever Paul Newman and I chance to meet,
we find ourselves talking about popcorn, the memory that
stands out most clearly from that day.

In September my children arrived, confused at their new
home and no doubt appalled. But at least we were together
again, and I was working. I starred in a *Studio One* show, got
a wonderful role on a *Robert Montgomery Presents*, followed
that with a solid *Lux Star Theater* part, and began to feel that
a whole new world was opening up for me.

That was when my old friend and onetime suitor, Gail
Smith, came to New York on business and, as he had throughout the years, invited me out to dinner. Gail was now head of
radio and television for Proctor & Gamble, the Cincinnati-based
company that was then the chief sponsor of daytime television
and the reason the serials are called soaps.

We dined at the Barberry Room, near CBS, where everybody in the room was Somebody. Gail was Somebody too,
even though he still looked boyish and preppy. Over my oysters
Rockefeller and entrecôte with béarnaise sauce I couldn't help
remembering that time when he'd sat across a table from me
and threatened that one day he'd be able to hire and fire me.
He had certainly made good on that boast, and I was happy
for his success.

I was happy generally, thrilled to be back in New York and pleased that everything was going so well. I told him about the television roles, expecting congratulations, but he surprised me.

"Okay, what next?" he asked.

"What do you mean?"

"Look, Ruth, you have to understand the current television scene. You've been on those shows, true. But they are just about *it*, the only dramatic shows there are now. And since you've had starring roles on them all, you won't be cast again for at least a year. What will you do till then?"

I felt a bit deflated, but still game. "Well, there's always Broadway," I told him. "That's really what I came back to New York *for*, you know."

"Yes, there's Broadway," he said. "And if you land a good part in a play, and if that play runs longer than two or three weeks, you will still have to start all over when it ends. And you know how many long-running plays there are around."

I groaned. "Please," I said. "You're ruining my evening. I don't want to talk about this."

"But I *do*. You've enrolled your children in Grace Church School, you tell me. Have you thought about how you're going to pay for it?"

I shrugged.

"Have you ever thought about daytime television?"

I was really shocked. "You mean soap operas?"

"Yes."

"What are you trying to do, ruin my career?" I could well imagine what all my Hollywood friends would say if they heard that Mrs. Citizen Kane was even considering such a thing.

"Ruth, I care too much about kids to let you wander around with your head in the clouds while your family goes down the drain," he said. Gail was now a father himself, and I knew how much he valued children, so this wasn't idle chatter. "The only way you can be sure of making a steady living as an actress is on the soaps."

"But—"

"Just be quiet and listen a minute."

For once in my life I shut up. It may have been the smartest thing I have ever done.

"Okay, tomorrow at ten o'clock I want you to go to Benton

and Bowles and see Lewis Titterton. He will take you to Liederkranz Hall and introduce you to Ted Corday, one of the best
producer-directors in the business. And whatever Ted Corday
asks you to do, say yes."

I must have looked skeptical, because he gave me a very
stern look indeed. "Ruth, I mean it. Don't argue or ask questions, just do it."

I did.

What Ted Corday asked me to do was incredible: I was to
do an "under-five" bit (that is, fewer than five lines of dialogue)
on an upcoming segment of *The Guiding Light*, so the creator
and head writer, Irna Phillips, could see me on the screen at
her home in Chicago.

"You're joking," I said. "Couldn't she screen a test, or just
watch one of my movies?"

"She could, but she won't. She needs to see how you'll
come across on *her* show. Or she thinks she does. And what
she wants, she gets. It's that or no job."

I did the bit, which consisted of wearing a nurse's uniform
and saying "Yes, doctor," and "No, doctor." (An under-five
in television is considered almost worse than being an extra,
where you can fade away into the background.) But evidently
Irna liked what she saw, because for the next six months I was
Nurse Janet—the "other woman" who seduced a doctor whose
young wife was pregnant—on the most successful daytime
serial of its day. One way or another, P&G saw my kids not
only through Grace Church School, but through college.

This new life in television was a far cry from the pampered
and publicized movie star image I had left behind, but I was
working regularly and I was happy about it. Never mind what
my Hollywood friends thought about the soaps. Hollywood
was in the past, and the future looked lively and interesting.
That was enough for me.

I would return to Hollywood in years to come, and even to
the marriage I had just fled, but if anyone had suggested such
a possibility in those months on *The Guiding Light* I would
have thought him insane. I loved living in New York. It was
a challenging new world, filled with interesting people.

One of those people was a brilliant young writer who worked
under the irascible Irna Phillips, the inventor of the modern

soap opera and then its reigning queen. This writer, who worked on scripts from her home in Philadelphia (and conferred by mail and phone with Irna, who remained in Chicago), was to play a large part in my future life, though I could not have known it then.

Her name was Agnes Nixon.

SEVEN

What are Soaps, and Why Do People Watch Them?

IN THE BEGINNING there was Irna Phillips. This formidable lady is generally credited with having literally invented soap opera, back in Chicago during the Depression years. A high-school speech teacher who had persuaded a radio station to let her read bits of poetry on the air, she was asked if she could make up a continuing story that would interest a wider audience among the many who couldn't afford movies or even magazines for entertainment. She agreed, and in 1930 the drab airwaves of the day were enlivened by a daily fifteen minutes of live radio called *Painted Dreams*, the first of the "family serials" that were to dominate daytime radio in the years to come, and daytime television almost from its birth. More serials quickly followed, until by the late thirties it was possible to spend an entire day in the lives of *Our Gal Sunday* and *Ma Perkins* and *Pepper Young's Family*, along with many others.

They even invaded the evening hours, normally reserved for dramatic programs or variety entertainment. (*One Man's Family* became so popular that it produced one of the earliest spin-offs, *I Love a Mystery*.) They were not the first shows to feature the same characters and locales: *The Amos and Andy Show*, *Fibber McGee and Molly*, and many others had done that. But the key to the serials—daytime or night—was the continuing story, which held listeners captive from one show to the next, eagerly awaiting the outcome of some plot development or the resolution of some crisis.

Irna Phillips did not invent the idea of a continuing story, of course. Writers had done that for generations, going back to such literary luminaries as Anthony Trollope, Henry James,

132

and even Dostoevski. Charles Dickens, who cranked out weekly installments of his novels for nineteenth-century newspapers, is usually credited with having invented the modern serial form, but the basic structure—the story told in separate installments—goes back at least to Scheherazade. What Dickens knew and the sponsors of the radio serials quickly learned was the power of the cliff-hanger, the incomplete episode that ends in a critical moment and keeps the reader/listener/viewer waiting avidly to learn what happens next. So powerful was Dickens' grasp of his audience that mid-nineteenth-century New Yorkers crowded the piers to await arrival of each new installment, and some daring souls even rowed out into the harbor to meet the incoming packet from England. As the boat approached, mobs began to cry for news of Little Nell.

I knew the lure of the serial firsthand in my own Missouri childhood. On afternoons when the newest installment of my story was due, you could find me fidgeting on the steps of our house, waiting for the sight of the paperboy's bike. I would snatch up the issue of the *News-Press* the instant it landed and unfold it with trembling fingers until I got to the inside back page of the front section, where an entire half page of my serial spread out before me like a feast. So when fans come up to me and blurt, "You're on *my* story!" I know exactly what they mean. That half page was *my* story, and it did not matter how many thousands of others read it. I lived its plots, and felt suspended in the time between one episode and the next.

Other writers followed Irna's lead, and material was produced in prodigious quantity for a market that grew in size and insatiability. When television came along, the serials moved quite naturally to this visual medium, where their tightly contained worlds fitted quite economically within the walls of a studio. With a kitchen and a living room (and later, when morality grew more flexible, a bedroom), a small cast could spin out weeks of plot that held viewers in thrall. Irna Phillips was the most succesful convert to the new medium, transferring *The Guiding Light* from radio and evolving *As the World Turns* and *Another World* specifically for television. In fact she was so successful that her projects quickly outgrew her ability to handle them alone, and assistants were hired to write dialogue. One of these helpers, hired in 1950 to write for a program

called *A Woman in White*, was an elfin blonde from Nashville
by way of Northwestern University's drama department. Barely
out of her teens, Agnes Eckhardt had already decided that
writing was to be her career, and three days after graduation
she submitted a script to Irna Phillips. She was hired on the
spot.

Ted Corday, who worked with Irna, once said that her chief
talent was an uncanny ability to "tie the largest number of knots
in the shortest possible piece of string." It was an ability the
young Agnes Eckhardt shared, along with a firm grasp of character and a sharp eye for the most worrisome and fascinating
problems of the day. She quickly rose to the position of head
writer on *The Guiding Light* and she created another long-
running soap, *Search for Tomorrow*, though she has never
received credit for it. Together, she and Irna created *As the
World Turns*, though by now Agnes had moved to New York
City and had met, and married, a young Chrysler Corporation
executive named Robert Nixon.

Irna stubbornly remained in Chicago throughout the remaining two decades of her life, keeping in close touch with
her New York-based shows by memos, letters, and almost
incessant telephone calls. This is a pattern Agnes Nixon has
repeated since moving to Philadelphia early in her marriage.
She, too, confers by phone, retaining tight control over her
"children" even though she rarely visits the sets. But since
Philadelphia is closer to New York than Chicago is, Agnes is
on hand for all important meetings and script conferences. In
between, she plots and writes the longterm and weekly outlines
from her home in Rosemont, near Bryn Mawr, providing the
guiding light that makes the world turn for the *All My Children*
writing staff.

Jacqueline Smith, the effervescent lady brought in by Freddie Silverman to head up ABC's daytime programming, says
she regards Agnes Nixon as "the Dickens of our time," and
she is dead serious. But when she first arrived, she was less
convinced of daytime's quality. "At CBS," she says, "I had
been Director of Prime-Time Specials and accustomed to working with large film budgets and the most sought-after writers
in the television film business. Frankly, I was concerned that
daytime drama might be less than substantial, many notches

down from the CBS Specials that had been my concern. To my delight, I discovered our drama on daytime at ABC is of no less quality in concept, writing, and performance than the nighttime I'd come from. We're the closest thing to live theater." And she adds, "We're fortunate to have Agnes Nixon. She's magic, a great lady who's far surpassed even the great Irna Phillips."

Wisner Washam, the show's longtime head writer, and the six dialoguists who work with him to convert Agnes Nixon's outlines into the daily scripts, would all agree. Her inventive mind spins out a constant skein of exciting and relevant plots that have made *All My Children* the leading show in the daytime lineup.

Why so many writers? The numbers will answer that: Five scripts per week, averaging seventy-five to eighty-three pages each, add up to about four hundred pages per week or well over twenty thousand pages per year! Obviously no one person could produce such a prodigious amount of sheer wordage alone (one polished script per week is par for most writers). However, one person *has* managed to produce the basic themes and the intricate interlacing of plot lines, though in recent years Wisner Washam has collaborated with Agnes on those outlines.

And where do those ideas and themes come from? From life, from the world around us, as perceived by a writer highly attuned to the problems and passions that move us all. This, without doubt, is Agnes Nixon's most valuable asset and greatest talent, this finely tuned sensibility both to the moods of the time and to its stresses. If her invention sometimes seems boundless, it is nevertheless highly disciplined. Truth is the criterion against which she measures her fiction—the changing truths of our time and society, the eternal truths of our hearts.

The basic human motives—love, hate, greed, jealousy—have always been with us and have always been grist for the writer's mill, but each moment of history tends to concentrate on certain social and personal problems it considers immediate and urgent. Divorce, for example, once taboo on daytime television, is now virtually epidemic in the serials, as it is in real life. Even more timely is the subject of abortion, which has moved from the back alleys of criminality into a clear light of public controversy that sharply divides the nation's opinion.

This split, between those who regard abortion as murder of an unborn human and those who regard a woman's right to control her own biological destiny as sacred, is reflected in the soaps. When Erica, who was clearly too neurotically immature for motherhood, opted for abortion, all the arguments—pro and con—were given careful and balanced presentation. (Many disagreed vehemently with her decision, but most would have to admit that the question was treated with scrupulous fairness and good taste.) Devon, on the other hand, decided to keep her child, even though her pregnancy had resulted from an immature attempt to get even with one boy by sleeping with another. Devon's choice, aided by Wally's devotion and her mother's loving support, was indeed an affirmation of life, though she (and viewers, one hopes) now sees how self-destructive her immature sexual behavior really was. Perhaps some of the show's young fans will get the message and avoid becoming one of the million-plus teenage mothers produced by this sexually permissive society every year.

Agnes Nixon has often said that she hopes to "open people's minds a little bit" by showing that many of life's situations are not so black and white as they may at first appear. When Donna Beck, the sweet-faced and earnest young runaway who had been coerced into teenage prostitution, became Mrs. Chuck Tyler, many fans condemned Phoebe for her refusal to accept the girl into the family. After all, Donna was trying so hard to straighten out her life and be a good wife. How could Phoebe not welcome her with open arms and a forgiving heart?

"What have you got against Donna?" one large and very irate woman asked me in a New York department store. "Aren't you *ever* going to accept that poor girl?" Her manner suggested that I had better do so, and right away.

I gulped, retreated a step, and then answered honestly: "I doubt that Phoebe ever will, but Ruth does. Candy Earley and I are good friends!"

But why *won't* Phoebe accept Donna? Another woman was very hard on Phoebe at one of our mall show appearances, demanding that I "leave that poor girl alone." Phoebe stared her down and asked her to answer one question with complete honesty: "If *your* grandson came to you and said the girl he was planning to marry was an ex-hooker, a woman who had

had sex with hundreds of men for money, how would you *really* feel?"

The woman was clearly torn by mixed emotions. Obviously she would not approve of such a thing in real life, yet she had sympathy for the guileless girl she'd come to know and love on *All My Children*. (Even poor Donna's obsessive attempts to better herself are seen as admirable, though her gaffes must leave viewers with a mixture of amusement and pain. When she tries to impress artistic Tara with her knowledge of painting, she comes up with the immortal line, "You could refer to this portrait as a real Gainesburger." It is funny, but she means well, and we feel for her even as we laugh.)

We may laugh at Billy Clyde and Benny, too, and sometimes even at Phoebe's somewhat boozy imperiousness, but we feel for them all. And that is the secret of a successful serial: characters. Real people, with real problems and pains you can share, living out their lives as we all must, by trial and error, through tragedy and triumph. They are us, the people of Pine Valley, and their world is a surrogate for ours. The problems we share with them are our problems too, and as we watch them cope we can learn from their mistakes as well as their successes. In fact, in this mobile, often isolated world we now inhabit, where the loving support of extended family and life-long neighbors is often unavailable, Pine Valley may well be a substitute for those things we have lost. In the Martin and Tyler families we see how people interact, how they blunder and hurt one another but remain close, how they work their problems through within the framework of their world. That is why for many—if not most—of *All My Children*'s millions of fans, Pine Valley actually is, in one sense, more real than their own neighborhood. They have unique access to those fictional lives and emotions, and can learn from them.

Because of this realism, and because the characters of *All My Children* are honestly drawn, therapists have found the show an excellent tool in helping patients recognize problems they may have unintentionally hidden from themselves. Watching the stories together in groups and discussing them afterward, patients often unwittingly drop illuminating clues to the underlying causes of their neuroses. A patient may identify with characters and situations that echo his own problems, often without conscious knowledge, and the emotions engendered will point like a compass needle to the hidden trouble.

One remarkable example of this identification came during the examination of David Berkowitz, the notorious Son of Sam killer who had shot young women at random in parked cars around the New York area. Throughout the questioning he remained calm and detached, admitting his guilt but showing no emotion at all. And then one day, while watching television, he began crying and screaming so violently he had to be forcibly subdued. What was he watching? A soap opera called *Days of Our Lives*. And what touched off the rampage? A discussion between two people on the show about committing a child to a mental institution, a threat David Berkowitz might have overheard in his own childhood. If so, Son of Sam's armor, which had withstood all attempts by judges, doctors and even parents of his victims to pierce it, was cracked by a soap opera.

Psychiatric patients are not the only ones who may profit from the soaps, however. According to Dr. Valentine Winsey, associate professor of anthropology/sociology at New York's Pace University, ordinary viewers may also find them helpful. "Learning to cope with problems is a major part of maturity," Dr. Winsey writes, "and soap writers work hard to insure that their characters constantly and overtly cope with problems. Each difficult situation is spelled out, episode by episode, not just from the viewpoint of one character, but from that of each family member and friend. We also hear, at length, from the person causing the problem about his own anger or frustration or helplessness. The 'solution' is skillfully, and often sensitively, detailed, step by step, from cause to effect. As each episode unfolds, viewers are guided on a remarkably clear tour of the many overlapping human emotions that every problem generates. This makes it possible for some viewers not only to achieve better understanding of their fears but perhaps even to resolve confusions over right or wrong, good or bad, in their personal attitudes and behavior. By dealing with some of the most relevant social issues of today, soaps indirectly prepare viewers to grapple with similar problems in their own lives."*

We know that fans react powerfully to *All My Children* because we hear from them when a story line or a character pleases or displeases them. In some cases fan reaction has had a direct effect, usually by keeping a character in the story beyond the original time planned for him. For instance, Phoebe's chauffeur, Benny Sago, was originally slated for a brief appearance, but fan interest won him a long-running part on the show. The same was true for the con man "professor," Langley Wallingford, whose British suavity evidently worked on the fans in much the same way that it did on Phoebe.

Fan letters are almost always interesting, sometimes quite surprising, and occasionally amusing, though the humor is not always intentional. One such letter, unsigned, came from a Canadian viewer who was clearly upset about Phoebe's dalliance with the charming Professor Wallingford. The writer grew quite overwrought and ended by calling Phoebe a "bitch" who thought she had kept her scandalous behavior a secret. "Well, I'm going to write every member of the cast and tell them what you did."

Phoebe, of course, was undaunted, and her relationship with Langley continued. But she was not to get away with it, because not long after the first warning from Canada, every member of the Tyler family—Charles, Lincoln, Chuck, and even Donna—got letters in the same hand revealing the sordid truth. I've received thousands of letters from people with an incredible range of backgrounds and occupations (doctors, professors, even priests). Many express strong convictions about the show, but the anonymous Canadian may have been the first to enter so completely—and so literally—into the spirit of Phoebe's world. For most, fortunately, Pine Valley remains dramatic entertainment, no matter how real we may manage to make it seem.

All of us in soap opera are aware, however, of the small minority for whom the line between enjoyment and outright belief becomes blurred. For me the awareness first came more than twenty-five years ago, during my stint as Nurse Janet on *The Guiding Light*, which was telecast live from that wonderful old concert and recording center, Liederkranz Hall.

In the show I was the confidante of Dr. James Lipton, a resident in the same hospital where I worked as a nurse. He was a man with domestic problems, and as he poured his troubles into my sympathetic ear it was clear that I was slowly falling in love. I even invited him to my apartment for a drink—innocent enough, but clearly the sort of thing that could lead to no good for a man with a hysterical, pregnant wife waiting at home.

A few days later, after I had finished the morning's show, I was rushing through the lobby on my way home. I never made it to the door, because there before me, glowering like a wrathful amazon, was a very pregnant young woman with a rolled-up umbrella and a wild look in her eyes. She advanced on me, glaring.

"You ought to be ashamed of yourself!" she screeched.

I looked around for the guard who normally did sentry duty in the lobby, but he was nowhere to be seen.

"That poor woman is expecting a *baby*!" the bulging lady yelled, brandishing the umbrella.

I backed up, but soon found myself in a corner.

"What do you mean, taking her husband to your apartment and getting him drunk?" she demanded, jabbing the point of the umbrella hard into my stomach. I was now beginning to be seriously alarmed.

I thought of calling for help, but I didn't want to upset her any more than she already was. I tried to smile reassuringly.

"You leave those people alone!" she said menacingly, prodding me again with the umbrella.

The missing guard returned at that moment and quickly hustled the screeching woman away, freeing me to flee from the scene. But in all the years since I have never forgotten the look on that woman's face as she defended a pregnant sister against the conniving of the "other woman." Clearly the show was reality to her, and she was prepared to deal with it. Luckily for Phoebe, most fans are less forceful.

The question of whether the soaps actually reflect the real world has always been hotly debated, though the attacks seem often to come from those who have never actually watched the shows they castigate. "How could anyone have all those problems, one after another and one on top of another, in real life?" We hear that sort of question all the time, and the best answer

I can give is: *One* couldn't, perhaps (though considering my own life I'm not so sure), but *All My Children* has at least thirty-nine continuing characters, plus dozens that have been written out, killed off, or left in some limbo from which they may or may not return. Altogether there have been close to a hundred major characters—and uncounted minor ones—on the show during the first decade; and with that many people interacting over that span of time, even real life would have come up with a respectable list of marriages, divorces, deaths, and personal conflicts both petty and tragic.

True, life is rarely placid for anyone in Pine Valley, at least not for very long. (Or not while they are active in the story, anyway. People do move away, usually to Seattle, or "Sea City," and presumably some of them live relatively calm lives there. But maybe not; maybe they are triumphing and suffering, marrying and divorcing and dying out there in Seattle, too, just like their real-life neighbors.) And the reason is obvious, if you think about it: A tranquil life might be nice to live, but most people don't lead tranquil lives; and in any case tranquility would probably be boring to watch. As Tolstoy said, "Happy families are all alike; every unhappy family is unhappy in its own way." It was not the happy familes about whom Tolstoy wrote.

When you consider it, isn't conflict the essence of all drama? *Macbeth* is not about marital devotion, and *Death of a Salesman* is not about the happy retirement of Willie Loman after a life of honorable toil, even though many real-life salesmen may be enjoying reasonably happy retirements all around us. It is in the turmoil and conflict of the Loman family that Arthur Miller finds meaning, and it is in his ability to make us feel and understand that turmoil that the play's strength lies. The same can be said of any play, to one degree or another, even of those plays that are lightweight froth. After all, "boy gets girl" would make for a very short and uninteresting evening. Even if we know the boy will regain the girl in the end, it is his momentary loss that keeps us in our seats.

The three-act play, like the nighttime dramatic show or the movie or the novel, distills experience into a single series of circumstances leading to a climax that will, one way or another, resolve the conflict. The soap opera, since it consists of many plot strands and since those many story lines will continue next week and next month, cannot achieve that cathartic resolution. What it *can* offer, however, is a *series* of catharses, with one story reaching a resolution (often temporary) while another one builds toward its own crisis. (And another, quite probably, moves to Seattle or takes a round-the-world cruise.) A continuing story is like a river: racing over rapids one moment and gliding tranquilly another; sometimes crashing over a waterfall or being stopped, temporarily, at a dam—but always going on toward the distant sea. A daytime serial, with its large cast and intricate braiding of plots, flows like a whole mapful of rivers, each feeding into or branching off of another, some growing stronger while others twist or turn or disappear altogether.

Ironically, those who argue that the soaps are not realistic seem determined to disregard the obvious: The two-hour movie, the three-act play, or the one-hour episode of a night-time dramatic show or situation comedy simplifies and isolates one set of characters and one chain of circumstances in a way that real life never does. The soaps, with their large casts and broad tapestry of stories, actually mirror at least one important aspect of reality in a far more direct fashion than any play ever could. But the soaps, too, are selective, since we are no more likely to relish dull trivia in a continuing story than we are to applaud if Macbeth spends the evening polishing his armor. But such selectivity is not unreal. It is simply a recognition of what we consider important enough to occupy our time and thought.

Yes, it may be true that the citizens of Pine Valley seem to have more problems than your family and neighbors confront, and they may seem to live at an emotional pitch few of us could endure for long. But look around you: How many salesmen do you know who suffer like Willie Loman, and how many cops face the perils of Kojak? For that matter, how many fathers have the problems that plagued King Lear? Life contains conflict, and drama is a distillation of life, a prism that refracts the moving and important while omitting the insignificant.

The soaps, undeniably, mirror a very large number of ordinary life's manifold problems. In addition to divorce, marital infidelity, abortion, teenage sex and pregnancy, and prostitution, *All My Children* has touched on such common human afflictions as alcoholism, drug addiction, impotency, mental retardation, various forms of insanity, venereal disease, and a host of medical problems from heart attacks and cancer to euthanasia and crib death. Pine Valley has seen battered wives, rapes, murders, kidnappings, thefts, arson, blackmail, and most of the other antisocial acts that afflict society. Such controversial subjects as interracial romance, interreligious marriage, and even antiwar activism have figured in the story, as they do in everyday life. Mary Fickett won an Emmy for Ruth Martin's impassioned plea to end the senseless killing of youth in Vietnam, a dramatic speech that expressed the feelings of many in the cast and a large part of the American public. Only homosexuality and child molestation remain untouched in daytime television, though neither will surprise me when it does appear. Times change, and the serials change with them. "We are first an entertainment medium," Agnes Nixon says, "but we are also a teaching medium. We don't set the tone, but we reflect the times and we encourage viewers to reflect on them."

Thus, *All My Children* is a teaching medium that neither preaches nor lectures. Rather, it permits viewers to *experience* problems vicariously and to measure their own beliefs against the decisions and actions of the characters. Perhaps this helps to explain why soaps are no longer solely the province of "bored housewives," if indeed they ever were. Recent surveys have shown that nearly forty-five million people watch soap operas daily, and a sizable percentage of that figure represents males, including everything from students to psychiatrists to long-shoremen. (*All My Children* boasts one of the highest percentages of viewers of all daytime serials.) In a period when prime time is losing viewers, daytime television has been steadily gaining them. The popularity of soap operas has become so substantial, in fact, that prime time has taken note, not only with such direct take offs as *Mary Hartman, Mary Hartman* and *Soap*, but also with such continuing stories as *Dallas*.

But if the soaps are popular entertainment, they are also ephemeral in a most literal way. Arthur Miller's plays will be performed and discussed for years to come, and even *I Love Lucy* seems destined to rerun forever, no doubt to amuse the grandchildren of its original viewers. Past episodes of *All My Children*, on the other hand, will never be seen by your grandchildren. In fact, they will not be seen again by anybody; the show's most moving or controversial moments can never be rerun for its critics or its supporters. Because videotape, unlike film, is reusable, and the sobering fact is that all the show's tapes have been recycled many times for simple economic reasons. (Tape is expensive, as is storage space, so only those scenes destined to be flashbacks are preserved even temporarily.) So cherish your favorite memories, because you'll never have a chance to enjoy those scenes in rerun.

The soaps differ from the nighttime shows in another more important way: For mass popular entertainment viewed by millions, they are produced on a remarkably small budget. (Literally hundreds of hours of *All My Children* are brought to you for what was spent on *Roots*.) And yet these shows, without benefit of reruns, account for a disproportionate percentage of network earnings. It has been said that even a popular hour-long evening dramatic show, costing upwards of two hundred thousand dollars to produce, will be doing well if it only *loses* fifty thousand dollars per show. A daytime serial, conversely, is expected to *earn* a profit (that may amount to many tens of thousands of dollars) each *week*—which *All My Children* regularly does. Thus, although daytime drama may not actually be aired on prime time, it is nevertheless clearly a prime moneymaker.

It has also supported some of the star performers from prime time, as well as a few from stage and screen. Any list I could provide would be enormous and probably incomplete anyway, but a few names that come to mind are: Ellen Burstyn, MacDonald Carey, Joan Bennett, Lee Grant, Warren Beatty, Sandy Dennis, Walter Slezak, Sheppard Strudwick, Joan Fontaine, Joan Crawford, and, of course, our own Eileen Herlie. Others, such as Carol Burnett and Sammy Davis, Jr., have made brief appearances, and Dick Cavett did a guest shot on our show last year to open Erica's ill-fated disco. Many actors have learned what my friend Gail Smith taught me long ago: A regular job not only helps pay the bills, it also allows a performer to work at his or her craft. And to work at acting day in and day out, is the best way to learn.

Now in its eleventh year and among the top three soaps in the ratings, *All My Children* has proven any original doubters wrong and Agnes Nixon, as usual, right. The show was originally criticized for being too family oriented, too old-fashioned in its treatment of complicated relationships among people of several generations, committed to one another by bonds of blood and love. But Agnes Nixon believed in those things, and she made believers of the networks, the sponsors, and ten million loyal fans. The Martins and Tylers and the others of Pine Valley may have problems and even deep conflicts, but they are held together by those ties of family and community that are uniquely American.

The original prospectus for the show, the famous "bible" written by Agnes Nixon during that vacation on St. Croix, begins with this description: "The community of Pine Valley is almost as important in our story as are the characters themselves. A settlement whose roots go deep into pre-Revolutionary soil, the valley has a distinctive personality and charm which affects all who live in or near it. . . . The Valley will be what everyone thinks of when they think of home. Home, because whether there or not, this verdant valley has in some way made them what they are and is to some extent part of them."

Home. In a vagabond nation where one family out of three moves each year, where two generations seldom live together or succeed each other in the same house, we still cling doggedly to the image of home and our roots.

Years ago, driving along the Pacific Coast Highway toward Malibu, I heard the car radio playing "The Green, Green Grass of Home." I stopped on the side of the road, staring across the semiarid southern California countryside where I often felt myself displaced, a stranger in a strange land. But in my mind I was in Missouri, on a bluff overlooking the gently rolling valley of the Platte River. There, beyond the white frame church and the great dark pines that whispered and sighed around it, lay the green, green grass of *my* home. Briefly in my mind, I was a child again, slipping out of that church to stand with my Mary Janes planted firmly in that grass, eyes closed, listening to the drone of bees, breathing deep, wondering if my great-grandparents and all my vanished great-aunts and -uncles knew I was standing among them. Somehow I was sure they did.

In September 1978 I went home to St. Joseph to receive the first annual Humanitarian Award, to be given each year in my name. My son, Jon Rolf, came with me, and together we attended a long press interview. He listened to the questions about my life there, heard me tell about my years as a girl in Central High, about the radio show and the church choir and the family picnics and the Civic Symphony Orchestra and the dozens of activities that had filled my young life. Later he told the reporters: "I understand my mother better today than I ever have. Though we children were raised in the Tinseltown of Hollywood and the canyons of New York, there was always something different about us. I think I've discovered why today: St. Joseph is not only her hometown, it's my hometown too."

For millions of Americans, Pine Valley is *their* hometown in much the same way, and from it they can draw guidance and comfort and reassurance that a common tie binds us all. As Agnes Nixon's bible for *All My Children* says, "The great and the least, the weak and the strong, in joy and sorrow, in hope and fear, in tragedy and triumph, you are all my children."

EIGHT

Detours and Excursions

The Guiding Light was not really my first soap opera. During my early years in New York I had made a number of appearances in a radio serial called *Joyce Jordan, Girl Interne*, a show that was to be revived some years later, with me in the lead role and the original radio Joyce Jordan in a supporting part. Such are the vagaries of show business.

However, during those summer months back in New York, my personal life was having its own vagaries, chief among them a laughing, singing, witty Irishman named Robert McNamara, known as Bibber to his legions of drinking buddies. I'd met him through some friends, we had hit it off, and I had accepted an invitation to spend the weekend at the Long Island house he'd rented, with another bachelor, for the summer. A younger, handsomer version of Pat O'Brien, Bibber's life revolved around his three brothers, Cornell football weekends, a joke and a song and—always—a bit of the gargle to make life go down easier.

That summer I came to look forward to the weekends at Amagansett, and to the touch-football games I was allowed to join. (I sometimes suspected that the real reason I fell for Bibber was because he let me play touch football, which had been considered improper for a girl back in Missouri and utterly unthinkable for my stiff-necked Scandinavian husbands.) But marriage was certainly not on my mind, especially since I had two children to consider. Besides, Bibber was a carefree bachelor pushing forty. I assumed such a man would flee from the responsibility of a ready-made family, especially when the children were already ten and twelve.

As summer neared its end I told him my children were arriving in New York, assuming my holiday was over. To my surprise he said, "Fine, bring them along next weekend."

When I arrived with Karen and Jon, Bibber appeared to greet us in a pair of Bermuda shorts, an uncommon sight to West Coast eyes, and wearing a World War I army hat much like the one worn by Smokey the Bear.

Jon sized up the vision and then said, "Okay, you must be the scoutmaster, but where are your troops?"

Bibber was delighted, and from that moment forward the three of us became his troops, whether in the inevitable football games, exploring the old whaling village of Sag Harbor or nearby Shelter Island, or just "ramicaking" around (an Irish version of "goofing off").

Almost by osmosis we became a family. In July 1953 I became Mrs. Bibber McNamara, and shortly afterward we moved to a converted carriage house in Westchester in whose cavernous living room the Jefferson Memorial monument had been sculpted. The enormous room, with its fireplace that had once been a blacksmith's forge, contained not one but two grand pianos. (It also contained, a bit later, a full set of drums for Bibber's virtuoso assaults. When a friend commented that he must have a very understanding wife to permit drums in the living room, Bibber said proudly, "Permit them? She *bought* them for me.")

For a time we commuted—Bibber to his job selling television advertising time, and I to *The Guiding Light*, various radio and television jobs, and a stint of several months as a spokeswoman for Prom home permanents on another soap opera called *Valiant Lady*. In Scarborough we lived the affluent suburban life, with golf at the country club and weekend cocktail and dinner parties featuring the unforgettable music of McNamara's Band, consisting of Bibber on drums, Karen on clarinet, Jon on trombone, and Mom on one of the pianos. The group amazed many a gathering with its renditions of "Bill Bailey, Won't You Please Come Home," and "Toot, Toot, Tootsie," which we attacked with great enthusiasm and the unspoken agreement that reaching the finish was the thing, regardless of what might happen along the way.

Early the following spring, my doctor phoned. "Tell Bibber there's going to be a new piccolo player for McNamara's Band," he said. I told Bibber, and Bibber told the world, or as much of it as he could reach on the platform of the Scarborough station the following morning. Though he'd come to fatherhood late in his life, he would greet it with open arms and beaming face. "A son," he announced. "I'm to have a great, fine son at last."

Meanwhile, life went on; so did the golf and the football weekends that fall, and the daily commercials—in the novel form of live interviews—for the home permanents. Since hair was the focus, the cameras were able to stay well above my growing midsection until it reached dimensions the producer found alarming. When she invited me to the inevitable lunch, I almost wept into my martini.

"You're going to fire me," I said. "Haven't I done a good job?"

"You've done a fine job, Ruth," she said. "It's just that we can't afford a standby obstetrician."

So I was sidelined for a time, both from work and at last even from the touch-football games I loved. (The latter ruling came from no less than Bob Kane, then director of athletics at Cornell and more recently head of the U. S. Olympic Committee. He was also my brother-in-law, but that didn't lessen his authority in matters of athletic fitness.) As the pregnancy went on into its ninth month I visited the library, causing a certain amount of amusement when I checked out *How to Get Your Child Into College* and *What Shall We Name the Baby?* on the same day. I was ecstatically happy and doing quite well physically for a woman of almost thirty-nine. In fact, on the day Tim was scheduled to be born, I was out in the backyard shooting baskets until a neighbor phoned and begged me to stop. She just couldn't stand to watch, she said.

True to his Irish heritage, Tim chose a pub for the delayed announcement of his imminent arrival. We were at Manero's with some weekend guests when I suddenly received the first unmistakable message that the new baby was on its way. I managed to get Bibber's attention and told him I thought we'd better leave.

"Why?" he said. "Come on, Big Red, it's early. Relax."
(I shared the nickname of the Cornell football team, a great
honor indeed.)

"It's not my idea, it's Tim's," I told him.

"Tim's?" He had been so certain the baby would be a boy
that he had already named him, so he knew who I meant. "You
don't mean . . . ? Are you sayin' that . . . ?"

When it finally sunk in, he leaped up onto a chair and yelled
for silence, then shouted to the crowded room; "Hey everybody,
I'm a father!" I had only heard such a note of jubilation in his
voice once before, when Cornell had run ninety yards for a
touchdown. "Drinks for everyone!" he yelled. "Bring me a box
of cigars!"

Finally the commotion subsided a bit and Bibber's brother,
already the father of four, managed to remind him about the
facts of the situation. We made an exit amidst cheers, some
of them even for the mere mother of the miraculous new
McNamara.

Tim must have been listening, because he decided to delay
his entrance into this madcap world as long as possible. Nothing
happened that night or next morning.

When I finally arrived at the hospital in Mt. Kisco, the labor
seemed to go on and on. I had refused drugs to lessen the pain
because I feared their effect on the baby. (Karen had been born
blue and almost dead because painkillers, given to me without
my knowledge or consent, had cut down the amount of oxygen
reaching her. I had no intention of risking a repetition of that.)
Finally the doctor, somewhat concerned, examined me again.

"There seems to be some obstruction," he said. "Have you
ever had surgery in that area?"

"Certainly," I said. "There was extensive repair work and
a suspension operation after my second child, years ago. I gave
all that information on my first visit."

I had given it to another doctor at this clinic, and it seemed
that the present doctor had not checked my records. His fore-
head was beaded with perspiration. "Good God, woman, you
should never have tried a natural birth after such surgery. It's
just not possible. You should have had a caesarean." He shook
his head. "It's too late now. The baby is already in the birth
canal, and we can't operate."

There was a look of fear on his face, and it was reflected on the other faces in the room. I was angry at them for letting this happen, but I was also battling to control a growing fear in myself as another violent contraction forced the baby toward the inflexible wall of scar tissue.

And then I sensed, and almost saw, a presence in that delivery room, a kind of brightness behind me that was somehow malevolent, as if someone or something did not want my baby to be born. I cannot account for this presence nor, I suppose, can I ask you to accept it as real. I only know that that moment galvanized me into battle. No longer passive, I banished all negative thoughts and began to concentrate on forming a mental image: the perfect birth of my perfect child.

I was concentrating so intensely I did not care that I was speaking aloud to my unborn child. "Don't be afraid, Tim," I said. "I swear it cannot harm you. I promise I will protect you. Come on out now, Tim, and don't be afraid of anything."

Whether my coaxing was heard, or whether it simply helped to relax my muscles into an elasticity that was not supposed to be possible, I shall never know. I only know that where there had been no movement and almost certain tragedy, there came movement and triumph. At last Tim entered the world, as hale and hearty as any Irishman could wish.

"This is one of the largest babies I've ever delivered," the doctor said, holding the red and howling Tim. "He'll be at least six feet three, I'll bet." (Tim McNamara, now a disc jockey in Colorado Springs, is six feet three inches tall.)

When they wheeled me at last back to my room, we found Bibber there, undressed and sound asleep in my bed, a shock to the nurses but not to me. Later, when Bibber had gone, I lay in the bed and held my precious baby, looking out the window at a glowing world, wonderfully happy and filled with gratitude. The phone rang, and I picked it up expecting to hear congratulations from a friend. Instead I heard the familiar voice of Ted Corday, who had directed me as Nurse Janet on *The Guiding Light*.

"Ruth, are you all right?" he asked. "They gave me this number."

"I'm just fine, Ted. It's so good to hear from you."

"I'm sorry I haven't been in touch lately," he said. "Irna

and I have been terribly busy writing a new show. And that's really why I called. We're ready to film a pilot now, and we want you with us."

I looked down at my son, whose incredibly long fingers were making a miniature fist. "Ted, it's awfully nice of you to think of me," I said to the phone. "But I have a brand-new baby, and I just can't do it."

"Nice to think of you!" Ted spluttered. "Irna and I wrote this show *for* you. You've got to do it!"

I really was flattered. Irna Phillips had once told me that I gave the "other woman" a whole new dimension, but I hadn't known she was that serious. "I really wish I could, Ted, but it's just not possible now," I told him.

Ted asked me to give it more thought, we chatted a bit more, and he congratulated me again on my new son and hung up. Later he told me he had been totally stunned at the news of the baby, since he had not heard about my marriage. He had thought me wonderfully daring and courageous to have a child out of wedlock, and at my age, too.

I was a bit unhappy to be saying no to Ted Corday, the man I'd been told always to say yes to, but I could not go back to work with a brand-new baby to care for. However, the show was delayed several times, and it was not until the following spring that Ted called and said they were actually ready to do the pilot. "Please," he said. "At least help us to sell the show to CBS. We won't ask you to sign a contract, and if you don't want to do it when we're ready to begin, we'll get somebody else."

I did the pilot, the show was sold, and *As the World Turns* went on the air in April 1955 with me as Penny's beloved Aunt Edie, the first sympathetic "other woman" in the soaps. Edith Hughes was a central figure on the show, written by Irna Phillips and Agnes Nixon, for the next three years, and she made guest appearances at family reunions for several years, even after I'd left the show. (She is still alive and well in Seattle, receiving visits from Nancy and Chris and anyone else in the show who needs some excuse to be absent from Oakdale for a time.) Once again, saying yes to Ted Corday proved to be one of my wiser moves.

I was beginning to have a few doubts about the wisdom of

having said yes to Bibber, though. He seemed to be drinking even more now, and ever since the birth of the baby he had been physically distant from me. At first I had assumed his disinterest was really consideration for the difficult time I'd had in childbirth, but as the months went by and he showed no inclination to resume our mutually enjoyed intimacy, I began to wonder what was wrong. Finally one night, as I snuggled up to him in bed and he turned away from me, I asked him what was the matter.

"Nothing," he said shortly.

"Bibber, when two people stop making love, something's wrong."

He jumped out of bed and grabbed his bathrobe. At the door he turned and said, "I have my son now. Why should I bother with you anymore?"

And that was that. From that day forward, although we remained outwardly a happily married couple, the warm and intimate physical love that is the heart of most marriages was gone. In truth, though, the Cornell football games and the country club and the ever-flowing booze were already crowding the center of Bibber's world. He admitted, years later, that I could have named the men's locker room as correspondent in our divorce, and there was truth to it: the men's locker room, the bar, the cocktail hour, the singing and the laughter and the dance. I'd gone from Carl Neubert's Viennese waltz to McNamara's Irish jig, danced at an ever-increasing tempo.

For a time my "other life" appeared to be part of our problem. He resented my commitment to my profession, even though we could never have afforded our life-style without my earnings. He didn't mind my daytime work in New York so much because he was also gone during the day. But he couldn't understand why I needed to spend time with my children, especially if that might interfere with a cocktail party or other socializing. Why couldn't I spend more time at the club, as other wives did, improving my golf game and making friends?

"You don't have any friends," he said in one argument. "You'll be sorry when the children are gone. Then you'll be lonesome."

"No, Bibber," I said sadly. "I'm afraid it may be you who'll be the lonesome one."

It was a prediction that was to prove tragically true, though no one would have believed it then of Bibber the Imbiber, the life of every party who could fracture a room with his Jack Benny impersonation. He had been a war hero and the U. S. Navy captain who had sailed the German heavy cruiser *Prinz Eugen* triumphantly into Boston Harbor. He had also been a brilliant salesman, picked by his boss to succeed him as the president of the company—until his "Monday morning flu" became a chronic problem that would cost him one job after another.

But despite our physical alienation, we stayed together, for we really did enjoy each other's company in every respect save one. And when the doors were opened for a wedding in the Catholic church, I decided to keep my promise and go through with the "real" wedding. Our original ceremony had been performed by a judge in the home of Bibber's boss, Pete Peters, whose wife was Virginia Church Peters, previously married to my first beau in Kansas City. (So soap operas are too free with coincidence?) But now, with my first husband dead, I was officially a widow (my second marriage had never occurred, in the eyes of the church) and eligible to marry in the Briarcliff Manor Catholic Church.

Though deliberately low-key, the wedding was attended by friends and relatives from far and wide. And in the front row, on my friend Sally Kemp's lap, sat three-year-old Tim, excited and happy even though he didn't quite understand the whole thing. As the bride and groom walked in from the side to face the priest, Tim's voice piped up loud and clear: "Hi, Mommy! Hi, Daddy!"

The church seemed to rock with silent laughter, but I didn't care. That is my beloved son, I wanted to tell everyone, and he belongs here more than any of you.

After the inevitable bash that followed, Bibber passed out on a couch somewhere. And the next morning he left, alone, on a business trip to California. Bibber had had his dream— a marriage performed before the altar and consecrated by the church—but alas, that marriage was to remain unconsummated.

I suppose that Bibber, at heart, was always more comfortable in the role of perennial sophomore than that of husband.

Often he'd call to say he'd missed the 8:03 and then, again, that he'd missed the 9:04 or the 10:59. Once, I remember, he called at 1:15 to say he was in the bar car of the *Montrealer* with some of the cutest Canadian chicks you ever saw, but not to worry because he was on his way home. At 2:00 he called from Harmon, a freezing cold half-hour's drive away, to ask me to come and get him. Since I had to get up at 5:30 to make a live performance of *As the World Turns*, I suggested that he ask the chicks to drive him home. An hour later, undaunted, he was under my bedroom window happily singing "Mother! Your wanderin' boy is home." Ah, the Irish.

I was happy in my role as Aunt Edie, but I still nursed a dream of doing a musical. Back in 1952, before I had even returned to the East Coast, I had learned most of the songs from *The King and I*, and one of my first actions on arriving in New York was to ask Rodgers and Hammerstein for an audition. They agreed, and I gave a performance of my own contrivance, made up of several songs and bits of scenes. They were sufficiently impressed to ask me to come in that afternoon to sign a contract.

And then, having done the hard part, I got cold feet and decided I needed an agent to negotiate for me. I got one, on advice from a friend who was a theatrical attorney, and he went to talk contract with a representative of the producers. What he was offered was something I had never heard of, a "standby star contract" stipulating that if Gertrude Lawrence should be unable to appear I would go on in her place—not as an understudy but as a replacement. The agent was a bit confused by this proposal and tried to get some guarantee about number of performances or matinees or something. But it was Friday, the bosses had gone to Bucks County for the weekend, and he was told to come back on Monday.

That same night Gertrude Lawrence died! She left the part, in her will, to her longtime understudy, Constance Carpenter.

So I never got to do the play on Broadway, but five years later, in 1957, when I was offered the opportunity to play Anna in a summer tour, I jumped at the chance. We opened in Albany, in a tent that took me back to Chatauqua days in Missouri, with three-year-old Tim in the front row singing softly along with every song. I was in heaven, with my family around me and the chance to do the part I had so long dreamed of doing.

The opening night went well enough until one number in which José Duval, as the king, marched toward me menacingly while I retreated from him across the stage. I had rehearsed the scene in a peasant skirt, but had never done it in the full six-foot-wide hoopskirt until that night. So, as I retreated and he advanced, the inevitable happened: I stepped on the bottom hoop, my heel caught and I went down in a heap, my leg tangled in the hoops so that I couldn't get my feet under me.

I waited for José to offer a helping hand, but he decided that would be out of character for the king, and marched away with his back turned disdainfully. I flailed about, growing angrier by the moment, imagining headlines about the star who couldn't finish her performance because she was attacked by a hoopskirt. I rocked back and forth, but I simply could not get untangled from the thing no matter what I did.

Finally José relented and came back to offer a hand. I grabbed it, bounced to my feet, and tore into a performance that was supercharged with anger and chagrin. Later it was suggested that I ought to fall every night, because I had practically brought the house down. The critics raved, and I went around for days on a high no drugs could possibly have matched. At long last I had proved to myself that I could do it.

And I did do it, through much of that summer and again the next. But right at the start I ran into trouble, when I was told of several cuts that were to be made in the matinee performance so that the rather long show could be performed twice without requiring that the actors be paid overtime. The Equity union deputy explained that such cuts were routine, so I did as I was told, even though some of the more effective bits had been lost, including Anna's soliloquy, my favorite part of the show.

The matinee performance ended, and immediately a major electrical storm began. A veritable cloudburst thundered on the tent roof and poured under the sides into my dressing room. But I was a former farm girl and not really bothered by the storm. I propped my feet up out of the mud and ate my dinner nonchalantly, hoping the rain would end before the evening performance so the audience could hear. And that was when the Equity deputy appeared again to announce that the same cuts were to be taken in the evening performance.

I was outraged. I knew that several important critics and theatrical people were to be in the audience, and I really felt it was unfair. I told the deputy I simply wouldn't do it.

"You *have* to do it," he said.

"No I don't. I happen to know Rodgers and Hammerstein specifically prohibit cuts in their shows, and I think they're right. It just isn't fair to the people who've paid to see the real thing." (Phoebe was warming up in the wings!)

I was adamant, so he went away wringing his hands. And in moments the owner of the tent was in my dressing room, stripped to the waist, drenched, and furious, waving a huge butcher knife.

"What the hell do you mean, you won't take the cuts?" he demanded.

I started to explain, eyeing the brandished knife, but he broke in angrily.

"Listen, dammit, I'm crawling around on top of that tent, which cost me twenty thousand dollars, cutting *holes* in it so it won't collapse from the water. And you're sitting here complaining about cutting a few lousy lines from the play? Goddammit, do as you're told!"

He stormed out, leaving me really up in the air. I had taken a stand that I truly believed was right on principle, but on the other hand I could see he was having real problems. What to do?

As the orchestra struck up the music of the overture, which never failed to thrill me, I stood near the edge of the tent, balanced on a board, surrounded by pools of water. Surveying the mud and rocks in the aisles I had to run through for my exits and entrances (there was even mud on the stage!) and looking at the musicians, huddled at the edge of an orchestra pit that was half filled with water, I prayed we'd make it through the performance.

Suddenly the producer appeared. "It's all right. You can do the whole show." He beamed. "I called New York. Equity said we won't have to pay overtime even if the show runs a little bit long, because the storm was an act of God."

We embraced warmly, the moon chose that moment to appear, and the show went on, intact and even inspired.

In 1959 I finally got the chance I had dreamed of—a part of my own in a Broadway musical. I had appeared on Broadway in *Miss Lonelyhearts* shortly after Tim's birth, but that was not a musical, despite my humming in one scene which seemed to become more like a production number with every performance. (I was finally complimented on my voice but told to remember this was *not* a musical, and to knock it off.) But this was different—a bona fide musical called *Take Me Along*, based on Eugene O'Neill's play *Ah, Wilderness*, and directed by Peter Glenville. Eileen Herlie, who now plays Myrtle Lum on *All My Children*, had already been cast in the part I had hoped to get, so I tried for the role of Essie, the mother. I outfitted myself with dowdy clothes and padding, grayed my hair, and managed to convince Peter that I was right for it, though I really was not.

We went into rehearsals, with me as Walter Pidgeon's wife, and instantly the excitement of the whole thing got to me. Working and lunching with Jackie Gleason and Walter began to bring the real me to the surface, and bit by bit the dowdiness was lost by the wayside and the years peeled away. My first number was a song called "I Can't Believe I'm That Man's Wife," and as rehearsals progressed several people commented that they too found it hard to believe I was that man's wife. Even so, I didn't realize until it was too late that I had committed the unforgivable sin: I had departed from the character I was supposed to portray. The result was inevitable.

I got the news that I was being replaced on a lovely summer day at our Scarborough home, with an incredible blue sky and the Hudson sparkling in the distance so brightly it was almost painful to look at. It was one of the most terrible moments of my life, to be told that the part I had wanted so much—and that I had actually *won*—was being taken away. I went into the yard, feeling almost physical pain, and ran around in circles like a wounded dog, wanting to scream and howl but afraid to alarm the neighbors and the children. I ran until I was panting, then stopped and stood still, trying to tell myself it was not as important as I knew it was.

As I stood there, actually wishing I were dead, the phone

rang. I went to answer it. And I listened, almost uncomprehending, as a calm voice informed me that my cousin, Sandra Warrick Reed, a beautiful girl in her twenties, had just committed suicide.

The shock was like a dousing of ice water, driving all thoughts of my disappointment out of my mind. While I had been pitying myself and thinking suicidal thoughts, that lovely young girl had actually ended her life, and would never again hold her child or see the sun sparkling on the river.

I called Karen and Jon to me and told them what had happened. I confessed that I had actually been wishing I were dead, and how terribly foolish and ashamed I now felt, hearing of a true and awful tragedy like that. Here was I, with a beautiful family and a good life, wanting to end it all over something as ephemeral as a part in a play. And yet, in honesty, I had to admit that my suicidal thoughts had been real, that for a short time I really had wanted to be dead.

"Someday, somewhere, the same thing may happen to you," I told them. "Something may hurt you so much you will truly wish you could die, as I just did. And yet I know now how foolish that was, how much I have to live for." I made them promise that if such a time ever should come for them, they would call me and talk about it, as I was talking to them then.

They listened, and promised. And in later years both Karen and Jon did make such calls, and we were able to share and deal with problems that seemed too great for one to bear alone. They learned what I had learned that day: Life, even when it hurts, is just too precious to throw away.

However, I now also had a practical problem that must be confronted. Over the past two years, what with summer tours and other commitments, I had given up my contract on *As the World Turns*. I had made occasional guest appearances, and would continue to do so for years to come, but Aunt Edie had been allowed to move to Seattle and was no longer a regular character on the show. So I swallowed my pride and accepted David Merrick's offer that I go with the show as understudy to both Eileen Herlie and Una Merkel, my replacement and fifteen years my senior.

When the train pulled out for tryouts in Boston with Jackie Gleason's Dixieland band on board, I was there too, determined to turn defeat into victory. I played each role several times during the year's run and became good friends with Mr. Merrick, who was kind enough to say that if only more actors loved the theater the way I did, he wouldn't find it necessary to hate them so much.

I learned a lot and became a combination den mother and Perle Mesta to the company, even applying some words of caution that may have saved Bobby Morse's job when Peter Glenville wanted to fire him. (Bobby was brilliant as the juvenile lead.) More persistent lobbying with the producer was required to save Onna White's marvelous choreography, when our ubiquitous director got the notion to dispense with her talents as well. (Phoebe was growing stronger every minute!)

With *Take Me Along* scheduled to close at the end of 1959, I could see I would soon be out of work again. What's worse, so was Bibber, having lost three jobs in a row because of his inability to make it to work on Monday. Things did not look good.

As usual when things looked bad, I began to think my most positive thoughts, affirming constantly that there was a job just right for me, and that the role and I would come together at the right moment. Sure enough, I was invited to lunch by a West Coast producer, who had been trying for six months to cast the part of the mother in a television situation comedy to be based on the novel and movie *Father of the Bride*. Finally the director, Fletcher Markel, had remembered the actress he'd worked with in a *Studio One* production years before.

"I don't know where she is or what's happened to her, but Ruth Warrick would be perfect for the part," he told the producer. Where I was, of course, was with *Take Me Along* at the Shubert Theatre in New York City, but for a Hollywood producer I might as well have been on the moon, so little did one coast know of the other in those days.

I went to the luncheon interview bearing pictures of my own daughter's recent wedding, and the producer was impressed with how well I suited the part. He was sold, he said, but I would have to pass muster with Leon Ames, who was to play the lead. That bothered me a bit because I knew that Leon, who was a bit shorter than I, was sensitive about his height. I agreed to a meeting if we could do it casually, rather than standing up to be measured together in front of a roomful of people at the MGM offices.

He agreed, and a lunch was arranged at Sardi's.

When I arrived Leon was seated behind a banquette table, so he couldn't rise entirely to greet me. We ate and chatted, and then I had to run to keep another appointment. Afterward we realized that, in the flurry of my exit, we had never actually stood up together. The agent insisted that another meeting be arranged, so this time we met for dinner.

And this time Leon got up, came out from behind the table, walked up to me, gave me a hug and a kiss, then stepped back and looked me up and down.

I had brought a pair of flat-heeled shoes with me and had slipped into them just before entering the restaurant. To my delight, Leon and I were about on eye level.

Leon grinned. "Dammit, you're not all *that* tall," he said. And we sat down with the deal done.

I was asked to do the pilot in California, and after conferring with Bibber I decided to give it a try. I flew out to the MGM studios in January and made the pilot. It was sold quickly to CBS, with General Foods as sponsor, and I was offered a contract. Again I talked with Bibber, and we agreed that I had better take the bird in hand, especially since things were looking no better for him.

In a few weeks I returned to Scarborough to arrange for the move West. Bibber had gone off to Florida with some friends, so I packed our most critical belongings, along with six-year-old Tim, our housekeeper, and a large boxer dog, into a compact car, and headed cross-country once again. This time, eighteen-year-old Jon, home on Easter vacation from Williston Academy, could do the driving. This trip was somewhat less carefree and relaxed than the earlier odyssey in the sky-blue Cadillac, but again I had the feeling of running *to* something instead of fleeing.

What I was running to, as it turned out, was a reunion with Carl Neubert that was destined to prove the old aphorism about people who do not learn from history being condemned to repeat it. Carl had also been married in the intervening years, to Lex Barker's sister Frederika, but that marriage had not worked out any better than ours had. He was currently un-

married, still living in the Mulholland Drive house we had
bought together, so it was probably inevitable that we should
meet again. Nine years older but no less handsome, he was as
ever the perfect escort, with tastes that matched my own. We
began to go places together and to enjoy each other's company
as we had a decade ago, before our marriage and its problems.

Bibber, meanwhile, had arranged a job in Los Angeles and
had come out to be near his son, though we had by now agreed
that we would no longer live together, and that the marrriage
was really over. He met Carl and even visited my former home.
So did Tim, who spent his first day there in wide-eyed wonder,
swimming in the pool, and playing with the German shepherds.
The day was capped with Carl's superb barbecued steaks on
the terrace at sunset, overlooking that incredible mountain
view. As we were changing from our bathing suits, Tim stroked
the lush wall-to-wall carpet and sighed wistfully.

"I wish we didn't ever have to leave," he said. "I wish we
could just stay here forever."

Those were pretty heady words for a mother to hear, especially since I had realized from my very first visit that Carl
was courting me again. I had no intention of falling into the
same trap. On the other hand, I had worked hard to forgive
and forget the old hurts, and now the pleasant memories were
very powerful and the emotions were deep.

On that visit he had led me on a tour of the garden, reminding
me when I had planted each bush and tree. To regain my
composure I had excused myself to use the powder room, but
Carl had stopped me.

"Don't be silly," he said. "You must use your own bathroom."

I found, to my utter amazement, that my bedroom and
bathroom had been restored to the exact state they'd been in
when I left, and that all traces of the intervening incumbent
had been removed. In fact, he had restored the entire house to
the decor we'd had, totally obliterating the last wife's redeco-
rating scheme. (Later, using a phone in the kitchen, I found
the book of numbers was my own, in my own handwriting.)

Carl said he felt he'd been entirely in the wrong in our
marriage, that he'd never stopped loving me, that he was sure
this time we could make it work—all very seductive words for

a woman to hear. "This is your home," he told me. "It always will be."

I reminded him of the problems we'd had, especially the arguments over my work, which I had come to realize would always be of major importance in my life. "I'm an actress and I will always be an actress," I told him. "And if that means I must be away from my husband for a night, or even a week, then that's the way it will have to be. I simply cannot be the 'shadow of her husband' a European housewife is supposed to be. You've every right to want that, but if you do, then please don't even consider marriage to me."

He assured me he had learned and grown. This time things would be different. I weakened as the summer went on, and weakened more when my divorce from Bibber McNamara became final. Finally, in September, a decade after our first wedding, Carl Neubert and I married once again, with "The Second Time Around" as our theme song.

Why on earth did we do it? In retrospect, it seems so clear that this remarriage was foredoomed. Since I cannot speak for Carl, I can only accuse myself. Myself and Phoebe, for surely that part of me that *is* Phoebe was then ruling my mind and heart. What I did was impulsive, romantic, and utterly foolish. No less foolish than Phoebe's "willing suspension of disbelief" in the promise of happiness represented by Langley's suavely manipulated charm. Phoebe and I may have many reasons for regretting our romantic errors, but we have no grounds for reproaching one another.

Within months of our marriage it became evident to me that I was not well, and a visit to my doctor confirmed it. I needed surgery, a double operation to correct internal problems that had grown worse since the last childbirth, problems which could have led to malignancy if not taken care of. The surgeon warned that this would constitute an unusual amount of surgery, but he decided to do both operations at once because I had some time off from *Father of the Bride* then, and couldn't know when another hiatus would come.

I wasn't really worried about the double surgery until I came to the interview with the anesthetist, who asked the usual questions about age, weight, and general health, and then sat there shaking his head and mumbling that no one should be under anesthesia for such a long time. With that bit of reassurance, I found myself waving good-bye to Tim from my hospital window, wondering if I would ever see him again.

As it turned out, I almost didn't. The surgery went well enough, but in one of the transfusions required because of the unusual blood loss, something went wrong with the valve and the blood was injected much too rapidly. I went into shock.

That night I woke to find myself floating up toward the ceiling. As I neared it I stopped, but somehow I knew that I could pass on through it and outward, into a place of peace and beauty. I wanted to go but for some reason turned back and looked down at the body on the bed below. The woman lying there looked so frail and vulnerable.

"I just can't leave her yet," I remember thinking as I looked down. "She still has so many things left to do."

With great regret I went back down and reentered the body. And the dream ended.

I went home a few days later with instructions to rest for at least a month, and I really meant to follow orders for once. But my resolve vanished only ten days later when my dear friend Sally Kemp became my houseguest. By an odd coincidence her husband, Howard Gossage, had just been admitted as a patient to the same hospital I had just left.

Taxis are impossible in the mountain reaches around Los Angeles, so I'd taken pity on her and driven her to the hospital. While waiting for her to finish her visit, I saw a resident doctor I had gotten to know while I was recovering. She and I had commiserated together over problems with our respective teenagers, so I smiled and waved hello. She rushed over with an alarmed look on her face.

"What are you doing here?" she asked me.

"Oh, it's all right," I said, explaining about my friend.

"You *drove* here?" she asked in amazement. "Get into my office where we can talk."

I went obediently, and sat down to face a very stern doctor.

"Are you crazy?" she asked. "Don't you know that less than two weeks ago you died?"

She explained that she had been in her office one night and suddenly had a feeling something was wrong. She had gone to my room and checked my pulse—which had stopped! A hurried injection had restarted my heart, but for a brief time I had actually ceased breathing.

Comparing notes further, I realized what I should have known instantly: That had been the night of my eerie dream.

I returned to *Father of the Bride*, but within a few months the show was canceled due to one of those decisions that leave performers confused and somewhat bitter. We had gotten quite respectable ratings in our two-year run, and General Foods was happy and prepared to continue their sponsorship. But CBS, in revamping its schedules, came up with some kind of imbalance in programming, which they "corrected" by dropping the show. That's television.

Unemployed again, I agreed to do a two-week summer stock production in Michigan. Carl was furious, and he all but forbade me to go away for such foolishness. I reminded him of the talk we'd had before this marriage, of how he had agreed that my career was important and that it would sometimes take me away from home.

"I remember," he said. "But I didn't mean it."

"What?"

"I didn't mean a word I said. I just said those things because you wanted me to, but I was counting on making you so happy you would never want to leave me for even a day."

I was stunned. This had been no casual promise, lightly made between a young couple with no knowledge of marriage. It had been a solemn reappraisal of the compatibility of two consenting adults. To hear him say childishly, "I didn't mean it," chilled me. It meant that he—and in a slightly different way, I—might have been deceiving ourselves. Perhaps our decision to remarry had not been as adult or carefully considered as we liked to suppose.

"Why can't you keep busy with charity work, as other wives do?" Carl asked. I had misgivings about this, but decided it was worth trying. If this marriage were to succeed, I was obviously going to have to make some concessions. As it happened, and somewhat to my surprise, I found social work both engrossing and enormously satisfying.

I became involved in working with dropouts, as a special consultant to the Labor Department's Job Corps, and that in turn involved me with a number of local officials and politicians. I decided to invite a group of them to our home to honor a visiting dignitary from Washington, and went to discuss my plans with Carl.

I had supposed he would be delighted; in fact, he was annoyed and rather contemptuous. He said he didn't wish to be there and that I would have to pay for the food and drink myself, since he was not about to feed a bunch of Democrats, who represented a position light-years removed from his own conservative Republicanism.

I was disappointed but respected (without agreeing with) his convictions. So I shopped for everything and took care to use nothing Carl might have paid for. And the evening went quite well, despite Carl's appearance midway through, his face set in an unmistakable look of disapproval. The guests departed, and nothing more was said about it.

A couple of days later, early on Sunday morning, I was startled when a man appeared at the front door with a packet of papers. He was a process server, it turned out, and the papers were Carl's petition for divorce. The grounds were that I had entertained Democrats in his home.

He had gone to his office, as he often did on Sunday, so I phoned him there to ask what in the world this meant.

"I just wanted to shake you up a bit and teach you a lesson," he said.

"Well, you succeeded," I told him. "But this time you can have the pleasure of going before the judge. See how you feel telling a court your reasons for dissolving a marriage."

He assured me that wasn't necessary, that he hadn't really meant to divorce me, that the papers had been meant only as a lesson. But the lesson had finally been learned, and I now saw that our life together simply could not work. With all his charm and intelligence, with all his social graces and generosity in small things, he just could not accept marriage as an equal partnership. There was in him an urge not merely to dominate, but to domineer. He was a mass of contradictions: a man who loved parties and who bought me glamorous clothes, but who would deliver an evening-long lecture over a chipped dinner plate; a man who enjoyed my modest celebrity at the same time that he resented it when he was not center stage. And a man who, though he worked hard and earned a respectable

income, was ironically in debt. And now this incredible trick,
if that's what it was. It was too unfeeling, too cruel.

So once again I left the lovely house I had helped to pay
for, taking only my clothes and paintings and a very modest
cash settlement from Carl. I moved Tim and myself into a
small apartment, with no servants, and began once more to
make sense of my life. At times like these it has always seemed
to me that I was lucky to have had the swimming pools and
minks and Cadillacs while I was still relatively young, so I
could learn how little those things contributed to real happiness.
Many women spend their lives believing they would be blissfully happy if only they had such material things; at least I
knew better.

However, I was now unemployed, having given up a brief
career as an ABC television interviewer when it became clear
to me that I was being groomed for a gossip-gathering role.
It really ended in Scandia, the Sunset Strip restaurant, where
I had tracked down Richard Burton and Elizabeth Taylor after
their unsuccessful attempt to be married in Mexico. I sat there,
decked out in my hidden mikes, and looked at those two beautiful people who had been hounded so mercilessly by the media
and other self-appointed moral watchdogs. They had even had
to watch while pickets paraded in front of their hotel carrying
insulting banners. Suddenly I knew I just could not go on with
this. I had the kitchen send them a silver platter with a bunch
of leeks, the symbol of Wales, and a note congratulating "the
first gentleman of the theater and his lady-in-waiting." They
invited me over to their table, and instead of getting my story
I found myself apologizing for the way they had been treated
and assuring them that most people loved them and sympathized
with their plight. I found later that they had been planning to
leave the country for good that same day but had changed their
minds and stayed on. And I also found out that day that I was
just not tempermentally suited to that kind of work. I resigned
from the job. If I left a void at ABC, Elton Rule was quick to
fill it, and with a very talented lady. Rona Barrett has turned
the job into a most enviable career indeed.

Now, with no series and no job, I kept house for Tim and
myself and looked for work. And for the first time, I was
scared. I was on my own, approaching my fiftieth birthday,

with a young son to support and no prospects. So I cooked and cleaned and prayed, and the months rolled by.

Then came an offer, one that both fascinated and frightened me: the lead in the then-controversial Albee play, *Who's Afraid of Virginia Woolf?* The controversy concerned language that was considered shocking, certainly not the sort of thing eleven-year-old Tim should hear from his mother, I felt. On the other hand, it was a terrific part, one that would certainly give my acting talents a test, and a chance to grow. I spent an entire night weighing my decision, then, at dawn knew I must take the job. After all, Tim didn't have to see the play. It was in the Los Angeles equivalent of Off Broadway (I called it "off La Cienega"), but in a good theater and sure to get some attention.

We got quite good reviews. More important, I felt I had achieved something important to me in this demanding role, and my confidence grew. I went from Albee to O'Neill, appearing in the long and rather murky *Long Day's Journey Into Night*, in a part I felt far less knowledgeable about. (The ravages of alcohol were all too familiar to me; drugs I knew little about.) But again, I was working and trying to make sense of my life.

Along the way I made friends with a manicurist, who would occasionally appear at our apartment with wine or even food for dinner. (The first time she explained that the store had been having a steak sale, a phrase I had never before encountered.) She had a friend at 20th Century-Fox, and through this friend she learned that a part was being cast in the nighttime soap opera *Peyton Place*, the highly successful serial version of Grace Metalious' best-selling novel, then in its third year on television. My friend's friend arranged an appointment for me at the studio, and I got the part, thus proving once again that success can depend on whom you know, even though it may be a manicurist rather than a tycoon.

I was to play Martin Peyton's housekeeper, Hannah Cord, a role that had originally been slated for Agnes Moorehead. The following year we were both nominated for an Emmy award, me for the role in *Peyton Place* and she for a single *tour de force* performance. Agnes, I believe deservedly, won, but all the way up to the stage she kept shaking her head and muttering, "No, I shouldn't be getting this." I think she felt it was a bit unfair to put one virtuoso scene up against a continuing role developed over hundreds of performances. (I was twice again nominated for Phoebe Tyler, but again I lost, both times to Helen Gallagher, a stunning Tony Award-winning actress. No quarrel with that, either. But I'm still around, and so is Phoebe, and maybe our time will yet come.)

But I'm getting ahead of myself. The contract was a good one, good enough that I could think of finding a home for us. On a camping trip to the beach, I came across a For Sale sign on a house that literally hung out over the breakers at Malibu. I called the agent next day, was shown the house, and bought it on the spot. As Tim and I stood in the rolling surf that day, I felt a serenity and satisfaction that was totally new to me. At that moment I took charge of my life. (Rock Hudson, who had originally owned the place, told me years later that he often thought selling that house was the greatest mistake he had ever made.)

The next few years were happy ones, working on a successful series and living in a place whose beauty was almost hypnotic. Bibber had an apartment in town, but he and his brother "Timmer" spent many weekends at the Malibu place, so young Tim had his father and his uncle on hand for the inevitable touch-football game, in addition to his mother. Bibber was drinking heavily, as his brother often bemoaned to me (not knowing that Bibber had worried aloud to me about Timmer's drinking), but the charm and laughter were still with him then. We were fond of each other still, in our own ways, and were bound by our love for Tim. We both knew marriage had long since been out of the question for us, just as we both knew, without speaking of it, that Bibber's drinking was now out of control. Still, the football games had their old magic, and the Malibu breakers, which crashed right under the dining room of our house, were a constant lullaby. It was almost a perfect life, with my family around me, work that I enjoyed, and the ocean, a lifelong love, outside my door.

Compared to ordinary daytime serials, *Peyton Place* was lavishly produced, since it was shot on film, with the full panoply of motion-picture production skills brought to bear. For two half-hour segments per week (and, for a brief time, three) we expended time, talent, and money that would have made any daytime producer green with envy. And it paid off. At a time when 20th Century-Fox was losing ground to television in the area of family-entertainment movies, *Peyton Place* began to soar in the ratings; the studio's stock began to take on a much healthier glow. The proven lure of the continuing story, which had always been thought to work only in daytime soaps, triumphed in prime time and held on for five years. In fact, the show might be running yet except for the restlessness of its producer, Paul Monash, and its executive producer, Richard Zanuck. Ratings had dropped somewhat but were still high enough to indicate a large and faithful audience, and there was no shortage of sponsors. But Zanuck wanted to move on, even if it meant killing the goose that had laid five years' worth of golden eggs. (He moved on to *Hello, Dolly!*, which nearly brought the studio to bankruptcy again. But one need not cry for him: Though he lost control of Fox, in partnership with David Brown he has since produced such blockbusters as *Jaws* and *The Sting*.)

Few shows have ever come to television with as much firepower as *Peyton Place*. Not only was it based on one of the most successful novels of all time (which had already been the basis for an all-star movie), it had a large budget and much outdoor location shooting, with all the production values possible in film. The heart of the Fox lot was *Peyton Place* exteriors. And it had a cast that, despite enough problems to fill several Grace Metalious novels, was loaded with talent. With such people as Ryan O'Neal, Dorothy Malone, Mia Farrow, Barbara Parkins, Leigh Taylor-Young, Lee Grant, and the cantankerous George Macready, how could the show not succeed?

As Hannah Cord, the somewhat mysterious housekeeper to the town's rich but eccentric leading citizen, I worked most often with George. He was a perfect Martin Peyton, since his off-screen personality was almost indistinguishable from the one he displayed as the crusty, invalid old tyrant of Peyton Place. I found it very difficult to break through his shell, but I was determined to try. Finally I began to resort to outrageous bits of horseplay on the set. George, who really did have a delightful sense of humor buried under his gruff exterior, was absolutely determined not to be broken up by my antics, so when Hannah appeared in one scene to bring him his medication and mail, he kept a straight face. Which was hard, because instead of the stiffly starched dress Hannah always wore, I was that day sporting the briefest of baby-doll nighties, and I wore that bit of froth through the whole scene without changing a word of dialogue. He, too, stuck grimly to his lines, but when I pulled back the covers and hopped into bed with him it was just too much. We both collapsed, helpless with laughter, and another outtake was born for our Christmas party.

To end *Peyton Place*, the authors had Hannah set Peyton's house on fire and disappear. Martin Peyton arrived in his Rolls to find smoke and fire belching from every window, and rushed up the steps in great distress. In one take of this scene, as George reached the top of the steps I burst out of the smoke and flames costumed as a witch, complete with broomstick and blackened teeth, and chased him across the lawn, yelling, "You'll never get away from me!" as I tackled him. And then, to everyone's amazement, the elderly and frail Martin Peyton turned into a tiger. As I brought him down he rolled us over and came up on top, and we went tumbling on across the lawn like a pair of rowdy children while the cameras whirred. A final outtake for our collection.

Not all relationships among the cast were smooth, however, and those of the handsome, young former stunt man, Ryan O'Neal, were sometimes bumpy indeed. Though married to beautiful Joanna Moore and already the father of a little girl, Ryan was ever alert for new conquests. The first was Barbara Parkins, a dark and delicate beauty who played the Erica Kane of the show, and who was, in real life, consumed with envious admiration for Mia Farrow. She imitated Mia's dress and even bought the same model foreign car and a similar poodle, but she could not quite copy her rival in the romance department. (There is, after all, only one Frank Sinatra.) Barbara tried Eddie Fisher for a time, but that didn't work out. And then came the young, handsome O'Neal, an actor with a promising career and enough charm to bowl over all but the toughest targets. Barbara was not tough, and she was soon madly in love.

Unlike movies, where an affair between stars might actually add intensity to the performances, the first rule in a serial is, Don't get involved with anyone at the office. A series goes on and on, while romances often do not. The demands are tough and tempers are often short, but you must do the job week after week and year after year with the same people. Love affairs do not help, especially when they are fleeting and shallow, as Ryan O'Neal's seem to be.

He was increasingly harsh with Barbara, dressing her down in public for trivial or imagined faux pas, but the real blow came when a new girl, Leigh Taylor-Young, arrived in Peyton Place. She played an innocent deaf-mute, but her innocence was short-lived as Ryan moved in to take her under his wing and show her the ropes, which were presumably stored in his bedroom.

Within months it became obvious that Leigh could no longer play the virginal innocent, and her story line had to be scrapped, along with several others. Hastily arranged divorces and marriages were engineered, and the two became man and wife, but it didn't last. Nor did Ryan's affairs with Anouk Aimée, Barbra Streisand, Julie Christie, Farrah Fawcett, and a host of others. It has often seemed, to Ryan watchers, that the only female who remains of lasting importance in his life is his daughter, Tatum, whom I first met at a cast Christmas party when the child was barely three. She had come with her mother, Joanna, who looked trim and quite provocative in a tiny leather mini-skirt with matching vest and boots. There were no other children there, but Ryan had insisted that she bring Tatum. It soon became clear why, because his relationship with the child was so intense as to exclude almost everyone else, including Tatum's mother. In fact, Joanna was sent home before the party was over, but Ryan and Tatum stayed on. He took over the little girl's life and career totally, and even now, in her teens, Tatum seems to wander imperiously through life with few friends. It is as if no one can compete with her favorite escort and companion, her handsome and charming father.

Mia Farrow provided one of the most highly publicized haircuts in the history of the media, during her tempestuous affair with Sinatra. One day, furious and hurt at having been excluded from Frank's fiftieth birthday party in favor of his first wife, Nancy (despite the consolation prize of a diamond bracelet, coyly concealed in a succulent roast squab), Mia retreated to her dressing room and hacked her long, blonde hair off to within an inch of her scalp. The event sent shock waves around the world, or so it seemed to those at the studio. Consternation reigned. And then someone got a bright idea, and a hair stylist was rushed in to trim the butchered stubble into a sleek, chic, little-boy hairdo that was promptly photographed and publicized worldwide. The self-mutilation was quickly converted into a new style, copied by armies of young girls who had no idea of its real origin.

Mia and Frank's attraction for one another, perhaps odd-seeming at first sight, may have had something to do with their personal histories. Mia worshipped her director-writer father, John Farrow, a brilliant but hot-tempered man who had died of a heart attack shortly after a bitter telephone quarrel with Mia. Frank, on the other hand, openly adored his daughter, "Nancy With the Laughing Face." Mia was even younger than Nancy; Frank was very like her father.

There was no doubting their mutual affection, but their life-styles simply didn't mesh. Frank invited a gang of his buddies (including Rosalind Russell) along on their honeymoon yacht trip, with what seemed like a photographer under every bunk.

"It was so boring," Mia said later. "All they ever do is play gin and talk about their old movies!"

One can easily imagine Maureen O'Sullivan's discomfiture and dismay at having Frank Sinatra for a son-in-law. "He should have been squiring me, not my daughter," she said disgustedly. "And I never could get used to the crude language of his blue jokes either. He would tell them deliberately just to make me blush."

However, Mia's later marriage to conductor-composer-arranger André Previn, again on the heels of some rather gamy headlines, did surprise me a bit—if not because of Mia then certainly because of André. I had known him from my earlier stint in Hollywood, and I still remembered the silent, stony-faced fifteen-year-old prodigy who sat like an automaton in his family's little bungalow while his parents discussed offers from MGM with one of the studio's producers. André had already gained fame as a child-virtuoso pianist, but he seemed almost disinterested in his fate as the adults haggled. The image of the shy, withdrawn boy, along with the image of the wispy, soft-spoken Mia, just did not add up to the kind of tabloid notoriety they engendered. Or perhaps it did add up; perhaps both felt set apart from the world around them, in a place where ordinary rules do not apply. With the birth of their children Mia became happy and fulfilled for the first time in her life. Adopted children from Vietnam augmented the family. Now a real woman, she becomes more beautiful and her talent grows with every role. Though currently separated from André, she is happy in her work and with her family, who flourish under the loving care of Mamma Mia and her devoted mother.

Dorothy Malone, the lovely leading lady of *Peyton Place*, provided the world with a real-life cliff-hanger that was followed by the fans as breathlessly as was the show itself. Dorothy had been suffering from a condition that was causing internal bleeding in her lungs, though she fought to conceal it over a period of several weeks in order to continue her work. The problem turned out to be more severe than she had realized, however, and as the lungs began to fill, she was rushed— belatedly—to the famed UCLA Medical Center. There the same brilliant team of doctors who had saved Patricia Neal's life worked together for five hours to repair the damaged veins and arteries in her chest. She survived and even managed to return to the show for a time, pale and so thin she seemed almost transparent. Her battle back to health was long and difficult, though, requiring several years of total retirement.

Last year Dorothy visited Pine Valley, along with her lovely daughters (by former husband Jacques Bergerac). As we embraced Dorothy said, "Can you believe, all the girls wanted to do in New York was visit the *All My Children* set? They even passed up sunbathing at the beach to watch the show." She shook her head in disbelief.

"We planned our entire college schedules around your show," the girls told me, echoing comments Phoebe has heard from college students all over the country.

Now happily married and living in Texas, Dorothy had just completed some television work in Canada and was heading home. Thank God she made it through that terrible time, back when we were in *Peyton Place* together.

Peyton Place, however, did not make it. In 1969, after five fabulous years, the show was allowed to die. It had given a new respectability to soap operas among people who had never watched daytime serials, and had opened the door for the miniseries and continuing stories (such as the successful *Dallas*) of today. It had also subsidized my Malibu house, which I had dubbed Peyton Place by the Sea, and a few years of life as perfect as any I've known. I shall be forever grateful to Zanuck and Monash and to the people I worked with on the show—and of course, to imperious Hannah Cord, who was another step on the road to Phoebe Tyler.

After the show ended, and I again found myself unemployed, it became immediately obvious that the Malibu house was too much for my tightened budget. With great regret I rented it out and moved Tim and myself into a place in nearby Topanga Canyon, a small but idyllic cottage on what had once been a huge estate, which had been willed to the state but not yet claimed as a park. We were happy enough there, with our own private stream and mountain and twenty-foot-high bamboo thicket, though I was somewhat puzzled by the great number of hippie types who seemed to come and go around the area. One of them, a small, bearded, rather intense young man who composed his own songs and played the guitar, spent a lot of his time in the vicinity, and got to be well known for his lectures on the world's shortcomings. Most people agreed that Charlie would never get very far, though, because he seemed to expend most of his energy on his numerous bedraggled girl friends, who lived with him in a converted black van. (It's true that he didn't save the world, but he did manage to attract considerable attention a few years later, to my horror and complete astonishment. The girls were pitiful, woebegone little things. That they could have assisted Manson in committing such monstrous crimes still seems almost impossible to me.)

With no work in sight, I sought out a lecture agent and inquired about bookings. I felt I could talk about Watts and the Operation Bootstrap program I had been deeply involved in for several years during the midsixties, but he quickly set me straight.

"That's the sort of thing people expect you to talk about *free*, as a civic duty," he said. "But you need to earn money, right? What they want to hear from you is *Peyton Place* gossip."

"Well, how about '*Peyton Place* and Beyond'?" I asked facetiously.

"That's it!" he cried in triumph.

So I agreed to lecture around the country on that title, privately deciding that the "beyond" would be my experiences in the Watts program, where I had helped establish a store-front job-training center and taught communication skills. And I did give the lecture many times over the next two years, which gave me personal satisfaction and at the same time paid some of the bills. Finally I was offered a role in a Warner Brothers movie, my first since I had left Hollywood back in the fifties. This one, called *The Great Bank Robbery*, was a camp western that may have been a bit before its time, though it has found a kind of cult audience in recent years, especially amongst college students.

In it I played a rather prim widow, much like the parts I had played in dozens of movies back in the forties. This dowager, however, was a bit different, because she was to be romanced by a phony preacher—played by the irrepressible Zero Mostel—and was to become a bit more "unbuttoned" in each scene as the movie progressed.

Mostel, who has come to town to rob the bank, poses as the preacher in order to tunnel from the church to the nearby bank vault. He is a spellbinder, but his sermons do not quite do the trick; the lady's suspicions flicker at various points in the movie and must be stifled by applications of Zero's ardor. In one scene late in the movie, the desperate preacher takes the lovesick lady behind a barn for some serious stifling, and much giggling and squealing is heard by the audience, who cannot see what is happening but can vividly imagine.

Zero, ever the naughty clown, had spent much of his time pinching, grabbing, and otherwise outraging most of the women involved in the movie, so when the behind-the-barn scene was to be shot I invited every female in the company to come and watch. And as Zero, whom I adored, whisked me out of camera range, I proceeded to give him the most thorough tickling of his life. The dozens of his past victims watched the performance in stitches.

After *The Great Bank Robbery* and the one-woman tours, which now included a show made up of my favorite roles, I began to feel an itch to find regular work again. But where? Then, in the fall of 1969, I went East for my annual visit with

At last! The spirit of Phoebe Tyler rises up in all her glory! (Well, not really. It's Ruth at a Halloween costume party.)

ALL MY CHILDREN

Here's the real Phoebe, talking with Nick Davis (Larry Keith), who changed so many lives in Pine Valley when he fathered Philip Brent.

(ABC)

(ABC)

(ABC)

Top: Philip's unwed mother, Amy, gave her son to her sister, Ruth, for adoption. Complications arising from the secret of Philip's birth formed the cornerstone of the original **AMC** storyline. Shown here: Amy (Rosemary Prinz), Ruth (Mary Fickett), Philip (Richard Hatch).

Top middle: The romance of Tara (Karen Gorney) and Philip was **AMC**'s first tale of young love, and one of its most poignant.

(ABC)

Bottom: Four actresses have played the part of Tara; and two actors, the part of Philip. Shown here: Nick Benedict and Stephanie Braxton.

Members of the **AMC** cast at the time of the 1,000th show (1974): Left to right, front row: Nick Benedict (Philip), Burt Douglass (detective), Charlie Frank (Jeff), Chris Hubbell (Chuck); 2nd row: Susan Lucci (Erica), Fra Heflin (Mona), Kay Campbell (Kate Martin), Susan Blanchard (Mary Kennicott), Ruth, Mary Fickett (Ruth), Francesca James (Kitty); top row: Ray MacDonnell (Joe), Eileen Letchworth (Margo), Hugh Franklin (Charles), Judith Barcroft (Anne), Larry Keith (Nick).

(ABC)

(ABC)

Top: A typical set: the Tyler library. *Bottom:* Offscreen movers and shakers. Two of our directors: Sherrell Hoffman and Henry Kaplan.

(ABC)

Top: Phoebe in her famous (infamous?) wheelchair. *Bottom:* One of **AMC**'s major triangles: An awkward moment for Phoebe, her husband, Dr. Charles Tyler (Hugh Franklin), and his mistress, Mona Kane (Fra Heflin).

Above: Lemonade in the shade: the cozy world of Kate Martin (Kay Campbell). With her are Joe (Ray MacDonnell) and wife, Ruth (Mary Fickett). (ABC)

(ABC)

Middle above: Paul Martin (William Mooney) marries Anne Tyler (Judith Barcroft), as Joe and Ruth stand up for them. *Bottom right:* Shattered by the death of her baby, Anne (Gwyn Gilliss) suffered an apparently irreversible mental breakdown (or as **AMC** would put it, "withdrawal from reality").

(ABC)

(ABC)

Impromptu party when **AMC** went to one hour. Left to right, first
row: William Mooney (Paul), Judith Barcroft (Anne), Nancy
Frangione (Tara), Lisa Wilkinson (Nancy Grant), Fra Heflin
(Mona); second row: John Danelle (Frank Grant), Richard van
Vleet (Chuck Tyler), Daren Kelly (Dan Kennicott); third row:
Paul Gleason (David Thornton), Candice Earley (Donna Tyler),
Laurence Fleischman (Benny Sago) and Mark LaMura (Mark
Dalton); top: guess who.

(ABC)

(ABC)

(ABC)

(ABC)

Top left: Paul's dream of divorcing Anne and marrying Ellen Shepherd (Kathleen Noone) collapsed when Anne returned after three years in Oak Haven Hospital. *Top right:* Phoebe with Tad Martin (John E. Dunn) and her beloved little Charlie (Brian Lima). *Bottom right:* Murderee and murderess: Eddie Dorrance (Warren Burton) and Claudette Montgomery (Susan Plantt-Winston). *Bottom left:* Erica Kane Martin Brent Cudahy (Susan Lucci), Pine Valley's most glamorous bad girl. (Some people thought Phoebe wouldn't allow this picture to be included, but she's no fool—she knows what sells books!)

(ABC)

(ABC)   ABC

Top: At the opening of Erica's disco: Phoebe finds a new lease on
life with husband-to-be Langley Wallingford (Louis Edmonds).
Bottom left: Myrtle Lum Fargate (Eileen Herlie) talks with
Phoebe's son, Lincoln (Peter White) and bride-to-be Kelly Cole
(Francesca James) in her dressing room at The Chateau. *Bottom
right:* In this intimate scene Brooke English (Julia Barr) got her
man, Mark Dalton (Mark LaMura)—but not for long. According to
Agnes Nixon, **AMC**'s creator, the show must always reflect
changing mores, leaving the viewer to judge their meaning
and value.

Top right: Phoebe and Benny Sago (Laurence Fleischman) indulging in a bit of horseplay on the set. Phoebe and Benny became one of **AMC**'s most popular teams. *Top left:* After Larry left the show, the part of Benny was taken by Vasili Bogazianos, shown here trying to drown his sorrows as he ponders the infidelity of his wife, Edna. *Bottom left:* Frank and Nancy Grant (John Danelle and Lisa Wilkinson) have had an unhappy on-screen marriage. Off-screen, John and Lisa have a very happy marriage indeed. *Bottom right:* Estelle (Kathleen Dezina), a reformed prostitute, married her onetime pimp, Billy Clyde Tuggle (Matthew Coles), but her true love is Benny Sago.

Top: Faithless Sean Cudahy (Alan Dysert) seems bent on seducing as many women as he can. Here he works his wiles on Devon (Tricia Pursley), wife of Wally McFadden. *Bottom:* Another of Sean's targets is nurse Sybil Thorne (Linda Gibboney) who still yearns for Cliff Warner.

Top right: One of the high points of the 1980 **AMC** season was the elaborate masked ball held at the Cortlandt mansion. Phoebe, appropriately, came as the Serpent of the Nile. *Top left:* Other Tylers at the ball, Donna (Candice Earley) and Chuck (Richard van Vleet). With them is Philip's widow, Tara (Mary Lynn Blanks). *Middle:* The mysterious "woman in red" at the masked ball. Known as Monique Jonvil, she is in reality Daisy Cortlandt, the mother whom Nina never knew and assumed was dead. *Bottom:* Here the peripatetic Chuck stands beside Betsy Kennicott (Carla Dragoni) and Nina Cortlandt (Taylor Miller).

(ABC)

(ABC)

Top: The troubled Cortlandts. Palmer Cortlandt (James Mitchell) clutches daughter Nina's (Taylor Miller) hand as suitor Cliff Warner (Peter Bergman) looks on. *Bottom:* Mrs. Murdock (Elizabeth Lawrence), the Cortlandt housekeeper, with Nina. Unknown to Nina, Mrs. Murdock is Daisy's mother, and, thus, Nina's grandmother.

Top: Agnes Nixon, the brilliant lady who created **All My Children.** Seated with her in the St. Croix house where **AMC** was conceived are Susan Lucci (Erica) and Richard Shoberg (Tom Cudahy). The occasion was the on-location taping of Erica and Tom's honeymoon. *Bottom:* Here, with his wife, Rosemary, and Ruth, is **AMC** producer Jørn Winther, the best and most distinguished mentor any TV show could ask for.

(ABC)

Phoebe's family, the cast party celebrating AMC's 3,000th show in 1978. From left to right: Susan Lucci, Candice Earley, Francesca James, Robin Strasser, Peter White, Lisa Wilkinson, Bill Griffis, Larry Keith, Tricia Pursley, Kathleen Noone, Hugh Franklin, Agnes Nixon, Richard van Vleet, Bill Mooney, Julia Barr, Ruth Warrick (boys Brian Lima, John E. Dunn), Daren Kelly, Paul Gleason, Frances Heflin, Kay Campbell, Sandy Gabriel, Mary Fickett, Ray MacDonnell.

my dear friend Rosemary Prinz, with whom I had worked in *As the World Turns*. I found her trying to decide whether to be flattered or annoyed by a job she had just accepted.

"It's a new soap by Agnes Nixon," she told me. "I swore I'd never do a soap opera again after fifteen years on *As the World Turns*, but they kept agreeing to every demand I made until I finally couldn't say no. So I've agreed to do it for six months."

"Hmmm," I said. "Do you suppose there might be a part for me in it?"

Rosemary didn't think so, but suggested I talk with Agnes myself. So I phoned her from Rosemary's kitchen and asked if the new show had anything in it for me.

"I'm afraid not," Agnes said. "There are two parts still open, but one is for a younger woman and the other is for one of the two grandmothers. We have one grandmother, and I really think you're too young to do the other one."

"But I *am* a grandmother," I told her.

"Really? How old is your grandchild?"

"About eighteen months."

"Ah, well! You see, this woman's grandson is in high school, and will soon go into college and med school to be a doctor."

I pointed out that some grandmothers now go to Elizabeth Arden and look younger than their daughters, and added (in case that didn't do it) that the show's grandmother might even be her husband's second wife and therefore younger.

"You sound serious about this," Agnes said. "Do you mean you would really give up your home and move back East to do this part?"

"Yes," I said. "With a one-year firm contract, I would." I was a bit surprised at my own enthusiasm, but I realized I really did want and need a new start in a new place.

Within hours a contract was being negotiated, not for a grand salary but for one full year, with the provision that I could continue for a second year or return to California when the first year was up. I agreed, and signed it.

I also agreed to return in January, when the show was to begin, and quickly applied for a studio apartment in Lincoln Towers, which was convenient to the studio but which also supposedly had a two-year waiting list. Within weeks, thanks to Rosemary's efforts, the agent called to say I had the apartment. In January I returned to set up housekeeping in my new home with a rented bed, a borrowed card table, and two chairs.

Ironically, as I prepared to begin my role in *All My Children*, I was setting up housekeeping for the first time without any of my own children. Karen and Jon now had separate lives of their own, but it was for Tim, then only fifteen, that my heart was aching. I remembered painfully our breakfast discussion in Malibu, as the sunrise began to change the Pacific from gray to blue-green.

"Do you really have to move?" Tim had asked. He was clearly upset and puzzled, since my work in the Mostel movie had allowed us to move back into our beloved beach house.

"Yes, I do," I told him. I explained some of the realities of my situation, with runaway production at its height and job opportunities growing scarce in California. I had already postponed the move East much too long, in fact, knowing that Tim would be torn in two directions.

His voice was husky now with emotion. "I love you," he said. "And I love Dad, too." He looked at me with real pain in his young eyes. "I know *you* will be all right, but I don't think Dad can make it without me."

His decision hurt, but it also filled me with pride: At an age when most adolescents are concerned only with their own needs and desires, Tim was acting out of selfless compassion. I feared that his efforts would lead to disillusionment, as all mine had, and part of me wanted to compel him to come East with me for his own good. He was doing well at Loyola, but I had always hoped he'd have a chance to attend Williston Academy, which had done so much for his brother. And he'd be near me, safe from the maelstrom of self-destruction around Bibber. But even if I could compel him (and he was old enough, legally, to choose life with his father), the effect might be to leave him feeling alienated and guilty.

He did come East with me for the Christmas holidays, and we had happy visits with my sister Margi and her family, near Boston, and with Jon and his family in Vermont. But Tim remained adamant about his decision. At the end of the holiday visits he flew back to California and Bibber.

And I reported for my new job as the snobbish and wealthy first lady of Pine Valley. For the first time I learned the name of the character I was to play. She was the wife of one of the town's leading physicians, one Dr. Charles Tyler.

NINE

All My Children's *Children*

MY FIRST DAY AT WORK was a cruelly cold one, with a knife-edged wind blowing off the Hudson River and seeming to slice right through me. It was a far cry from Malibu's sunny days and sparkling breakers, and my new salary was a far cry from the palmy days of movies and *Peyton Place*. Still, I was eager to plunge into this new world, so I battled my way through wind and traffic to the drafty old studio on West Sixty-seventh Street where the show was to be taped.

This building, unlike our present studio, was somewhat makeshift. It had once been a stable and later a roller-skating rink, and it was so huge and so lacking in soundproofing that street noises ruined many scenes. Often the actors, weary of retakes, would try to convince the producer that tooting taxi horns or banging garbage can lids added realism, but we never got away with it. And we never managed so simple a thing as a trip to the bathroom without the most careful planning and the utmost endurance, since the dressing and makeup rooms were on the second floor and the rest rooms were in the basement, with long corridors to be traversed before one got to either destination.

The first day was memorable in many ways, not the least of which concerned my wardrobe. I had slipped on an icy patch on my way to the studio, ripping the zipper of my slacks, and since we rehearse in our street clothes the gaping zipper was a problem. The wardrobe lady kindly volunteered to fix it, but she had barely started when the call, "Phoebe on set," came over the speakers. When that call comes, you go, so I slipped on the jacket of my pantsuit and sprinted for the set sans slacks.

Luckily the jacket was cut in Edwardian style, covering the censorable parts of me, and I was wearing panty hose, which kept me looking reasonably decent.

Later, Mary Fickett told me that everyone had figured if that was my idea of rehearsal clothes, they were all in for some interesting times indeed. (And I guess they were at that. For instance, there was the time during the "flashing" fad when the crew decided to liven up the silent beauty spot at the end of the show and dared me to join them. The control rooms across the ABC network were startled indeed to get an almost-sub-liminal flash of a skimpily clad Phoebe Tyler whizzing across the set behind the titles. It was only dress rehearsal, on closed-circuit, so the censors could recover from their heart arrest.

Censorship is a curious thing, a complex procedure practiced by the network according to rules that are often difficult to understand. Too-low-cut dresses or any undue exposure are *out*, but an allowable bedroom scene may nevertheless suggest much to a viewer's imagination, despite the mandatory visi-bility of all four hands at all times outside the covers. All language is guarded most carefully: *Damn* or *hell* may be per-mitted, though only in extreme situations and never with any great frequency or regularity. And the Lord's name will never be taken in vain, or used in any other way except in a direct prayer to the Almighty. Phrases like *good Lord* and *for God's sake* are not allowed, though the writers sometimes forget and have to be reminded, usually by the performer given the line to read. (At the end of one especially long and difficult scene when Charles slammed out the door "forever," I got carried away, and, in my extremity, cried, "Oh dear God!" Instantly realizing what I'd done, I quickly added "—help me!" thus making it into a prayer instead of an exclamation. Even so, I was surprised when they let it get by.)

Another area of "censorship" is particularly tricky: ordinary words that are subject to special interpretation or misinterpre-tation by viewers. For example, we on *All My Children* tend to be shy of using words connoting mental illness. You might call this a kind of self-censorship. The number of people who might be disturbed by words such as *crazy, idiotic, imbecile, insane* or *mad* (even when used to mean *angry*) is probably small, but we try to be alert to their sensitivities. I agree with this, but I'm less sympathetic to the need to ban certain words simply because they sound like other words. Once I ad-libbed the word *niggardly*, in place of a word I had temporarily blanked on. It was declared "possibly offensive," although it had nothing whatsoever to do with a racial slur. (The root word comes from the old Norse *nygrd*, meaning stingy.) Similarly, Edna's "Honest Injun" was quickly axed. Censorship is clearly necessary in a mass-entertainment medium, but at a time when the subject matter of television drama is becoming increasingly frank, the standards of censors are bound to strike some viewers as too restrictive. On the other hand, that may be precisely the time when vigilance is required most.

As I plunged, half dressed, into that first day of *All My Children*, I could never have guessed that Phoebe Tyler would be such a large part of my life for so long. The cast was fairly small at first—an average of about eight characters appeared each day—but it grew as characters were added, and when we went to an hour-long format a few years ago, still more characters were brought in. Now an average episode will include about twenty characters. Their stories, interwoven so that each touches upon all others, could not possibly be synopsized in anything less than a book of twice this length. Much has happened in Pine Valley, to many people in many changing relationships, all in some way inter-related.

This complexity makes casting especially difficult, and this tricky job has been handled most skillfully by Joan D'Incecco for all the years we've been on—with Agnes Nixon paying close attention and reserving final say on any important character, as befits the show's creator and guiding spirit. And how does Joan spot the right actor for the part out of the dozens or even hundreds who apply? "The person has to have a *look*," Joan says. "There has to be something there beyond talent and technique, even beyond energy and vitality. A quality has to shine through, so the viewer will care about that person. Because a good actor really manipulates the viewer, and that requires something beyond a convincing performance."

A character must be cast with many things in mind beyond whether he or she looks right for the part. Will the person play well against the other actors? Is the chemistry right for scenes of passion or conflict? More important, will the person being

cast be convincing in future turns of the story, most of which
are known only to Agnes and a very few others? I can think
of no dramatic medium in which characters are allowed more
scope for change than in the daytime serial. Suppose you are
casting a girl to play a sweet, compliant wife, for instance. It
may be that the story will call for that wife to commit a crime,
or to betray her husband, or perhaps even to suffer some kind
of severe emotional disorientation. Will the sweet, soft-voiced
girl you are interviewing be convincing in those situations as
well as the present one? So when a new performer appears,
don't be too quick to say, "She doesn't *look* like Anne." Remember, you don't know what will happen to Anne in the next
month or year. Neither do I. And neither does the performer,
for that matter, a fact that can cause occasional problems.

It is for those reasons that performers' contracts are written
for two-year periods, but with the producer retaining the option
to drop the performer at the end of any thirteen-week period
along the way, with only six weeks dismissal notice required.
This lopsided contract, a carry-over from movie contracts
where option periods were six months and then yearly, is a
bone of contention between actors and management, but I feel
there is some justification because of the unique demands of
the medium. If a character—or a whole story line—fails to
click, or perhaps becomes dated by events, the producers must
have the flexibility to make changes. On the other hand, if a
character works out especially well, or a story develops dimensions not originally foreseen, it is important that the actors
be available to continue, especially since it may take over a
year for a major story line to develop and for a performer to
become totally wedded to the character in the viewer's mind.
To change this system would probably result in chaos, though
it may well come to pass. Some formula for a more reasonable
equity is inevitable, since other unions have almost total job
security. As a veteran in this business (which no one expecting
total security should even think of entering), I am aware of the
fantastic amounts of time and money—running into the millions of dollars—required to mount and produce such a show.
A painter can paint alone, a writer needs only his own imagination and a piece of paper, but an actor is dependent on a
production in which to display his talents. As his value to the

show becomes an observable fact, then he can negotiate a contract in which equity is a reasonable expectation.

So, having told you all I can about how and why a soap opera works, and having admitted that I cannot begin to summarize the decade of *All My Children* plots or even list all the performers who have figured in them, what *can* I do?

Well, why don't you come with me to a family reunion with those of us who have hung around long enough to have had some lasting effect on the story. Naturally, Kate Martin will greet us with freshly squeezed lemonade and cookies right from the oven.

THE MARTINS:

Kate Martin (Kay Campbell), mother of Dr. Joe Martin and Paul Martin; grandmother of Tara Martin Tyler Brent and Jeff Martin, and of Joe and Ruth's baby; is also great-grandmother to Little Charlie Tyler, son of Tara and Phil Brent, and to Tad Martin, formerly Tad Gardner, the child she's helped raise since Ruth and Joe adopted him. Kate is the prototype of the homey grandmother, found most often in the kitchen whipping up a batch of brownies. She is solid, supportive, wise in the way of a woman who has lived well and kept to her faith.

After a very brief stint by Kate Harrington, the role was taken over by Kay Campbell, whose Irish warmth is quite real off screen as well as before the cameras. For fifteen years she played the part of Fay on one of radio's all-time great soaps, *Ma Perkins*. Now she divides her time between a New York apartment and a home in Connecticut, where she gardens avidly and plays real-life grandmother. However, unlike Kate, she has been known to down a martini and laugh uproariously at a slightly off-color joke.

Kay is a theater buff who can always be counted on to show up when any friend opens anywhere in anything. When I played *The Madwoman of Chaillot* in New Jersey and chartered a bus to haul my New York friends there (complete with on-board champagne), Kay was in the thick of things and having a ball.

Dr. Joe Martin (Ray MacDonnell), husband of Ruth Martin, is the father of Tara and Jeff by a previous marriage and of Ruth's baby—an unexpected gift in their middle years. He is on the staff of Pine Valley Hospital and often involved, professionally as well as personally, in the lives of many other characters.

Ray went from Lawrence, Massachusetts, through Amherst College and then on to London, on a Fulbright Scholarship, to study at the Royal Academy of Dramatic Arts. When he returned to America he appeared in many television dramas such as *Studio One* and *Armstrong Circle Theater* before discovering the lure of a regular paycheck. As I had done with *As the World Turns*, he accepted a role to keep his growing family fed, then stayed in daytime television ever after, going from eight years of *Edge of Night* to more than a decade in *All My Children*.

Although Ray is often outspoken about the subordinate role of men in the soaps and the stodginess of Dr. Joe, the character he plays radiates great warmth and compassion for his wife and daughter in traumatic moments. Ray commutes happily from his home in Pleasantville, New York, reading prodigiously on the trains and leaving books all over the studio, where the rest of us can sometimes grab them up for quick doses of self-enlightenment between takes.

Ruth Martin (Mary Fickett), "Nurse Noble" of Pine Valley Hospital and wife of Dr. Joe, adopted Phil Brent, Nick Davis' child by her sister, Amy. She also shocked the nation by having an affair with the defrocked surgeon, David Thornton, and very nearly breaking up her marriage in the process. But she and Dr. Joe weathered the storm and have been rewarded by the most wonderful gift of all—a baby named Joey.

Mary Fickett, a winner of both Tony and Emmy awards, is often called the first lady of television, and not without cause. She won her Tony (named for Antoinette Perry) while still in her twenties for her dazzling performance as Eleanor Roosevelt in *Sunrise at Campobello*, and her Emmy was awarded for Ruth Martin's soul-searching speech against the slaughter of youth in senseless wars. Between those two awards she has established herself as one of the most talented and versatile performers in our business.

Her private life, too, has been something close to pure soap opera. While still playing Eleanor Roosevelt on Broadway she fell madly in love with a handsome actor several years her senior. He proposed, and they went to get the blessing of her

father, the well-known director of *Lux Radio Theater* on radio
and television, and a man of mercurial but authoritarian tem-
perament. Homer Fickett, outraged that a divorced man dare
woo his beloved daughter, accused him of evil intent and flatly
forbade the marriage.

Mary, as usual, bent to her father's strong will and broke
up the relationship with the actor named Brian Keith; but soon
after, she went to California and there—away from Homer's
watchful eye—she met another actor who wooed and wed her.
Together they became parents of the two children, Bronwynn
and Kenyon, who are the lights of her life. The marriage was
not destined to last, but with the help of her friends Mary has
come through the anguish of a divorce. Moving from her elegant but burdensome town house into the same family-oriented
apartment building where Fra lives may have helped to give
her a new lease on life. In any event she is now blissfully happy
married to television director Allen Fristoe, who shares her
Scottish ancestry and affection for the Highlands. They claim
their honeymoon in Scotland was almost like a homecoming.

Mary played a central role in one of the most poignant and
thought-provoking sequences ever shown on daytime television. This concerned the sadistic, unprovoked rape of Ruth
Martin by Ray Gardner. The act itself was of course not ex-
plicitly shown, but, more to the point, its pathological motivations and appalling personal and legal consequences—all
carefully researched by Agnes—were explored in depth. Society has too often failed to understand the essential nature of
rape: a hate-filled crime that has nothing to do with normal
sexuality. Agnes has done many admirable things, but her
tasteful, yet unflinchingly candid treatment of this repellent
social problem must be one of her finest achievements.

Paul Martin (William Mooney), attorney and brother of
Dr. Joe, was married first to Anne Tyler, then to Margo Flax,
then again to Anne, from whom he sought a divorce in order
to marry Ellen Shepherd. With Anne's return from her years
in Oak Haven Hospital, the divorce has been abandoned, but
not Paul's dreams of a life with Ellen.

If Paul Martin is moody and sometimes petulant, Bill Mooney is the direct opposite—a cheerful, confident man addicted
to jogging and devoted to his opera-singer wife, Valerie, and

their twin sons, Sean and Will. He lives in New Brunswick, New Jersey, and is very active in his church, where he supervises an annual fund-raising dinner of Cordon Bleu caliber which is always oversubscribed. He has also branched out into directing, staging *The Robber Bridegroom* in an outdoor amphitheater before four thousand appreciative New Jerseyites. He has gotten rave reviews for his imaginative direction of the Off-Broadway musical *Jazz*.

Perhaps more remarkable than Bill's accomplishments, however, is the generosity that led the Mooneys to take a Vietnamese family into their home for over a year, until these refugees could learn English and establish their own life. Characteristically, Paul dismisses the whole experience as no big deal. "We had extra room in our house, and we felt it would be a good experience for the boys. Besides, sometimes you have to do more than just talk about ideals."

Tara Martin Tyler Brent (orginally Karen Gorney, presently Mary Lynn Blanks) is daughter of Dr. Joe and the mother of Little Charlie by Phil Brent. Married to and divorced from Chuck Tyler, and then married to Phil Brent, she is currently widowed but probably not for long. One of the pivotal characters in the show's story line, Tara is the marrying kind, a woman forever in need of a strong man's support and love, and men invariably respond to her need.

There have been several Taras in the show's long run, including Karen Gorney, Stephanie Braxton, and Nancy Frangione. The incumbent joined us in 1979, after Tara's six-month absence during which she and Phil had moved to Washington where his hush-hush job with a CIA-type agency was based. When Phil went off on a mysterious Caribbean mission, Tara returned to Pine Valley with Little Charlie, thus complicating life for Chuck Tyler and his chronically insecure wife, Donna. With Phil's death, Donna's worst fears will be realized, and Chuck will once again be drawn into the world of the wife and son he has never stopped loving.

Karen Gorney, the original Tara, was the perfect, ethereal, love-struck maiden, though she was already married and a full ten years older than her on-screen age. She and Richard Hatch (the original Phil Brent) were beautiful and totally believable together, but when—after two years—Richard left for California, Karen began to get restless, and when her contract was up, she too decided to head West.

I had private doubts about whether intellectual Karen would really like living in California. A Brandeis graduate, she came from a cosmopolitan, musically talented family, and music and painting were her real passions, with acting running third. "You have a brain," I told her. "You are used to intelligent, cultivated people."

She went anyway. When she returned a year later, to resume the part of Tara as Stephanie Braxton's replacement, she admitted I had been right. "I think that for every six months you spend in California, you lose another IQ point," she said ruefully.

She had come back home the hard way, having left both Hollywood and her marriage behind to sing and play her guitar across the country, often literally singing for her supper. She arrived, exhausted and broke, eager to resume a steady job in television, and the fans' "real" Tara returned to Pine Valley.

However, her heart was still in her music. That preoccupation, plus some life experiences of a harsher nature, made it difficult for her to be the sweet, compliant, nonassertive Tara, ever following the advice of father, brother, lover—any male in her life. Karen had outgrown "Juliet," and she now found the romanticism of Agnes Nixon's beloved Wordsworth sometimes difficult to take, though that poet's "Ode: Intimations of Immortality" was virtually a theme song for Tara and Phil.

One day in her script she encountered once again the familiar lines:

> What though the radiance which was once so bright
> Be now forever taken from my sight,
>   Though nothing can bring back the hour
> Of splendour in the grass, of glory in the flower;
>   We will grieve not, rather find
>   Strength in what remains behind . . .

This day, bored with the lines, Karen gave them an intentionally singsong reading. Although the scene was allowed to air, afterwards there was a good deal of criticism of the liberty

Karen had taken. In fact it was the final symptom of her growing estrangement from the part of Tara, and soon thereafter, by mutual agreement, she left the show.

Karen's abrupt dismissal was probably a good thing for all concerned—herself included. She had done an amateurish and self-indulgent thing (as, I suppose, I had done years before when I misplayed my part in *Take Me Along*), and now she was going to have to pay for it by going out into the world and proving she could be professional. And prove it she did! First with a solid, demanding part in the hit movie *Saturday Night Fever*, and more recently with the publication of an album of her own music. I'd say that she is now well on the road to success and I am delighted: She has earned it and she deserves it.

Mary Lynn Blanks is our present Tara. An accomplished actress with a considerable amount of regional theater behind her, she was born and educated in Florida and, until she reached college age, never doubted that she was going to be a scientist. Then she took a drama course at Miami University and suddenly knew that she could only be happy in the theater. "I auditioned for Tara no less than three times," Mary Lynn told me, "beginning way back in 1969. Now, at last, I've got my dream role." With tears that are ever accessible and absolutely genuine, she may be closest of all to Agnes' basic concept of Tara as a sweet maiden grown into a tender, compassionate, vulnerable young woman and mother.

If it is true that America is turning back to romance in its popular entertainments, I'd have to say that *All My Children* has been there all along. Tara and Phil, Jeff and Mary, Cliff and Nina—at no time have we been without at least one story line dealing with idealized young love. There are conflicts, problems, even tragedies, to be sure, but through it all the emotions of the young lovers run pure, intense, and full of yearning. Agnes Nixon may have a sharp eye for timely issues, but she also has a heart that understands the simple things that always move us most.

Dr. Jeff Martin (Charles Frank), son of Dr. Joe and brother of Tara, first married Erica, who fiercely resented having to live in the Martin household and forced him to establish a separate home of their own. When Erica realized she could never command Jeff's undivided attention, she sought a career. Their marriage ended when she aborted their child rather than jeopardize her job as television's "Lacy Girl." A bit later Jeff found his perfect mate in the sweet, wholesome young nurse, Mary Kennicott, the very antithesis of the sophisticated, ego-centric Erica.

Mary Kennicott Martin (Susan Blanchard), was a nurse at Pine Valley Hospital and the sister of Dan Kennicott. The fans went into deep shock and mourning when Mary was killed by kidnappers holding Little Phillip hostage in her apartment. However, it had become necessary to remove Jeff and Mary from Pine Valley, since Susan Blanchard and the man who played her on-screen husband, Charles Frank, were both de-termined to move to the West Coast and tackle the world of nighttime television. Charles landed the lead in *Young Maverick* and Susan became the No Nonsense Panty Hose girl, at a salary certain to turn her ex-colleagues green with envy. Eventually Charles and Susan became man and wife in real life.

A few years later James Sullivan played Jeff Martin opposite Robin Strasser as Dr. Christina Karras. Jeff helped her to overcome her neurotic attachment to her father, and married her, but once again the Martin family influence was too great and they moved to San Francisco.

Tad Martin (John E. Dunn), is the son of blackmailer and rapist Ray Gardner, adopted by Ruth and Joe Martin after his father's imprisonment. He lives in the Martin household. (Orig-inally Matthew Anton played the part, but he left for a role in a movie with Brooke Shields.) Now in adolescence, Tad is discovering girls, to the everlasting disgust of his younger "cousin," Charlie. Ruth's fanatical protectiveness of her natural baby makes adopted Tad feel an outsider.

John E. Dunn, who has already won an award as Best Juvenile Actor on Television, is a charming and very serious young man who is scrupulously saving his salary for college (Fordham is his goal). One of his greatest assets is the loving support he unfailingly gets from his large, ever-joyful family.

Margo Flax Martin (Eileen Letchworth), was the mother of Claudette Montgomery and briefly was the (much older) wife of Paul Martin, in between his marriages to Anne Tyler. The role of Margo was written specifically to lure the fine stage actress Eileen Letchworth back to the soaps, and it provided Agnes Nixon with an opportunity to weave the theme of cosmetic surgery into the plot of the show. Margo's doomed attempt to retain a younger man's love culminated in the dramatic unveiling of Eileen's "new" face, a moving moment for viewers and cast alike. Margo's desperate, last-gasp ploy of faking a pregnancy and bargaining to buy a black-market baby was just too much, and the marriage ended. She went off to the Caribbean and there (offscreen) wed a "banana baron."

THE TYLERS:

Phoebe Tyler (Ruth Warrick), second wife of Dr. Charles Tyler, mother of Anne and Lincoln, and step-grandmother of Dr. Chuck Tyler, has most recently become the wife of "Professor" Langley Wallingford. Phoebe is opinionated, imperious, sometimes even arrogant, but she stands up for her beliefs and fights for her family's welfare, according to her own lights. Her reverence for marriage and home led her to refuse Charles his divorce for many years, even though they were separated and he made no secret of his love for Mona Kane, the femme fatale of the desk set. Only under the spell of the slick con artist, Langley, did Phoebe permit her convictions to waver, and she will no doubt pay for that slip dearly.

As you might expect, I'll have a good deal more to say about Phoebe later on. But for now, let's go on to meet the other members of the Tyler clan.

Dr. Charles Tyler (Hugh Franklin), chief of staff at Pine Valley Hospital and longtime husband of Phoebe, recently married Mona Kane, his secretary for many years. He is father of Anne and Lincoln, and grandfather of Chuck. His preoccupation with his career, and later with Mona, made it impossible for him to fulfill his role of father and husband to Phoebe's satisfaction, though she refused to hear of divorce for many years. Now married to Mona, the soft-spoken and devoted woman who represents almost the direct opposite of Phoebe, it remains to be seen if he will be happy.

Hugh Franklin, the handsome and distinguished actor who returned from a premature retirement to play Charles Tyler, has had a long and remarkable career that included roles opposite Jane Cowl, Ina Claire, and Katharine Cornell. He is a dignified, very literate man and a most serious actor, respected by everyone in the cast. However, his sobriety has occasionally brought out the imp in me.

Once, after one of Charles and Phoebe's classic fight scenes had begun to seem just a bit too familiar to me, I added a line. Charles had just announced that he wanted a divorce, and Phoebe, as usual, had shouted "Never, never, never!" Then, as he was turning to stalk out of the room, I added, "You can't leave me, Charles. I'm pregnant."

Hugh gaped at me as if I'd gone mad, and you could almost see him reviewing the script in his mind to see if such a pre-posterous line might have escaped him. And then he heard the chortling from the crew, and he broke into loud guffaws.

Hugh is a man of total concentration, and once on a flight to the West Coast, where we were to appear on the game show *Family Feud*, the stewardess bent over Hugh to ask him his name.

Lost in the crossword puzzle, he said, "Dry martini."

Our roars of laughter snapped him to attention, and when the other stewardess appeared a few minutes later to take his luncheon order, he was ready. "Hugh Franklin," he announced firmly.

Hugh is a dear man. He is most proud of his real wife, author Madeleine l'Engle, whose longtime classic, *A Wrinkle in Time*, will soon be a Disney movie. I just don't know what Phoebe will *do* without him.

Anne Tyler Martin (Gwyn Gilliss), Charles and Phoebe's daughter, has been much married—to a European count before our story began, to Nick Davis, to Paul Martin, and a second time to Paul after his marriage to Margo. After the crib death of their baby, Anne withdrew from reality and was confined to Oak Haven Hospital, unaware of her marriage or mother-hood. During the three years of her illness, Paul fell in love with Ellen Shepherd, a friend from their high-school days, and planned to marry her. Anne's recovery and return to Pine Valley brought great pain to all three.

There have been several Annes over the years, including Diana de Vegh, Joanna Miles, and Judith Barcroft, who is married to our head writer, Wisner Washam. (Wisner had been Neil Simon's executive stage manager and met Judith when she rehearsed for a part in a Simon play.) She is also the mother of our first Little Phillip. Ian Washam was a pink-cheeked, golden-curled cherub of four, and Judith was quite apprehensive about what effect all that unreal attention might have on him. He was marvelous on the set, but a short while later the powers that be decided to accelerate the story line and make Little Phillip several years older, so he could be given dialogue beyond a four-year-old's abilities.

This situation was explained to Ian, but he was crushed. Wisner and Judith even let him watch his replacement, Brian Lima, so it would be clear that the part now called for a much older boy. Still he was hurt, and he continued to bring it up for some time afterward. Judith's motherly instincts had been correct: Fame did have its price. How many people are has-beens at the age of four?

Judith's instincts about her son may have been good, but her judgment about men was not always quite so reliable. In the years before she met and married Wisner, she had a mad crush on a young actor named Darren McGavin. They became engaged and talked seriously of marriage. (Later Darren moved to the West Coast and she remained in New York, so the relationship began to simmer down.) At about this same time another close friend of mine, Sally Kemp, was doing summer stock with a handsome young Irish actor and fell madly in love with him. As she told me about it during a visit, I had an eerie sense of déjà vu. Sure enough, her great love was the very same Darren McGavin! And you think soap operas are too free with coincidence?

When Judith retired from *All My Children* to resume work in the theater (she recently took over the lead in the award-winning *The Elephant Man*), Anne went offscreen for three years—the period of her incarceration in Oak Haven Hospital. When Anne was pronounced cured and reentered Pine Valley society, her role had been assumed by a young actress named Gwyn Gilliss. Gwyn's initial appearances were startling in that she actually looked heartrendingly like someone in the throes of a serious illness. She later confessed to me that it wasn't all acting. "This show actually saved my life," she said. "I was so pale and emaciated because I was recently divorced, couldn't find work, and had run out of residuals and had used up all my unemployment payments. I was discouraged and exhausted, so the part of Anne really was a 'life saver' for me."

I am happy to report that both Anne and Gwyn have recovered beautifully since those first trying days. Recently Gwyn asked a fellow passenger on a bus if he could change a dollar bill. He said he was sorry that he couldn't but added that he was "glad you got your mind back." Speaking for the entire cast, so say we all.

Lincoln Tyler (Peter White), attorney and brother of Anne, was married to Ruth Martin's sister Amy and later to Kitty Shea, a girl from the wrong side of the tracks. After Kitty died he fell in love with her twin sister, Kelly Cole, defended her in the Eddie Dorrance murder trial, eventually obtained her release, and married her.

Lanky, prematurely gray, Peter White has that patrician look befitting a Tyler, though he has appeared as the villain in countless movies and television plays. From Cape Cod by way of Northwestern, Agnes Nixon's alma mater, Peter won great acclaim in the stage and movie versions of *Boys in the Band*, in which he played the only straight man at the gay party. However, it was his role as a murderer on one television show that led to his most memorable encounter with a fan.

"I came home from an audition to find this guy standing behind my refrigerator with a gun pointed at me," he says. "The kid had ransacked the apartment without finding anything he wanted, but when I came in he recognized me from that part and started asking me what it felt like to kill someone. Naturally that didn't reassure me very much." Pete smiles wryly, shivering a bit at the memory. "He stayed for a long time, alternately threatening me and admiring me. Then he came across my bank book and found out I had less money than he did, so he decided to take pity on me. He left, but he made me autograph a picture for him first."

I'm sure Pete kept his cool, as he has done when modeling agencies seeking a "Peter White type" have turned him down: Too recognizable, they say. It's a curiosity of the business that Peter White can't make the grade as a Peter White type.

Peter was not the original Lincoln Tyler. Jimmy Karen was an early casualty, mainly because he was only a few years younger than I. He went on to be, for years, the spokesman for Pathmark in television commercials. Paul Dumont, who followed in the role, was an urbane and handsome French Canadian, but he was undone by strange accents on wrong English syllables. I would coach him carefully, but in emotional scenes the odd pronunciations always emerged. We are still close personal friends and we often laugh about those times— in between his musical comedy engagements, the commercials (whose audiences adore his French accent), and his brilliant conversions of lofts in New York's Soho district. After Paul, Nicholas Pryor had a brief tenure, then he moved to Seattle.

But once Peter came on the scene he *was* Lincoln Tyler. People even assured me we bore a strong family resemblance to each other. All the more reason, then, for me to be so downcast when learned the dismaying news that Peter was to be written out of the show. Apparently it was felt that the Lincoln Tyler story line, having exhausted all the possible Kitty/Kelly combinations, and having reached a kind of climax in the solving of the Eddie Dorrance murder, had no place to go. Thus Lincoln is to move to the nearby town of King's Cross (from which, I hope, he may someday return). Ironically, the producers had had to fight to keep Peter on for the last two contract periods because he wanted to move to California.

Certainly we all miss the pleasure of working with this gentle, talented man who had originally been educated to become an Episcopalian minister. ("When I informed my bishop that I thought I oughtn't to take my vows because my heart lay with the theater," Peter once told me, "he was wonderful—no recrimination, no effort to coerce or persuade, no guilt. In fact, he told me I'd be surprised to learn how many crossovers there were between the divinity school and the drama department. Both ways.") The warm compassionate nature that would have made Peter such a fine minister has made him a wonderful human being. With his departure I felt as though I had lost a valued friend, and Phoebe a beloved son.

Dr. Chuck Tyler (Richard van Vleet), grandson of Dr. Charles Tyler and step-grandson of Phoebe, formerly married to Tara and currently married to onetime hooker Donna Beck. A close high-school chum of both Phil Brent and Tara, Chuck married Tara when Phil was lost in Vietnam so that her child, Little Phillip, could have a father. When Phil returned, both

Tara and the child were torn between the two, and eventually Tara divorced Chuck and married Phil. (Little Phillip meanwhile had become Little Charlie, since he believed Chuck to be his father. The boy's confusion has been doubly compounded with Phil's death, as shown by his confused desire to take Phil's last name—Brent—while retaining Chuck's first name. In truth, the boy has neither Brent nor Tyler blood in his veins since his father, Phil, was Nick Davis' illegitimate son by Amy, before she married a Tyler. I trust you are following all this.) Chuck has never stopped loving Tara and Little Charlie, though he respected her position as his friend's wife. Phil's death will complicate life for them all, just as the question of Phil's origin provided the original complications for the families of Pine Valley.

The original Chuck was played by Jack Stauffer. Though probably much in fashion now, Jack was something of an anachronism in the early seventies, flawlessly projecting the image of the young man who is square, preppy, and proud of it. Though the best of friends, he and I argued endlessly about Vietnam. Jack loyally supported the administration's war policies, whereas I—who played the part of his conservative grandmother—in real life was an ardent attender of peace rallies and regularly appeared on the set wearing "Make Love, Not War" T-shirts.

After Jack married and left the show, the part of Chuck was given to a blond, strapping young actor named Chris Hubbell. Chris was amiable, hardworking, and serious about his part, but he simply hadn't yet had the professional experience to enable him to cope easily with the fearsome pressures to which actors in soaps are subjected. He developed a thing about live cameras. Whenever the red light went on, his normally strong voice would dwindle away to near inaudibility. In an effort to bring his voice level up, I encouraged him to shout all his lines at rehearsals, and Chris worked diligently with outside voice teachers to try to achieve the same result. But it's hard trying to acquire overnight techniques most actors spend a lifetime developing, and eventually Chris left the show to return to his home on the West Coast.

Our present Chuck, Richard van Vleet, called Van by his friends, hails from Colorado. He too has served his time on the West Coast. After touring with a USO troupe in *Gigi,* Van settled in Los Angeles and played everything from farce to Shakespeare there, but ended up teaching drama at Central Arizona College to support his family.

"Talk about irony," he says. "One day some of my students heard Fernando Lamas and Florence Henderson talking about new talent on the Merv Griffin show. They both mentioned a guy named Richard van Vleet as one of the most talented newcomers they'd seen. And where was this talented newcomer? Sitting in Arizona because he couldn't get an acting job."

Van, who now lives in central Connecticut with his wife, Kris, and their two children, commutes over a hundred miles to and from work.

"You know, when I took the part on *All My Children* I thought I had sold out." He smiled. "I was surprised and delighted to find myself involved in the first ensemble acting company I'd come across outside of stock companies. It's demanding work and I love it."

Most of us feel that way. If we didn't, we wouldn't have been around for so long, and the show wouldn't be number one among the soaps.

Donna Beck Tyler (Candice Earley) is a runaway teenager coerced into prostitution but "redeemed" by Chuck, who married her for the wrong reasons and now regrets it. Recovering from the shock of a stillborn baby, Donna launched a tentative career as a singer at The Chateau, replacing the imprisoned Kelly Cole.

Candy *is* a singer, in supper clubs and in the Broadway show *Grease.* She's an Oklahoma girl, though her parents traveled much during her childhood (her father was an army officer) and her roots are everywhere.

Another of those odd coincidences that are supposed to happen only in soap operas occurred on the day of a party for Candy, arranged on the set of *All My Children* to celebrate her wedding, scheduled for a few days later.

It was lunch break, and she had only one scene left to do. It was a difficult one in which Donna wanders forlornly in a Center City rainstorm, clutching a bottle of sleeping pills and planning suicide. Candy wasn't looking forward to it; none of us like to stand under the studio rain machines, which catch water in a tarpaulin and recycle it through overhead pipes onto the dripping, shivering actors. But today she was too happy to care. She and her husband-to-be—a young ABC business-controls expert—were to leave for Fort Sills the next day to be married in the post chapel. She was positively glowing, and I found myself wondering how she could bring herself down enough to do Donna's tragic scene.

Someone told her her mother was on the phone, and Candy trotted off to take it, to discuss last-minute wedding arrangements.

In moments we heard a scream, and when she returned she was pale and trembling. And we learned, then, what news her mother had called to deliver: The previous evening Candy's brother had died tragically.

Though still in near shock, Candy somehow got through Donna's scene, clutching the bottle of pills with white knuckles and crying tears we knew were all too real. When it was over she stood there, dripping wet and with tears still streaming. I went to her and gathered her into my arms.

"You'll get all wet," she sobbed.

"Never mind that," I said. "Just listen to me. Nothing can bring your brother back, and only time can ease your pain. But you mustn't let this tragedy scuttle your life. You've got to hold on to love more fiercely than ever now, and say yes to life with all your strength."

Still sobbing, she fled to her dressing room, leaving me to wonder if I had done the right thing. Although I believed in the truth of what I had said, this might not be the proper moment to offer such advice. With all my heart I hoped I hadn't unintentionally added to her distress.

We all left for the weekend. On Monday the following telegram arrived:

Dear All: There is no way we can thank you enough for your kindness, understanding, and concern on Friday. Peter and I have decided to go ahead with all the plans for the wedding as all of us here feel that life is to be lived. What a comfort to know that the people I work with are so loving and caring. Again, many thanks.

—Candy and Peter

Amy Tyler (Rosemary Prinz), sister of Ruth Martin and once married to Lincoln Tyler, is mother of Phil Brent out of wedlock. Amy had gone away to have the baby in secret, and Ruth then arranged to adopt it, keeping the child's origins hidden for many years, even from her then-husband. That husband died in an auto accident, and Ruth married Joe Martin, though young Phil retained the Brent name. It was this secret illegitimate birth, and the consequent complications, that was really the genesis of *All My Children*. However, when the six-month contract expired, Rosemary elected to withdraw. Phil's doting "Aunt Amy" (my beloved friend in real life) has been lost to *All My Children* in the tangled skein of plotting, but Phil and his natural father, Nick Davis, remained in Pine Valley for many years.

Brooke English (Julia Barr), Phoebe's niece and permanent guest in the Tyler mansion, has had affairs with Benny Sago, Dan Kennicott, and Mark Dalton, for whom she still harbors an unrequited love. To punish Mark for his rejection of her, Brooke flirted with Eddie Dorrance, a foolish playing-with-fire that led to her rape, which in turn gave rise to the show's second abortion. (Rape is one of the reasons most often accepted for abortion, since it might be impossible to love and nurture a child born of such brutal violation, as even most adamant right-to-lifers are forced to agree.) Brooke, the spoiled brat who brought Benny home to horrify Phoebe years ago, has shown signs of maturity of late, and Phoebe has hopes for her eventual recognition of Phoebe's values. Meanwhile, Brooke's broken heart has gotten some help in mending from Erica's ex-husband Tom Cudahy, though the two had to cope with Erica's attempt to part them.

Julia is an adorable girl and a fine actress (nominated for an Emmy in 1980), growing steadily in her role just as Brooke is growing in her life. However, she inadvertently caused a Phoebe-Ruth identity crisis when Brooke went away for that abortion, because it happened while I was briefly absent from the show, and I was not aware of the plot development. (This often happens even when we are not away, since each performer receives only those scripts in which he or she appears. If something happens in a script we didn't see, we may not learn about it until we see the actual show.)

In this case, the subject came up in a casual conversation

with a new acquaintance who was telling me the plot of the show. (People often do that, though I cannot imagine how they could believe us ignorant of the very story in which we appear. In this case, however, the storyteller was right.) When he got to Brooke's abortion, I stopped him.

"No, that was *Erica*," I said. "*She* had the abortion, not Brooke."

"No, I mean the one *Brooke* had," he insisted.

"My niece did *not* have an abortion," I found myself saying in Phoebe's sharpest no-nonsense voice.

He looked at me rather uneasily, as if unsure of whether his leg were being pulled. "Don't you remember?" he said. "Eddie Dorrance raped her, and she had the abortion right away, and..."

I felt my heart stop, my stomach turned over, my face flushed, and my palms grew damp. My Brooke! Oh, poor baby—and I wasn't with her! So *that's* why she went to stay with Mark!

My head was trying to tell me I was reacting irrationally, but my emotions paid no attention. Somewhere deep inside, Ruth knew Brooke's abortion was fiction, but for a brief time Phoebe took over, and our nervous system registered quite real shock and pain. In moments such as that, Ruth has to take a firm grip on reality until Phoebe has subsided.

OTHERS IN PINE VALLEY:

Nick Davis (Larry Keith) was the stranger in town who changed so many lives when he fathered Phil Brent. Since this was the original story line of the show, it bears repeating here in some detail.

As a teenager, Nick had conveniently left Pine Valley to join the Navy, assuming that Amy's pregnancy would be taken care of. When he returned twenty years later, every effort was made to keep the secret of his paternity from him, but when he learned the truth he insisted on claiming his son, much to the boy's confusion. Fatherhood did bring a degree of maturity to this amoral, egocentric, self-gratifying man, but not much. His arrant charm held a fascination for women, including even the discriminating Phoebe Tyler, whose involvement in one of his schemes almost ended in her seduction. However, when he abruptly transferred his amorous attentions to Anne, he incurred Phoebe's undying enmity.

Phoebe, who understands sexual attraction quite well, urged the shy and withdrawn Anne to indulge herself if she felt the need but not to mistake passion for love, and above all not to marry such an unlikely life partner. But Anne, weary of proper types, was brought alive by Nick's carnality, and the two were wed.

Once married into this socially prominent family, Nick made the mistake of trying to become part of the very world Anne had grown sick of, though his attempts to become a stock-broker, to lunch at the club, succeeded only in displaying his inadequacies. Frustrated, drinking heavily, he decided Anne needed a child, but that effort also failed. As his new life slipped away, he reacted by retreating into his old amoral ways and treating Anne with increasing harshness.

Returning to his first business, a dance studio, he promptly got his assistant, Kitty Shea, pregnant. Kitty's problems were aided by therapy, which helped her gain confidence in herself, and in time she met and married Linc, while Anne (aided by Phoebe) turned to her safe and civilized high-school beau, Paul Martin, the man she should have married in the first place.

But Nick was not out of her blood, and on a New York buying trip for her boutique, she ran into Nick and again fell under his spell. (A trip to New York usually signals a fall from grace for the people of Pine Valley.) Nevertheless, in the end she managed to resist Nick's importunate advances and asked that he drive her home. On the return trip they were in a car crash, resulting in a near-fatal head injury for Anne, requiring a long recovery. (Which allowed Judith Barcroft to produce her second child, Amy, in real life.) During this time Paul, already disillusioned by Anne's seeming infidelity, fell into Margo's trap, leading to his divorce from Anne and marriage to Margo.

Eventually Anne and Paul were remarried, but this time they were hit by the double tragedy of their child's mental retardation, followed by her crib death. And this, in turn, led to Anne's withdrawal from reality and her commitment to Oak Haven Hospital, from which she emerged three years later. Nick Davis, meanwhile, started a supper club, The Chateau, moved on to an affair with Erica, then moved from Pine Valley altogether, to take a position with a Chicago restaurant chain. The Chateau, however, remains one of Pine Valley's favorite gathering spots and the scene of many dramatic incidents.

Thus, as I have said, Nick Davis, as played by Larry Keith, was one of the central figures in a basic story from which has evolved ten years of ever-expanding, highly complex plotting.

Larry Keith is a fun-loving man, and once, during one of our early scenes, his lines had to do with the only proper way to mix a martini. As we rehearsed I jokingly told the prop man to make mine Beefeater's, and Larry overheard. Unbeknownst to anyone, he substituted a real bottle of Beefeater gin for the prop bottle, and in run-through I was startled to taste a very real martini instead of the water I had expected.

I went along with the gag. The next scene, in which several people arrived for dinner, involved more martinis. By the time we got to the taping, the cocktail-party atmosphere was extraordinarily convincing, but when Larry confessed to our producer afterward, Bud Kloss turned absolutely purple. We never did it again.

Larry may just be the most relaxed actor I have ever worked with. Once he fell sound asleep during one of Mona's long recaps over coffee in the kitchen. "I couldn't believe it," Fra said later. "I kicked him under the table. He woke up, carried on as though nothing had happened, and actually made his siesta work for him in the scene."

Larry's case illustrates one way in which teamwork operates the show. Agnes had originally seen Nick's role as more pivotal than central—that is, his actions were needed to set in motion a basic story line, yet thereafter, his personal involvement was not strictly necessary to the story. But everyone connected with the show was so impressed with the way Larry was playing Nick that by a kind of mutual accord it was decided that Nick should be included in the long-term story projections. Thus Nick Davis stayed on, to be the source of years of additional fascinating complications in the lives of Pine Valley's citizens.

Opening The Chateau was Larry's idea, and Agnes Nixon went along with it gladly because it gave us a chance to use his fine singing voice in the show. He had sung the Professor Higgins role in *My Fair Lady* on Broadway and in touring companies, and it would have been a shame to waste all that talent. Larry was also a hotshot pilot, a *bon vivant*, and a man with sartorial flair (much of Nick Davis' memorable wardrobe was actually Larry's own), but over the years he has settled down considerably, just as Nick Davis did in Pine Valley. Larry has worked in both SAG and AFTRA (two theatrical unions), and has served as president of the New York chapter of the Screen Actors' Guild, where he has labored indefatigably for better pay and treatment for daytime performers.

When Larry decided to leave the show, we all gathered, at his invitation, in the Belasco Room at Sardi's for a farewell party. The drinks flowed and the world-famous cannelloni was too tempting to resist, as were the shrimps creole, the Virginia baked ham, the rare roast beef, and the infamous Sardi's cheesecake, the ruination of many a girlish figure.

Larry did a masterly performance as master of ceremonies. I still recall his toast to darling Rosemary Prinz, who had been gone from our show for years. She had appeared in *Prisoner of Second Avenue* for six months in Chicago, and then in national tours across America. The following night she was to open in a Broadway play opposite Jack Lemmon. Said Larry, lifting his glass, "Rosemary is living proof that there is life after soap opera."

Larry has been sorely missed. His Rhett Butler brand of masculinity and his sardonic sense of humor are rare. Who knows—maybe one day Nick Davis will return once again to Pine Valley. And frankly, my dear, we *will* give a damn.

Erica Kane Martin Brent Cudahy (Susan Lucci) is the much-married, beautiful "bad woman" of Pine Valley. Her immoderate selfishness causes constant problems for all who have to deal with her, as well as regularly denying her the happiness she is sure she deserves. She has been married to Dr. Jeff Martin, to Phil Brent, and most recently to the football hero Tom Cudahy, proprietor of Pine Valley's other restaurant, The Goalpost. In each marriage, as in her abortive modeling and acting careers, her conniving and duplicity have cost her dearly. She has returned to Pine Valley from a disastrous attempt to breach the walls of Hollywood, so we can assume that yet another man will be smitten, and will live to regret it. (As did Nick Davis, her lover after her divorce from Phil Brent, though Nick was at least her match. Erica still dreams that he will return, though she isn't sure whether to be thrilled or frightened at the thought.)

One of Erica's greatest coups had to do with the opening of the disco she had long dreamed of owning. For the gala occasion we invited Dick Cavett to make a guest appearance on the show, which he did with his usual witty aplomb.

Susan Lucci, perhaps more than anyone on the show except myself, bears the stigma of the character she plays in the minds of fans. When Phoebe makes a public appearance she can be sure of one question, asked without fail by some quite serious fan: "Is Susan Lucci really like Erica?"

The questioner quite often seems to expect—even to want—to hear that Susan *is* the bitchy Erica, so convincingly has she built the character over the years. Besides, just look at her. With all that chiseled beauty, how could she not be spoiled and manipulative?

Sorry, but the answer is no, Susan is not the least bit like Erica. In the early days of *All My Children* she could light up a room just by entering it, and nothing has changed in the ten years we've worked together. But Susan has changed in other ways, has matured in her work and her marriage.

Born of an Italian father and a mother of Swedish descent, Susan grew up in Westchester County, near New York City. She was educated at Marymount College in Tarrytown, a prestigious Catholic girls' school that emphasizes the traditional roles of wife and mother for its students. Though no slave to convention, Susan has followed those traditions in many ways, especially in her happy marriage to Swiss hotel executive Helmuth Huber and in her role as mother to blonde and beautiful Liza Victoria and young Andreas, born recently during Erica's absence in Hollywood. (Susan left the show on January 17, had her baby February 28, and returned in May, as Erica returned to Pine Valley.)

Susan has a charming husband, two lovely children, a perfectly gorgeous home on Long Island, and a career that most actresses would envy whether they admit it or not. (When asked if she yearned to leave soap opera she said, "Why should I? Where else could I play Scarlett O'Hara fifty-two weeks a year for ten years?")

Susan is beautiful, and that never hurts. But she is much too talented and far too nice ever to have to try to gain happiness by means of Erica's childish manipulations. Yet the stigma of her role remains. She and I once received what must be the ultimate hate letter. Our correspondent had cut out pictures of us, pasted them on a sheet of paper, and drawn long forked tongues protruding from our mouths. "You and your serpent tongues will be punished," read the irate caption.

Tom Cudahy (Richard Shoberg), former football star and proprietor of The Goalpost Restaurant, is still trying to untangle himself from his many problems with Erica, to whom he was married before her disco failed and she fled Pine Valley for a short-lived career in Hollywood.

Richard hails from Michigan. I had somehow gotten the idea that he came from a typically conservative midwestern background, so I was curious how his family had reacted to his marriage to an exquisitely beautiful Vietnamese girl, Var-\porn. When I asked him, he grinned. "Frankly, they didn't \urn a hair," he said. "When I'd come home from college, I'd generally brought a black girl with me. So they weren't surprised that I finally decided on an interracial marriage."

Before settling down in Pine Valley, Dick spent an entire year roaming the country, making his way by singing and playing his guitar. "You really learn a lot out there," he told me. "It got a little hairy sometimes, but it was a great experience."

Sean Cudahy (Alan Dysert) is Tom's free-and-easy kid brother. He has come to live with Tom while attending college, but he is spending more time with girls than with textbooks—especially the shy teenage wife and mother, Devon McFadden.

Alan grew up in central Illinois, where he fell in love with Liz, his high-school sweetheart. After graduation from college, Alan entered real estate but soon decided he would prefer to try his wings in show business. While working as a stand-up comedian in San Francisco he again encountered Liz, who had also moved west to become an actress. Before long Liz had opted to exchange her theatrical career for marriage and home-making and Alan had begun to find life as a comedian a bit too frantic for a family man. "So," says Alan, "we moved to New York and eventually joined the AMC family."

And it *is* a family, as he quickly learned when his neighbor Peter White waited on a street corner for several hours to catch him and deliver a message from the studio. (Alan's phone was not yet connected. His shower wasn't working, either, which led to an invitation from Peter to use his shower. Alan and Liz declined, but Peter still jokes that Liz so preferred his shower that she has taken all her showers there since.)

With his easy charm and lanky good looks, Alan may well be slated to fill the gap left by the amoral, sexy Nick Davis.

Mona Kane (Frances Heflin) is the mother of Erica and secretary and longtime lover of Dr. Charles Tyler. Her patience has finally been rewarded. After Phoebe's decision to marry Langley Wallingford freed Charles from the limbo of their protracted separation, he and Mona were married at last.

Thirteen years younger than her famous brother, Van, Fra Heflin spent her school years in Oklahoma, though she raced through them in record time so she could come to New York. "Van had said I could live with him when I finished high school, but I don't think he expected me to do it at sixteen," she says now.

The theater was in her blood. Her first job was playing the young daughter of Fredric March and Florence Eldridge in Thornton Wilder's *The Skin of Our Teeth*, which I saw during my first year in New York. I also saw Fra in the world premier of Bertolt Brecht's *Galileo* in Los Angeles some years later and admired her performance, little realizing we were to be mortal enemies in *All My Children*. (Fra could never be anyone's enemy, but Mona Kane will forever cause fire to flash from Phoebe Tyler's eyes.)

Fra's passion is needlework, and from her busy hands pours forth a staunchless torrent of baby blankets, hoods, booties, jackets, sweaters, afghans, bedspreads, and even a lovely lacy blouse for Susan Lucci (who, unlike Erica, could not have been more appreciative). Her most ambitious project was a rust-colored cape, in seventeen pieces, which seemed to go on interminably and which drove our temperamental director, Henry Kaplan, even wilder than usual. He called her Madame Defarge, and practically gnashed his teeth every time he saw her needles clicking away. Then one day her knitting needles mysteriously disappeared, and we all looked high and low for them all day, at every break in our rehearsals and our run-throughs. At the end of the day they as mysteriously reappeared. The sly and somewhat guilty smile on Henry's face told us all we needed to know.

Another day Henry was especially snappish with Mona during red chairs. "It's bad enough that you keep clicking away at that thing while I'm giving notes," he said, "but did you have to pick such an ugly color?" A few hours later, on emerging from the control room, he found to his utter disgust that the entire cast was now knitting away en masse, all with the same colored yarn. When at last the rust-colored cape was finished, or at least had disappeared from the set, I asked Fra if she ever wore it.

"Are you kidding?" she said. "By the time I finished that thing I was sick of looking at it myself."

Fra is married to Sol Kaplan, who composes music scores for motion pictures, and they have been exceptional parents to three exceptional children, Jonathan, Nora, and Maidy, all involved in the theater. Fra had a cameo role in *Mr. Billions*, directed by son Jonathan, so the whole *All My Children* cast went to see it. At one point in the film Fra's character answers the phone and says, "Hello, Erica? How are you, honey?" Naturally we all broke up, and later Jonathan told us the scene got the same reaction everywhere it was shown.

Speaking about parenthood, Fra says, "People are always saying, 'Oh, I never interfere with my child's life.' Well *I* interfere all the time. That's a parent's job." ("Here, here," echoes Phoebe—particularly when the parents are as special as Fra and Sol.)

Phil Brent (Nick Benedict), adopted son of Ruth Martin but natural son of Nick Davis, worked in the Environmental Protection Administration, in the Pine Valley police force, as maître d' in his father's restaurant, and as an agent for an unnamed organization resembling the CIA, in whose service he lost his life.

Phil is another pivotal character, essential to an understanding of the basic story line. Let me try to explain: Phil Brent and Tara were childhood sweethearts, but when he went off to Vietnam, unaware that he was leaving her pregnant (caught in a snowstorm on the way to be married, they had "married" themselves in an abandoned chapel just before he left), Chuck Tyler married her to give the child a name, for by this time Phil had been reported missing in action. The child was first called Little Phillip Tyler, later Little Charlie to honor the man he really felt was his father. Now he has changed his last name from Tyler to Brent, to honor his actual father's memory, though he has retained Charlie as his first name.

Phil may be gone from Pine Valley, but Nick Benedict will be long remembered by all of us. From a show business family (his father was a movie director and his mother a queen of burlesque comedy), Nick is a restless, energetic man whose release from tension is a vigorous set on the skins. (He's a drummer of professional caliber, having played the lounges of Las Vegas.) His role as the rather passive, often frustrated Phil seemed to leave him feeling personally frustrated, and at last he begged Agnes Nixon to give Phil something a bit more exciting to do than his job with EPA.

Agnes agreed and made him a policeman, but that job set up other stresses for Phil and Tara because of his frequent absences and his increasingly authoritarian attitude toward her and Little Phillip. These stresses caused Tara to draw close once again to ex-husband, Chuck Tyler, and this emotional turmoil culminated in a scene at the lake, when Little Charlie's near-drowning threw Tara into Chuck's arms and bed.

This development, surprisingly, produced shock waves throughout America, though few fans had seemed shocked when Phil was passionately reunited with Tara some years before. At that time Tara had been married to Chuck, so it wasn't simply a reaction against adultery per se in the Chuck-Tara affair. What was the added factor? Donna, of course, sitting at home simply oozing mute adoration for Chuck, the husband whose love she feels unworthy of holding. Viewers were pulling for Donna, and they couldn't stomach Tara's latest romantic turnaround. "If she can't make up her mind after all these years and marriages, what kind of girl *is* she?" fans asked.

As a result, it was decided to retire the whole triangle for a time. Chuck returned to Donna and Phil moved to Washington, to be nearer his work, taking Tara and Little Charlie with him. Nancy Frangione, the then-current Tara, who had come to us from the stage play *Equus*, left for California with dreams of nighttime television, and Agnes wrote Phil a regretful Dear Nick letter, telling him Phil was to disappear on foreign assignment.

Undaunted, Nick left for the West Coast in his new Jeep, and a few months later he had a role in *The Young and the Restless*. And a month after that, Phil Brent was buried in Pine Valley with full military honors, the Ceremonial Guard from Fort Hamilton, New York, officiating. If you have been following this tangled story, you will see why Phil's death was, in many ways, a momentous event in *All My Children*. In burying Phil Brent, Agnes Nixon had lain to rest the show's first decade. The major characters remain, but we are all off onto other tangents now.

The original Phil Brent was Richard Hatch, a remarkable part-Indian flower child whose expressive blue eyes and boyish sweetness had a lasting effect on viewers. He and Karen Gorney (the original Tara) worked long and hard together, examining motivations and exploring the depths and shadings of their roles. As a result, no other relationship has ever evoked the amount of fan mail that the first Phil and Tara duo did. They were young love personified, shy and yearning and intense, and they struck a universal chord in viewers.

When Richard decided to leave the show, the producers urged him to stay on. After all, they said, he had put a lot of work into creating a most successful characterization. And they advised him—perhaps with some reason—that he would do well to stay with the show, since he needed more experience under his belt before he rushed off to tackle the West Coast. But he was determined, and off he went to climb the Big Rock Candy Mountain, with everyone hoping that the producers' warnings about his inexperience wouldn't prove to be true.

The next year he replaced Michael Douglas during the last gasp of *The Streets of San Francisco*. Shortly after that he gave a moving performance as a brain-damaged young man in a movie made for television, and the following year he won the plum role of Apollo in the much-ballyhooed science fiction series, *Battlestar Galactica*. When I visited him on the *Galactica* set, he said, "Tell everyone at *All My Children* to thank their lucky stars they are with that show. At least it has some continuity. Here I do a scene, and my fellow actor in the same scene may be working in another studio. Or I learn one scene and they shoot a different one. It's crazy."

That series had had its ups and downs, but Richard—who declined a second year—is doing quite well in his career, making other movies for the home screen. One of them, *The Hustler of Muscle Beach*, directed by Jonathan Kaplan, Fra Heflin's son, elevated Richard to his greatest heights yet. Our extended *All My Children* family goes on and on.

Little Charlie/Phillip Tyler Brent (Brian Lima) is the confused natural son of Tara and Phil. He has always thought of Chuck Tyler as his real father, and Chuck has always loved him as a son, to Donna's everlasting chagrin.

Though Phoebe Tyler was profoundly shocked at learning that Little Charlie is not a true Tyler, there was never any doubt about my feelings for Brian Lima, who plays the role. He is my pal, my sometime partner for catch-up ball games in the corridors of the ABC studios, and he was my "date" when thirty cast members attended Candy Earley's opening in *Grease* a few years back. On his tenth birthday I took him to lunch at the elegant fantasyland restaurant in Central Park, Tavern on the Green, and found him one of the most articulate and interesting luncheon partners I can remember. But then, perhaps he feels at home dining out: His grandparents own one of New York's finest French restaurants, Le Champignon.

Little Charlie is currently recovering from the shock of his father's death, and also dealing with the puzzling phenomenon of girls, who seem to be messing up his friendship with his slightly older "cousin" Tad Martin. But I'm betting he'll work both problems out, and that my darling Brian Lima will be around to play ball with me for quite a while.

Eddie Dorrance (Warren Burton) was a hustler and the manager of singer Kelly Cole. He maneuvered his way into Claudette's job at The Chateau and began to blackmail several Pine Valley citizens, including Phoebe Tyler. His murder precipitated a lengthy trial ending in Kelly's conviction and death sentence.

Warren Burton loved his role on *All My Children*, as most actors love roles that allow them to play charming villains. When the character of Eddie began to change for the worse, and he started blackmailing virtually everyone in sight, Warren

realized the end had to be near. (A character can be bad, but
when he becomes a truly vicious menace the end is usually not
far off.) He protested the newly harsh dialogue and the brutal
acts Eddie was now performing, including the rape of Brooke
English and the brandishing of a loaded gun at various characters. But to no avail. As Eddie's behavior got worse, Warren's performance reflected not only the growing desperation
of Eddie Dorrance but the parallel desperation of Warren Burton, who saw the part he loved winding down to a certain end.
By the time Eddie was murdured, Warren, after what must
have been a nerve-wracking time for him, was probably relieved when it was all over.

However, no one stays dead for long in the land of daytime
television, and before Eddie Dorrance's body was cold Warren
was appearing (where else?) in *Another World*.

Shortly after Eddie's demise, Warren returned to visit us
on the set. On the way, he told us, a man stopped in the middle
of the street, looked at Warren, and said, "My God, you're
dead!"

"You will be, too, if you don't wake up," replied Warren
as he snatched the man out of the way of an oncoming bus.

Claudette Flax Montgomery (originally Paulette Breen,
then played by Susan Plantt-Winston), former drug addict and
convicted dealer, was most recently manager of The Chateau,
before and after her murder of Eddie Dorrance and before her
death in an auto accident. (She was the spoiled daughter of
Margo Flax Martin, formerly married to Paul.)

Claudette's role changed somewhat over the years, from the
tough conniver who finagled a job as Phoebe's secretary and
then stole her diamond earrings to pay for her drug habit, to
the calmer and more self-possessed manager of The Chateau.
Paulette Breen also changed in the years she played the part,
from the former Playboy Bunny and model woefully lacking
in acting experience to the competent professional she became.
But the change was no accident. From the first days on the set,
when she was yelled at and humiliated for her inexperience,
she hung on tenaciously and worked hard to learn the craft.

Susan Plantt-Winston, statuesque where Paulette had been
diminutive, is a California beauty, a former dancer, and Dyan
Cannon's close friend and stand-in. The day Lisa Wilkinson

(Nancy) and John Danelle (Frank) brought their new baby to visit the studio, Susan cornered me in my dressing room with a wistful look in her eye.

"I want to have a baby so badly," she told me. "If I wait until Christmas to get pregnant, do you think I can work till April, when my new contract is up? Will they be mad at me?"

I said I thought she could swing it, but as it turned out, she didn't wait. Instead, Cameron Scott Winston, a perfect replica of his strapping Scottish father, joined the *All My Children* family, spending many days at the studio among his adoring "relatives." "Maternity leave" is an accepted fact of life on our show.

When Susan overheard speculation that it was she who had murdered Eddie Dorrance, she was furious. "I won't do it," she insisted. "They didn't ask me, and no one's going to railroad me into the electric chair! I have a husband and a baby! They can just get someone else to play those scenes."

Before she had recovered from that shock, she got an even worse one, overheard from stagehands: She was to be killed in an auto crash! (The prop men have to know.) What's more, she was to confess to the murder with her dying gasp. Almost hysterical, Susan made a speech before the assembled cast, protesting how cruel and unfair she felt it was to do such a terrible thing to her without warning.

This is a recurring argument, with management claiming they are afraid an actor's performance will be affected if he or she knows what is ahead. (When Mona killed the modeling agent who had seduced Erica, she was told of her guilt only days before her scene on the witness stand.) So the cast is kept in the dark for their own protection. Probably a thousand people asked me who killed Eddie Dorrance, and it was comforting to be able to say quite truthfully, "I don't know."

Of course Susan calmed down, though she did demand a rewrite of her final scene. That done, she gave an excellent performance, celebrated with champagne, Cokes, and a huge cake for all hands.

If it all sounds strange, I can only tell you that years in a continuing role do create a strong identification with the character. To have that character become a murderess, or die, is a real trauma.

If they ever try to do that to Phoebe they'll have a real battle on their hands, of *that* you can be sure.

Kitty Shea (Francesca James) was married to Lincoln Tyler and is now deceased. *Kelly Cole*, her twin sister, is the current wife of the same Lincoln Tyler. Kelly, the pill-popping singer at The Chateau, was convicted of Eddie's murder but was later released when Claudette confessed.

Francesca James has loved music since her Michigan childhood, when she would sing and tap-dance on tabletops in her family's restaurant to enchant the customers. As Kelly Cole she has come full circle, again enchanting customers in a restaurant in Pine Valley. (And lest you think singing is only a minor interest for this talented actress, consider this: How many professional opera singers would venture into Alice Tully Hall at Lincoln Center with a solo program composed entirely of difficult German *lieder*? Francesca did it, looking like a fragile Dresden figurine but sailing through the demanding program without turning a hair!)

When Kitty's funeral was attended by all of Pine Valley, this elaborate scene, with crowds of extras, was scheduled for just after lunch. During lunch break, when no one was around, Francesca slipped in and lay down in the coffin. Peter closed the lid, leaving a corner propped open with a tiny piece of wood so she could get air. And she stayed there for over an hour while the scene went on. Then, as the minister was finishing the closing prayer, we all heard a knocking from the coffin.

Lincoln stood up and said, "Wait a moment. There's something wrong here." He went forward and threw open the coffin, whereupon Kitty sat up with a daisy in her mouth.

It took five minutes to get everyone quieted down so we could do a retake.

After Kitty died in Pine Valley, Francesca went off to pursue her singing and composing careers. However, she still felt some separation anxieties, and she expressed them to Agnes Nixon at a sumptuous dinner party Agnes gave for the cast and production staff at "21." Agnes reassured her, adding that if Francesca ever wanted to come back to *All My Children* she should let us know. "I've always wanted to do a twin story," she said.

Famous last words. Francesca did decide to return, and

Agnes, true to her word, "discovered" a missing twin sister of the dead Kitty Shea—and a singer to boot! And thus was born Kelly Cole, destined to fall in love and marry her dead twin's widower.

I've no way of knowing, of course, but I have a feeling that things will not go well for them. As Phoebe keeps saying, the girl is simply not up to the Tyler family's high standards.

Myrtle Lum Fargate (Eileen Herlie), the down-and-almost-out ex-carnival lady hired by Phoebe to impersonate Kitty Shea's mother, is now living in Pine Valley as a kind of surrogate mother to Kelly and as manager of Ellen Shepherd's boutique.

"If it hadn't been raining on a certain summer afternoon in Brighton many years ago, my life would have been quite different," says the distinguished actress, who has played opposite Laurence Olivier, Richard Burton, and a host of stage luminaries. It seems that Eileen, then in her early twenties, was appearing in a provincial repertory company's production of *The Little Foxes*, and the distinguished British director Peter Glenville decided to take in the show to pass a rainy afternoon. He was so electrified by the young girl's performance in the role made famous by Tallulah Bankhead that he insisted Tyrone Guthrie, head of the prestigious Old Vic company in London, come down to see her. Tony Guthrie agreed and invited her to join the company, which led quickly to Eileen's enormous success in Cocteau's *The Eagle With Two Heads*.

"Had the sun shone on that Wednesday matinee day, I'd probably have spent my life touring the provinces," Eileen muses now. Instead, after her London triumph, she came to America, where she appeared in Tony Guthrie's production of *The Matchmaker* on Broadway. Her performance as the milliner, Mrs. Malloy, established her in the American theater, and she remained in her adopted country to perform in a long succession of stage roles. And how does she like playing the tough ex-carny lady on *All My Children*, after having played queens in no less than four major stage productions? "Only in America..." she says, her eyes twinkling as she puts on Myrtle's orange wig and somewhat garish clothes.

Eileen simply loves acting, which is no secret to anyone who knows her. In fact, she gave the secret away early in her life, as her first repertory company was arriving in Liverpool.

"As we pulled into the station I saw a poster announcing our play, and at the bottom it said, in big letters, 'Twice Nightly.' I turned to the stage manager and burbled, 'Oh, good! We get to do it twice every night!'

"The man looked at me as if I were quite mad, but I was really just in love."

She still is, with the theater and *All My Children*, and with her darkly handsome Egyptian sculptor, Hassan, with whom she has had a most remarkable long-distance love affair for many years now.

Professor Langley Wallingford (Louis Edmonds) is an elegant con man whose real name, Lenny Wlasuk, was only known in Pine Valley to the deceased Eddie Dorrance until he was at last identified by Myrtle as "a purse snatcher" from the old carny days. He is now married to Phoebe and busily scheming to relieve her of the Tyler fortune.

Another case of an actor whose role was extended due to fan response, Langley remains a constant reminder that Phoebe's lifelong abhorrence of divorce was well-founded. The poor lady's head was turned by Langley's suavely calculated charm, but her momentary lapse in judgment will no doubt cost her dearly. As Louis says, "Poor Phoebe. She thinks of nothing but love, and Langley thinks of nothing but money."

To the manor born on a Louisiana plantation, Louis made his debut in the Leonard Bernstein/Lillian Hellman *Candide*, followed by appearances in works by Oscar Wilde, George Bernard Shaw, and Shakespeare. He is a close friend of Carrie Nye and Dick Cavett, and we are all neighbors, sometimes confusing reel and real life.

Benny Sago (established by Larry Fleischman, currently played by Vasili Bogazianos) is the onetime leather-jacketed boyfriend of Brooke English who became Phoebe's chauffeur and sometime confidant. Benny has had a rocky marriage to Edna Thornton, whom he married on the rebound when his true love, Estelle, decided to return to her husband and former pimp, Billy Clyde Tuggle.

Though Benny was initially Phoebe's servant and barely tolerated for his "common" behavior, a bond has grown between the autocratic lady and the coarse but caring young man.

When Anne was committed to the sanatorium and Phoebe let her true emotions break through, Benny responded with a genuine concern that touched her deeply. Since then, despite Phoebe's haughty treatment, Benny has regarded her as a friend, and she has welcomed his friendship. This genuine bond, underlying the often funny byplay between this ill-matched pair, grew so popular with the fans that people began to suggest a *Phoebe and Benny* spinoff show. In one memorable scene (for which I was certainly unprepared) he simply tucked the ranting Phoebe under his arm and carried her, fuming, from the courtroom. I'm sure I owe Larry a good tenth of Phoebe's character and more than half her appeal.

Originally brought into *All My Children* by his buddy Nick Benedict for a three-day role as Brooke's raunchy weekend guest, Larry Fleischman quickly drew an enthusiastic response from viewers. Here was someone who wasn't threatened or impressed by Phoebe, and his scenes with her gave off sparks. As usual, Agnes Nixon knew when she had struck gold; Larry was quickly written into the show, and he remained there for many years, providing that much-needed foil against which Phoebe plays so well. They have seen each other through many a crisis, from Phoebe's bouts with alcoholism to Benny's troubles with Estelle and the gun-wielding Billy Clyde.

When Larry left the show he was replaced by Vasili Bogazianos, who is first-generation Greek and extremely proud of it. Vasili was working in regional theater when he learned he was being given the part. He got some inkling of how tough the job might be from his colleagues. Instead of congratulating him, they all wailed, "You mean *Benny*'s left the show?" But Vasili needn't have worried—he's doing fine.

Edna Thornton Sago (Sandy Gabriel), once marrried to Dr. David Thornton, who was the father of her daughter, has most recently married Benny Sago, though she has a roving eye. Profoundly upset by Benny's departure, Sandy decided to leave the show.

Sandy Gabriel is a sexy-looking dish indeed, and she plays her somewhat funky female-on-the-make role superbly. In real life she is the wife of John Gabriel, who plays Seneca on *Ryan's Hope*, and is the mother of two little girls.

Dr. David Thornton (Paul Gleason) was a defrocked surgeon and former husband of Edna Thornton Sago. Though he has gone to that great Seattle in the sky, David Thornton's bearded charm very nearly wrecked the marriage of Ruth and Dr. Joe Martin. When his affair with Ruth fizzled, David left Pine Valley, only to reappear some time later, beardless and somewhat subdued, as Edna's husband and the lover of Dr. Christina Karras. His plot to kill Edna with poisoned wine was thwarted when their little daughter Dottie, setting the table for Mommy, accidentally exchanged the glasses. In the original story outline, Edna was to have been done in. However, the fans preferred her to him (as did the cast and producers), so once again there was a switch.

It always seemed to me that Paul believed in the virtue of making waves. Possibly he felt, as some other actors do, that the stimulus provided by keeping things stirred up on the set helped to sharpen everyone's performance. If so, it's not a theory I subscribe to. The high-pressure environment of a show like ours creates quite enough tensions, thank you, without my feeling the need for any artificial ones.

Estelle LaTour Tuggle (Kathleen Dezina), a former prostitute now married to her former pimp, Billy Clyde, is still in love with Benny Sago. She and Billy Clyde have moved to Sea City (which somewhat resembles Atlantic City), but she finds frequent excuses to visit her old friend from the streets, Donna, and to bump into Benny. Her old benefactress Maggie tells her in a dream to go back to Benny, since Edna has run away with a wealthy Texan.

Billy Clyde Tuggle (Matthew Cowles) is a former pimp who is now supposedly going straight, though his compulsive gambling makes that improbable.

Equally improbable is the fact that the low-down Billy Clyde is played by blue-blooded Matthew Cowles, nephew of famed publisher Gardner Cowles, and grandson of a Philadelphia Biddle. He grew up on the Riviera and in Connecticut, but learned his southern accent from a bartender while playing in *Sweet Bird of Youth*. So charismatic was his characterization of Billy Clyde that girls actually accosted him on the street and begged him to make them part of his stable. By dubbing his hand-carved club his "persuadiator," he coined a word that has become a street term.

Ellen Tucker Shepherd (Kathleen Noone) is a Pine Valley girl who went away, married and divorced, and then returned to become engaged to Mark Dalton, many years her junior, though that relationship was aborted by the crisis of Devon's untimely pregnancy. Ellen's subsequent love affair with Paul Martin was doomed by Anne's recovery, after three years in Oak Haven Hospital, but Mark Dalton is forever waiting in the wings.

Kathleen O'Meara Noone and I have several things in common, including both Missouri and a consuming interest in metaphysics. She was born on Long Island, but the family moved to St. Louis for a year, which she remembers as having been spent mainly sitting on the school steps at St. Mary's eating ice cream.

Like me, Kathleen felt under tremendous pressure to succeed in school. And like me, she paid a physical price for it— in ulcers and a collapse in a corridor of Southern Methodist University, where she was working for her master's degree. She too took to acting early, and she also had a too-early marriage that ended badly. And we both play grandmothers on *All My Children*, though Ellen has got to be one of the most dazzling grandmothers in all daytime television. She is indefatigable in her support for the Special Olympics for retarded children.

Harlan Tucker (William Griffis) is Ellen's father. He appears only infrequently on the show because William Griffis, a very fine actor and singer, spends most of his time in his dream house in Costa Rica.

Devon Shepherd McFadden (Tricia Pursley) is the daughter of Ellen Shepherd and wife of Wally McFadden, with whom she slept in order to spite Dan Kennicott, accidentally becoming pregnant in the process. Devon is probably still too immature for either marriage or motherhood, as her affair with Sean Cudahy illustrates. But at least Sean has taught her that "there is nothing wrong with her as a woman," something she had genuinely feared.

During high school Tricia trained at the Ringling Brothers and Barnum & Bailey Circus school near her home in Florida, but then went on to get her master's degree in drama. About her affair with Wally, one knowledgeable young fan wrote,

"We know you aren't *really* pregnant, because you didn't even take your pajamas off, and neither did Wally."

Wally McFadden (Jack Magee) is Devon's young husband. He hopes to complete college while supporting his wife and child. Wally is torn between his love for Devon and his anger at her inability to return that love. (Hugh Franklin, watching them in one connubial scene, commented loftily, "No wonder that boy's having problems with lovemaking. He has no *technique!*") Poor Devon, and poor little Bonnie, their infant daughter, who may also be hurt in the emotional turmoil of her too-young parents.

Jack Magee, who came to the attention of *All My Children* while playing in *Galileo* (with Francesca James) at Columbia University, has felt so frustrated playing the fumbling Wally that he recently took off on a European vacation with Francesca.

Mark Dalton (Mark LaMura), is a professor of music at a nearby university, half-brother of Erica, and for a time Brooke English's somewhat reluctant lover, though still in love with his former fiancée, Ellen Shepherd. (Ellen ended their engagement because of the difference in their ages and the worry that her behavior might be having a bad influence on her daughter.)

Mark LaMura tested for the role of Jeff Martin, and even though he was not right for that part, Agnes liked him so much that she created Mark Dalton expressly for him, even giving the character the same first name. As you might suspect, anyone that handsome is bound to have a girl in every port. In fact, this Club Med playboy seems to use his free time to shoot for a new Guinness record. In his characterization of Mark Dalton's new relationship with Ellen, however, he has emphasized tender and supportive friendship rather then sexiness. The result is most attractive.

Dr. Frank Grant (John Danelle), another member of the Pine Valley Hospital staff, was once married to Nancy Blair, who moved to Chicago when she got the offer of a much better job, expecting Frank to keep his promise to relocate there too. When he reneged, the couple became estranged and were eventually divorced. Unknown to Frank, Nancy was pregnant at the time of the divorce. To give the child a father, she married Carl Blair, but Carl was later killed in an air crash. Frank subsequently learned that he was little Carl Blair's true father and wanted to reclaim both the boy and his mother, but Nancy would have none of this, wishing instead to marry Dr. Russ Anderson. Whatever happens, it is clear that their lives will be forever entangled.

John Danelle is the son of a cop, and he had planned a career in the military, but instead he graduated from Carnegie Tech, one of the world's best schools for theater. He is an outspoken man who talks back to the brass as few others do. Once, enraged over a bit of "stupid censorship," he kicked over a chair and glared around as if he might tear apart the whole studio. Instantly, Lisa (who plays Nancy, and is also John's real-life wife) was at his side to calm him. "He's the agitator and I'm the mediator," she says. "Still, he's one of the few people I know who has a large circle of friends, all of whom have only good things to say about him." Yes, John is dependable and kind; also volatile and explosive—and very talented.

Nancy Grant Blair (Lisa Wilkinson) social worker and former wife of Dr. Frank Grant and Carl Blair, mother of Little Carl, was until recently engaged to Dr. Russ Anderson, who planned to adopt Little Carl after their marriage—thus giving the confused child yet another father to sort out.

Lisa's mother started her in ballet at four, but at fourteen she saw the Broadway show *Oliver*, and that was it. While still in high school she did stock and community theater, then spent a year at Ithaca College. "But I saw they'd never let me play anything except maids, so I came back to New York University's School of Fine Arts, which was great. I got the first commercial I auditioned for, which supported me for two years while I got started." She met John in a play and six months later they were married.

Lisa has left *All My Children* twice because she felt the role lacked substance. During her time away she played a principal role in the revival of *Candide* and worked in an extraordinary one-woman show called *After Happily Ever After*, a story of a woman's self-discovery, which led Lisa to the discovery that she wanted a child as well as a career. With John's help she produced Amanda, who quickly wrapped her daddy around her little finger. Back in *All My Children* with a more substantial story line, Lisa and John proudly bring little Amanda along to the studio, where she enchants us all.

Caroline Murray Grant (Pat Dixon), Frank Grant's former wife, is not currently involved in Pine Valley life.

Pat Dixon, a graduate of Juilliard School of Music, has a sensational voice, which she displays in a supper club act she and Candy Earley have put together. The two, billed as *Cafe au Lait*, are gorgeous together.

Dr. Russ Anderson (Charles Brown) was Frank Grant's colleague at Pine Valley Hospital and for a time the fiancé of Nancy Grant Blair. When he saw—better than Nancy—that she still loved Frank and that the facts of Little Carl's parenting would always be an obstacle, he withdrew from Pine Valley (and Charles Brown left the show).

An award-winning actor with the famed Negro Ensemble Theater, Charles Brown's tremendous talent was never fully tapped in his *All My Children* role. In *Home*, he played a South Carolinian who comes north to improve his life and is almost destroyed there, returning to savor and celebrate his rural life and roots. Charles' performance was superb.

Carl Blair, Jr. (Billy Mack) is the child over whom a storm continues to rage, though he is unaware of the reasons.

If you think Little Carl looks familiar, it is because you've seen him only a thousand or so times on those marvelous Jell-O commercials with Bill Cosby. At six, Billy is already a veteran of Sesame Street, though he is not sold on acting as a life's work. Then what *does* he want to do when he grows up? "I want to build things, like bridges and buildings," he says. When asked if he likes his Uncle Frank or his Uncle Russ best, he grins noncommittally and says, "I like them both." Maybe he'll grow up to be a diplomat.

Palmer Cortlandt (James Mitchell) is a multimillionaire tycoon who has returned to Pine Valley with his sheltered diabetic daughter, Nina, to resume residence in the vast and gloomy Cortlandt mansion.

Playing a gothic "Elizabeth Barrett Browning father" is a far cry from Jimmy Mitchell's beginning as Curly, the major dancer in the original *Oklahoma*. Jimmy is a sweetheart—urbane, witty, the very opposite of the coldly menacing Palmer Cortlandt.

Nina Cortlandt (Taylor Miller), nineteen-year-old daughter of Palmer and Daisy, is in love with handsome Dr. Cliff Warner despite her father's vociferous objections. Palmer, the psychotically protective father, will stop at virtually nothing to keep Nina with him and keep her from discovering that her mother, whom she was told had died as a result of complications from childbirth, is very much alive and actually living, incognito, in Pine Valley.

A Texas girl, Taylor was educated at Sarah Newcomb College, Tulane University, the Bryn Mawr of the South. But don't let that wispy girlishness fool you; she's a bit of an intellectual and a marvelous cook, who lugs in pans of brownies and delicious carrot cakes from her oven.

Daisy Cortlandt (Gillian Spencer), Palmer's supposedly dead wife, reappeared in a seance to reassure Nina and she decided to hang around Pine Valley (though Palmer believes her back in Europe with her jet set pals). Instead, she has cut her hair and enrolled in the university, where she has struck up a friendship with the unsuspecting Nina, determined to see that Palmer doesn't ruin his daughter's chance for marriage.

Gillian is a daytime veteran, not only as an actress on *As the World Turns*, but also as a writer for four years on that show. "That worked well at the time, when my sons were young and needed me at home more. But after a while writing got pretty lonely, and I decided I had to get back with people again. Since I had to lose about thirty pounds for the role, I went on the Scarsdale diet. I'd heard about it from my next-door neighbor, who is the 'nurse' mentioned in the rather lurid press accounts of the author's murder. It's so strange to find such a lovely person even peripherally involved in such an ugly business. In fact," she adds, "it's like a soap opera."

Myra Murdock (Elizabeth Lawrence) is the Cortlandt housekeeper and (unbeknownst to Nina) mother of the gadabout Daisy, which also makes her Nina's grandmother. Mrs. Murdock is a fearless protector of Nina's welfare and a roadblock to Palmer's ruthless schemes.

Liz and I share a dressing room, and we also share a rather odd distinction of having played the two sides of Irna Phillips, the difficult queen of the early soaps. In *As the World Turns* I played a role Irna saw as an idealized version of herself (she told me so), and in *Another World* Liz played the real Irna Phillips. That show was based directly on the lives of Irna and her two adopted children, one of whom was a writer on the show under Irna's dictatorial guidance. "It was just too painful," Liz moans, remembering. "It was Albee and Pinter and *Mommie Dearest* all rolled into one."

Another interest we share is in teaching, especially working with disadvantaged or learning-handicapped children.

Dr. Cliff Warner (Peter Bergman), a young resident at Pine Valley Hospital, is in love with Nina despite her father's attempts to smear, bribe, or intimidate him.

Peter is a Gemini who fell into acting because the girl he was dating was in the senior play. He tagged along to rehearsal, and before he knew it he was playing the lead, and to his amazement, loving it. "I was a real hell raiser," he says. "I was the son of a career army officer, and I had never really taken anything seriously, but acting intrigued me. And now I have great respect for the profession."

Peter is a selection of our producer, Jørn Winther, who beams all over the control room when he sees Cliff Warner in close-up. "Look at those eyes!" Jørn says. "They have *lights* that go on inside them." Viewers agree.

Sybil Thorne (Linda Gibboney) is a conniving nurse who is in love with Cliff Warner and sometimes in league with Palmer Cortlandt in his machinations to break up his daughter's engagement.

Linda's exotic looks are a heritage from her Philippine mother and Scottish father. A stage actress and graduate of the New York Academy of Dramatic Arts, she lives for fun and excitement, and is the possessor of one of the most entrancing, gurgling giggles I've ever heard. (I wish she'd use it on camera.)

Betsy Kennicott (Carla Dragoni), wholesome younger sister of Dan Kennicott and Mary Kennicott Martin, is now a nurse at Pine Valley Hospital and roommate of Sybil Thorne.

As we assembled for the masked ball at the Cortlandt mansion (one of the most elaborate bits of location shooting in the history of the soaps), Carla looked at Phoebe's glamorous Cleopatra costume and sighed. "Wouldn't you know they'd make me Little Bo Peep," she said. She looked totally adorable in the costume, which may have made things even worse.

Bubbly Carla, half Irish and half Italian, is notoriously accident prone, appearing constantly with bandages on one part
of her or another. But she's very famous in the building where
I live, having done a Pamper commercial with the baby daughter of Bill Stack, our elevator man.

There have been many minor characters and a few fairly
major ones in the show's ten-year life, but to list them all would
be impossible. Dr. Christina Karras (played by the soap opera
veteran Robin Strasser, now Dorian Lord in *One Life to Live*)
and her spectral father Anatole (C. M. Gampel) will be remembered, as will the hair-raising menace of the pimp Tyrone
(played by Sesame Street veteran Roscoe Orman), and the
vicious brutality of Tad Gardner's deranged father, Ray (Gil
Rogers). And there was Dan Kennicott (Daren Kelly) and Dr.
Nigel Fargate (Alexander Scourby) and Mark Dalton's mother
(Rosemary Murphy).

There are mainstay characters such as Mrs. Valentine (Alyce
Webb), Aunt Bessie (Frances Foster), Hughes (Bill Cain), res-
ident priest Father Tierney (Mel Boudrot), fatherly psychiatrist
Dr. Polk (Norman Rose), and Freddie Porcelli, maître d' at
The Chateau (and in real life, at "21," where he is often asked
to autograph menus).

New characters will appear between this writing and the
time you read it, no doubt, and no doubt some of the present
ones will depart from Pine Valley, one way or another. But
you can be sure that the Tylers and Martins will survive, and
that we will all continue to face our many problems. Whether
we meet triumph or tragedy, and whether we meet them with
wisdom or foolishness, life in Pine Valley will go on.

Now that you have met some of the people who make up
Phoebe Tyler's imaginary world, as well as the flesh-and-blood
actors and actresses who play their parts, I wonder if you aren't
struck—as I always am—by the complex ways in which performers' characters relate to their characterizations. In some
cases, of course, the two may seem to be very close, but in
many other cases they appear so different as to be almost
contradictory.

Take Erica, for example. We know that the way Susan Lucci

behaves in real life is exactly opposite to the relentlessly bitchy way Erica behaves in Pine Valley. How, then, can Susan be so totally convincing as Erica? The obvious—and correct—answer is that Susan is a superb actress. But what, exactly, do we mean by that? Much more, surely, than that Susan is a gifted mimic. The fact is that Susan *understands* Erica, can actually feel what Erica is feeling, knows instinctively what Erica will do or say in any given situation. Does this mean that, after all, there is something of Erica buried deep down in Susan's character? Of course it does. There is something of Erica in all of us—and something of Mona and Chuck and Benny and Brooke and every other inhabitant of Pine Valley. It was Agnes Nixon's genius to isolate and identify those somethings, to clothe them with imagined personalities and to turn them into vivid, believable characters. In Susan's case, it was her art—her performer's art—that permitted her first to understand what Agnes had done, and then to reach back into her own personality (I am tempted to say *humanity*, for *personality* is almost too weak a word), find those elements that correspond to Agnes' model and bring them forth as a full-fledged characterization.

Does this help you (or, for that matter, me) to understand the relationship between Phoebe Tyler and Ruth Warrick? I hope so, for as I review my life—that strange amalgam of inherited characteristics and varied experiences, of failures and triumphs, of lessons learned and lessons still to be learned—I think I see a thousand clues to Phoebe's origins. I also think that is why I am probably, for all her faults, Phoebe's staunchest defender. I understand her. I may not be all Phoebe, but she is all me.

I'm bound to say, however, that the process of extracting Phoebe's character from my own wasn't altogether easy or natural. At first I was much too inclined to pass judgment on her. In the early days of the show I found Phoebe's snobbery offensive, and I began to play her as a foolish, empty-headed, rather useless woman (I, who had always involved myself deeply in causes I believe in, from Operation Bootstrap in Watts to my work with disadvantaged students at Julia Richman High School). More and more I began to play on her ridiculous aspects, feeling I was making a comment about the sort of person Phoebe was. And to make things worse, I got laughs, especially from Ray MacDonnell, who thought the whole thing was hilarious, like Restoration comedy.

I was still basking in those laughs when Jack Wood, one of our directors, invited me out to dinner. We went to Le Poulailler, near Lincoln Center, and had a truly elegant three-wine meal. By dessert I was as relaxed as anyone could possibly get. What a lovely evening!

"Ruth, if you don't stop being funny on the show, we're going to have to replace you," he said as I sipped my brandy.

I nearly choked on it. All I could do was stare at him, totally stunned.

"You just don't seem to understand," he said. "Phoebe is the *menace* on the show. People are supposed to be scared of her, so terrified that they shiver at the sound of her name. You're playing her so light and amusing there's nothing to be afraid of."

While I was still looking for my voice, he went on to explain that Agnes had been distressed for some time, though no one had given me so much as a hint about it. At last it sunk in, and I was furious.

"Well, for heaven's sake!" I snapped. "I'm an actress and you're the director. So *direct* me! Why haven't you ever said anything about this in rehearsals?"

"Well, I tried to give you hints," he said.

"Hints! What kind of direction is that?"

I was getting angrier by the second, thinking about it. Finally I banged my hand down on the table, raised my chin, lowered my voice about an octave, and said, "All right! You want a troublemaker? You've *got* a troublemaker. And you'd better batten down the hatches, all of you!"

And so the real Phoebe Tyler was born, much to the delight of the writers, the cast, and the fans, who loved her more than ever before. For oddly, as time passed, Phoebe did begin to seem more likeable. Agnes, insightful as ever, had realized that if the more human Phoebe were ever to emerge, I was going to have to stop prejudging her.

That was not only a good lesson in acting, it was also a good lesson in self-understanding. My world is much different from Phoebe's, certainly, and my beliefs—political, ethical, philosophical, social—would rarely mesh with hers. Phoebe would not have rushed about as I have done in pursuit of a career, nor would she have worked with disadvantaged people in Watts or Harlem in the ways I have done. Her views on social class are extreme, to say the least, and she is often somewhat arrogant in her dealings with others, which I hope I am not.

And yet, when all the differences are listed, I find there is still a kinship that somehow transcends them. We do share much, Phoebe and I, including a love for our children, a belief in the importance of family, and a conviction that people must be held accountable for their acts. She may be unyielding, but she is often right, as events in Pine Valley prove. She may be too hard on Donna, or on Kitty or Kelly, but it is because she wants her children to have good and happy marriages. And has she been so wrong?

True, she was duped by the specious charm of Langley. But even then, it was only because she wanted and needed to believe that he was the courtly, thoughtful, caring man he pretended so convincingly to be. What woman is not vulnerable to such human needs? (Certainly I have been, often to my regret. And I hope I shall never change.) She is not the first woman to have been deceived by a man, and she will certainly not be the last.

Some people make the mistake of trying to sum up Phoebe simply by dismissing her as a bitch. Not only is that a judgment, similar to the one I wrongly made when I first began to play the part, it is, when you stop to think about it, almost self-evidently beside the point. If it were the central truth about Phoebe, how can we account for the millions of viewers who persist in loving and admiring her? No, there is more to Phoebe than that, something at the core of her personality that transcends any symptoms of willfulness, error, selfishness, or even malice. I don't quite know how to define this quality. Strength, candor, courage, identity—all are somehow involved. It is what enables Phoebe to stand up for what she believes, no matter how unfashionable the conviction. It is what impels her always to speak her mind openly (and sometimes outrageously), without regard to whether her words are politic. It is perhaps what makes her so attractive to so many younger viewers. Phoebe, when all is said and done, is up front. Which is not a bad place to be.

Am I like that? Well, there is a part of me that certainly

wishes I were. I'd like to think I had the courage to say aloud the things that most people feel but are afraid to articulate. I'd like to think I had the strength to demand what I know to be my (or other people's) rights, regardless of the consequences. I'd like to think that I was always as true to my standards as it is humanly possible to be. If Phoebe draws part of her character from what is potentially worst in me, she also draws part from what is potentially best. How can I not forgive her, and how can I not love her?

And apparently many other people, feeling that Phoebe represents a very human mixture of the bad and good in all of us, forgive and love her too. I experienced one memorably unexpected instance of this at, of all places, the prestigious and proper International Debutantes Ball held at New York's Waldorf Astoria. As I was leaving the receiving line, one of the official escorts, a strapping young man resplendent in white tie and gloves, approached me. "Excuse me, ma'am, I just had to speak to you," he said in a charming Texas drawl. "I'm with a pro football team, the Dallas Cowboys, and I just want to tell you we think you're great. We come runnin' off the field all hot and sweaty and can't wait to watch you. *Ma'am, we sure do love to watch Phoebe kick ass!*"

I laughed, but Phoebe almost fainted.

Where does Phoebe get all her never-say-die strength and stamina? Some of it, I hope, from me. At age seven, a curvature of my spine required me to wear a back brace for two years, plus take two hours of daily therapeutic exercises, a boring drill for a child. (Later, I was warned that I should not expect to have children, a cheering thought for a young girl.) At eighteen came the nervous breakdown, and warnings that I would never be able to cope with much stress.

Then, as the thirty-year-old mother of two, and their sole support, I began to look somewhat strange in movie scenes. In the mornings I would have to roll out of bed, crawl to a doorknob to pull myself upright, and spend thirty minutes in a hot shower before I could move naturally. Back to the orthopedists, whose verdict this time was, "Get ready for the wheelchair." I had some sort of strange degenerative disease, they said, and they could do nothing for me. And again I ignored the pronouncements of doom. I learned to ski, staying with Jim and Robert Stack at their lodge in Lake Tahoe, crying from the pain but *moving*.

As the condition continued, my mother suggested I try her chiropractor. "What have you got to lose?" she said when I hesitated. What, indeed? I went.

"You are simply lacking in natural lubrication in your joints," the chiropractor told me. "But that's no great problem," he added. "Movement, constant adjustment of every one of them, lots of exercise, sensible food, and a less restrictive attitude toward life, and you'll be fine."

His advice and my instincts were correct, it turned out: Movement, exercise, and healthy fun were the antidote. Yet if I had accepted the orthopedist's verdict, *that* prognosis might well have turned out to be correct. Instead of faking paralysis in a wheelchair, Phoebe might well have been confined to one!

However, neither Phoebe nor I has been successful in overcoming emotional stresses. Where are the exercises that strengthen one's judgment in choosing a mate? Why don't we learn from our past mistakes? Why do we repeat patterns that hurt and destroy?

Certainly I've not done well in marriage. It would seem that I have an unerring instinct for choosing the wrong mate, in fact. But who would be Mr. Right? Being married to an independent, strong-willed, high-spirited, highly volatile and ambitious woman (who is not exactly low profile) can't be easy, especially when she expects as much from a relationship as she is constantly demanding of herself. As one therapist put it, "You scare most men out of their socks! They know they'd never be able to live up to your standards, so why try? And those who could, might simply find it too exhausting, so they abstain."

So who *is* attracted to this perpetual motion machine? Those who need and want a tower of strength. Why doesn't it work out, then? Because under that fiercely spinning dynamo is a very feminine woman, someone who enters marriage looking for strength and wanting to be taken care of, at least emotionally. When she doesn't get it, she cheerfully assumes responsibility (that was taught her in the cradle) and takes over. But sooner or later the woman in her asserts her right to have *her* needs satisfied, too.

> I am asham'd that women are so simple
> To offer war where they should kneel for peace,
> Or seek for rule, supremacy, and sway,
> When they are bound to serve, love, and obey.

So said the poet and psychologist Shakespeare through Kate in *The Taming of the Shrew*. (And there was a shrew to give Phoebe a run for the money!) But to what is she to be obedient? "... obedient to his *honest* will," says Kate, "In token of which duty, if he please,/My hand is ready; may it do him ease."

Though skeptics may snort and libbers shout "Treason!" I have to wonder. A researcher in the high mountains of Tibet once asked the head matriarch of a village about the most puzzling aspect of that society: "Though you women have the power, you control the property, and the children receive their mother's family name, I can't help noticing that, in their daily lives, the women nevertheless cook for the men, serve them graciously, and seem to defer to them, seeking always to please them."

"Ah! That is only natural for a woman," the matriarch told him. "If she is *required* to do all these things as an inferior, it is servitude and intolerable. But because she is his equal, indeed more than his equal, she gives him pleasure gladly. Only between equals does it have meaning for a woman to do for a man what her nature takes joy in doing."

Phoebe understands that. How girlish and pliable she has become while in love with Langley! And though now she resists seeing his duplicity with all her might, when she is finally forced to confront it, how can anyone imagine that she will remain compliant to his *dis*honest will?

What does a woman do with her energies when there is no man in her life? Phoebe turned to drink. Ruth learned, from Erich Fromm in *The Art of Loving*, that "love is not primarily a relationship to a specific person: it is an attitude, an orientation of character, which determines the relatedness of a person to the world as a whole, not toward one love object." To love one person and be indifferent to the rest of one's fellowman is not love, it is egotism.

In my early years in Hollywood I had asked the European directors and producers what it had been like to live in Germany while the ovens were going, and I had been startled by the vehemence with which they denied any knowledge of such things. And yet, when Watts exploded in my own backyard, I could say with all honesty that I had known nothing about it. This sobered me considerably, and I decided I must put my actions where my mouth had been.

I attended some seminars and workshops to fill in the gaps, and then I met two young black men who seemed to me to be moving in a positive direction: Lou Smith, who had been through all the troubled times in the South with SNCC and CORE; and Robert Hall, a successful salesman who had kept in touch with the ghetto boys through athletic programs he had sponsored. Strangers, they had joined to save the life of a white television cameraman during the violence, and in the following dawn they had sat together on a curb amidst the rubble and had decided to join forces to found Operation Bootstrap, to be run by and for blacks. "We'll never learn until we take responsibility for ourselves," they argued. *"Learn, Baby, Learn* must replace *Burn, Baby, Burn,*" they vowed. White friends could help, but not dictate or set policy.

I helped finance the conversion of a storefront into a job-training center, and became the first teacher. Enrollment day was long and hectic, and I prayed hard we could deliver half of what we were promising. It was growing dark outside, and the sounds of Saturday night were coming in from Central Avenue. "Well, they're beginning to get drunk," I muttered, and instantly the cliché blinked like neon in my mind. I quickly added, ". . . just like they are in Beverly Hills and Bel Air and Malibu too." Talk about hardening of the categories!

And then I became aware of a face pressed against the plate-glass window, contorted by anger, and heard the harsh shout: "What are you doin' in there, blue-eyed witch? Go back where you belong, white bitch!"

I looked around the room. Everyone was working, evidently oblivious to the shouts. And then it hit me: I was now the *only* white person in that room. There had been others, but they had gone home. Slowly I realized that *I* was the object of the man's fury, and my stomach began to curl like the edges of an egg dropped into hot grease. How could he say those things when he didn't even know me?

And then, beset as I was with gathering feelings of fear, anger, and humiliation, I began to understand what it must be like to be black, what a black-skinned person faced every moment of his life. I looked at the shouting, angry face at the window, and then around the room where the other workers sat, pretending not to hear. Slowly I gathered myself to leave, some of the day's enthusiasm draining away.

As I got up, one of the men said, quite casually, "I'll walk you to your car." I didn't object.

It was a silent walk. As he opened the car door he said, "Well, I suppose this is the last we'll see of you down here."

"Only if you tell me you don't want me to come," I said. "But you must answer me honestly about that. Because if my being here stops some of the people from coming who need what Bootstrap is offering, then I'm a liability and I *should* stay away."

He considered it. "Don't you think there need to be some bridges built?" he asked finally. "Don't people need to learn that prejudice comes in more than one flavor—not only vanilla but chocolate too? It won't always be easy, but you're sure as hell needed."

It wasn't always easy, but one tall young man who firmly believed "you can't trust Whitey" gave me my graduation certificate. We were singing "We Shall Overcome" on the sidewalk one Saturday night when I said, "Cornell, you can trust me, can't you?"

"Why hell, *yes*," he said. "Man, I *know* you!"

I taught there two years, while playing Hannah Cord on *Peyton Place*. Those years, with block parties on the street and Nellie Lutcher singing and playing in front of the house where she was born, with Stevie Wonder performing and then insisting the children let him feel their faces while they felt his, taught me much about myself, about living, and about the senselessness of an unlived life. I'd learned that love can be an expansiveness, an activity of the soul that transcends self.

Operation Bootstrap now owns, runs, and trains operators for gas stations, body-repair shops, a co-op market, and—our pride and joy—a black-doll factory. I have many good memories of that time.

Later I worked at Synanon, as a volunteer and "square"

Game Player, a sort of gestalt therapy group interaction that produced incredible, almost miraculous insights and character breakthroughs. I also taught there, and seriously considered becoming a member of the community. But that would have required my living there and relinquishing my sole right to my son's upbringing, since all children became wards of the group. When one wants desperately to contribute something of meaning in life, sacrifices have to be expected, but to entrust my son to others...?

Swimming in the sea before my Malibu home, I could see, across the bay some miles away, the old resort hotel Synanon had taken over. I looked at the institution and then looked at my splendid young son swimming beside me. The decision was no contest: In light of the organization's later deterioration, it would seem that the angels were watching over me.

Under John Kennedy and his brother Robert, then attorney general, I worked on the Dropout Program for a time. When the incredible news came from Dallas, I was sitting with a carbon copy of a letter I had written to JFK, reading the phrase: "It's fine that you share Lincoln's enthusiasm for the rocking chair, but *please*, don't go to too many theater parties."

During Lyndon Johnson's term I was made a consultant to the Department of Labor for the Youth Job Corps. (To be sworn in, one raises one's hand and repeats the same oath as the President of the United States.) Under President Carter my work continued, with Job Corps and with the Cities in School pilot program, under which I teach part-time at Julia Richman High School in New York City. We write soap operas, based on the students' lives; and perform them, incorporating creativity, grammar, punctuation, spelling, and experience in group interaction and sensitivity; with a field trip to the *All My Children* studio thrown in to liven things up. Fifteen-year-olds who at first would not even speak performed before a thousand people in Washington Square Park at the end of the semester. Blacks and Puerto Ricans also learned to forget their cliques and enjoy each other in a group effort.

At first glance, no aspect of my own life seems further removed from Phoebe Tyler's concerns than does my continuing, passionate involvement with social work. Yet who is to say that Phoebe hasn't the *potential* to become involved? In that respect, is she so unlike many people whose capacity to help their fellow human beings exceeds their willingness to do so? Is she so different from what I was before Watts? Perhaps she, like most of us, only needs some catalyst to unleash creative energies she does not even suspect she possesses.

But like Phoebe, I never give up the dream of love and romance so dear to the hearts of all moon-child Cancer creatures. I married once again, only to see that marriage fail, in a pattern I must admit has some disheartening déjà vu aspects to it.

Jarvis Cushing and I were wed amidst great pomp and ceremony and attendant publicity, due as much to his social position as to my modest celebrity. But it was just not destined to be, and the memories of how we failed each other are a bit too painful still for sharing.

When introduced to Jarvis by mutual friend Joan Lowther, I had been wearing a small cloche hat with a twenties look. The intensity of Jarvis' gaze was unnerving, and later his sister Pam asked if I realized how closely I resembled their mother, Barbara Brokaw Cushing. That sent shock waves through my psyche: As a girl I had studied Pond's Cold Cream ads of beautiful young society women with the slogan, "She's lovely, she's engaged, she uses Pond's." Barbara Brokaw, with her elegant assurance, rope of pearls, and direct gaze, had been my heroine. "If only I could be like her when I grow up," I had daydreamed. Jarvis had lost his beloved mother to cancer when he was only twenty; I was still seeking that elevated selfhood—symbiosis had set its subtle trap quite skillfully. Unfortunately for Jarvis, I was *not* his mother, nor did marrying him transform me into Barbara Brokaw. Another failed dream.

Still, we had one happy-ever-after accomplishment to take pride in. Jarvis had gone to work in Puerto Rico a month after we met, and I had planned my two-week vacation from *Irene* to visit him there. Unbeknownst to us, his fifteen-year-old son, Harry, had been dispatched by his ex-wife to live with Jarvis. Handsome, loaded with energy and high spirits, the boy won me over on the spot, and I found it hard to see in him the "irresponsibility" I'd heard about. After several midnight heart-to-heart talks with him, I called Williston Academy, where his ability as a top hockey player would have opportunity to bloom, and made an appointment with the admissions officer. When I left Puerto Rico, Harry was with me. Jarvis came too, and when we arrived in New York his daughter, Chi, joined us for the weekend, making an instant family I had not really planned on. But I had not planned on Harry, either, or the role I felt I had to play in trying to give his life some more satisfying direction.

It wasn't easy for any of us. There were hard lessons to learn. But we persevered, and in his senior year he was elected to the inner circle of the student council, the scene of many reprimands and even a suspension he'd suffered along the way. When he received his diploma, the whole student body cheered. The headmaster summed it up: "Harry is the best example of what Williston is here to accomplish. Take an unruly, mischievous boy on a disaster course and teach him the *self*-discipline that will allow him to realize his real potential."

Marriage may not have been my strong suit, but I have seen my children grow strong and thrive, and from them I draw immense satisfaction. Karen is settled into a gratifying life teaching music (all instruments) and directing a band in Keystone School District in La Grange, Ohio, near Oberlin, her alma mater. She makes costumes and props for halftime shows (including a twenty-foot fire-breathing dragon) in her basement playroom, and helps supervise trips to Disney World and the Indianapolis 500. Any disciplinary-problem child who enters the music program seems to find himself under her guidance.

Jon, a clinical psychologist (A.B., Amherst, Ph.D., U. of Minnesota), is presently on leave from a professorship at the University of Vermont to head a program of research studies in schizophrenia for the National Institute of Mental Health in Washington. But with all his activities, it does not surprise me that he has found time to be an extraordinarily devoted and sensitive father to Erik and Eliza, for those traits surfaced early in his boyhood.

Tim has chosen to be a communicator, and—overcoming his natural reticence—is a disc jockey in Colorado Springs. He has also written some very good material for the show, à la Bob and Ray, and he could be headed for a wider career. At age twelve he had sent away for one of those Great Writers' Schools applications, and in answer to a question about the kind of writing he most enjoyed, he'd written, "I like a story that builds quickly to a climax, then takes off from there."

In 1977 Tim was to come to New York for Christmas, his first vacation in two years, but in mid-November he called from New Mexico to say that he was thinking of visiting his father instead. "Please don't be upset," he said. "I haven't been in touch with Dad for two years, and I have a feeling I'd better go see him."

"I *know* you should," I said, swallowing my disappointment, "But don't wait till Christmas. Can you make it on Thanksgiving?"

On Thanksgiving Day Jon, Karen, and I talked with Bibber and Tim long distance from Vermont. Bibber was just out the hospital, recovering from his seventh internal hemorrhage.

"Isn't Tim beautiful," Bibber said, trying hard for the old hearty bravado but not quite making it.

"We have a wonderful son," I said. "Thank God for him."

Bibber was silent for a moment, then said quietly, "You know, Red, you were right when you said someday I'd be a lonely old man. Sometimes I think I just can't..." His voice trailed off.

After a moment he said, "I love you, Big Red. I always have, I always will." This time his voice broke.

"I know. I love you, too," I said, fighting to control the tears that threatened to drown my voice.

On December 22, the Los Angeles police called Tim, who was on the air at the time, to tell him his father was dead. Bibber had died alone. His body had not been discovered for two days in the squalid apartment where he had been living.

Tim and I stood side by side, together after all, as Bibber was laid to rest on Christmas Eve in Holy Name Cemetery— near Bing Crosby, which would have pleased him. On a wreath of green and white flowers was a card that said, "We know you were in heaven ten minutes before the devil knew you were dead. Erin go bragh forever. Love from McNamara's Band: Ruth, Tim, Karen and Jon."

There have been good times and bad, happy and sad, but all in all, life has been benevolent to Mrs. Citizen Kane, and I owe much of my good fortune to two women: the very real Agnes Nixon and her creation, the sometimes-very-real Phoebe

Tyler, whose name I gladly sign along with my own whenever fans ask for autographs.

She's quite a lady, that Phoebe. I don't know what I'd do without her.

EPILOGUE:

Plains, Georgia, 1977

THE TELEPHONE RANG.

"Excuse me," Miss Lillian said, "that'll probably be my daughter Ruth calling from North Carolina. All my children are so good to me."

While she was on the phone I hurried back into the kitchen to see about the dinner I had cooked earlier in New York and had then brought with me on the flight down to Plains. There wasn't much left to do except heat and serve, but I was still a little nervous.

It was now about six months since that August day when I first met Miss Lillian, and in the interval we had become fast friends. As she had been hospitalized for two weeks during the holidays and was still in the process of getting her strength back, I had thought it might be nice if I prepared a fancy dinner for her—roast duck à l'orange, wild rice with mushrooms, pea pods with water chestnuts, watercress salad, orange soufflé with anise-flavored cookie crumbs, and even a bottle of champagne.

While I was fussing about in the kitchen, searching for pots and pans, Miss Lillian appeared in the doorway. "I wish I had a picture of this," she laughed. "Phoebe Tyler on her hands and knees in my kitchen. Why, you've never even been inside your own kitchen in Pine Valley." She was still chuckling when we sat down to dinner.

"Would you mind saying the blessing?" she asked. "Not that I'm terribly righteous, but we always do it. At Jimmy's house they always hold hands and Amy does it."

I bowed my head and said, "Dear Father, we thank Thee

for the blessings that pour forth from Thee—greater than we would ever know to ask for. We thank Thee for the beautiful friends we know and love. We ask Your blessings for the man You have given us to lead this country. May he understand Your words—Not with might, not with power, but with My Spirit, sayeth the Lord. Bless this food to our use and us to Thy service. In Jesus' name we ask it. Amen."

"Amen," Miss Lillian said.

Then she smiled and put her hand on mine. "Now I'll never be able to think of you as Phoebe again. You're Ruth to me now."